P9-DNN-044

PRAISE FOR THE MRS. MURPHY SERIES

CATCH AS CAT CAN

"This latest is as good as its predecessors . . . thoroughly enjoyable." —*Winston-Salem Journal*

"Light, fun, and quite possibly addictive to fans of the cozy mystery, especially to those who believe in the high intelligence of our four-footed friends. And who among pet owners does not?" —*Romance Reviews Today*

"Brown's proven brand of murder and mayhem played out against a background of Virginia gentility and idealized animals is once again up to scratch." —*Publishers Weekly*

"Any new Mrs. Murphy is a joyful reading experience, and *Catch as Cat Can* is no exception. . . . An adult mystery that appeals to the child in all of us." —*The Midwest Book Review*

"The[se] mysteries continue to be a true treat." —*The Post & Courier,* Charleston, SC

"An entertaining read in a fun series." —*Mystery News*

CLAWS AND EFFECT

"Mrs. Murphy, the incomparable feline sleuth with attitude, returns to captivate readers. . . . An intriguing and well-executed mystery . . . Grateful fans will relish this charming addition by a master of the cozy cat genre." —*Publishers Weekly*

"Reading a Mrs. Murphy mystery is like eating a potato chip. You always go back for more. . . . Whimsical and enchanting . . . The latest expert tale from a deserving bestselling series." —*The Midwest Book Review*

THE BOOK RACK
55 PARDONE ROAD
TRIONIUM MD 21058
410-667-6897
FAX 410-666-1269

"As charming as ever." —*The Tennessean*

"With intricate plot twists that will keep readers guessing right up until the end, *Claws and Effect* once again blends murder and mayhem with animal antics." —*Pet Life*

"Fans old and new will enjoy this witty and suspenseful installment." —*Cats & Kittens*

"Another charming and elegantly spun yarn."
—*The Providence Sunday Journal*

"Excellent series . . . Another murder in Crozet would be most welcome." —*Winston-Salem Journal*

PAWING THROUGH THE PAST

"This is a cat-lover's dream of a mystery. . . . 'Harry' is simply irresistible. . . . [Rita Mae] Brown once again proves herself 'Queen of Cat Crimes.'. . . Don't miss out on this lively series, for it's one of the best around." —*Old Book Barn Gazette*

"Apparently eight's the charm for Rita Mae Brown and her cat, Sneaky Pie, whose latest adventure just may be the best in this long-running series." —*Booklist*

"Another delightful mystery . . . Once again, Rita Mae Brown proves she can capture the ambiance of life in a small southern town and, more impressively, get readers to accept thinking, mystery-solving cats and dogs." —*The Virginian Pilot*

"Cleverly crafted . . . Fans of the Mrs. Murphy series will want to immediately read this novel, while newcomers will search for the previous books." —*The Midwest Book Review*

"A delightful cozy mystery, all the more so because of the active role the pets take in solving the crime . . . [The] puzzling mystery will shock and delight you." —*Romantic Times*

"Rita Mae Brown's books are always well written, always entertaining, always full of interesting people becoming involved with plots, plans and emotional entanglements. *Pawing Through the Past* is no exception." —*I Love a Mystery*

CAT ON THE SCENT

"Rita and Sneaky Pie know how to grab a reader. This fun-loving and delightful mystery is a must even if you're not a cat lover." —*The Pilot,* Southern Pines, NC

"These provocative mysteries just glow." —*Mystery Lovers Bookshop News*

"Features all the traits of purebred fun. . . . The antics of the animals, Brown's witty observations, the history-revering Virginians, and the Blue Ridge setting make this a pleasurable read for lovers of this popular genre." —*BookPage*

"Animal antics and criminal capers combine captivatingly in *Cat on the Scent.*" —*The San Diego Union-Tribune*

"A charming and keen-eyed take on human misdeeds and animal shenanigans . . . Told with spunk and plenty of whimsy, this is another delightful entry in a very popular series." —*Publishers Weekly*

"A fine murder mystery . . . For fans of Mrs. Murphy and her pals, both two- and four-legged, *Cat on the Scent* smells like a winner." —*The Virginian-Pilot*

"Charming." —*People*

MURDER ON THE PROWL

"Leave it to a cat to grasp the essence of the cozy mystery: namely, murder among friends." —*The New York Times Book Review*

"Will charm even the reader generally indifferent to animals, while animal lovers and those who enjoy a good cozy will simply lap this one up." —*Publishers Weekly*

MURDER, SHE MEOWED

"As feline collaborators go, you couldn't ask for better than Sneaky Pie Brown, the canny tiger cat.... Solid storytelling." —*The New York Times Book Review*

"The intriguing characters in this much-loved series continue to entertain." —*Nashville Banner*

PAY DIRT

"If you must work with a collaborator, you want it to be someone with intelligence, wit and an infinite capacity for subtlety— someone, in fact, very much like a cat. It's always a pleasure to visit this cozy world. [T]here's no resisting Harry's droll sense of humor...or Mrs. Murphy's tart commentary." —*The New York Times Book Review*

"The superb narration...resonates with small-town intimacy and wit.... Sure to delight anyone who loves cozy mysteries." —*Mostly Murder*

Catch as Cat Can

RITA MAE BROWN

& SNEAKY PIE BROWN

ILLUSTRATIONS BY MICHAEL GELLATLY

BANTAM BOOKS NEW YORK • TORONTO • LONDON • SYDNEY • AUCKLAND

CATCH AS CAT CAN
A Bantam Book

PUBLISHING HISTORY

Bantam hardcover edition published March 2002
Bantam mass market edition / February 2003

Published by
Bantam Dell
A Division of Random House, Inc.
New York, New York

All rights reserved.
Copyright © 2002 by American Artists, Inc.
Cover illustration copyright © 2002 by Jack Unruh
Cover design by Jamie S. Warren Youll

Illustrations by Michael Gellatly

Library of Congress Catalog Card Number: 2001035741.
No part of this book may be reproduced or transmitted in any form or
by any means, electronic or mechanical, including photocopying,
recording, or by any information storage and retrieval system, without
permission in writing from the publisher, except where permitted by
law. For information address: Bantam Books, New York, New York.

If you purchased this book without a cover you should be aware
that this book is stolen property. It was reported as "unsold and
destroyed" to the publisher and neither the author nor the publisher has received any payment for this "stripped book."

ISBN: 0-553-58028-0

Published simultaneously in the United States and Canada

Bantam Books and the rooster colophon are registered trademarks of
Random House, Inc.

PRINTED IN THE UNITED STATES OF AMERICA

OPM   10 9 8 7 6 5 4 3 2 1

Dedicated to
John Morris and Robert Steppe
When they're good, they're good
but when they're bad, they're better!

Cast of Characters and Events

Mary Minor Haristeen (Harry) The young postmistress of Crozet.

Mrs. Murphy Harry's gray tiger cat.

Tee Tucker Harry's Welsh corgi, Mrs. Murphy's friend and confidante.

Pewter Harry's shamelessly fat gray cat.

Pharamond Haristeen (Fair) Veterinarian, formerly married to Harry.

Mrs. George Hogendobber (Miranda) A widow who works with Harry in the post office.

Susan Tucker Harry's best friend.

BoomBoom Craycroft A tall, beautiful blonde who irritates Harry.

Big Marilyn Sanburne (Mim) The undisputed queen of Crozet society.

Little Mim Sanburne The daughter of Big Mim, struggling for her own identity.

Tally Urquhart Older than dirt, she says what she thinks when she thinks it, even to her niece, Mim the Magnificent.

Rick Shaw Sheriff.

Cynthia Cooper Sheriff's deputy.

Herbert C. Jones Pastor of St. Luke's Lutheran Church.

Lottie Pearson Assistant Director for Major Gifts at the university. She is in her mid-thirties, ambitious, well connected, looking for Mr. Right. If she can't find Mr. Right she might weaken and take Mr. Right Now.

Thomas Steinmetz Second-in-command to the Ambassador from Uruguay. He is suave, very wealthy, and always ready for a good time. He doesn't discuss his age but he's probably in his mid-forties.

Diego Aybar Under-Counsel to the Ambassador of Uruguay. He most often assists Thomas Steinmetz. He is as handsome as a swarthy Apollo; women fall all over him.

Sean O'Bannon The proprietor with his brother, Roger, of O'Bannon Salvage. Taking over the business after his father's death a year ago, Sean has increased profits by catering to the restoration trade. He's a good businessman, single, late thirties.

Roger O'Bannon Outgoing, raucous, besotted with Lottie Pearson, he works hard at the salvage yard but he plays hard, too. He tries Sean's patience at times.

Don Clatterbuck He repairs leather items such as tack or leather sofas. He also practices taxidermy as a hobby. He's a low-key working-class guy.

Pope Rat A disreputable rat living at the O'Bannon Salvage yard. He knows how to steal food out of the vending machines.

Abraham A very old, courtly bluetick hound.

The Dogwood Festival A spring celebration with wine tastings, parties, and parades organized by many communities in central Virginia. Crozet hosts a parade.

The Wrecker's Ball A fund-raiser for a charity selected each year by members of the salvage and building trades. The O'Bannons are currently in charge of the ball.

Catch as Cat Can

1

Long, low strips of silver fog filled the green hollows and ravines of the Blue Ridge Mountains. The mists feathered over the creeks and rivers at six-thirty in the morning. Redbud was blooming, the tulips had opened. The white and pink dogwoods would explode in another week.

Mrs. Murphy, awake since five-thirty, snuggled next to Pewter, whose small snore sounded like a mud dauber at work, a low buzz. The two cats rested in the hollow of Mary Minor Haristeen's back while Tucker, the corgi, stretched out to her full length, most impressive, on the hooked rug next to the bed. She, too, snored slightly.

Murphy loved spring. Her undercoat would shed out, making her look sleeker and feel lighter. The robins returned, indigo buntings and bluebirds filled the skies. Down by the creek the redwing blackbirds snatched insects, gobbling them in one swallow. The scarlet tanagers flew into the orchards for their forays. The rise in the bird population excited the tiger cat even though she rarely caught one. Both she and Pewter dreamed of killing the blue jay who made their lives miserable. Hateful and aggressive, he would dart at them in a nosedive, scream as he got close, then pull up at the last moment just out of paw's reach. This particular blue jay also made a point of pooping on the clean clothes hung on the line to dry. Harry hated him, too. Harry was Mary Minor's nickname, which often surprised people upon meeting the young, good-looking woman.

People assumed her nickname derived from her married name but she had earned it in grade school because her clothes were liberally decorated with cat and dog hair. Her little friends hadn't yet mastered spelling, so hairy became harry. To this day some of her classmates remained on uneasy terms with spelling but rarely with Harry.

Outside the opened window, the cat heard the loud *rat-ta-tat-tat* of woodpeckers. She couldn't remember a spring with so many woodpeckers or so many yellow swallowtail butterflies.

The giant pileated woodpecker, close to two feet in length, proved a fearsome sight. This bird, found throughout the hickory and oak forests of central Virginia, was a primitive life-form and in repose one could almost see his flying reptile ancestors reflected in his visage.

The smaller woodpeckers, though large enough, seemed less fearsome. Mrs. Murphy enjoyed watching woodpeckers circle a tree, stop, peck for insects, then circle again. She noticed that some birds circled up and some circled down and she wondered why. She couldn't get close enough to one to ask because as soon as they'd see her, they'd fly off to another juicy tree.

As a rule, birds disdained conversation with cats. The mice, moles, and shrews happily chattered away from the safety of their holes. "Chattered" being a polite term, because they'd taunt the cats. The barn mice even sang, because their high-pitched voices drove Mrs. Murphy crazy.

The tiger glanced over at the clock. Harry, usually up at five-thirty, had overslept. Fortunately, today was Saturday, so she wouldn't have to rush in to work at the post office in Crozet. A part-time worker took care of Saturday's mail. But Harry, an organized soul, hated to waste daylight. Murphy knew she'd fret when she awoke and discovered how late it was.

Pewter opened one chartreuse eye. *"I'm hungry."*

"There are crunchies in the bowl."

"Tuna." The fat gray cat opened the other eye, slightly lifting her pretty round head.

"I wouldn't mind some myself. Let's wake up our can opener." Murphy laughed.

Pewter stretched, then gleefully sat, her back to Harry's face. She gently swept her tail over the woman's nose.

Mrs. Murphy walked up and down Harry's back. When that didn't produce the desired effect she jumped up and down.

"Uh." Harry sneezed as she pushed the tail out of her face. "Pewter."

"I'm hungry."

"Me, too," Murphy sang out.

The dog, awake now, yawned. *"Chunky beef."*

"You guys." Harry sat up as Murphy stepped off her back. "Oh, my gosh, it's six-forty. Why did you let me sleep so late?" She threw off the covers. Her bare feet hit the hooked rug and she sprinted to the bathroom.

"I'm standing vigil at the food bowl." Pewter zipped to the kitchen.

Murphy, in line behind her, jumped onto the kitchen counter.

Tucker, much more obedient, accompanied Harry to the

bathroom, looked quizzically while she brushed her teeth, then quietly followed the human into the kitchen, where she put a pot of water on the stove for tea.

"All right, what is it?"

"Tuna!" came the chorus.

"M-m-m, chicken and rice." She put that can back on the shelf.

"Tuna!"

"Liver." She hesitated.

"Tuna!"

"Tuna," Tucker chimed in. *"If you don't feed them tuna they'll make a mess and it will take me that much longer to get my breakfast,"* she grumbled.

Harry reached into the cupboard, lifting out another can. "Tuna."

"Hooray." Pewter turned little tight circles.

"Okay, okay." Harry laughed and opened the can with the same hand opener her mother had used. The Hepworths, Harry's mother's family, thought fashion absurd. Buy something of good quality and use it until it dies. The can opener was older than Harry.

The Minors, her father's family, also practical people, proved a bit more willing to let loose of money than the Hepworths. Harry fell somewhere in the middle.

After feeding the cats and dog, she turned on the stove, pulled out an iron skillet, and fried up two eggs. Breakfast was her favorite meal.

"Well, I've got Mr. Maupin's seeder for the weekend so I'd better overseed those pastures," she said to the animals, good listeners. "I was lucky to get it. Anyone with a seeder can rent it out for good money, you know. I'd love to buy one but we'd need almost twenty thousand dollars and, you know, I'd rather stand in line and wait to rent Mr. Maupin's. Even a used one is expensive and you only use it in the spring and, in the fall, depending..." Her voice trailed off, then rose again. "The trouble is, when you need it, you need it. We were lucky this year." She reached over to stroke Mrs. Murphy's silken head, as the cat had joined her at the table. "I just feel it's going to be a lucky spring. Worms to turn and eggs to lay."

She washed her dishes, walked out on the screened-in porch, and threw on her barn jacket which hung on a peg. The temperature was in the forties but by noon would near sixty-five.

As Harry stepped outside into the refreshingly cool air the first thing she noticed was the fog on the mountains. The sun, rising, reflected onto the fog, creating millions of tiny rainbows. The sight was so beautiful that Harry stopped in her tracks and held her breath for an instant.

The cats noticed the rainbows but their attention was diverted by a huge pileated woodpecker, lying in the dust, just off the screened-in porch.

"Cool." Pewter hurried over, tried to pick up the freshly dead bird in her jaws. It was quite heavy. She gave up.

"I could help you with that," Tucker offered.

"Touch my bird and you die," Pewter hissed.

Mrs. Murphy laughed. *"It's not like you brought it down, Pewter."*

"I found it. That's almost as good."

"Yeah, the great gray hunter." Tucker curled her upper lip.

"I don't see you catching anything, fat bum." Pewter's eyes narrowed to slits.

"I'm not fat. I don't have a tail. That makes me look fat," Tucker replied sharply. *"Bubble butt, you should know."*

Pewter lashed out, catching the dog squarely on the nose. *"Weenie."*

"Ouch."

"What is going on with you two?" Harry walked over to

the fighting animals. "Oh, no." She knelt down to examine the giant woodpecker. "You hardly ever see one of these up close."

"I found it first." Pewter put her paw on its plump breast, claws out for emphasis.

"Pewter, let go," Harry commanded her.

"Only if I get my birdie back." She swished her tail.

"You'd better let go, Pewts," Mrs. Murphy advised.

"Oh, sure, so you can grab my woodpecker."

" *'Cause she's top dog,"* Tucker wisely noted.

"I'm not a dog." The gray cat said this with a supercilious air.

"Good, because I'd hate to claim you."

"You're being a real snot," the cat said but she relinquished the bird, retracting her claws.

Harry first felt the woodpecker's neck because a bird will sometimes fly into a windowpane and break its neck. The woodpecker's neck was fine and woodpeckers usually don't fly that close to houses. She turned the bird over. Not a mark.

"This guy is heavy."

"Tell me," Pewter agreed.

"In perfect condition. Strange. Really strange." Harry lifted the bird by its feet as she stood up. "Taxidermist," was all she said.

"I can pull the feathers off a stuffed bird as well as a live one." Pewter smiled.

"Indulge her, Pewter," Tucker growled, her nose still hurting.

The cat said nothing, following Harry closely as the human located her old large cooler, filled it with ice, wrapped the woodpecker in a plastic bag, then placed it in the cooler. She would visit the taxidermist after overseeding.

She then walked to the barn, turned the three horses out,

picked stalls, scrubbed water buckets, and was on the tractor in no time, happy as she could be.

The animals had no desire to run after the tractor as Harry monotonously rolled up and down the fields, so they reposed under a huge white lilac bush, blooms half-opened. Pewter and Tucker called a truce.

"It was weird—that woodpecker." Mrs. Murphy watched a swarm of ladybugs head their way.

"An omen. Found treasure," Pewter purred.

Tucker rested her head on her paws. *"A bad omen if you're the woodpecker."*

2

What do you think?" Harry leaned over the heavy wooden table where Don Clatterbuck studied the recently deceased pileated woodpecker.

"I can do it. Sure can." His smile revealed teeth stained by chewing tobacco, a habit learned from his maternal grandfather, Riley "Booty" Mawyer, who was old but still farming.

She folded her arms across her chest. "Lots?"

"Not for you." He smiled again.

"Well—?"

"Oh, how about a hundred dollars and you give my card out when foxhunting starts again? At the meets."

"Really?" Harry knew she was getting a good deal because stuffing birds was more difficult than stuffing deer heads.

"Yeah. We go back a ways, Skeezits." He called her by a childhood nickname.

"Guess we do." She smiled back and pointed to coffee tables, the tops covered with old license plates, some dating back to the 1920s. "These are good. You ought to carry them up to Middleburg and put them in those expensive shops there."

His shop, a converted garage, overflowed with hides, knives to cut leather, and a heavy-duty sewing machine to sew leather, though usually he employed hand tools even for sewing. Donald repaired tack, leather chairs, car upholstery, even leather skirts and high-fashion stuff.

He made a decent living from that and his taxidermy but he also exhibited a creative streak. The license-plate-covered coffee tables were his latest idea.

"Not satisfied. I want to make some using the color for design. The old New York plates used to be orange so what if I used orange and, say, the old California plates, black. I don't know. Something different."

"These are good. The ones right here. Where do you get these cool old plates?"

"Yard sales mostly. Junkyards. Scratchin'."

As they'd known one another since they were toddlers, they employed a shorthand. Scratchin' meant he'd scratch up stuff like a chicken scratches up grubs. Many of Harry's friends did this, as they all had known one another all their lives. In the case of the older generation, this shorthand contracted into orders. The Virginia way was that older people gave orders, young people carried them out. "Worship of youth is for other parts," as Virginians said. And what any true Virginian would never say was that those "other parts" of the country didn't count.

Another fundamental of Virginia life was that society was ruled by women. The entire state was a matriarchy, carefully concealed, of course. It would never do for men to know they were being directed, guided, cajoled, or sometimes openly threatened to do what the Queen wanted, the Queen being the reigning woman of every locality.

What the men never told the women was that they knew that. Hunting, fishing, and golf provided a respite from the continual improvements of the ladies. Despite the occasional irritations, interruptions, and exhaustion of pleasing women, Virginia men bore this burden for reasons they did not share with those same women. The men felt they were bigger, stronger, and more inclined to fight, which also meant they could protect those who were smaller, weaker, and who needed them. They declined to let the women know that those ladies needed them or that they knew full well what the ladies were doing.

The system worked most times. When it didn't there was hell to pay.

Harry and Don, in their late thirties, actually believed they weren't part of this dance. Of course they were, and in time they'd understand just how much they'd been influenced by their elders and by the very ethos of Virginia.

"You're the craftsman." She smiled.

"I get by." He wiped his hand across his chin, leaving a faint streak of light brown stain, as he'd been coloring calfskin before Harry came into his shop.

"You've always done good work. I don't know where you get your ideas. I remember the Homecoming float with the stallion that bucked. I still don't know how you built that bucking horse. No one's ever topped that."

"Wasn't bad." He grinned.

"Where do you get all this stuff?" She pointed to a broken pediment, good stone, too; a huge pile of ancient license plates; an old gas pump, the kind with a whirling ball on the top; a massive enameled safe with a central lock like a pilot's wheel; and a beautiful old Brewster phaeton, badly in need of repair but an example of the coach builder's art.

Mrs. Murphy and Pewter sat in the cracked, deep green leather of the phaeton seat. The body of the coach itself was dark green enamel with red and gold piping, quite lovely even if faded and cracked.

"O'Bannon's."

"The salvage yard? I haven't been there since the old man died."

"Opened up four acres in the back. The boys are good businessmen. Sean really runs the business and Roger runs the garage, old cars. He still spends half his time at the stock-car races. You ought to go over there." Don carefully put the woodpecker into a large freezer he had for game. "They've even got a caboose on the old railroad siding. Must have been fun in the old days when businesses all had railroad sidings."

"When did Sean expand?" Harry asked, knowing Sean O'Bannon was the older of the two brothers and seemed more commanding than Roger.

"He started about a month after his dad died. Said he could never get his father to see how the business could grow. He borrowed some money from the bank. It's a big expansion."

"Thought I knew everything." She scratched her head.

"You gonna be another Big Mim?" Don laughed, naming Mim Sanburne, in her late sixties although not broadcasting her age. Mim was wealthy, beautiful, imperious, and prepared to rule Crozet and all of Virginia if permitted to do so—and even if not permitted. She had to know everything.

"Thanks," Harry dryly replied.

"Mom likes to give orders as much as Mim, secretly," Pewter giggled.

Murphy disagreed with her companion. *"I don't think so. I think she likes to go her own way but if she has to work in a group of humans she wants to get the job done. Mother doesn't want to hear a lot of personal stuff about people's lives—girl talk. Hates it."*

"I think she could run Crozet every bit as much as Big Mim."

"She has the ability but not the desire." Mrs. Murphy sat up and thought how civilized it would be to travel in a phaeton on a perfect spring day such as this.

"Don't forget Little Mim." Tucker, who had been inspecting every item on the floor of the shop, walked over.

"True." Pewter considered the social and political ambitions of Mim's sole daughter. *"She's vice-mayor now, too."*

Jim Sanburne, husband to Mim, father to Little Mim, was mayor and had been mayor since the middle of the 1960s. His daughter challenged him for the mayoralty in the last city election but they compromised and she became vice-mayor, appointed by her father, approved by the City Council. Had she gone through with the campaign it would have divided the community. This way harmony was preserved and she was mayor-in-training.

"Go over to O'Bannon's," Don suggested. "Artists go there. Not just motorheads. BoomBoom Craycroft is there once a week, sifting through scrap metal."

"What?"

"She's welding artistic pieces. Says it grounds her."

"Give me a break." Harry grimaced. "BoomBoom can't stick to anything and every new activity is her salvation and ought to be yours, too. Well, at least she's out of her group therapy phase."

"Ready for the Dogwood Festival next weekend? Our mid-April rites of spring?" He changed the subject.

"No." She pursed her lips. "Damn that Susan. She suckers me every time."

"What do you have to do this time?"

"Parade coordinator."

"Yeah?"

"Means I have to line everyone up at the starting place, Crozet High School, space them correctly, use the bullhorn, and get them marching. It's easy enough until you consider who's marching in the parade. The clash of egos—our version of *Clash of the Titans*."

Don laughed. "BoomBoom especially. Your favorite person."

Harry started laughing so hard she couldn't talk. "She's leading a delegation of disease-of-the-week. I forget which disease."

"Last year it was MS."

BoomBoom Craycroft, a beautiful woman and an ambitious one, each year selected a charity. She would then lead this group in the annual parade, a celebration of spring and Crozet. It wasn't just that she wished to perform good deeds and help the sick, she also wanted to be the center of attention. She was too old to be the head majorette for the high school, obviously, so this was her venue.

"I suppose we wouldn't laugh so hard if we had whatever illness it was but I can't help it. I really can't. I think she should lead a contingent for breast reduction." Harry giggled. BoomBoom carried a lot of freight upstairs.

Don gasped. "Don't do that."

"Spoken just like a man. You twit." She made a gun out of her thumb and forefinger and "shot" him. She walked over to the huge safe. "Got your millions in there?"

"Nah, just half a million." He laughed, then thought a moment. "Give me two weeks on the woodpecker. You've hit me at a good time."

"Great." She gave him a high five and picked up her brood to head to O'Bannon's. "See you at the parade."

3

With the exception of the interstates, the roads in Virginia were paved-over Indian trails. They twisted through the mountains, leveled out along the riverbeds and streams, proving a joy to those fortunate enough to own sports cars.

Harry, on the other hand, was the proud owner of two trucks. One truck, a dually F350, was expensive to run due to its big engine but she needed the power to pull her horse trailer. Thanks to a long-term loan she could afford the payments. She had three years left.

For everyday use she drove her old 1978 Ford half-ton, ran like a top, was cheap to operate and repair.

Today she curled around the hills and valleys in the old Superman-blue Ford, the two cats and Tucker cheerfully riding in the cab, commenting on the unfolding countryside.

Don Clatterbuck's business rested just past the intersection with Route 240 on Whitehall Road. The O'Bannon Salvage yard was located east of town on that same Route

240, tucked off the highway so as not to offend intensely aesthetic souls. To further promote good community relations, the O'Bannon brothers had put up a high, solid, paled fence around the four acres, a considerable expense. A large, pretty, hand-painted sign swayed on a wrought iron post at the driveway, right by the big double gate. A black background with white lettering read "O'Bannon Salvage," and a red border completed the sign. What made everyone notice the salvage yard, though, wasn't the sign but the black wrecker's ball hanging from a crane positioned next to the sign. Each morning Sean or Roger opened the heavy chain-link fence gate and each evening they locked it, the wrecker's ball and crane standing like a skeletal sentinel.

As the postmistress of Crozet and born and bred there, Harry knew every side street and every resident, too. There was no shortcut to O'Bannon's. She'd have to go through town. Don had aroused her curiosity. She wanted to see Sean's improvements.

She no sooner turned east than she passed the supermarket and spied Miranda Hogendobber, her coworker and friend, in the parking lot. Her paper bags of groceries were perched on the hood of the Ford Falcon, an antique that Miranda used daily, seeing no reason to spend money on a new car if the old one operated efficiently.

Miranda seemed upset. Harry turned into the parking lot, found a space, and hurried over to her friend, the animals behind her.

"Oh, Harry, I'm so glad to see you. Look. Would you look!" Miranda pointed to her tires, hubcaps missing. "I've never had anything like this happen—and at the supermarket."

"It's all right, Mrs. Hogendobber." Mrs. Murphy rubbed against her leg, feeling certain this would calm the lady.

"What's the big noise about a hubcap?" Pewter shrugged.

"Car's from 1961. How can she replace them?" Tucker replied.

"The car runs fine without hubcaps." Pewter struggled to understand human reactions, since she often felt they missed the point.

"You know how she is. Everything has to be just so. Not a weed in her garden. She doesn't want to cruise around with her lug nuts showing, you'll pardon the expression." Murphy circled Miranda, rubbing on the opposite leg.

"Did you call the sheriff?"

"No. I just walked out this very minute." Miranda, crestfallen, stepped back to view her naked wheels again.

"Tell you what, you stay here and I'll run over to the pay phone." Harry started to move away, then stopped. "Do you have anything that needs to go into the freezer? I can take it home for you."

"No."

Harry called the sheriff's office and before she hung up the phone to rejoin Miranda, Cynthia Cooper, a deputy with the sheriff's department, pulled into the lot.

"That was fast." Harry smiled at the young, attractive deputy.

"Just around the corner at the firehouse going over the parade route for the thousandth time."

"Look." Miranda pointed to her car as Cynthia, notebook in hand, walked over.

"That's just heinous." Cynthia put her arm around Miranda. "Do you have any idea how much they're worth?"

"Not a clue." Miranda's pink lips, shiny with lipstick, pursed together.

"That's probably why someone stole them. Because they're hard to find. They must be worth something," Harry thought out loud.

"Why can't she put on new hubcaps?" Pewter, irritated, wanted to get on the road again.

"Not the same." Tucker sniffed the wheels hoping for human scent but the perpetrator had pried off the hubcaps with something other than his hands.

"Piffle," the gray cat yawned.

"Are we keeping you up?" Harry noticed the large yawn accompanied by a tiny gurgle. "Why don't you go back and sleep in the truck?"

"Ha, ha," Mrs. Murphy laughed.

"Aren't we the perfect puss?" Pewter growled at the tiger cat.

"Don't start. I'd like to have one Saturday where you two don't fight." Tucker sat between the two cats.

"Tell you what, while I write this up, Harry, pick up the mobile in the squad car and call O'Bannon's. Ask Sean if he has any Falcon hubcaps."

"Funny, I was just on my way over there." Harry trotted over to the squad car, slipped behind the wheel, and dialed on the mobile unit. She punched in the numbers feeling envious. She'd love a mobile phone herself but thought it too expensive. "Hi, Sean, Harry."

"How you doing, Harry?"

"I'm just fine but Mrs. Hogendobber isn't. Someone this very minute stole the hubcaps off her Ford Falcon. Coop's here at the scene of the crime, if you will, and she told me to call you. You wouldn't have any Ford Falcon hubcaps, would you?"

"Yeah," Sean's voice lowered. "I just bought them from the dude who must have stolen them. Dammit."

"We'll be right over." Harry clicked the end button on the phone. "Hey, Coop. He's got them."

"My hubcaps?" Miranda's hand fluttered to her throat.

"He said he just bought them off someone. If they aren't yours it's an odd coincidence. I said we'd be right over."

"Mrs. Hogendobber, do you feel settled enough to drive your car over there? I'll follow in the squad car."

"Of course I feel settled enough." Miranda couldn't believe the deputy thought she was that ruffled by the theft.

"I'll tag along, too, if you don't mind." Harry picked up Pewter, who was wandering in the direction of the supermarket. "I was going that way anyway."

"Fine." Cynthia opened the door to the squad car.

Mrs. Murphy sat in Harry's lap as she backed out of the parking space. *First the woodpecker, now the hubcaps. What next?*

"Extinction by death ray." Pewter giggled.

4

Like ants at a picnic." Mrs. Murphy marveled at the humans, about twenty, walking through lots of elaborate broken columns, pediments, sarcophagi all neatly divided according to function.

The short drive to the building was dotted with large terra-cotta, stone, and ceramic pots. Next to the stone lot was a marble lot with large sheets of roseate marble that must have come from an old hotel lobby, smaller pieces of veined green marble, a bar top perhaps, which rested next to jet-black marble, again all neatly stacked. The largest outdoor lot was filled with rubble from stone walls, building foundations, some blocks hewn square and others natural.

The indoor rooms of the main building contained wooden cornices, fireplace mantels, pilasters, handblown glass, hand-hammered nails, a cornucopia of treasures.

A railroad siding ran parallel to the main building. A flatcar filled with heavy stone cornices, lintels, and copings was near the building. Flatbeds delivered materials and perhaps an old car once a week. Behind that was an old red caboose which stayed as yet unrestored.

Sequestered in the rear of the four acres was Roger's garage shop. Fast-growing pines shielded it from view. Dotted around the various outdoor lots were small neat buildings. They looked like garden sheds and contained tools, old tractor parts, and other items needing protection from the elements.

The animals found the debris less fascinating than the humans but occasionally a whiff of a former occupant, another dog or cat, lingered. Such olfactory information was recent, of course. No such signature wafted from shards saved from the late seventeenth and early eighteenth centuries.

Harry was amazed at the salvage yard's transformation into a kind of architectural dumping ground. The last time she had visited, Sean's father, Tiny Tim, who was tight as a tick with his money, jovially presided over the place, one big yard filled with rusting cars. Tim collected old gravestones as he was interested in the stonemasons' carvings. He'd talk about the tombstones, then move to the broader subject of death. Tiny Tim vehemently opposed autopsies. When he died his wife and sons did not request one so no one knew exactly what he died from, but a lifetime of smoking, drinking, and eating anything that didn't eat him first probably did him in.

Sean, long and lean, wore a faded orange canvas shirt tucked into carpenter's pants. Grease was not ground into his hands, no smears of oil or dirt besmirched his shirt. He could have been a greengrocer except for the carpenter's pants.

One wall displayed specialized tools used in restoration: elegant chisels, small hammers, larger ones, tiny butane torches for peeling back layers of leaded paint. The choices were overwhelming and expensive.

Cynthia and Miranda approached the counter.

Sean asked his assistant, Isabella Rojas, to take care of the customer he was serving and he strode across the expanse to greet the two women. "Welcome. I think you're in luck."

Harry caught up with them, the three animals lagging behind. "This is wonderful."

"Thanks." He focused on Miranda. "Mrs. Hogendobber, follow me."

The humans and animals left the main building, walking about four hundred yards to the rear where thousands of hubcaps, sparkling in the sunlight, hung on wires. They were organized according to car model and year.

The glare from the shiny surfaces caused Mrs. Hogendobber to shield her eyes with her hand. "My word, I had no idea there were this many hubcaps in the world."

"Let's cruise the outbuildings." Tucker wagged her nonexistent tail. *"Bet they're full of vermin."*

"You're a ratter, are you?" Pewter sashayed, a superior air exuding from her gray fur. *"You couldn't catch a comatose mouse."*

"Look who's talking," the corgi called over her shoulder as she sprinted toward the garage building followed by Mrs. Murphy. A trail of fading beer cans gave evidence of Roger O'Bannon's progress. Sobriety was not a virtue associated with Roger.

Pewter declined. For one thing she really didn't care much about mousing or Roger O'Bannon. Birding was her game and she was still put out that Harry had saved the woodpecker for Don Clatterbuck's skills. She wanted to pull the feathers off. Truth be told, Pewter had never killed a bird but she picked up those who died or fell from the nest. She liked yanking out the feathers. She wouldn't eat one. Pewter wouldn't eat anything that wasn't well cooked except for sushi. Something about the darting and dodging of birds excited her and she dreamed of killing the blue jay housed in the maple tree. One day the arrogant fellow would fly too close, run his mouth too loud. She knew her day would come and she'd end his foul abuse. But for the moment she was content to sit at Harry's feet and listen to the tale of the hubcaps.

"My hubcaps!" Miranda reached for the only set of Ford Falcon hubcaps on the line.

"Now, Mrs. H, if you file a theft report I have to impound the hubcaps as evidence. If you don't file, you can put them right back on your car," Cynthia counseled her.

"No!" Miranda shook her head in disbelief.

"That's the law."

"How long will that take?"

"It depends on whether we find the suspect or not. If we do and he comes up for a hearing and then a trial, it could take months—many months." Cooper sighed, for the clogging of the courts wore her out as well as her sister and brother officers. She often thought to herself that people would be far better off trying to solve problems themselves instead of running to the sheriff's department or a lawyer to do it for them. Somehow Americans had lost the ability to sit down and talk to one another, or so it seemed to her.

"Oh, dear, what will the girls at church say?" Miranda worried about driving around undressed, as it were. "Well . . ."

"Maybe we can solve this together." Cynthia focused on Sean, now removing the hubcaps from the line. "The obvious question: who sold you the hubcaps?"

"Usually Roger takes care of the car end of the business but he's not here at the moment," Sean said. "I just happened to be outside when a kid drove up with the hubcaps."

"Know him?"

"No. Never saw him before in my life. I knew the Falcons were rare so I paid fifty dollars for them, wholesale. I priced them at one hundred and twenty and hung them right on the line. If I'd taken a moment to think about it, I might have realized they were Miranda's but the kid said they came off his grandmother's Falcon that had breathed its last."

"What did he look like?"

"Slight. Early twenties. Sandy hair, a pathetic attempt at a mustache." Sean sported a red mustache and closely clipped beard of luxurious density but the curly hair on his head was black and long. He tied it in a ponytail at the nape of his neck. Harry called this a dork knob behind his back.

"Any distinguishing features? Do you remember his clothes or his car?"

"1987 GMC truck. Gray. Virginia plates. Uh, a Dallas Cowboys windbreaker maybe as old as the car and—yes, there was one distinguishing feature. His left eye sagged, an old wound. It was half-closed and a small red scar ran from over the eyebrow to below the eye itself."

"Runny nose? Jumpy?" Cynthia was looking for a fuller picture of the "perp," as she called him.

"No. Calm. Didn't smell alcohol either."

Miranda took out her checkbook as Harry held the hubcaps that Sean had handed to her. The older woman fished around in the bottom of her purse. "I've got a pen in here, I know it."

"Put that away," Sean chided her gently. "I'm not having you pay for what's yours."

"But you paid the thief."

"My problem. I mean it, Miranda. You put that checkbook away right now."

Cynthia thought a moment. "Why don't we do this? You

put the hubcaps back on your car. I'll fill out this report and I'll look for the kid. If Rick Shaw"—she mentioned her boss, the sheriff—"wants to see the evidence, I'll send him to you. I just don't see the point of impounding your hubcaps where they'll sit until God knows when. Just let me handle this."

"I don't want to get you in trouble." Miranda appreciated Cynthia Cooper's concern. She had become friends with the young deputy over the last few years.

"A little trouble won't hurt me." She smiled.

"I'm sorry about this." Sean genuinely liked Miranda, as did most people in Crozet.

"Times change and it would appear not for the better. You had nothing to do with it." Miranda smiled back at him.

"If you all don't need me anymore I'll get back to the store. Saturdays are always our busiest day." He took a few steps, then stopped. "You all are coming to the Wrecker's Ball, aren't you? First Saturday in May. It's our fund-raiser for the project Building for Life, which helps poor people who need homes."

"Wouldn't miss it." Cynthia closed her notebook.

"My ex-husband asked me to your ball months ago. I was so proud of him for planning ahead but," Harry laughed, "it's foaling season so for all I know right in the middle of the dance his beeper will go off. The perils of veterinary medicine, I guess."

Fair Haristeen, Harry's former mate, was a much-sought-after equine practitioner. He'd built up a fine practice, constructing a modern clinic with an operating room.

"Eradicating vermin. Ha," Pewter cackled, trying to direct Harry to her furry pals.

Harry looked down at the gray cannonball of a cat. She

would have scooped her up but her arms were full of hub-caps.

Miranda whistled for Tucker.

A yip told them where Tucker was and also that the dog was in no hurry to return to the humans.

"Let me put these by your car, Miranda. I'll even put them on for you but I'd better find those two first. Do you mind?"

"Of course not. I'm taking up your Saturday afternoon."

"I was coming here anyway, really I was." Harry walked briskly back to the Falcon, parked in front of the new main building. She stacked the hubcaps by the driver's door.

"Hey, I'll put the hubcaps on. How do we know some-one else won't pick them up or try to buy them?" Cynthia came over. "You get the kids."

Harry put Pewter in the truck cab, careful to roll down the window partway even though it wasn't that warm, only in the low fifties. She then hurried back to the garage. "Tucker!"

"I've got a rat!" Tucker crowed.

"A rathole. Be accurate," Mrs. Murphy corrected the dog but she, too, knew the rat was in the hole and her tail fluffed out a little. A rat could be a formidable enemy, with teeth that could tear a hunk of flesh right out of you.

Harry opened the large sliding door and slipped in. Three old cars, in various states of interior and exterior re-birth, sat side by side. The walls were hung with tools, an air compressor sat in the corner, and the pièce de résistance, an expensive hydraulic lift in a pit, bore testimony to Roger O'Bannon's passion. Just as Sean loved old buildings, Roger loved old cars; and fortunately for both brothers, the market for old cars and trucks was soaring just like the restoration business.

One wall was filled with tools, vises, rubber fan belts hung on pegboard. Everything was organized and neat except for the garbage can overflowing with beer cans.

Tucker and Murphy crouched in the back right-hand corner of the shop.

"Come on. Time to go," Harry ordered.

"He's in here. He's got a bag of popcorn." Tucker's nose never failed her.

"Wonder where he got the popcorn," Mrs. Murphy said.

A voice much deeper than expected startled them. *"The vending machine. I know how to get in and out. Now leave me alone before I tear your face off."*

"I'll rip your throat out first!" Tucker ferociously replied.

"Listen, you nipshit, I've got lots of ways in and out of this joint. If I want to I can just slip out and you won't even know it. But this is my living room and I want you out."

"You can't talk to me that way. I'm Tucker Haristeen!"

"Yeah, and I'm the Pope. Look, Tucker, you're on my turf, I'm not on yours. And take that cat with you before I get really mean."

"You two are pushing the envelope!" Harry grunted as she lifted an uncooperative Tucker. "Now we're going and I mean it. Mrs. Murphy, if I have to come back here for you, no catnip tonight. Is that clearly understood?"

"Mean. You can be so mean sometimes," Mrs. Murphy grumbled.

"Pope Rat, I will come back here and get you! Your days are numbered," Tucker promised.

"Dream on." Laughter emanated from the hole.

Two disgruntled creatures joined a languid Pewter on the front seat, the driver's window rolled down partway. Miranda had waited for them. Cynthia had left to respond to a fender bender at Wyant's store in Whitehall.

"Thank you again, Harry."

"Please." Harry waved her hand as if to say it was nothing. "What are you going to do for the rest of the day?"

"I'm going to plant pink dogwoods at the edge of my front yard. It needs an anchor. Did you know that the Romans planted quince trees at their property corners? It's a good plan but I'm going to plant dogwoods, pink." She drew out the word "pink" until it sounded like "pa-ank."

"Pretty."

"What are you going to do?"

"Plow the garden. It's about time."

"We might have one more frost but I doubt it. Although I remember one year back in the fifties when we had a frost in May. Don't forget to plant okra for me."

Before either woman could get in her vehicle, Roger rumbled through the opened front gates. A shiny trailer rolled behind his Ford dually. Unlike a horse trailer, this one had no side windows, slats, or side doors.

He screeched to a stop. "Hey, babe."

"Am I the fourteenth woman you've called 'babe' this morning?"

"Nah, the ninth." He pulled over so traffic could get in and out, cut the motor, and stepped out of the rig. "Mrs. Hogendobber, you're a babe, too, but your boyfriend would knock my teeth down my throat so how about if I just say, 'Hi, lovely lady.'"

"Roger, you're an original." The good woman smiled.

They filled him in on the hubcap episode. He was delighted the hubcaps had been recovered immediately.

As the humans chatted Pewter remarked, *"If he'd lose twenty pounds, trim up his hair, and take a little more care about his person he'd pass."*

"As what?" Mrs. Murphy snickered.

That made Pewter and Tucker laugh. Tucker stuck her nose out the slightly opened driver's window.

"Kinda chilly." Pewter ruffled her fur.

"Yep," Tucker replied, watching Roger drop the tailgate to proudly display his stock car. They stepped up the tailgate ramp for a closer look at this latest incarnation of the Pontiac Trans Am.

"—someday." Roger crossed his arms over his chest.

"Well, I hope you do get into big-time racing but, Roger, it's so dangerous."

"Your green Hornet is impressive." Harry admired the brilliant metallic-green Pontiac.

"Oh, I love this machine, I do, but it's kind of the difference between"—he thought a minute—"a real nice horse and a great horse. NASCAR is the top of the top, you know. I'm down here in the bush league."

"You've got a lot of horses right here." She patted the long hood of the car, then stepped back onto the ramp. "Grease monkey."

He turned up his palms, grease deep in the skin. "Daddy had me swinging that wrecker's ball by the time I was twelve. In the blood. 'Chines." He looked up at the steel giraffe. "Still works." Then he looked at Harry. "Come on."

If it had a motor in it, Harry was enthralled. She clambered up the metal steps ringing with each footfall, up to the operator's cab.

"What is she doing?" Pewter crossly complained, paws on the dash as she peered upward through the windshield.

Mrs. Murphy and Tucker followed her example. They heard the motor fire up.

"You know," Miranda said out loud, "I believe I'll move my car."

"If she's getting out of here, we should do the same." Pewter headed for the open driver's-side window.

"Worrywart." Mrs. Murphy barely got the words out of

her mouth when the wrecker's ball swung over the roof of the truck, over part of the new main building's roof.

"Adios!" Pewter flew out the window.

"Damn." Tucker scrambled to the window; it was a long drop for the dog.

"Don't worry, Tucker, I can open the door." Murphy leaned hard on the door handle, pressing with all her weight.

Hearing the click, the corgi pushed against the door, which opened, Tucker nearly tumbling out. Once on the ground, cat and dog bolted just as the ball passed over on its way back.

"Every cat for herself," Pewter called from under a neatly stacked crosshatched pile of railroad ties.

Miranda crouched in her Falcon, which she'd parked next to those railroad ties. "Tell you what, I hope that boy is sober." She emerged from her car thinking if anything did go wrong she'd have a better chance on foot.

"Me, too," Pewter concurred.

Up in the operator's cab, Roger brought the ball back up to the nose of the crane. "Your turn."

She sat on the cracked black leather seat, warm from Roger. "Ready."

"If you want the ball to go down—no, don't grab them yet—you squeeze these calipers. Closing them completely dumps the ball straight down. Smash.

"If you want to swing the ball use this set of calipers here, here on the left, and the wheel"—he pointed to the steering wheel—"will move the whole deal, turn the cab and the crane, see. Got it?"

"Piece of cake." She smiled as she swung the ball, slowly, over the other side of the fence, keeping her eyes glued to the ball. "Bet you get to a point where you can work the calipers, the wheel, the pedals kind of like a drummer."

" 'Zactly, but I say if you can drive a tractor you can learn to do most any heavy equipment work."

She brought the ball back up, let it down a little bit, then brought it up to the nose. "This is so cool."

"Yeah."

Sean strode outside, looking upward along with his customers who were outside. He shouted, trying to be heard over the heavy diesel motor, "Roger!"

Roger leaned out of the cab, saluting his brother, then he swung back in. "He is so old. Turned into an old man. I'm telling you, I love my brother but, Jesus H. Christ, he is such a pain in the ass. Like this business is the center of the universe. Ever since Dad passed. Okay, okay, everyone has to make a living but Sean thinks he's the indispensable person. Hey, the cemeteries are filled with indispensable people, you know what I mean, Harry Barry?" He sighed. "Miss seeing you around."

"Thanks, Rog. What a nice thing to say."

He shook his head. "We've got the yard on an even keel. Working like dogs but all I ask"—he waved again to his gesticulating brother, then cut the motor—"is to go to the tracks Friday and Saturday nights." He glanced down. Sean hadn't moved. "Big Brother is watching you. Well, babe, lesson's over."

"I loved it."

As they climbed down, the three animals hurried back to the truck, jumped in, and together using the armrest pulled the door back.

Tucker had to jump onto the floorboard first but she scratched up on the seat and helped pull the door back with the kitties.

"She doesn't need to know I can open the door." Mrs. Murphy raised her long silky eyebrows.

"What she doesn't know won't hurt her." Pewter giggled.

"I'm thrilled to be alive," Tucker exhaled. *"Seeing that black ball swoosh over my head did not inspire confidence."*

Harry, enthusiastically reporting her lesson to Miranda, didn't notice the animals shutting the truck door. She hadn't even noticed it was open in the first place and she was so excited when she was up with the wrecker's ball she missed the people scattered below.

Sean fired off a few choice words to Roger, who shrugged. Sean turned on his heel, stalking back into the main building.

Roger smiled at the two women. "The only question worth asking yourself is, 'Am I having fun?' "

Harry drove home feeling the day had improved considerably. As she turned down her long farm road to the house she noticed a gleaming BMW 740il parked in front of the barn. The car belonged to BoomBoom Craycroft, a marvelously beautiful woman who had had an affair with Harry's ex-husband, making her a least-favorite of Harry's. Granted, BoomBoom had slept with Fair Haristeen after Harry had separated from him. Still, the affair had lasted for about six months. Harry was devastated. Of all women, BoomBoom! She had competed against the tall beauty since grade school. Harry usually won the athletic and intellectual events, although BoomBoom ran a close second along with Harry's best friend, Susan Tucker. But where no female classmate could compete with Boom was her effect on the male of the species. Most men, especially when they were young and not wise in feminine wiles, fell for BoomBoom like the proverbial ton of bricks.

The two women had managed an accord over the last few years but that was the extent of it.

"Damn, damn, damn," Harry whispered under her breath.

"If you'd let me catch that rat she would have come and gone," Tucker unhelpfully suggested.

"Tucker, shut up. You know how they can get. It's all hands on deck." Mrs. Murphy put her paws on the dash.

5

I'm so glad you're here. I was just about to leave," Boom-Boom effused as the three horses watched her from the paddock.

"We're in luck," Harry dryly replied as Mrs. Murphy, Pewter, and Tucker scrambled to see who could get out of the truck first.

Pewter won only because she used Mrs. Murphy's back, banking off her to touch the edge of the seat, then slide down, front paws onto the running board and onto the ground.

"I don't believe you did that!" Murphy was furious.

"Toodle-oo." The gray cat made a beeline for the house, where she knew a large bowl of crunchies waited on the kitchen counter.

"Pretty good for a fat girl." Tucker eased herself down.

"Don't take up for her."

"I'm not but it is amazing."

The cat replied with a laugh, *"You're right, though, she can be agile when she has to be. After all, she is a cat."*

"Self-regarding, you cats." Tucker walked over to greet BoomBoom, who leaned over, petting the dog's glossy head.

Mrs. Murphy, now out of sorts, thumped into the barn, walked into the tack room, sat down hard, and shouted at the tiny mouse-hole in the wall, *"I know you're in there. I tell you, you'll be mouse soufflé before Memorial Day."*

The mice, sound asleep, didn't reply. Further agitated, the cat returned to the house, where the humans had now repaired. Maybe she could irritate someone in there.

Despite her antipathy, Harry had minded her manners and invited BoomBoom into the house for tea or a soft drink.

BoomBoom sat in the living room, ensconced in one of the old wing chairs Harry's parents had bought forty years ago for five dollars apiece because they were circa 1930s, unfashionable at the time, and beat-up. Since then they'd been re-covered five times; the last time, before her death, Harry's mother had had them redone in soft green leather, an extravagance on the one hand but a prudent expense if one considered the long run. The chances were that Harry would never have to re-cover the chairs in her lifetime.

"I have a teeny-weeny problem." BoomBoom cast her eyes downward, which meant the problem had just increased in size. "I'm hoping you'll help me."

"Oh. Why not ask Susan?" Harry volunteered her best friend, who got along with BoomBoom better than Harry did.

"Susan is married."

"Ah." Harry was getting the picture.

Mrs. Murphy strode into the room, sat down on the coffee table, and yelled, *"Everybody is horrible! Only I am perfect."*

"Murphy, what's the matter with you?" Harry swatted at her to leave the room.

The tiger cat eluded this clumsy effort by jumping onto the wing chair, taking up residence on the back behind BoomBoom's beautiful, long blond hair, held up in a simple swirled French twist. Having just left the hairdresser's, BoomBoom's tresses were lighter than usual. *"BoomBoom has big bosoms. Bet she blacks her eye when she jogs. Bet it's hard to bend over and stand up again. Maybe her face just hits the floor,"* she warbled, quite pleased with herself.

"Boom, push her off of there. She's being naughty."

"I don't mind the noise. The tuna breath is what gets me." BoomBoom laughed.

"Tuna breath?" Mrs. Murphy's eyes widened, the beautiful electric color seemingly brighter. She unleashed one dagger claw, expertly hooking it into the pretty tortoiseshell clip holding up Boom's hair. With a flick she dislodged half of it so Boom's golden hair fell out of place.

"Now that is enough!" Harry, angry, stood up, grabbed the cat—who offered no resistance—and dropped her to the floor. "One more stunt like that and you're sleeping in the barn tonight."

Pewter, observing the display, coolly said, *"She's only doing what you'd like to do, Mom. You can't stand BoomBoom."*

"Right." Mrs. Murphy, emboldened by the support of Pewter, emitted another yowl.

"First you fight and now you're best friends. You two are infantile." The dog rolled her eyes. She had squeezed next to Harry on the sofa.

"Big word, Tucker. Congratulations," Mrs. Murphy said sarcastically as she turned her back on the company and lifted the tip of her tail in her right paw, bringing it to her lips for grooming.

"Hee hee." Pewter couldn't resist laughing because it was funny to her but also because it would make the dog mad.

Tucker ignored them, placing her head in Harry's lap, looking as adorable as possible.

"You know what I'm doing, I'm venting. Humans vent all the time," Murphy said.

"I wouldn't imitate humans." Pewter thought about grooming but then decided she was too tired. *"It's a species that has as its motto: I can't always do it the hard way but I can try. They make everything so complicated, no wonder they vent, bitch, and moan. It's their own fault."*

"There is that," the tiger cat agreed with her.

BoomBoom had just finished an elliptical tangent that finally returned to its starting point, her need of Harry's help—"... so you see Susan wouldn't be quite right and Lottie Pearson is too eager, if you know what I mean. She parties in D.C., Richmond, and Charlotte, all in search for a man of means. She's beginning to get panicky about marriage, I swear. Of course she says she's canvassing for contributors to the university. Her job as a fund-raiser covers a multitude of sins, I swear." Lottie Pearson was a social acquaintance of BoomBoom's, whom she sometimes liked and sometimes didn't. Today was a didn't.

Harry, fearing what was coming, quickly interjected, "But Lottie Pearson is single and Susan is not. That's a plus." Harry echoed BoomBoom's earlier dismissal of turning to Susan for help. She wished BoomBoom would get to the point. Exactly what did she want?

"Lottie Pearson will complicate things. I really don't want my friends interviewed about their net worth."

"Boom, you're losing me here. What friends? What net worth?"

After a long, refreshing draft of steaming-hot Plantation Mint tea, the tall woman placed the china cup in the matching saucer and laid them on the coffee table. "Your grandmother's china. I remember your grandmother."

"Mom's mom." Harry smiled, an image of a lean, silver-haired lady crossing her mind.

"She was a good teacher. Pony Club."

Pony Club teaches young people all aspects of horsemanship. Riding is but a small portion of one's skills.

Harry leaned forward. "Remember when she made us take apart a bridle, strip it, dip it, put it back together, and she inspected everyone's work? Susan tried to cheat and used a toothbrush to clean around the bit instead of totally dismantling it?"

BoomBoom laughed. "And then she gave that lecture on shortcuts. Hey, I can still hear her voice when I'm considering the lazy way—'the shortest way around is often the longest.'"

As they neared forty both women were slowly realizing that shared experiences were binding. Time possesses the greatest power. Men who fought on opposite sides in a war, in old age, often felt closer to their former enemies than people of their own nationality who were younger.

"You know." BoomBoom lowered her voice, a sweet, dark soprano, a counterpoint to Harry's liquid alto. If the two had sung together they would have sounded heavenly. "I've been seeing this divine man. He's so interesting. He's urbane, speaks four languages, and he's tremendously intelligent. He's coming down this weekend and at the last minute his assistant at the embassy said he could come and—"

"Embassy?"

"Yes. He's Under-Secretary to the Ambassador for Uruguay."

"Who?" Harry was fighting exasperation.

"My friend, Thomas Steinmetz, is Under-Secretary."

BoomBoom threw up her hands. "I'm going in circles. Will you escort my friend's friend? That's what I'm trying to ask."

Now this was interesting. The two cats and dog turned their heads to stare at Harry, who blinked.

"Say something," Mrs. Murphy suggested to Harry.

"Uh—"

BoomBoom tried to be more organized now that the cat was out of the bag, so to speak. "Handsome. Fun. A lot of fun really. Recently divorced."

"How recently?"

"U-m-m, a year."

"Why are you asking me, really?"

"Because you're fun, you're very attractive, and because, well, you never know." She held up her hand, her large diamond reflecting the light.

"Know what?"

"When lightning will strike."

Harry scrunched down in the sofa a bit. Tucker refused to budge. "Tucker."

"I don't want to miss a thing," the bright-eyed corgi replied to the complaint.

"Ha," both cats giggled.

"Harry, you need to get out more." BoomBoom picked up the teacup once more.

"How ironic coming from you."

When Harry and Fair separated and filed for divorce, his brief affair with BoomBoom kept tongues wagging in Crozet. It was like the small-town version of being splashed across the front page of the tabloids.

Harry always felt that Fair could have picked someone out of town or that BoomBoom could have refused him. The fact that both Fair and BoomBoom were great-looking people, in the prime of life, escaped her.

"You're still angry with me and I've done all but grovel,

and I repeat for the thousandth time, he was separated from you. Separated."

Ignoring this because she didn't believe BoomBoom's version of the timing of the affair, Harry plunged in. "Well, it hurt like hell. And just why didn't you stay with him?"

"I could never be a veterinarian's wife."

Truer words were never spoken. Not only could Boom-Boom not stand the schedule of an equine vet, those calls for colic coming right in the middle of a romantic evening, she needed more position, more power, more money.

BoomBoom's affair with Pharamond "Fair" Haristeen, DVM, owed something to putting herself back together after the shock of her young husband's sudden death. To her credit, though, she never used her loneliness as an excuse.

On Fair's part, the affair was a flight from responsibility, pure and simple. He realized it. Broke it off after six months and went into therapy—a tremendously difficult thing for him to do, to ask for help. After the first year of therapy, he begged his ex-wife's forgiveness. He still hoped to win Harry back. She was the best mate he could find and he knew it. She understood horses. She understood him. She expected to work hard in this life and what she asked in return was a partner who also worked hard, remained faithful, and had a good sense of humor. He knew he could do that now.

She remained diffident, although at times she would be pulled back toward him not just emotionally but physically, and that only stirred the pot. Not that she told BoomBoom but Susan knew, of course, and Mrs. Hogendobber suspected.

The animals remained discreet on the subject.

Harry, silent for a while, finally spoke. "What I don't get is why you won't leave me alone? Why is it so important that we be—something?"

"Because we're part of one another's lives. We grew up together. And because we're women and women are smarter than men about these things."

"I don't think I'm smarter than a man about infidelity."

"But he wasn't unfaithful, Harry. You were separated." BoomBoom made this point again, as though speaking to a slow child.

"Can we table this?" Harry rolled her eyes heavenward.

"You've been tabling it for years. Surely we can coexist. We work on all the same projects."

"So does everyone else. It's a small town," Harry said peevishly.

"We hunt together, we play golf and tennis together."

"I hardly ever play golf and tennis. I haven't got the time." Harry fidgeted.

"Okay." BoomBoom took a deep breath. "Will you be Diego Aybar's date?"

"That's his name?"

"Diego Aybar. And trust me, he is handsome, full of energy—even if lightning doesn't strike, you'll enjoy his company. Please say yes, Harry. I know he'll like you and it will be an unforgettable weekend for all of us."

"Fair asked me to the Wrecker's Ball. I could go to everything but that and I'm parade coordinator for the festival"— she paused—"but you know that. 'Course once that last float pushes off—"

"*Say yes,*" Pewter meowed. *"A little shake-up in the status quo can't hurt."*

"All status and no quo." Mrs. Murphy watched her human struggle with conflicting emotions, the most obvious being mistrust of BoomBoom.

"Harry, if you don't like this, if you suffer through the weekend I'll buy you that new Wilson tennis racquet everyone is raving about. Then you can beat me."

"I beat you anyway. You don't have to bribe me, Boom-Boom."

"Well?"

"Clothes?"

"God, she's a hard nut to crack." Pewter exhaled.

"And lacking in all spontaneity but I love her," Mrs. Murphy purred as she leaned into Pewter who'd come up right next to her.

"Don't you two make a pretty picture, but I'm next to Mom and you aren't."

Rising to the little dog's challenge, the cats leapt onto the back of the sofa. They plopped down behind Harry's head.

"It will be fun. All you need is a spring dress for the tea. Your white evening gown looks lovely on you. You need only one new dress. I know how you hate to shop."

"That evening gown was Mother's."

"Classic. Christian Dior classic. Your mother had fabulous taste."

"And no money. She won the gown." Harry smiled, remembering her mother and her pride in the gown that she had, in fact, won in a contest to design the Christmas Ball for the United Way. Christian Dior, a friend of Tally's—Big Mim's aunt who knew everyone and anyone—put up the gown as a reward.

"Come on. It will wake up Fair. He has no competition."

Harry uncrossed her arms. "That's a fact." Her eyebrows twitched together a moment. "All right, BoomBoom. I'll do it. I don't exactly know why I'm doing it but I'm doing it."

"Thank you."

"Spring fever," Pewter laconically said, a small burp following.

"Excuse yourself, pig." Mrs. Murphy reached out and touched Pewter on the shoulder.

"Excuse me. Spring fever."

"Pewter, what are you talking about?" Tucker wanted an answer. She hated it when the cats got "airy," as she called it.

"Spring fever. That's why Harry is going out with this new guy."

"You might be right," Mrs. Murphy agreed. *"This will get Lottie Pearson's knickers in a twist. She's on the man hunt and BoomBoom ignored her in favor of Mom. She'll have her revenge. Just wait."*

"On whom? Mom or BoomBoom?" Tucker lifted her head.

"Both, if I know Lottie. Her social ambitions seethe. Being escorted by a handsome man working on Washington's Embassy Row is her idea of perfect. She'd get to meet more important people and she'd look important. She cultivates people, I guess that's how you put it, before she asks them for hundreds of thousands of dollars for the university. She'd like to run this town someday, too. Never happen. Big Mim will live to be one hundred and fifty. Look how old Aunt Tally is. They never die, I swear. But you mark my words, Lottie Pearson is smart and devious. She'll get her revenge."

"It's so petty!" Pewter exclaimed.

"Precisely but that's the way people are. They're further and further removed from nature, and they get weird, major weird." Mrs. Murphy watched as Harry walked BoomBoom to the back door in the kitchen.

"Spring fever." Pewter marched back into the kitchen for more crunchies.

6

The work week rolled along without incident. Harry and Miranda sorted mail, light this time of year. Big Mim made pronouncements about how to improve the Dogwood Festival before Saturday's parade. Everyone smiled, said, "You're right," and went about their business.

Fair, Harry's ex-husband, was just wrapping up foaling and breeding season. Upon hearing that Harry would be accompanying Diego Aybar to the tea party and then the dance, he fumed; but Fair had committed the mistake of thinking he didn't need to ask Harry. He assumed she would be his date if he could shake free of work. Usually a low-key and reasonable man, he slammed the door to her kitchen, upsetting the cats and secretly delighting Harry.

Miranda glowed for her high-school beau, who would be returning from Hawaii, where he had finally settled his estate, would be her escort for all festivities. She was to pick him up at the airport Friday morning and she figured he'd bounce back from his travails and travel by Saturday, the big day. Tracy Raz, former star athlete of Crozet High, class of 1950, was a tough guy and an interesting one, too.

Reverend Herbert C. Jones, pastor of the Lutheran church and parade marshal this year, was the most jovial anyone had ever seen him, which was saying something as the good pastor was normally an upbeat fellow.

Little Mim, as vice-mayor of Crozet, used this opportunity to insist more trash barrels be placed on the parade route. She endeared herself to the merchants in town by having flags made up at her own expense for them to hang over their doorways. The flags, "Crozet" emblazoned across a French-blue background, also had a railroad track embroidered on the bottom right-hand side. As Crozet was named for Claudius Crozet, former engineering officer with Napoleon's army, she hoped out-of-towners would ask about the tracks. Crozet, after capture in Russia, again rejoined the emperor for Waterloo, managing to escape the Royalists and sail to America. He cut four tunnels into the Blue Ridge Mountains, an engineering feat considered one of the wonders of the nineteenth century. His work—sans dynamite, using only picks, shovels, and axes—stands to this day, as do the roads he built from the Tidewater into the Shenandoah Valley.

The town itself never became a glamorous depot but remained a quiet stop before one plunged into the mountains themselves. Most residents worked hard for a living, but a few enjoyed inherited wealth, Little Mim being one, which is why she paid for the flags herself. She thought if merchants hung the flags out it would create further color for the day, showing pride in the community. Not that residents of the small, unpretentious town lacked pride but rather, in that quiet Virginia way, they didn't speak of it. The surrounding countryside, dotted with apple orchards, drew tourists from all over the world, as did Albemarle County itself, laboring under the ghosts of Jefferson and Monroe, to say nothing of all the movie stars, sports stars, and literary lights who had moved there, enticed by the natural beauty of the place and the University of Virginia. As it was only an hour by air from New York City, some of the richest residents commuted daily in their private jets.

Crozetians, although part of Albemarle County, more or less ignored Charlottesville, the county seat.

Little Mim, a Republican, and her father, a Democrat, now ran the town together. He was grooming her as well as pressuring her to jump parties. So far, she had resisted.

The merchants adored her, not just because of the flags. Like her father, she had a natural flair for politics.

Lottie Pearson assisted Little Mim. Both women were five feet six inches, slender, and well-groomed. Since both favored bright spring sweaters, khaki slacks, and flats, the only way you could tell them apart from the back was that Lottie's hair was honey brown while Little Mim's was ash blond this week. Lottie was much in evidence throughout the week as she climbed on a ladder watering and inspecting the huge hanging baskets at each street corner. Like Fair, she wasn't thrilled about Harry escorting Diego Aybar but she put a good face on it. Little Mim was so busy preparing for the festival that she really hadn't the time to tell anyone what she thought even if she was so inclined. Little Mim, divorced, was beginning to feel lonely. Diego would have been a suitable escort for her, too.

The last task before the parade was hanging the bunting. Everyone pitched in, so the blue and gold colors streamed across Route 240 and Whitehall Road. Bunting hung from buildings. Blue and gold flags and streamers waved from people's windows. Blue and gold were the colors of the French army under Napoleon, or so the town felt. White and gold with the fleur-de-lis was the emblem of the Royalists, so there wasn't a fleur-de-lis in sight.

In addition to the big wrecker's ball crane, which the O'Bannon brothers used to carry the heavier items through town, they owned a smaller, second crane. Roger perfected the knack of appearing wherever Lottie happened to be, always using the excuse that he had a job to do. He asked her to be his date at the Wrecker's Ball, held the first weekend in May, but she put him off, saying she needed to get through the Dogwood Festival first.

Since she didn't give him a flat no, he felt hopeful. Sean told him to give it up, as did Don Clatterbuck, his fishing buddy. Roger swore he'd win her over.

By Friday night Harry crawled home. She'd womanned the post office by herself since Miranda had to go to the airport. She also thought Miranda and Tracy would have a lot to talk about, so she forbade Miranda from coming back to work. The irony was that Miranda wasn't a postal employee. Her long-deceased husband had been the postmaster and she helped out now to keep busy. When George died she drifted in and out of the post office through force of habit. Harry performed many small services for Miranda but felt she could never adequately repay the older woman's boundless generosity.

Determined to go to bed early, Harry slipped into bed by nine; Mrs. Murphy, Pewter, and Tucker, too.

Just as the animals fell asleep, Pewter murmured, *"I have this feeling it's going to be a big, big day tomorrow."*

"The Dogwood Festival's always big." Tucker rolled over on her side.

"Something more." The gray cat closed her beautiful chartreuse eyes.

Mrs. Murphy, on her back next to Harry, turned her head up to look at Pewter reposing on the pillow. *"Cat intuition."*

7

Saturday dawned bright and clear, the temperature at five-thirty a.m. being forty-seven degrees Fahrenheit. The red-buds opened in full bloom, although those in the hollows where it was cooler stayed the dark raspberry color before full flowering. The apple trees still had some blooms but the pear trees were finished, as were the peaches. Tulips and pansies filled gardens in town. But the glory, the highlight, the beauty of spring resided in the dogwoods, which fortuitously chose that exact day to open. The mountains were filled with wild dogwoods. Creamy-pink flowering trees dotted bright green lawns. White and pink dogwoods lined driveways. Everywhere one looked dogwoods bloomed, and to complete the perfection, the azaleas opened, too. Hot pink, soft purple, flaming orange, pure white, and radiant pink azaleas announced their presence heralding high spring in Virginia. The wisteria swaying from doorways and pergolas added lavender and white to the unbelievable color. Old ruins, smothered in wisteria, became a focal point for photographers.

Spring had arrived but not just any spring, spring in the Blue Ridge, the apotheosis of springs.

Harry smiled as she drove to her old high school at nine A.M. The parade would start at ten. Her concession to this task was to apply mascara and to iron her jeans as well as a crisp white shirt. A red crewneck sweater kept her warm. The temperature was fiftyish. Mrs. Murphy, Pewter, and Tucker, old hands at the parade, had been groomed to perfection.

When Harry parked the old truck the temperature had climbed to sixty degrees. By noon she figured it would reach seventy degrees and stay close to that comfortable temperature throughout the day.

Despite the jitters, everyone was smiling as they lined up on the tarmac at Crozet High School. On a day like today not smiling was impossible.

Mrs. Murphy and Pewter sat on a wooden milk crate placed in the bed of the truck. As Harry had parked by the head of the parade, they had the best view. Tucker couldn't stand not being with Harry so she tagged along at her human's heels.

"How do I look?" Reverend Jones held out his arms full-length, a blue and gold marshal's sash covering his chest.

"A million bucks." She smiled. "Are you ready?"

"What do I do but wave?" The older man laughed.

Sean and Roger O'Bannon walked up. Roger, a touch shorter than his brother, had obviously just buzz-cut his sandy hair.

"Time?"

"You've got time." Harry smiled at him. "Like your new haircut."

"Make time." Roger snapped his fingers, ever the

younger brother, slightly rebellious. "Do you know this is the fifteenth year I've driven a float? Do I get a medal?"

"No, Roger. It means you're a glutton for punishment." Harry laughed at him.

"Ever since I got my driver's license."

"Liar." Sean poked his brother. "You drove before you had your license."

"Not a float."

"If Dad were here he'd settle this."

"Well, he's not." Roger smacked Harry on the small of her back. "Talk to Lottie for me."

"Why?"

"She's playing hard to get."

"Smart girl." Sean laughed.

Roger growled at him, baring his teeth as fangs. It startled Tucker, who growled back. "I want her to be my date at the Wrecker's Ball."

"You're upsetting my dog," Harry said to Roger.

"Same effect he has on Lottie."

"Sean." Roger threw up his hands in mock despair. "What do women want?"

"Ask us one at a time," Harry swiftly replied.

Roger laughed, "Good answer."

Sean spoke to Roger. "Be persistent and send presents. Always works for me."

"Oh? Since when?" Roger pulled Sean's ponytail.

"You're driving her float. That ought to spike your hormones." Sean readjusted his ponytail. "Make her special."

"Guys, would you like me to leave?"

"I said hormones. I didn't mention his sperm count." Sean smirked. "No help for that."

Harry threw up her hands. "Too much information! Go back to your respective floats."

"You're worse with women than I am," Roger swirled right back at his brother.

"Well?" Harry crossed her arms over her chest.

"I'm going." Roger turned on his heel.

"I'm not." Waiting until his brother was out of earshot, Sean whispered, "Do you think it would do any good if you spoke to Lottie?"

"Hell, no. She's pissed because BoomBoom fixed me up with someone she wanted to go to the dance with."

"Who?"

"I don't know. A friend from Washington. Lottie doesn't know him either but he's new and he has a good position at an embassy. Guess the idea excited her. Anyway, she won't listen to me. Ask Little Mim to help you, since Lottie's been working with her for the festival. Worth a try."

Sean smiled weakly. "Thanks, Har." He took a few steps, then turned back to her. "He's an okay guy, a little rough around the edges. Typical motorhead."

"I know." She winked as Sean set out to find Little Mim.

Harry checked her watch, then her clipboard. She scanned the floats. The O'Bannon Salvage float was an elaborate reconstruction of Monticello made out of salvage.

"They'll win the prize for sure," Reverend Herb whispered in her ear, coming up behind her.

Harry returned to her list. "Herb, you look terrific and you'll pull out in about fifteen minutes. We've got the St. Elizabeth band right behind you and the Mah-Jongg Club."

The Mah-Jongg ladies, most of them in rickshaws being pulled by sturdy-legged youngsters, wore Chinese clothes. The club had been running strong since the 1920s and these were the survivors, Aunt Tally Urquhart among them in an electric-blue dress.

Harry grabbed the bullhorn as she ascended the three-foot-square wooden stand that served as her command post.

"Hey, gang." They chattered still. "Earth to parade. Earth to parade." Slowly the assembled, perhaps five hundred strong, quieted. "We are ten minutes from blastoff. If you have to go to the bathroom, do it now." A titter of laughter followed. "Remember, the parade always takes longer than we think it will. There are people with buckets filled with ice, bottled water, Gatorade, along the route. They are there for you. If you feel even a tiny bit thirsty, call out and they'll bring you your drink."

"Scotch on the rocks," Aunt Tally hollered, her voice strong and youthful for a woman in her nineties.

"Oh, you spoiled my present." Reverend Herb Jones trotted over, handing her a bottle of good scotch as everyone around screamed with laughter and the news was passed down the line, with more laughter following in ripples.

"I could use some catnip." Pewter was grateful that Harry had put a huge bowl of water in the truck as well as crunchies but she wanted catnip, too.

"Get in a rickshaw then. Your chances will improve." Murphy laughed.

"I just might." The gray cat leaned over the edge of the truck.

Harry checked her watch again. "Eight minutes."

An athletic figure jogged alongside the assembled floats.

"Welcome home!" Harry beamed, seeing Tracy Raz.

"Hey, girl." He kissed her as she leaned down. "I'll catch up with you later. Cuddles is nervous. I think she's blown every note on her pitch pipe." He laughed at Miranda, whom he sometimes called Cuddles, her high-school nickname.

Miranda was the lead singer for the Church of the Holy Light and the choir was arranged on a float called Stairway to Paradise, which was just what you would expect.

"Have you seen Boom?"

"I did a minute ago. Primping." He smiled.

"Big surprise. Hey, you'll be at the tea dance. I'll find you there."

"You got it." He kissed her again and jogged back down the line, where Miranda could be seen in her choir robes, her back turned toward Harry. The other choir members were taking their places on the stairway to paradise. A few appeared as though their Maker might call them soon enough.

"Mom, don't forget to drink water yourself," Tucker, ever solicitous, barked.

Harry stepped down, lifted the dog, and climbed back up. She didn't understand a word the corgi had said.

Jim Sanburne and Little Mim sat in an open convertible behind Herb's float.

Harry smiled at them and they smiled back. "Little Mim, Sean's looking for you."

"He found me. I'll do what I can," came the unenthusiastic reply.

Lottie was on the third float, Daughters of Time, sponsored by the United Daughters of the Confederacy. Lottie's hoopskirt was so big a stiff wind would send her airborne. Roger was driving that float while Sean was driving the O'Bannon float.

"Four minutes," Harry called out.

A tug at her jeans behind her turned her around. Boom-Boom, dressed as a 1920s flapper for the Heart Fund float, said, "I want you to meet Diego before the tea. Mary Minor Haristeen, please meet Diego Aybar."

Harry's mouth moved but nothing came out. She was staring into the liquid brown eyes of one of the most gorgeous men she had ever seen. "Uh—welcome to Crozet."

"My pleasure. BoomBoom tells me I should meet you at Aunt Tally's"—he said "Aunt Tally's" with a Spanish accent and a hint of good humor—"garden. She says everyone falls in love in the garden."

"With the garden." Harry smiled.

"No, in the garden," BoomBoom corrected. "Listen, I've got to get back on my float. Diego, the two best places to see the parade are from the back of Harry's truck or on the corner of Route 240 and Whitehall Road."

"Try the truck," Harry stammered. "The two cats are good companions."

The two cats at that very moment were laughing at their mother, who was in a state. Neither could ever remember seeing Harry like that.

"The best friends come on four feet," he said in his beguiling light baritone.

"Now there's a man with sense." Mrs. Murphy walked forward to greet him as he gracefully bounded into the truck bed.

"One minute," Harry called into the bullhorn.

Reverend Herb Jones straightened up, took a deep breath. In the car behind him, Little Mim leaned over and kissed her father on the cheek. The drivers started their motors. Some band members threw back their shoulders, others licked their reeds, while the drummers spun their drumsticks in anticipation.

"Ten, nine, eight, seven, six, five, four, three, two, one— showtime!" Harry called.

The drummers clicked their sticks in rhythm. The four different high-school bands interspersed throughout the parade marched in place. The Reverend Jones cruised first, slowly out of the school lot. The St. Elizabeth band, first with the music, initially walked out to bass drums only, *boom, boom, boom;* then the snare drums kicked in and within a minute they all burst forth with the ever-popular theme song from *Rocky.*

Harry waved as each group passed her. She heard the roar from all the people crowded along the path. Tears sprang into her eyes. She felt as if her own life were parading before her. The sight of Tally Urquhart in her rickshaw, participating in her ninety-second parade (Tally was a star even as a toddler) brought the tears rolling down.

What great good fortune to be where you know people, you love people, and hopefully they love you. The fact that her family had nested here immediately after the Revolutionary War, having drifted over from the Tidewater, where they'd lived since 1640, only deepened the experience of home.

Tucker crowded next to Harry. Tucker loved music. The cats had leapt to the roof of the truck so as not to miss a single thing.

Harry waved as friends and neighbors passed, and then she glanced back at Diego. His smile was five thousand megawatts. She smiled back at him, grateful that this small slice of Virginia pleased him. It hadn't occurred to her that she pleased him, too.

Harry felt as though her chest would burst. The joy, as high as grief was deep, nearly overwhelmed her.

8

Although covering less than two miles from the high school to the town's main intersection, the route was hilly. The float builders, knowing this, had devised railings and props such as fake boulders with little handholds on them, so that the people on the floats could grab them when the floats rolled downhill.

Lottie Pearson forgot this. When the Daughters of the Confederacy float dipped into the decline just before the fire department, she lurched off the float, saved only by the metal in her hoopskirt, which hit the pavement first. Unhurt, she was helped back on the float by friends standing along the parade route. Roger couldn't leave the truck. Lottie's skirt was bent, which meant her pantaloons showed. Each time she pushed the skirt back into place it popped up on the back side. The result drew cheers and laughter but not of the sort she hoped to hear. As she was the leading lady on the float, the one right up front, she was loath to relinquish her position. If the choice was between obscurity and showing her ass, Lottie bravely decided to show her ass.

As the last band marched out of the parking lot, the black and red of Albemarle High, Harry hopped down from her perch.

"Mom's got a little tan. Looks good against her white T-shirt," Pewter noted as Harry removed her sweater with the day's warming. Pewter giggled, remembering the sight of Harry ironing her jeans and T-shirt.

"Nobody looks better in jeans than Harry," Tucker called out from behind her mother. *"I mean, if this fellow likes a fit body then he has to like Mom."*

Mrs. Murphy loved her mother, but she realized that not all men like natural women. Many, attracted by artifice, want lots of hair, preferably blond, boobs pushed up to the max, long fingernails, expensive clothes, and perfect makeup. In a word, BoomBoom.

Harry actually was a beautiful woman but she had no sense of it. High cheekbones accentuated wonderful facial bone structure. Her long black eyelashes drew attention to her soft brown eyes. She rarely wore lipstick on her full lips. Her hair, short and black, curled just above the nape of her neck. But one had to study Harry to recognize her beauty. A woman like BoomBoom hit one over the head with it.

As Harry had no vanity she was able to concentrate on whomever she encountered. She didn't think she was pretty. She didn't worry about the impression she was making. Her focus was on the other person. This quality beguiled more men than her looks once they got around to really studying her. There was an innocence about her. It never occurred to her, not once, that she might be attractive to men. She had known her ex-husband since kindergarten. The art of flirting, of luring men, seemed irrelevant to her since she had always loved Fair. When he left her she assumed she'd never love again. She didn't launch into tirades about how awful men were, how they used women and dumped them, the usual cry of the abandoned female. Harry had seen women behave execrably toward men. As far as she was concerned one gender was as bad as the other.

Fair's attempts to reconcile touched her. She truly loved him but now in quite a different way. At first she felt she could never trust him again. Lately, she thought maybe she could. He'd learned and she'd learned but the difficult part was that she didn't know if she'd feel romantic about him again. Certainly she could go to bed with him. She knew his body the way a blind woman knows Braille. However, that didn't constitute romantic desire.

She didn't share these thoughts with Susan or Miranda. Harry kept her deepest thoughts to herself, sometimes asking the animals for their opinion.

As Mrs. Murphy watched Harry approach the truck she felt the lightness in her step, the surge of energy that illuminated her human's face.

"How could Diego not like Mom . . . but is he good enough?" Mrs. Murphy stretched. "After all, we are better judges of character than humans. We need to check out this situation."

"You're right and I should have thought of that straight off." Tucker felt guilty.

"You would have eventually." Mrs. Murphy hopped into the bed of the truck just as Diego, of average height and muscular, hopped out.

"Oh, balls," Pewter disagreed. "One human is pretty much like any other. They make a big deal out of these tiny, tiny differences but as a species they're all cut from the same cloth."

"Mother's better." Tucker defended Harry, whom she loved with all her heart.

"They do fuss over nits and nit-picking but I think they're very different from one another and that's their challenge. They *are herd animals and they need one another to survive but they can't build communities to include everyone. It's a real mess. They don't understand their fundamental nature, which is to be part of the herd,"* Murphy stated.

"I'm not part of any herd." Pewter proudly jumped down next to Murphy.

"Of course not. You're a cat," Murphy said.

"Murphy, this herd idea sounds good but you once said that dogs are pack animals and here I am—not with other dogs." Tucker waited for Harry to put her in the cab of the truck.

"We're your pack." Mrs. Murphy drove home her point. *"The fact that we're cats plus one human is beside the point."*

"H-m-m." Tucker pondered this as the humans chatted. *"I never thought of that."*

"Mrs. Murphy, Cat Supreme." Murphy pushed out her chest, then laughed.

"... merrier." Diego finished his sentence, which had started out "The more." He had agreed to ride in the cab of the truck with two cats, one dog, and Harry. He didn't seem to mind at all.

Harry drove them around the back way. They parked near the main intersection, walking the last block. The cats remained in the truck with the windows open. Neither one liked crowds, although they usually rode on Harry's shoulders if they had to enter a fray. Pewter complained about the marching music. She preferred Mozart. Furthermore, the trumpets hurt her ears. Mrs. Murphy thought it was time for her noon nap.

Tucker eagerly accompanied Harry and Diego. As they reached the main intersection the people lined the road four deep, a lot for Crozet. At five feet ten inches, Diego could see over most of the crowd, but Harry, at five feet six, had to stand on her tiptoes.

Diego gently worked his way to the front, reached back

for Harry's hand, and pulled her up with him. When people saw it was their postmistress carrying Tucker they gladly gave way.

They'd no sooner reached their place than the United Daughters of the Confederacy float rolled by, with Lottie and her pantaloons evoking comment.

Harry heard Roger O'Bannon yell to a bystander, "Give me twenty bucks and I'll dump them all on the road."

Laughter greeted this offer. Lottie ignored it, of course.

Spurred on by the laughter Roger stuck his head farther out of the truck, artfully concealed by the float. "Hey, Lottie, why don't you ditch the hoop?"

"Shut up, Roger."

"You'd better be good to me. I'm driving this boat." He laughed loudly. She ignored him again so he catcalled, "Lottie, oh, Lottie Pearson."

"Roger, for God's sake, watch where you're going."

They were cruising close to the side of the road.

"Just trying to get you girls a nice cold drink."

Danny Tucker, Susan's son, rushed up, two drinks in each hand. The ladies eagerly reached down.

"How did women wear these things?" one young lady grumbled, for the finery was heavier than anything she had ever worn before.

"They didn't wear them every day," Lottie snapped, then remembered her attention should focus on the crowd. She smiled big and waved, then she saw, really saw, Diego Aybar. Her smile froze. She recovered and continued to ignore Roger, whose suggestions grew ever more risqué.

By the end of the parade the mood of the participants and the crowd was even more elevated than at the beginning. The reason for this was that the Veterans of Foreign Wars had a small brass band with two snares and they peeled out of the parade as it ended, marching and playing all the while. They marched straight into a small bar where they continued to hold forth.

BoomBoom was taking a Polaroid of Don Clatterbuck and Roger at the float. The "belles" had all fled. The minute she clicked the picture both men made a beeline for the bar.

"Is it always like this?" Diego asked.

"More or less, which means either they're more drunk or less." Harry smiled.

"Ah yes." He smiled back at her and it was obvious he liked her. There weren't a lot of women like Harry hovering about the embassy. She intrigued him. "You know for us the seasons are opposite. Spring fever comes in late October and early November."

"I imagine it's beautiful in South America."

"Yes—not every centimeter but—yes."

"Did BoomBoom give you today's schedule?"

"We are to go to a tea party. BoomBoom wanted me to meet you in the garden. She suggested I see the parade and meet you afterward but I wanted to meet you as soon as possible and I'm glad I did."

"Me, too. I guess BoomBoom wanted us to meet in the garden because I'd have a dress on. I rarely do." Harry blushed for a moment. "The truth is I'm 'most always in jeans."

"Señorita, you are beautiful no matter what you wear." He bowed his head slightly.

"*Oh, this is good.*" Tucker happily drooled.

Harry burst out laughing. "Mr. Aybar—"

"Diego."

"Diego, you are very kind." She took a deep breath. "We have a few hours before dressing for the party. If you'd like I could drive you around, show you a bit of the county. I don't think there's any way we could get to Monticello and back on time, though."

He held up his hand. "I have seen it. Mr. Jefferson has my full admiration."

"Cruise?"

"Cruise." He echoed her word. Diego was a quick study.

And cruise they did, chatting all the while. She drove by estates, apple orchards, cattle farms. To her delight she learned that the Aybars maintained a residence in Montevideo but the family had an *estancia* where they bred cattle.

Diego, educated at Duke, studied law at Yale and then studied back home in Uruguay. His father propelled him toward diplomacy but his heart was in farming.

"I'm at a crossroads."

"And your father will be upset?"

"Ballistic." Diego smiled wanly. "Family is, oh, I can't say more important in my country but tighter, a deeper sense of obligation, perhaps. Here the job comes first—or so it seems to me. Home, it's family. And like everything, that's both good and bad. You see, we have ruling families and they ask not what is best for Uruguay but what is best for the family."

"I think I understand. And you come from such a family."

"My father and grandfather would like to think so."

"Perhaps the weekend can take your mind off your crossroads."

"Or help me make a decision. One hates to disappoint one's family, no?—but one hates to violate one's self."

"Entire novels have been written about that." Harry turned back toward the mountains. "Where is Thomas Steinmetz?"

Diego replied, "He had some business to attend to but will be at the tea. You must know that your county is overflowing with retired ambassadors, diplomats, senior officials, and senior officers of the military."

By the time Harry dropped Diego back at the guest

house at BoomBoom's place, they had learned a lot about one another. Perhaps the most important thing was that they both had a sense of humor.

The phone rang as Harry struggled with her panty hose.

"How do you like Diego?" BoomBoom asked.

"He's handsome and charming."

"I thought you'd like him. His passion is farming."

"Yes, we discovered that. Are you calling me just to find out if I like him?" Harry remained suspicious of Boom.

"Well, no. I need your help. Roger O'Bannon insulted Lottie Pearson and she's mad at me anyway—all the more so since she laid eyes on Diego. I asked Aunt Tally if she might disinvite Roger and she wouldn't hear of it, but you know how Aunt Tally likes a scene. I thought you might speak to her. She likes you better than she likes me."

"BoomBoom, since when are you solicitous of Lottie Pearson? There's more than you're telling me."

"No, really there isn't. I was hoping to spare Aunt Tally a scene."

"For God's sake, BoomBoom, as you said, Aunt Tally lives for a scene." Harry started to laugh.

"You're right. I contradicted myself." BoomBoom sighed deeply. "I was hoping to spare myself."

Aunt Tally was about to get her scene all right but it wasn't the one BoomBoom anticipated.

9

In order for a Virginia party to be a success certain things must occur. First, someone has to leave in tears. Second, someone has to pass out due to overindulgence. Third, there has to be a fistfight, and last, someone has to fall in love.

If pressed on these qualities most Virginians would decry the fistfight, the tears, and the drunkenness, but not Aunt Tally. Forthright about life being theater, or at least her parties being theater, she mixed her guests like water and sulfuric acid, then waited for the explosion.

Her advancing years only whetted her appetite for drama. Her beloved yet criticized niece, Big Mim, said it was because Aunt Tally had no sex life. She stirred up other people's hormones.

Upon hearing this, Tally snapped, "Of course I have no sex life. There are no men over ninety and those under ninety won't look at me. You find me a beau and I'll wear him out. I'm still hell in bed, Marilyn, and don't you forget it!"

"Dear God, spare me," Big Mim murmured through her frosted-bronze lipstick.

This was said in front of Reverend Jones, Miranda, Susan and Ned Tucker, as well as Lottie Pearson, who arrived early so as to mix with the older crowd, ever trolling for major donors to the university. There was no way Big Mim could be spared.

"Well, what are you all staring at with your mouths hanging open? Catch flies that way." Tally flicked out her silver hound's-head cane at the assembled. Before she could further berate the small gathering, the doors were flung open and everyone else seemed to arrive at once. The O'Bannons, extremely merry, roared in. Roger wore a sprig of mint in his sports coat for reasons known only to himself and Jim Beam. Sean kissed Aunt Tally repeatedly. She was loath to let him go.

Ned Tucker realized that Aunt Tally's servants, almost as old as the great lady herself, would never be able to pass the hors d'oeuvres and drinks fast enough. He hastily directed people to the bar, a temporary measure. He then called the band director of Crozet High School, an old friend, telling him to send a couple of kids over to pass food around. He'd make a contribution to Crozet High.

He no sooner hung up the phone when BoomBoom swirled in, the diaphanous skirt of her spring dress, a pastel lavender, catching light and the breeze. Next to Boom-Boom, in line to meet Aunt Tally, stood Thomas Steinmetz, blond, middle-aged, impeccably dressed. This was a man who flew to London at a whim to be measured for shirts at Turnbull & Asser, suits from shops on Jermyn Street, and shoes from Lobb's or Maxwells. Standing behind Thomas was Diego, also impeccably turned out, a bright turquoise handkerchief in his silk-and-linen jacket breast pocket.

Tally's sharp eye missed nothing. "Harrow?" she asked Thomas.

"Yes." He nodded slightly to the American, who recognized his old school tie from England. Most Americans hadn't a clue.

"Well, you're a wise man then—wise enough to escort one of the most beautiful women in Virginia." She was taking his measure.

"Madam, I am speaking to one of the most beautiful women in Virginia." Thomas bowed low and Tally pursed her lips, all ready to say something about being The Ancient of Days, but at the last minute she decided to enjoy the praise.

"You are very kind, Mr. Ambassador." BoomBoom had given Tally his bio before, of course, but she bumped him up from being counsel to number one. He didn't mind. She turned her attentions now to Diego, being introduced by BoomBoom. When she took a moment to focus on him, his light brown eyes, his jet-black hair, she breathed in. Oh, if only she were young again!

She and Diego chatted and laughed as two cats and one dog tore through the house.

"Quick. Let's get past the receiving line!" Mrs. Murphy led her friends. *"Aunt Tally will insist we do tricks."*

"I smell ham biscuits." A dreamy look came over Pewter.

"Later. We've got to dodge the humans." Tucker nudged Pewter with her nose, for the fat kitty had slowed down.

"They can just get out of my way," she replied with a saucy toss of her gray head, but she did move.

Tally said, "Where's Harry?"

BoomBoom called over her shoulder for Tally was now greeting Tracy Raz, who'd stopped off to buy an orchid corsage for Miranda as well as one for Aunt Tally. "She's in the garden."

"She can't go in the garden before she goes through the receiving line. You tell her to get her bucket back here or she'll hear from me."

"I will but—" BoomBoom glanced around, then walked back, whispering something in the old lady's ear.

"Oh, well, all right, but tell her she has to come back here then." She smiled a moment. "Harry. H-m-m."

Diego strode into the garden, where Harry waited in a simple but very becoming dress. She leaned against a handsome bench built in the eighteenth century, worth a small fortune. Tally believed things should be used. Her only concession to the bench's value was to bring the outdoor furniture into the huge mudroom each night. Her George II silver, her Hepplewhite sofa, chairs, all the paraphernalia of old Virginia wealth pleased her, but she wasn't possessed by her possessions. Nor did she call attention to them. Only new people did that.

Diego bowed, then kissed Harry's right hand, brushing the back of her hand with his lips, the proper way. "In the future, I shall equate spring with you."

"Diego, you know how to turn a girl's head." She laughed.

"May I bring you a drink?"

"I think you'll have to because Aunt Tally's butler probably can't make it from the bar to the garden." She noted his puzzled look, then she pointed out the butler, who happened to be slowly passing the opened French doors.

"Ah, a gentleman in the fullness of his years."

"Before you fetch me a drink I must pay honors to Aunt Tally. I ran around the back of the house and didn't go through the receiving line because I wanted you to find me in the garden. I guess I spoiled the effect by telling. I was running late because my neighbor's cows crashed through the fence and I had to drive them back. My neighbor knows next to nothing about farming plus he's in Seattle on a photo shoot for Nordstrom's. I just made it!"

"A photographer?"

"A model. Little Mim was mad for him. You've met Marilyn?"

"Only just, on my way to you."

Harry stood up, a little unsteady on her heels. "I don't know why I'm talking so much. I'm actually a fairly quiet person. Everyone will tell you that and lots else, I guess." She smiled, her white teeth enhancing her clean, open features.

"I'll walk you back to the grand Aunt Tally. I take it she earned her name hunting?"

Harry positively beamed. "Oh, you know about fox-hunting?"

"Tally champagne." He called out as they passed the bar and Ned Tucker held up a bottle of violently expensive champagne.

They both laughed as Roger said a bit too loudly, "Come on, Ned. Stop telling me how great it is and pour, dammit."

"An artist?" Diego noted Roger's attire ... just off, despite his wearing a sports coat. The cowboy boots didn't help.

"Uh, a mechanic. He and his brother Sean own a salvage yard filled with architectural pieces, columns, that stuff. It's quite interesting." They'd reached the line for Aunt Tally. Big Mim had rejoined her aunt on the receiving line.

No sooner had Harry and Diego taken their place than who should walk up behind them but Fair, at six foot five towering over everyone.

"Harry." He leaned down and kissed his ex-wife. He knew thanks to BoomBoom that she was "helping out" with the South Americans as BoomBoom put it, but of course Boom had neglected to describe Diego. When Harry introduced them, Fair struggled to contain his surprise and dismay. He collected himself. "Welcome to Crozet."

"Thank you." Diego firmly shook his hand.

At that moment Harry reached Aunt Tally and Big Mim. Both ladies took in the situation. A sly smile crossed Aunt Tally's lips, Lancôme lipstick generously but not sloppily applied.

"Aunt Tally, I cheated."

"I know you did but in a good cause." She turned her cheek for Harry to kiss her. "I saw your animals rip through here so I knew you couldn't be far behind. That cat of yours, the gray one, will eat me out of house and home."

"Be glad she doesn't drink."

Tally laughed. "There is that. And Mr. Aybar, you may kiss me now, too, since you've met me." She turned her other cheek and Diego kissed it, then kissed the back of her hand.

He bowed and also kissed Big Mim's hand. She brightened considerably.

As they moved away both Aunt Tally and Big Mim made a fuss over Fair, how good he was to forgo a date with Harry so the Uruguayan gentleman wouldn't be lonesome, how's foaling, how are you, etc.

As Fair moved away, quickly intercepted by Lottie Pearson wearing a flowered hat, Tally whispered to her niece, "I just lo-o-ove my parties. Uh-huh."

"You're incorrigible." Big Mim laughed, then reached out to greet Deputy Cynthia Cooper, herself in a spring dress. "I don't think I've ever seen you look so lovely."

The tall woman replied with humor, "Mrs. Sanburne, I don't think you've ever seen me in a dress."

"Well...yes."

"You're a tall girl. You'd look good in anything, even chain mail," Aunt Tally said. "Is your boss coming by?"

"The sheriff said he'd try to make it but he's a little behind today."

"It was good of him to let you join us." Tally let go of her hand and Cynthia headed for her friend Harry.

Big Mim whispered, "Security. You didn't tell me you hired security."

"I didn't. I like Cynthia Cooper." Tally beamed at Lynne Beegle, a prominent local rider, as she moved up in the receiving line.

Harry, Diego, and Cooper chatted away, soon joined by Miranda Hogendobber, Tracy Raz, Susan Tucker, and Ned. They celebrated Tracy's return, found out that Diego had a great sense of humor, and thoroughly enjoyed one another.

Over in a corner, Lottie Pearson fended off Roger O'Bannon. She had a smile on her face as she refused his advances. She'd never admit it but she liked the attention. Fair, not being her date, had gotten her a drink, then circulated. He was currently talking to Little Mim about zoning ordinances, not his favorite subject but one of hers.

Lottie pulled a cigarette from her small beaded clutch bag. "Damn." She couldn't find a light.

Roger pulled a brightly colored matchbook from his sports coat, struck a match, lighting her cigarette. "Here, take the pack." He paused. "I'll pick you up at eight," he declared.

"No, you won't." She tossed her head back.

"I'll take you to Mim's dance tonight, too. You don't have a date. And I'll escort you to the Wrecker's Ball."

"Who told you that?" Lottie crossly said. "I have a date for tonight."

"A little bird."

She eyed BoomBoom across the room. "A big robin redbreast. Wait until I get my hands on her."

"I'd rather you get your hands on me."

Eavesdroppers stifled a giggle, making certain not to stare at the impending drama.

"Roger, dream on."

"You know what's wrong with you, Lottie? You're a god-damned snob. And you know what else? I've never seen a snob who was really happy because there are so few people they can lower themselves to be with, you know? And you need friends in this world. You need friends. It's a cruel world sometimes. You need friends and you need a drink."

"You've had enough to drink, which is why I'll forgive you calling me a snob. If you want me to go out with you, Roger, you're sure going about it in a bizarre manner."

"I'm not drunk." A whiff of belligerence filled his voice. "And I'm getting rich. You forget that. How many F.F.V.'s have money? Look at Harry. Great blood and not a penny." He liked Harry but he didn't mind using her as an example of First Families of Virginia. "Business is booming. I'm not a poor man. Didn't your mother tell you it's just as easy to fall in love with a rich man as a poor one? Well, I'm rich."

Lottie at the moment wasn't pleased with Harry because she thought Diego should have been her date. BoomBoom was heartless in assigning Diego to Harry. After all, Harry could have gone to the parties with her ex-husband. Everyone knew he was still in love with her and was dying to get her back.

"Lottie, maybe you've had too much to drink." Roger touched her arm as she was lost in thought.

"Huh. No!"

"Well, let me get you one. The world looks a lot better after you've belted back some Jim Beam."

The John D'earth band started playing out in the garden. Aunt Tally had set up her outdoor dance floor. People drifted outside.

Sean, wearing a sports jacket and tie, walked over. "Roger, lay off for a little bit or you'll be useless by tonight."

"Big Brother is watching you," Roger said with no malice as Sean moved away, Lottie in tow.

"Thank you, Sean," Lottie said, her voice low.

"He's always had this crush on you, Lottie. I wish you could see past his exterior. Roger is a good man and he'd be a good provider, solid. He needs a woman to anchor him. He drinks because he's lonely."

"This is said by a man still single." Lottie thought Sean the better-looking of the brothers.

"The business has taken up so much of my time, a lot more than I thought. I'll tell you, I've sure learned to respect my father and grandfather. They started the business and they changed with the times although at the end Dad was set in his ways. Rog and I have to put everything we've got in the business. But you know, I like the challenge." He exhaled a long deep breath. "But I do have to get out more. I'm not going to find a wife in the junkyard."

"Oh, if BoomBoom, now the artiste, comes to your lot I imagine other women do, too."

"You'd be surprised at the people who come out there." He grinned in semi-agreement. "BoomBoom surprises me. She really is welding." He held up his hand. "Honestly. She's making sculptures out of scraps and they aren't bad. Kind of whimsical. But I still don't think I'm going to meet the love of my life at the salvage yard."

"BoomBoom with a welding torch." Lottie's eyebrows rose.

Aunt Tally followed her guests into the garden as the marching-band members served drinks and hors d'oeuvres. "Where did all these children come from? Have people been reproducing behind my back?"

"Ned Tucker called for some extra help," Big Mim told her.

"He should run for office. He's a smart man."

"What kind of office?" Big Mim wanted no interference for her daughter's career. She was relieved that Marilyn finally had some direction in life.

"Congress."

"Yes, he'd be good but let's see how Little Mim does."

"She's vice-mayor and she's young. Give her time."

"But Ned's young, too," Big Mim said.

"He's in his late forties. Marilyn's in her thirties. Let Ned pave the way." Aunt Tally rapped the brick path with her cane, betraying her impatience as well as her intelligence. If Ned ran for Congress and won, then Tally and others like her could push him toward the Senate someday and Little Mim could inherit his seat. It would be less of a fight and that way they'd have two politicians in their pockets. A lot of ifs but most endeavors started that way and Tally paid little mind to ifs.

"May I have this dance?" Reverend Jones held out his hand to Aunt Tally.

"I thought you'd never get me away from her." Tally laughed as they stepped onto the floor. "She hovers around me. What does she think? I'm going to keel over in her presence because I'm older than dirt?"

"She hovers over you because she loves you."

"Oh, that," Tally answered the Reverend.

Diego held Harry. She felt a chill run down her spine. Fair, dancing with Lottie, glared.

Thomas Steinmetz made the rounds of the ladies, always returning to BoomBoom, as was proper.

"You're making a lot of women happy." BoomBoom smiled at him.

"So long as I make you happy." He smiled at her as one who is accustomed to getting his way with women.

Roger wandered over, a bit more sober. "Are you really an ambassador?"

"Thomas Steinmetz, Roger O'Bannon, proprietor with his brother of O'Bannon Salvage," BoomBoom said.

"Pleased to meet you." Thomas held out his hand.

Roger blinked, then shook it. "Likewise. You guys have tin mines in Uruguay?"

"Bolivia has more of those than we do." He noticed Aunt Tally being led back to a table. "If you will excuse me, it's my turn to dance with Aunt Tally."

"Lucky dog," Roger replied noncommittally.

Lottie passed by BoomBoom and hissed. "You're a real shit to fix up Harry with Diego. You want Fair back."

BoomBoom turned on her heel. "Lottie, you are so small and so off course. I ought to smack you right in the mouth."

"You've got a violent streak. You had it in high school. Go ahead. Just go ahead," Lottie baited her.

Roger grabbed Lottie by the elbow. "Come on, Lots. Let's talk."

"No." She shook him off.

Roger stood there for a moment, indecisive, then walked away, a slight sway to his gait.

"Lottie, don't be an ass. I put Harry and Diego together because I knew he loved farming. How was I to know they'd hit it off? Because you're unhappy you don't want anyone else to be happy."

"Bitch." Lottie's voice rose a bit.

"Yes," Susan answered as a joke for she could overhear part of the exchange. "I can go from zero to bitch in three point six seconds. Ask my husband."

Lottie fixed her gaze on Susan standing with Cooper,

then decided to allow Roger to lead her away. The two
women joined BoomBoom.

"You certainly have an effect on women." Cooper
laughed at BoomBoom.

"Usually negative." She smiled, though, as Thomas was
returning to her.

"She'll wear us all out." He indicated Aunt Tally.

"First woman to fly a plane in Albemarle County as well
as other things," Susan remarked.

Under the long table inside the house Pewter had fallen
fast asleep. Stuffed with turkey, ham, smoked salmon, and
other delicacies, she needed a snooze to aid her digestion.
Tucker lay beside her, a little bubble escaping her lips.

Murphy sampled everything but she wasn't a big eater.
She'd walked back into the kitchen.

The caterer's assistant fussed over the large silver samovar,
filling it with coffee. He sniped at one of the kids. "Keep the
coffee coming—for obvious reasons."

"*Crab.*" Murphy curled her tail around her as she
watched.

"Be sure and put out the raw sugar. I noticed most of it
was gone."

"Yes, sir," Brooks Tucker, Susan and Ned's daughter, said.
She walked through the pantry filled with china and silver
to go back to the kitchen. She carried the near-empty silver
sugar bowl, which she filled with raw sugar, hurrying back
to the dining room to put it on the table. Another sugar
bowl with cubed white sugar was on the table. That, too,
was getting used up fast. Honey was also on the table. She
wondered if Aunt Tally would mind if she filled up a few
nonmatching bowls with sugar to meet the demand but forgot about it as Chef Ted, the caterer himself, called for her
to come back in and take a tray of moist carrot cake out.

"Want to help me, Mrs. Murphy?" Brooks asked.

"Sure." The cat trotted after Brooks, then remained in the dining room sitting on the fireplace mantel so she could see everything.

Back out on the dance floor, Diego inadvertently bumped Fair as the dark man danced yet another dance with Harry.

"Watch it, buddy, and while you're at it you could move away from my wife."

"I am not your wife." Harry was appalled.

Fair then tapped Diego on the shoulder. Diego quizzically looked to Harry, who indicated she'd dance with Fair. They didn't dance so much as they quietly moved back and forth. Neither one said a word.

Diego joined BoomBoom, Thomas, and Susan, who gave the men a two-sentence description of the marriage and its unraveling.

"They were high-school sweethearts. They got married and, well, it didn't work."

"Ah, I see," Diego said with some feeling. "He seems still to care."

"He does," Susan flatly stated. "He wants her back. She was the best thing that ever happened to him and he lost her. Those things happen."

"To lose Harry would be quite a loss," Diego murmured.

"Everyone grows at their own rate." BoomBoom had no desire to remain on this topic.

Susan understood, of course. Their attention was diverted by Sean propelling his brother back into the house.

"She's not interested," Sean said with the little group overhearing.

"She is, too. You don't get women, Sean," Roger said.

The music ended and Diego walked out, taking Harry's hand. Fair stood there a moment.

"M-m-m, I can see steam coming out of those ears," Aunt Tally noticed, but then she noticed everything, most

especially that Miranda Hogendobber was happier than she'd seen her since girlhood and Tracy Raz looked twenty years younger. They were obviously in love.

Sean sat Roger down and got him a cup of coffee. Many people crowded around the table for coffee and tea. The desserts had been brought out.

Mrs. Murphy thought about waking up Pewter and Tucker but they were sound asleep. She noted from her high position how many of the men had bald spots.

Roger was loaded, but not as loaded as Sean made out. After all, he could still recognize people, he could still speak. He drank his cup of coffee in silence.

Sean bent over, whispering to Lottie now at the desserts. She glanced at Roger, then sighed.

"It would mean so much," Sean said. "And he could use a second cup."

Mrs. Murphy watched as Lottie picked up a piece of Black Forest cake, then moved over to the samovar, poured a cup of coffee. She reached for the cubed sugar in a silver bowl. She paused for a second, and Thomas just behind her handed her the china bowl with raw sugar. He had just dipped a spoon into it but being a gentleman he handed it to Lottie first. She dumped three heaping spoonfuls of sugar into the cup and turned to hand it back to Thomas just as he reached for it. She lost her grip and the bowl clattered to the floor, breaking and spilling sugar all over the random-width heart-pine flooring.

"I am sorry," Lottie said.

"I'm the clumsy one. This gives me the opportunity to ask you for a dance when you're finished with dessert." He smoothed over the incident.

"I won't be long." Lottie smiled and hoped it would up-set BoomBoom.

People noticed and approved as she walked over to

Roger, handing him the coffee and the cake. "Roger, I'm sorry I was cross but sometimes you're a pest. Try to think of less blunt ways to approach women, all right?"

He liked the idea of being served and said in a low voice, "I'm like a bull in a china shop. But really, Lottie, we'd have a good time if you'd go with me to the ball. I promise not to drink. I'll buy you a corsage and, well—it took me a long time to work up my nerve."

"It did?"

"Yes, you scare me half to death." He sipped the coffee. "Just because I'm a pest doesn't mean I'm not scared."

"Well—let me think about it while I dance with Thomas Steinmetz."

"I'll sit right here. I won't move." He smiled genuinely for the first time that afternoon.

"Some men really don't get it," Mrs. Murphy thought to herself. *"It's one thing to show a woman you like her. It's another thing to push her. Men need to be a little mysterious. They ought to study cats."*

The party rolled on and a few more men asked Lottie to dance. Aunt Tally danced every dance.

When Lottie returned to Roger he was fast asleep, his head resting on his chest.

"Roger. Roger." She shook him. "Roger, you lazy sod, wake up," she said lightheartedly. "Roger." Lottie stepped back. "Oh, my God."

Little Mim came over and without thinking said, "What'd you put in his coffee? He's out cold."

"He's either passed out or—dead." Lottie's face registered horror.

"Oh, Lottie, don't be a drama queen. He's been drinking since the parade." Little Mim grabbed his arm to pull him up. "He's warm. Really." With a touch of disgust and determination she gave him a yank and he pitched forward, falling flat on his face.

Little Mim looked at Roger and back at Lottie. "Roger!"

Mrs. Murphy jumped off the mantel, ran under the table, and woke up Pewter and Tucker. Tucker hurried over to Roger, sniffed, then backed away.

Cynthia Cooper was brought in from the dance floor. She walked into the room thinking he was out cold. She felt for a pulse in his neck. Nothing. She tried again. By now other guests were gathering around. She pressed her forefinger and middle finger on his neck again. Nothing. "He's dead."

10

Why does everything happen to me?" Tally grumbled as she watched her guests struggle with the situation.

Then again, what does a hostess do when someone dies at her party? Dispose of the corpse after the festivities? Haul him out and dump him on the lawn so no one has to look at him? Comfort the family members? But years of cotillion plus years of running Crozet before stepping aside for her niece had given Tally a sure touch.

She listened as the ambulance wailed about a mile away. In the quiet of the country sounds carried.

"Ladies and gentlemen, if you would all repair to the garden, please." She nodded to Ned Tucker, who shepherded them out the opened French doors. Then she walked over to Sean, leaning against the chair in which Roger had been sitting before Little Mim yanked him off of it. Sean's mouth hung slack. "Sean, come over here and sit with me." The nonagenarian led the tall, lean man into the formal living room. Big Mim helped her as they gently sat him on the peach-colored satin Hepplewhite sofa.

"Aunt Tally, I'll get the door."

"Thank you, dear."

But Cynthia Cooper reached it first, opening it for Diana Robb and her Crozet Rescue Squad assistants, Dick and Susan Montjoy. Big Mim joined them as they walked over to the body.

Diana said under her breath to Cynthia and Big Mim, "I knew the coke would kill him sooner or later."

"I had no idea," Big Mim whispered, surprised since she thought she knew everything about everybody.

Cooper shrugged. "People use the better part of their intelligence hiding their habits. I see it every day."

"Yes, I guess you do," a troubled Mim replied. "Sean's in a state of shock. I wonder if he knew."

As Diana and Dick carefully lifted Roger into the body bag and then onto the gurney, Big Mim quietly walked into the formal room.

"Sean." Aunt Tally patted his hand. "Sean, honey, they're taking Roger away."

Big Mim leaned over. "I know this is difficult. Is there a funeral home you—"

He jerked his head up. "Hill and Woods."

"Yes. I'll go tell them." She paused a moment longer. "For the sake of your health, Sean, you might want to request an autopsy."

He dropped his head into his hands. "No. I don't want anyone cutting my brother."

Tally and Big Mim exchanged glances and then Big Mim returned to Diana Robb and the Montjoys. "Hill and Woods. Tell them Sean's in no condition to make decisions at this moment."

"Okay." Diana rolled out the gurney as Susan opened the door.

When the door shut, Big Mim folded her hands together, her seven-carat emerald ring shining like green fire. "I wish he'd order an autopsy. When young people die like that you want to know. It could run in the family."

"Yes, but when young people do drugs, especially cocaine, it wreaks havoc on the body," Cooper said.

"The only thing I ever saw Roger do was drink beer and bourbon, a bit too much of it." The older, perfectly groomed woman stared out the front window, watching as Diana shut the ambulance door.

"That's just it. You don't see people do these things. Albemarle County is a wealthy, wealthy county, Mrs. Sanburne. You can buy anything here and there's a group that does drugs. They know one another and they protect one another," the deputy whispered.

"But surely we'd have some sign, Cynthia. A deterioration of behavior. A sudden drop in weight or the reverse. He seemed so normal. Not the most brilliant man but well—normal."

"He was." She sighed. "Now, I can't prove he took cocaine, but we have Diana's word on it and she's rarely wrong." She thought a moment. "Some people can take a line or two of cocaine and enjoy it just like some people can take a drink or two. One of the reasons the anti-drug campaign doesn't work is it really doesn't tell people the truth. It just demonizes drugs instead of explaining that different people have different chemistries. One person can drink and not become an alcoholic and another is lost with one drink. There's so much we don't know and it would appear we don't want to know."

"Are you condoning drugs?" Mim was incredulous.

"No. But aren't we hypocritical? One drug, alcohol, is

legal. Either legalize them all or ban them all. That's how I see it, and it would make my job a great deal easier."

"I'll have to think about that. In the meantime I'd better find someone to take Sean home. And I'd better release the guests from the garden. This will put a crimp in my dance tonight." She said this without rancor but more in the spirit of how life throws curveballs to everyone from time to time.

"I'll tote Sean home," Cynthia offered.

"Thank you."

As Big Mim headed for the garden, Mrs. Murphy, Pewter, and Tucker emerged, breaking their silence.

Pewter crossly complained, *"You didn't wake me up in time. Lottie Pearson's shrieking woke me up. You saw the whole thing!"* Mrs. Murphy had told her what happened.

Mrs. Murphy padded over, not focusing on the spilt raw sugar, a small amount, that had fallen into the cracks on the floor. *"How was I to know he'd just died? I didn't know until he flopped on the floor. As it was I did come get you two."*

Tucker blinked. *"He just keeled over?"*

"Here today, gone tomorrow." Pewter giggled.

"Diana thinks the cocaine did him in. Humans lower their voices but it's so easy for us to hear." Mrs. Murphy ignored Pewter's merriment. *"I never smelled cocaine on Roger, though."*

"Easy to determine. Bitter. They sweat it out." Tucker wrinkled her nose.

"Pope Rat would know." Pewter mentioned the rat in Roger's shop. *"He lived with Roger ... not that Roger knew."*

"It really doesn't matter." Tucker watched Sean being helped to his feet by Fair Haristeen and Reverend Jones. *"He's done for and that's the end of it."*

But it wasn't, of course.

11

Bumblebees buzzed around the wisteria, their fat bodies a triumph over physics and logic. Yet there they were, a squadron of them, their black and yellow bodies purposefully darting here and there in the late afternoon sun.

Harry and Susan sat out on the lawn. Mim's dance for charity would be in two hours. Both women were bemoaning the occasion. Mim had little choice but to go forward since it was a fund-raiser. Then, too, it wasn't a death in her family. No one expected her to cancel.

"We have to do it," Susan said.

"I know. We do. Everyone will be there but it's going to be leaden. And you know how Big Mim gets if a fund-raiser doesn't take off."

"She'll be sensible about this party. After all, no one can control these things." Susan plucked out the mint leaf from her tea and chewed it. "Love mint. You have the best mint patch."

"I grew those mint plants on the windowsill. It will be

another month before my herb garden does much." She shielded her eyes to watch her three horses in the meadow. She'd turned them out in the larger pasture.

"It was kind of awful that Little Mim pulled Roger off the chair." Susan lowered her eyes, which produced a giggle from Harry. "Harry, you're horrible."

"Well—it was funny. Who said death couldn't be funny? Not that I wished him dead," Harry hastily added. "After all, he showed me how to run the wrecker's ball and he could be fun when he wasn't—you know what I mean. If he could have seen his death he'd have a sense of humor about it. *Really.*"

"You're terrible."

"No, I'm not. I'm honest. Lottie Pearson screaming her silly head off just added to it, you know. And I'll give Boom-Boom credit." She smiled knowingly at Susan. "She hauled Lottie's silly ass out of the room. If Lottie had screamed any louder, she would have shattered the crystal."

Susan considered this as Mrs. Murphy rolled over in the freshly cut grass. "Murphy, what a lovely tummy."

"Mine's better." Pewter rolled over, too.

"Fatter."

"Better." Mrs. Murphy closed her eyes.

"Mine's whiter." Tucker rolled over as well.

"Would you look at that. Three spoiled children. Oh, to be one of my animals." Harry smiled. "What a life."

"No bills. No taxes. No stress. No unrealistic expectations about the future. They live in the moment." Susan sighed. "I'd be better off if I could be more like them."

"Me, too." Harry shifted in her seat. "Miranda and Tracy said they'd take food over to Sean and then go on to Big Mim's. Think we should take food?"

"Tomorrow. This is going to be hard on Ida O'Bannon. She hasn't fully recovered from her husband's death. I don't

know if Sean can handle all this. Men usually aren't too good at these things."

"No." Harry squinted as a bumblebee flew up to her, decided she wasn't a flower, then zoomed off. "Lottie Pearson's mad at BoomBoom." She didn't need to explain since Susan knew why. "But she let Boom lead her off. She wants something but I can't figure out what it is."

"Your mind is a grasshopper."

"I know. Always was. I didn't mean to change the subject, and I am sorry for Ida and Sean."

"Do you think Thomas Steinmetz is married?"

"Now who's changing the subject?" Harry touched Susan's leg with her foot.

Susan laughed. "Well, anyway, do you think he's married?"

Harry shrugged. "I don't know. If he is, he's bold as brass coming down here and staying with Boom. Washington's not that far away. He strikes me as the bold type anyway."

"Honey, with the telephone, e-mail, and television, nothing is that far away. It's both wonderful and dreadful."

They sat in silence for a few moments as the killdeers called on the meadows, their high-pitched voices distinctive.

"Did Roger have any enemies?"

"Harry." Susan's voice rose, filled with humor and a touch of censure. "You watch too much *Mystery Theater*."

Sheepishly, the slim woman replied, "It's good."

"Who would want to kill Roger O'Bannon? If he had any enemies it would be himself. He sat back there in his garage like a doodlebug in its hole. His socializing was at the stock-car races. I mean he was pleasant enough but you can't be covered in grease and expect someone like Lottie Pearson to fall for you."

"Lottie's a snob."

"So is half of Albemarle County."

"I guess." Harry exhaled. "Anyway, it crossed my mind, that's all. Oh, did you notice the flying blue heron sculpture in Aunt Tally's garden?"

"Yes."

"BoomBoom made it out of scraps. Kind of amazing."

"H-m-m." Susan enjoyed another long sip. "Diego Aybar." Given the length of her relationship with Harry, Susan didn't need a transition. She could hop around subjects as rapidly as Harry, although her concept of herself was as a logical, linear person.

"Yes?"

"You're smitten with him."

"You're soft as a grape."

"I suppose I'd have to be to be your best friend. Share a little, Harry, it's part of friendship, you know."

"Oh—he's handsome—"

"Gorgeous."

"Okay, Susan, he's gorgeous."

"And charming."

"Yes, but you know he has a quality, a sweetness, really, I can't think of another word but sweetness. I wish American men would get over trying to be so, uh, manly and just be themselves, you know."

"Well, that was a little outburst," Susan laughed, "for you, anyway."

"But Diego has"—she thought hard but couldn't find a substitute word—"sweetness." She inhaled. "But I hardly know him."

"True."

"Do I detect something acidic in your voice?"

"No, you don't actually. I'm only hoping that someday you'll fly. You'll let yourself go. Anyway, I don't believe in mistakes anymore." Susan set her glass down hard enough to make the ice cubes collide.

"Huh?"

"Mistakes. There are no mistakes. No matter what you do, no matter how awful it seems at the time, it's not a mistake because you needed to learn that lesson so—let go."

"I don't believe that."

"Harry, I knew you'd say that."

"Well, I don't. Murder is a mistake. You can't murder someone and then say you needed to learn that lesson. The lesson being, I suppose, that human life is valuable and no one has the right to take it except in self-defense, naturally."

"We aren't talking about murder."

"I'm carrying forward your theory about mistakes to its extreme conclusion."

"Thereby proving my point." Susan threw her head back, peals of laughter filling the fragrant air. "You need to let go."

Harry sat quietly for a moment, considered Susan's thought, then smiled slowly. No need to reply.

12

Flaming torches lined the long, curving driveway to Dal-
mally, Mim Sanburne's estate. The pinpoints of red-orange
against the twilight created the eerie sensation of going back
in time. Cool night air arrived with the sunset. The temperature plunged to fifty-two degrees Fahrenheit and would
probably wind up close to freezing.

BoomBoom arrived shimmering in a raspberry chiffon
evening gown, with a silver fox stole wrapped around her
shoulders. Thomas would have cut the motor and leapt out
of his Mercedes sports car to open the door for her, but
Mim, leaving nothing to chance, had hired a valet parking
service from Charlottesville. She demanded that no car
jockey take the expensive cars for a joyride. The valet company signed a contract to that effect. Mim always made a
point of marshaling staff before a party and reading them
the law, the law of Virginia and Mim's law. Her Aunt Tally
and her mother had taught her this.

Not all the guests wallowed in riches. Tracy Raz drove

Miranda in her Ford Falcon. People laughed, saying that Miranda would be buried in that car, which itself was over forty years old. Slimmed down, a smiling Miranda emerged from the car. She wore a red gown, almost medieval in style, which looked fabulous on her. She wasn't afraid to show off a bit, now that she had lost so much weight. As she passed along the receiving line, Big Mim, Little Mim, Jim, and Aunt Tally murmured to one another how youthful Miranda looked. Tracy, too, had lost some weight, scaling down to one hundred and seventy, what he had weighed when he made All-State from Crozet High.

As Miranda and Susan had helped Harry make up and dress up, the young postmistress dazzled as she glided along the receiving line. A simple royal-blue sheath, with a plunging neckline made all the more daring by long sleeves, was perfect on her. Diego, in white tie at her shoulder, couldn't take his eyes off her.

Nor could Fair Haristeen. Vowing to himself that he would win his ex-wife back before midsummer, he smiled, walked over, and made a point of engaging Diego in conversation.

As they chatted, Lottie Pearson arrived with a subdued Donald Clatterbuck in tow. Uncomfortable in white tie, obviously rented at the last minute, Don smiled sheepishly as people recognized him, which took a moment. Don hadn't even dressed up for his high-school graduation. As Roger O'Bannon had been a buddy, Don was dumbfounded by the news of his death. He wasn't at all sure he should be at Big Mim's. Lottie threw a fit when he tried to back out so he reluctantly accompanied the forceful woman.

Thomas bent over and breathed into BoomBoom's ear, "Americans must learn never to rent evening wear. Good clothes last your whole life."

"Provided you stay in shape, which you have," she

breathed right back into his ear, the color rising in his cheeks.

"Ah, Diego." Thomas waved him over. "I didn't see you come in." He bowed low to Harry. "The beauty of Virginia's countryside is exceeded only by the beauty of her women."

Even BoomBoom, mouth slightly agape, blinked and said, "Mary Minor, if only your mother could see you now."

Harry laughed. "I'm not sure she'd believe it." Noting Thomas's and Diego's puzzled expressions she hastily added, "Mother despaired of transforming me into a proper lady. She would have been happier with a daughter like Boom-Boom."

"Harry, don't say that. Your mother loved you."

"Boom, she loved me but she would have rather gone shopping with you."

They laughed as Lottie Pearson, dragging Don, flounced by. Not able to resist Diego's handsome face, she stopped and made a point of introducing Don. The two Uruguayans made Don feel immediately at ease. They even pretended interest when Don held forth on the wonders of taxidermy. Lottie ignored him. He was occupied anyway. She wanted to corral Diego but had to settle for talking to him with Harry. She'd never thought much about Harry one way or the other but at that precise moment, Lottie loathed Harry Haristeen. Even the sidelong, knowing glances to Fair fell short of their intention. Fair did not pull Harry away from the dark handsome man nor did he make an effort to assist Lottie in her flirtations.

"I know you all are wondering how I could come here tonight after Aunt Tally's but, well, I called Reverend Jones and he said I should follow my heart. After all, the O'Bannons aren't close friends and Roger, poor fellow, could be a pest. It's not like he was family and, well, people do die. What about all those football players who drop before they're forty?" Her hand fluttered to her throat. "And you know how Big Mim gets if you miss one of her parties."

"We know," Harry and Fair said in unison, then blushed. The years together often meant their thoughts were similar.

"Is Big Mim such a dragon?" Thomas's pleasant voice coated each word like honey. "She's so gracious."

"As long as you do things her way." Lottie's lips formed a pout.

Don, running his finger under his neckband, said with sense, "Ought not to criticize the hostess when you're enjoying her hospitality."

Thomas bowed his head slightly to Don. "A Virginia gentleman."

"Don?" Lottie said with surprise.

Harry deflected the conversation, speaking directly to Don Clatterbuck. "How's my woodpecker?"

"Frozen stiff." He laughed.

"Woodpecker?" Thomas inquired.

"When I woke up a few days ago, I found, well, actually, my gray cat, Pewter, found a pileated woodpecker. One of those huge woodpeckers. Dead. She pretended it was her kill, which if you know Pewter is absurd, but I finally convinced her to give it to me. Made a beeline for Don. He's the best. You should see his work." She paused and said, "Museum quality."

Don blushed as Lottie's eyes darted about. How would she ever extricate Diego from Harry? She wanted to ask him to accompany her to a huge alumni fund-raising dinner and dance, but he was glued to Harry. She believed Harry would look much less attractive if he could see her covered in grease as she repaired her ancient tractor. Harry was just too butch.

"What's a peel—?" Diego smiled, groping for the next syllable.

"Pileated woodpecker." Fair Haristeen's deep voice finished the word. "The largest woodpecker in America, close to twenty inches. You've seen the Woody Woodpecker cartoons?"

"Yes." Diego laughed.

"They're based on the pileated woodpecker, which has a brilliant red crest and red mustache as well as a distinctive loud call. Woody Woodpecker borrowed a bit of that, too."

"Can one see such a bird?" Thomas asked.

"Actually, you can. They don't hide. And they fly in an odd manner." Fair, as a vet, held the floor, which he liked. "They flap a few times, gaining speed rapidly, then fold their wings flat to their sides and zoom like a rocket. You'll hear them before you see them. They're noisy."

"Rapping into dead trees echoes in the woods. Fair's right. It's loud." BoomBoom was glad they'd steered away from Roger O'Bannon's demise. She'd felt a bit detached about it as he moved in a different circle. But when Lottie brought up the subject of Roger, BoomBoom decided she was both stupid and vain.

"They eat ants in the trees." Harry smiled at the two visitors. "You fellows don't really want to know about woodpeckers, do you?"

"I do. I'm an amateur naturalist. North America has many unusual animals."

Jim Sanburne strode by, clapping Fair on the back. "Going coon hunting tomorrow? Jack Ragland's bringing out Red Cloud."

"Red Cloud?" Diego was thoroughly enjoying himself, as this really was different from Embassy Row.

"Fabulous hound, brother, fabulous hound. Won about everything there is to win in this country in hunt trials." Jim's voice carried over the room.

"Like foxhunting?" Diego asked curiously.

"Oh, you don't want to go coon hunting. It's so country." Lottie rolled her eyes.

Jim Sanburne cleared his throat. "Music." The one word explained coon hunting to the locals. Jim loved the sound of the hounds, those deep, high, and middling voices. It was music.

Lottie grimaced. "You can break your ankle running around in the dark."

"That's what flashlights are for." Harry found Lottie as welcome as prickly heat.

"Women coon hunt?" Thomas wondered.

"Yes. Anyone can go so long as the hound owners invite them. It's not like foxhunting where an engraved card is sent out. You know?" Thomas nodded that he was familiar with foxhunting so Harry continued. "People can hunt one hound or two, called a brace. They can even hunt coon with a pack, it's up to the hunter or hunters. They'll often run their hounds together so the sound is better and oh, how the sound carries at night. It will make the hair stand up on the back of your neck."

"What happens when you find the raccoon?" Diego thought he'd like to see this unique Southern practice.

"Coon climbs up a tree, sits there, and looks at you. You can shoot him down or leave him be. I leave the coon alone so I have the pleasure of his or her acquaintance another time." Jim folded his arms across his chest, then added, "Never sporting to kill a female, especially in spring. She might have babies back home."

"Ah, yes." Diego smiled.

"Does one have to pay to participate?" Thomas wanted to go.

"Not at all, brother, not at all. Tell you what, I'll call Jack right now and ask him if you all can come along tomorrow night. What about you, Harry? Fair?"

They nodded yes.

"You'll hate it," Lottie declared.

"I'm going, too." BoomBoom, for all her perfect fingernails, clothes, etc., was a country girl, after all.

"All right. Jack should have been here tonight along with his wife, Joyce, but when I told him it was white tie he begged off. He said if I put a gun to his head maybe he'd wear a monkey suit—actually, Joyce would be the one to make him do it—but he's not wearing tails." Jim's deep laugh rumbled. "Tell you one thing, the man can hunt. Wife can, too. And gentlemen, I'll bring along a little something to cut the night's chill, a little something we do better in the mountains than they do anywhere else."

"Better keep your voice low." Fair winked. "Cooper's right behind you."

The deputy was talking to Tracy and Miranda and turned when she heard her name. "I didn't hear a thing."

"Good. Always thought a deaf woman would be an advantage." Jim winked.

"You mean dumb, don't you? One who can't talk." BoomBoom winked back.

"Is that what I meant?"

"Sexist pig." Harry stuck her finger in Jim's stomach.

"Awful. You can dress me up but you can't take me out. Come to think of it, I'm not out. This is my home." Jim roared with laughter, then shambled off to the telephone.

"How can he say that?" Lottie fumed.

"He's pulling your leg, our legs." Harry's eyes returned to Diego. "Every woman in this room knows that Jim Sanburne would do anything to help; his heart is bigger than he is."

"That doesn't excuse sexism." Lottie pursed her lips. "You make excuses for men, Harry." The "you" was loaded with innuendo.

"Lighten up." Don stifled a giggle. "Otherwise I'll have to give you a stuffed shirt."

At this they all laughed except for Lottie.

Miranda and Tracy joined the group just as Gretchen, the majordomo, butler, servant, you name it, strolled through playing the glockenspiel. She repeated the same three notes, which meant time to go to the dining room.

Mim and Jim Sanburne enjoyed the resources to host a sit-down dinner for sixty guests, seven courses, each with a different wine, champagne, sherbets, and cakes at the end. Mim had grown up with wealth, never knowing anything but abundance although she'd suffered bouts of emotional famine. She married Jim Sanburne on the rebound. He was big, strong, handsome, poor. Over the years he'd proved hot as a forty-balled tomcat. His licentiousness had as much to do with his sex drive as the fact that having a rich wife isn't all it's cracked up to be. In time they worked it out. He stopped running after women, she stopped giving him orders.

After dinner the orchestra played in the ballroom, which was decorated with dogwoods, pink and white, and viburnum, providing fragrance as well as beauty. Lottie sat next to Don, who didn't ask her to dance. Finally she pulled him onto the dance floor, hissing, "Getting cold feet?"

"No, I'm just not much of a dancer," Don replied.

Miranda had left her purse in the Falcon. Needing her lipstick, she rose from one of the small tables arranged on the sides of the dance floor. "Honey, do you have the car ticket?"

Tracy reached inside his cutaway, the inside pocket. "I do. But you sit right here. I'll get your bag, sweetie."

"Why don't we get it together?" She winked.

The older couple strolled through the rooms to the front of the house, where they gave the attendant the ticket. He picked up a cell phone and called in the number. In the distance they heard the old engine fire up.

When the car was delivered, the parking lot driver emerged, a young, slender man with sandy hair and a thin mustache.

"Wait, don't get out. I just need to grab the lady's purse. You can take the car right back."

"All right, sir."

As Tracy reached in for her small, beaded purse Miranda fixed her gaze on the young man driving her precious vehicle. She noticed that his left eye sagged and there was a red scar over his eyebrow running through to below the eye. It took a moment for this to register, then she blurted out, "You, you stole my hubcaps!"

He blanched, shot out of the car, running flat out into the darkness.

Tracy tore out after him. He hadn't been a star halfback for nothing and he was still in great shape. Although the kid had a head start he was no match for the older man. When he turned to see Tracy gaining on him he misstepped and rolled, got up, tried to pick up speed, but Tracy knew how to throw a block. He leaned down and pushed off his right foot, sailing into the back of the young man. Tracy hit him so hard that the kid's body flew up in the air like a rag doll, then fell to earth with a sickening thud. Tracy was on him fast, squeezing his head in a hammerlock. A heavy object on a chain around the young man's neck popped out of his shirt when he was blocked by Tracy. It was a Mercedes star hood ornament.

"I didn't steal nothin'."

"We'll see about that."

13

As Tracy forced the young man back toward the house, he took no chances. Holding the kid's left arm up behind him with his other hand on the young man's collar, his grip was tight. Each time the kid tried to shake free, Tracy jerked the bent left arm upward, which evoked a howl. In the cool night air thunder over the mountains presaged an approaching spring storm.

The main attendant had the presence of mind to find Big Mim, who in turn corralled Cynthia Cooper. The two women were waiting with Miranda Hogendobber as Tracy delivered his quarry.

"It's the man Sean described," Miranda said. What upset her as much as anything was the fact that a young person would steal.

Cynthia stepped forward. "I'm Deputy Cynthia Cooper. Cooperate and maybe we can make this less unpleasant."

"I didn't steal nothin'," he sullenly defended himself.

"Why don't we start with your name?" Cynthia then turned to Tracy. "You can release him. And thanks."

The scared youth grumbled, "Fast for an old man."

Miranda couldn't help but smile. "Son, you've been brought down by one of the best halfbacks this state ever produced."

The youth warily studied Tracy, who beamed thanks to Miranda's praise.

"What's your name?" Big Mim betrayed irritation.

"Wesley Partlow."

"Mr. Partlow, your address," Cooper methodically asked.

"Got none."

"You must sleep somewhere," she pressed.

He shrugged. "When I get tired I—"

"Come on. Where do you live? You're clean. You're wearing a white shirt and black pants," Big Mim said.

"They gave me the shirt." He nodded to the head attendant. "Company policy. All valet attendants wear a white shirt and black pants. The logo is over the pocket."

"So it is." Mim crossed her arms over her chest.

"Let's try this again. Where do you live?" Cooper patiently repeated her question knowing she'd hear more lies. She'd seen this type many times before: young, sullen, rebellious.

"Noplace."

"You're homeless?"

"Yeah," he smirked.

"Where's the 1987 GMC truck you drove to O'Bannon's Salvage yard? The one with the Dallas Cowboys jacket in it."

His eyes opened wider.

"Where is it?" Cooper wished she could slap the smirk right off his white face.

His eyes dropped to the ground.

"Are you hungry?" Miranda, kind even under these circumstances, thought food might help him.

"No, ma'am."

"I know you didn't mean to upset me but my Falcon means the world to me. If you'd cooperate with us we can settle this . . ." Miranda's voice trailed off.

Tracy put his arm around Miranda's waist. "Honey, don't fret over it."

"There's a quick way to settle this before I take Mr. Partlow into custody. I'll run him over to Sean O'Bannon's."

Wesley's eyes darkened, his jaw clamped shut.

Big Mim, not realizing that Cooper was laying a trap, said, "Cynthia, you can't do that. Not tonight. Not now. After all, Roger's not even cold yet. I don't think Sean is in any condition to identify a thief."

Wesley's head jerked up, senses alert, a flicker of fear in his eyes now. "Who's dead?"

"Roger O'Bannon. Did you know him?" Cooper inquired.

"No," he unconvincingly answered. He became even more wary.

Cooper sighed. No more dancing for her. "I have the strangest feeling, Mr. Partlow, that you and trouble are well acquainted. Tracy, will you stay with him while I call in for a squad car? I can't trust him to stay in the Jeep. He'd be out at the first stoplight."

14

The Dogwood Festival, celebrating the state tree and spring-time, provided ample opportunity for revelers to over-indulge each mid-April. Automobile accidents, property destruction, and fights kept the sheriff's department busy.

Sheriff Rick Shaw had the whole force out working tonight. When Cooper called him concerning Partlow he drove out in a squad car himself. It would never do for Big Mim to be unhappy. His presence as the highest elected law-enforcement official in the county usually mollified the grand lady. He'd also learned when he'd been elected twenty years ago to call Mim first when something broke. It made his life easier but also with her wide net she often could help him.

As a man ages his judgment usually improves. If it doesn't he's either dead or a drunk. Rick Shaw had learned to trust his judgment. He followed procedure to the letter of the law but he also trusted his instinct. In the past, when Mary Minor Haristeen would blunder onto a crime scene accom-panied by her animals, he used to fume. Over time he had learned that help comes from unusual quarters. Once the corgi found a human hand, which eventually led him to a murderer. Harry and her furry cohorts had a funny way of blundering onto things.

So he wasn't surprised when he drove up to Mim's front door to find Big Mim, Miranda, Tracy Raz, Harry, and Diego, to whom he was introduced.

Harry couldn't resist an event. When she saw Mim head for Coop she knew something was up so she followed the deputy. Diego found her curiosity amusing.

Rick smiled at his favorite deputy. "Coop, enjoy yourself. This is the only night off you've had in two months. I'll take the perp back."

"You can't lock me up for stealing hubcaps—which I didn't do." He snarled as he put the Mercedes star, which had slipped out again, back under his shirt.

"Boy, I can lock you up for just about anything." Rick genially pulled Wesley's arms behind his back, cuffing his hands together.

BoomBoom and Thomas happened to walk out front.

"Mim, there you are. We had a wonderful time." Boom-Boom noticed Rick pushing Wesley into the back of the squad car as she finished her sentence. "What's happening?"

"Miranda thinks he stole the hubcaps off her Falcon earlier," Harry said.

"We're lucky he didn't steal our jewels." BoomBoom's hand protectively covered the priceless sapphire and diamond necklace at her throat.

"The jewels are nothing. The woman is everything. I'd be afraid that he'd steal you." Thomas kissed her on the cheek after casting a jaundiced eye at Wesley, who cast it right back.

"That would be a first," Mim wryly responded, as Thomas gave the head attendant his parking ticket.

Diego whispered to Harry, Silver tongue."

"How long have you known Thomas?"

Diego shrugged. "Our families know one another. He's a bit older so we didn't go to school together. Since working at the embassy I've gotten to know him. Before that," he shrugged again, "social. Like tonight."

"A lady-killer," she whispered, eyebrows lifting upward.

"He thinks so," Diego giggled back, a giggle that made him irresistible, especially since American men rarely allow themselves a good giggle.

"BoomBoom eats it up."

"There is a type of woman who does, and you're not that type," Diego said with insight.

"Well—no."

Their attention was drawn away from one another as Wesley Partlow turned around in the backseat of the squad car and with his handcuffed hands managed to shoot the bird as Rick started the motor.

"What an asshole," Coop muttered under her breath.

Tracy, next to her, said, "Used to see guys like that all the time in the service. We had the draft back then so there was always a small percent who thought the rules didn't apply to them. Usually that was beat out of them during basic training. Seems to me that Wesley Partlow will miss the experience of being in the armed services. Too bad. Makes a man out of punks like that."

"Well, there's one thing for sure, he's going nowhere." Cooper removed her left high heel to shake out a small pebble. "Miranda, I didn't think we'd find your hubcap desecrator so soon."

"Me neither. I bet he stole the truck, too."

"That's a given." Cooper rubbed her bare arms as the lightning flashed on the side of the mountains. "Looks like the storm finally rolled up over the Blue Ridge."

15

Within seconds the wind roared through Crozet at forty miles an hour, lifting party tents into the heavens, shredding striped awnings, sending Big Mim's guests shivering to the fireplaces as the temperature dropped violently.

Overhead, black clouds, blacker than night, scudded over treetops; white, pink, and even bluish lightning ripped through the swirling clouds to strike below. A brilliant bolt hit the tin roof of Mim's gardening shed, the flash temporarily blinding those who beheld it. Luckily the shed didn't catch fire.

The usual quota of car accidents for the Dogwood Festival dropped, because most people had the sense to get off the roads. Those few that stayed out skidded into guardrails. The sheriff's department and the wrecker services were working as fast as they could.

Although she had looked forward to this night, Cynthia Cooper, overcome with a sense of duty and knowing that Rick Shaw would be on overload, bid her host and hostess good-bye, hopped in her Jeep, and drove to headquarters. She changed into her uniform and grabbed the lone squad car remaining, driving out into the lashing rains.

"Coop to Sheriff Shaw."

"Hey," came the familiar, tired voice.

"I'm heading out to Boonesville. Accident at the crossroads."

"What are you doing at work?"

"All hands on deck on a night like tonight. Yancy's squad car was lonesome. Where's Yancy?"

"In the hospital with a broken jaw."

"What?"

"Stopped a speeder, Din Marks, weaving all over the road. Guy got out of the car, Yancy shined the flashlight in his face, and the guy hit him broadside with a hammer. Held it behind his back, black as pitch tonight and Yancy never saw it coming."

"Damn."

"Filthy night. But Yancy will be okay. With his jaw wired shut he's bound to lose weight."

"There is that." She smiled. "Did he nail the perp?"

"Oh yeah. Sitting in the same cell with that little asshole, Partlow. Hey, I don't know when we'll wrap up this night but I'll buy you coffee and a doughnut when we do."

"Best offer I've had all week."

"Over and out," he replied.

As Cooper headed up to Boonesville, a small community north of Charlottesville proper, Harry and Diego danced the last dance at midnight. Big Mim invited everyone back to the library for coffee. Her eagle eyes noted if anyone was beyond driving. Her husband whisked off those few to the apartments above the stable. Jim's size and bulk guaranteed little resistance.

Thunder roared overhead, the lightning illuminated the

fields with eerie colors. The horses sensibly retreated to their run-in sheds. Even the cattle withdrew to the run-in sheds, standing patiently with the horses, who felt superior to cattle.

Tucker covered her eyes in the bedroom at Harry's home. Pewter made a big show of not caring about the storm.

Mrs. Murphy, curled up on the bed, said, *"This is a bad one. I'm surprised there isn't hail."*

The words were no sooner out of her mouth than a tremendous rattle pelted the roof. Hailstones the size of golf balls pounded down, bouncing high off anything they hit.

"Wow!" Pewter hurried to the window.

"It was a dark and stormy night," Mrs. Murphy chanted in a ghostly voice.

"That's not funny." Tucker shivered.

"Wimp." Pewter tossed her head in the air.

"Don't pick on her. She really hates these things and this is a hateful storm. Bet the horses are glad Mom opened their outside stall doors. She's got a sixth sense about the weather."

"She watches the Weather Channel." Pewter, never one to be impressed with humans, jumped as a big hailstone smashed against the window.

"Wasn't on the Weather Channel. I watched it with her. This is one of those wild storms that comes out of nowhere." Mrs. Murphy knew how swiftly weather could change in the mountains. *"People are lucky their crops aren't high enough to beat down but this will tear the dogwood blossoms right off the trees."*

The sound of Harry's truck coming down the driveway sent them all to the back door. She floated through the door heedless of the weather. "Hello, babies."

"I'm glad you're home," Pewter confessed.

Tucker, thrilled that Harry was home, followed her human closely. *"I hate this."* Pewter decided to follow Harry, too.

Mrs. Murphy scampered ahead of them as the hail sounded like artillery fire. *"Let's be glad we're inside tonight, safe and sound."*

That was the same feeling Cynthia Cooper had when she finally pulled back into department headquarters. At four-thirty in the morning her eyes burned, her mouth was dry. It had been one fender bender after another.

She pushed open the heavy swinging door. The odor of fresh coffee greeted her.

Rick smiled. "Doughnuts right here. Krispy Kremes."

"I could eat a bug." She poured coffee, grabbed a glazed doughnut, and slumped into her desk chair. "Where is everybody?"

"Out. I called Krispy Kreme and told them to give everyone doughnuts and coffee. I'd pick up the tab. Mercifully, things are slowing down. Next shift comes on at six. Hey, want a jelly doughnut?"

"No. You don't fool me. You bought those for you."

"Uh—yes. I even bought a carton of cigarettes, which I am stashing in your desk."

"Why?"

"Because if my wife comes in she'll check my desk."

"Little lies lead to big ones." Coop rolled her eyes.

"It's my one vice. I've tried to give it up and I finally decided, to hell with it. I might as well enjoy it."

"Yeah." She reached for another glazed doughnut. "My problem is I enjoy the first two puffs, then I can't stand the taste. Lot of money to spend for two puffs. I'm hungry. I think I'll call Miranda and ask her to make her orange-glazed cinnamon buns tomorrow."

"It is tomorrow."

"Oh—well, the next tomorrow." She licked her fingers. "Mim threw another grand party. She was afraid it would be subdued because of Roger O'Bannon's death but it wasn't. Not really Roger's crowd."

"I wouldn't think so. What happened?"

"He keeled over in his chair. Pretty much like you heard over the radio." She mentioned the radios in the squad cars. "Makes you think. I mean about stuff like smoking and eating doughnuts and greasy hamburgers."

"Coop, when your number's up, it's up." Rick folded his hands over his chest as he leaned back in his big chair. "And Sean won't agree to an autopsy?"

"No, unless he's changed his mind. He was, well, you can imagine. Held it together but what a shock."

"People have strong feelings about autopsies. If it were my brother I'd do it. In case it's something hereditary, something I could attend to."

"Now wait a minute. You just said you're smoking, to hell with it and when your number's up, it's up."

He grinned. "Me?"

"Wasn't it Emerson who said, 'Consistency is the hobgoblin of small minds'?"

"You're the reader but it sounds good to me." He cocked his head. "Christ, the storm is getting worse."

She polished off the last of her doughnut. "Who's back in the Taj Mahal?" she said, referring to the jail.

"A full house. Students. People who should know better and Din Marks, the jerk who smashed Yancy."

"Din? Well, I suppose it's better than Spirit-Moves-Us. Remember him?"

"Easy wardrobe. Bedsheets." Rick laughed. "And people give money to guys like that. Religious nuts. I'm in the wrong business. I'll shave my head, put a dot in the middle of my forehead, wear bedsheets, and chant 'Om'—instant riches. Tell people they're stressed out and need to find inner peace."

"Spirit-Moves-Us did, with prepubescent girls."

Rick grimaced, shaking his head. "Said it was part of his religion. He won't be out of jail for years."

"Is the guy's real name Din?"

"That's what his driver's license said. Oh, can't really hold that Partlow kid on hubcaps. I'll let him go later. Actually, I ought to release him now. Kick his sorry ass right out in the storm. I'll run him by the salvage yard first."

"I think I'll pay him a visit." She glanced at the clock. "A five o'clock wake-up call ought to bring a smile to his face." She walked into the cell block, Rick with her. The arrested were sprawled in cells, dead drunk, sleeping it off. Wesley, though, sat straight up, listening to the storm. "Good morning, glory," Cynthia said teasingly.

"Sounds like a tornado."

"They're louder," Rick answered him. "We're going to take you over to O'Bannon's Salvage later this morning. If Sean makes a positive I.D. your ass is grass. If not, you're free."

"I didn't steal nothin'. He'll tell you." Wesley listened as the hail intensified.

"Okay." Rick shrugged.

"Wesley, if you cooperate things will go easy."

He glared at her. "Nothin's easy."

"Fine." She turned and walked out, Rick with her.

Once outside the cell block they paused for a moment.

Rick sighed. "I need to pay my respects anyway. I'll ask Sean if he's up to identifying the little jerk. If he's not, we let him go."

Unexpectedly, Sean agreed to do it, said he could handle it. When Rick brought Wesley to him he swore he'd never seen the kid though Wesley matched the description he'd given. Either there were two young men with a pronounced scar over the left eye or Sean was too rattled to make sense of anything. Then again, in his vulnerable state he could have figured nailing a kid for hubcaps wasn't worth it.

Rick released Wesley Partlow. He'd already run a check with DMV on the kid's license, which was current and clean. His address was Randolph Street, Waynesboro. He didn't really think too much about it. Small-fry.

16

At seven o'clock Sunday morning, Fair Haristeen drove through the puddles in Harry's driveway. He stopped in front of the barn because he knew she'd be feeding the horses. At the slam of his truck door, Tucker joyously dashed out to greet the vet. Tucker loved Fair.

"Wasn't that an awful storm?" The corgi wagged her tail-less bottom.

Small tree limbs were scattered over the yard and dogwood petals covered the ground.

"You're the best dog." Fair bent over to pat the silky head.

"I'm in here," Harry called out from the center aisle of the attractive old barn.

"Figured." Fair jumped over a puddle. "You should see the roof of BoomBoom's barn. Swiss cheese."

"Your first call?"

"Not exactly. When I drove by I saw her and Thomas standing out by the barn so I pulled up. You know when Kelly"—Fair mentioned BoomBoom's deceased husband—

"built that barn I couldn't believe he'd put on such a cheap roof. The man was a paving contractor. He knew better."

"Yeah, but riding wasn't his thing so he built a cheap barn. Pretty tacky of him."

Fair removed his baseball cap. "Never thought of it. He had more money than God."

"Just a little revenge on his part. Control. And to what do I owe your company?"

"Does the word 'control' have anything to do with it?"

Mrs. Murphy, lounging in the hayloft with Simon, the opossum, remarked, *"You know, I think he's gaining insight."*

"M-m-m." Simon evidenced scant interest in human couplings and uncouplings. *"Did I show you the beads I found?"* He rolled out his treasure.

"Simon, those aren't beads, they're ball bearings, and if you found them around here it means a piece of Mom's equipment is about to die a horrible death."

"Really?"

"Really. Where did you find them? And I assume this had to be a few days ago. You weren't fool enough to go out in that storm."

"I'm not telling."

"All right. Don't tell but put them back—maybe she'll see them before the damage is done. Something's broken."

"I'm not putting them back and I'm not telling. Anyway, maybe I didn't find them here. They're shiny and I found them fair and square. I like shiny things."

"Marsupials are weird." Mrs. Murphy lashed her beautiful tail to and fro. She didn't like being disobeyed.

"Pewter grabbing a dead woodpecker and then Harry picking it up is pretty weird."

"She took it to the taxidermist." Mrs. Murphy laughed, her good humor restored. *"And you know that Pewter will tear it to shreds the minute that stuffed bird is brought back into the*

house." The cat tiptoed over to the edge of the hayloft, having decided that the human conversation might be more interesting than her own. Not that she didn't like Simon, but he was a bit simpleminded at times.

Pewter reposed in the tack room on a neatly folded Baker blanket. She'd gorged herself at breakfast and would need half the day to digest.

"It's been quite a Dogwood Festival." Fair dipped a clean old towel in water, rubbed it on a glycerin bar, and began wiping down Harry's hunt saddle.

"You don't have to do that."

"No, but I like to be useful." He hummed a Billy Ray Cyrus tune, then cleared his throat. "You seem to have hit it off with Diego."

"Yes," came the terse reply.

Fair knew better than to expect an explanation out of Harry. He'd known her all his life and having been married to her he felt he knew her better than anyone except maybe Susan Tucker. But women's friendships existed on a separate plane from spousal relationships. He often laughed to himself when he'd hear idle chatter about the differences between men and women. Women, according to the experts, were more forthcoming about their emotions than men and they bonded through sharing emotions whereas men bonded through activity. In all the years he'd known Mary Minor she'd never volunteered an emotion. You had to pry them out of her. She'd happily tell you what she thought, read, saw, did, but not what she felt. Susan used to harangue her over it but Harry was Harry and that was that. "Take me or leave me" was her attitude, and when Fair thought about it, he concluded she was right. You either accept someone or you don't and no amount of jawing about it will change them or bring you closer.

"The guy looks like a movie star." Fair flipped the stirrup

iron up over the saddle seat so he could better clean the flaps. The saddle was clean but he needed a task.

"He does but you're pretty great-looking yourself." She winked.

"You say that to all the boys." He laughed, glad to be in her presence. "Lottie Pearson is on the warpath, by the way."

"Against me or BoomBoom?"

"Anyone that gets in her way but I think you and BoomBoom are, well, let's just say, hold on to your scalps."

"What is Lottie's problem?" Harry scrubbed out a water bucket in the sink in the tack room. It had hot and cold water, a nice feature in a tack room. "I mean it's not like I woke up one morning and said, 'Today I will piss off Lottie Pearson.' And I only agreed to be Diego's date after pressure from BoomBoom. She said Lottie would bore him to tears whereas I could talk about farming."

"Lottie's getting scared and she's getting bitter."

Harry tipped her head up to stare into Fair's blue eyes. "Scared about what?"

"She's in her thirties, never been married, and no prospects in sight."

Dropping the bucket in the sink, Harry put her hands on her hips. "Oh, come on, you don't believe that."

"About Lottie I do. Man-hungry."

"Said by a man." Harry giggled.

"Hey, we may be the slower sex but I don't know any man who doesn't have radar for a woman crazed to get married. The pheromone of fear or mating or something is what she sends out. Nothing turns a man off faster than that except personal uncleanliness, I guess."

Harry resumed scrubbing. "Never thought about it but you're probably right. What's to get scared about, Fair? You can't just go out and find a mate. It's not like shopping for a car."

"No, but it is a big-ticket item." He smiled. "What I find offensive about Lottie is that she wants to get married but no one is good enough. Roger O'Bannon was crazy about her and, well, now he's dead. He wasn't right for her." Fair lost his train of thought. "It's hard to talk about him in the past tense."

"I know what you're trying to say."

"She wants someone who is First Family of Virginia. That stuff is so superficial."

"Easy for us to say because we are."

"Have you ever cared for one moment that your ancestors arrived here in 1620? No, 1640. Good memory." He tapped his forehead.

"No. I'm proud of them but it doesn't make me better than anyone. And the slave trade really picked up at the end of the seventeenth century so as far as I'm concerned those African-American families are F.F.V., too."

"If there's one thing that I really hate about Virginia it's the great game of ancestor worship." He flipped over the other stirrup. "On the other hand, it gives us stability, I suppose. Anyway, even if Lottie marries one of us she's not F.F.V."

"No, but her children will be."

"Great. Another generation of snobs." Fair laughed again. "My favorite low moment for Virginians was when the descendants of Thomas Jefferson had a reunion and argued about whether to let Sally Hemings's descendants join when the DNA tests proved they carried Jefferson's blood. I mean here we are in the twenty-first century and someone is going to argue about this."

"You're expressive this morning." She shook her head.

"Actually," he exhaled, "I'm so glad I didn't find Diego here."

She shot him a searing look. "Oh, like I'd go to bed with him on the first date, so to speak?"

"Uh—yes."

"Fair, it's my body."

"I love your body."

"Oh, Fair—" She threw up her hands.

"I love your mind, too."

"This is getting good." Mrs. Murphy leaned way over the edge of the hayloft.

Even Pewter woke up. Tucker sat, tongue out, listening to every syllable.

"You can be real smooth when you want to be. Now look, I'm doing what I want, when I want, and with whom I want. Don't fence me in."

"I haven't."

"Yeah, and you haven't had any rivals either."

"Oh, now I do?"

"Might."

"I hate it when you're coy."

"Well, I hate it when you try to manage me."

"I'm not managing you." He leaned over the saddle. "I'm being truthful."

"Then I'll be truthful right back. I like Diego and I'll see him again, most likely. Other than that, I don't know squat."

"Don't go to bed with him." Fair's voice grew stronger.

"I'll do as I damn well please."

"Latin-American men are faithful to their mothers and no one else. You don't know who he's slept with. You can't be too careful."

"That's pretty racist." Acid dripped from her voice.

"It's true. They're dominated by their mothers!"

"Fair, you are so full of shit." Harry laughed. He was unintentionally funny.

"I'm trying to protect you."

"No, you're not. You don't want me to go to bed with anyone but you."

"I admit that."

"Get over yourself."

"Harry, go slow. Think things through. What kind of future would you have with a man from a country full of ex-Nazis?"

"Fair, for Chrissake!"

"It is."

"So are Argentina and Paraguay and, for that matter, the United States. After the war didn't our government spirit out any German who had knowledge we needed or wanted? And furthermore, that was over fifty years ago. Somehow I think most of those dudes are dead. Now you're an expert on Uruguay?"

"Can't blame a guy for trying."

"Yeah, yeah. To change the subject, are you going on the coon hunt tonight?"

"Thought I would."

The best time to hunt coons is the fall but sometimes a hunter would train his young hounds with an older hound before then. Summer was too hot so spring often was a good time to work young hounds. The female coons, "heavy," usually gave birth in April through May to litters of between one and eight. They'd only be hunting males.

She filled the cleaned-out bucket with clean sponges, placing the bucket under the sink. "I wonder when Roger's funeral will be."

"Wednesday or Thursday. Unless Sean thinks he'll have to wait for the weekend because of out-of-towners. I doubt it though. Herb will know. Brings death a little closer, doesn't it?"

"Nah." She shook her head. "Can't think about it. It

doesn't do any good. You can die at four years of age or one hundred. But you can't think about it."

"Sounds like your dad."

"It's true, though."

"I suppose, but Roger's death makes me think about it. One minute he's sitting in the chair and the next minute he's on the floor with Little Mim pulling on his arm and Lottie screaming."

"Been quite a weekend. Lottie falls off the float. Oh, wait, it started with Miranda's hubcaps getting stolen and winding up at O'Bannon's. Then Lottie bounces off the float. Given the hoopskirt I'm surprised she didn't bounce right back or she could be our own living Taco Bell symbol. Then Roger goes to his reward. The twerp who stole Miranda's hubcaps shows up parking cars at Big Mim's party. Tracy tackles him. Then the storm from hell rips through Albemarle County. And you're worried that I'm going to sleep with someone other than you? Isn't there a Chinese curse, 'May you live in interesting times'?"

17

Diego and Thomas spent the day at Windy Ridge, an estate owned by the retired Ambassador to the Court of St. James's. Since she didn't need to be a tour guide for the visitors, Harry worked, suppressing her excitement about the coming evening's coon hunt. She loved to hunt. Picking up the debris around her house took two hours. Then she walked her fence lines to make certain they weren't torn up. Blair Bainbridge's cattle loved to amble over onto her lush pastures. Not that she minded herding them back but she didn't always have the time to drive them across the creek, repair the fence, check for injuries. Also, her three horses, Poptart, Tomahawk, and Gin Fizz, disliked the cattle. They'd pin back their ears, bare their teeth, hurl crude insults usually involving the fact that cows have four stomachs.

Mrs. Murphy and Tucker accompanied Harry on her rounds. Pewter declared the storm frayed her nerves; she needed to rest in the house. The offending blue jay swooped around the kitchen windowsill. Seeing Pewter asleep on the kitchen table, he unleashed a torrent of abuse.

After a day's work the tiger cat and Tucker felt entitled to participate in the coon hunt. Both waxed furious when Harry shut them in the house, closing off the animal door, then driving off in her 1978 blue Ford pickup.

"You'll pay for this!" Murphy threatened as the red taillights receded into the gathering twilight.

"Pipe down." Pewter rolled over.

"You've slept all day. Don't tell me you're tired."

"I didn't sleep all day. That horrid blue jay perched on the windowsill. He called me a fat gray sow, a sea cow, a ponderous pachyderm. I'll kill him!"

Mrs. Murphy walked back from the door, jumped onto the kitchen counter, trotting to the window over the sink. *"I can't believe she left me! We worked today. We deserve a party."*

"We were invited to Aunt Tally's tea party. Of course, that didn't turn out so good, did it?" Tucker thoughtfully added.

"That's not the point." Mrs. Murphy batted at the windowpane.

Pewter jumped up on the counter, too. She headed for the large bowl of crunchies, stuck her head in, and munched away.

"Noisy eater." Tucker giggled.

"Tailless wonder." Pewter flicked a nugget on the floor for the dog. *"I've endured enough insult for one day."*

"It's a dumb time to coon hunt." Murphy hoped to find a way to make her loss less. She adored any form of hunting, even if only to watch from the bed of the pickup. After all, she was the best hunter in central Virginia, maybe all of Virginia.

Put out as she was, she should have been grateful to be left behind.

The sodden ground sucked the boots right off the

hunters' feet. The bushes and branches, loaded with droplets, soaked each person who brushed by. Durant Creek, a tributary of Beaver Creek, roared like a diesel dump truck on full throttle.

Harry, hardened by outdoor life, didn't much mind. BoomBoom was a surprising trouper. Thomas bravely soldiered on in his expensive Holland and Holland outfit. Diego wore what Harry told him. He had bought a pair of Red Wing work boots after leaving the former ambassador to Great Britain and topped his outfit off with a pair of old jeans and a canvas shirt. Thomas thought Diego's boots were too country and not English enough. He regretted it now, though, as he tried to keep up in his green wellies, a wonderful high rubber boot for country chores but not for running behind hounds. Thomas was hard put to keep up, his flashlight bobbing as he labored. Boom stayed back with him, a sacrifice for her since she liked being up front.

Jack's hounds treed two coons in rapid succession. He called them off, walked about a quarter of a mile, and set them to work again. Joyce, his wife, walked along, too.

Fair enjoyed good hound work and was pleased to see shiny coats on the hounds. He wanted to stay behind Harry and Diego but forced himself to run ahead of them.

Jim Sanburne brought up the rear along with Don Clatterbuck, both men moving at a leisurely pace, happy to listen to the music.

Harry held the flashlight as she and Diego ran behind Fair.

"They're on another one. Picked him up by the creek," Harry said, but the words were no sooner out of her mouth than a rumble overhead surprised her.

Low clouds moving fast presaged another storm. She'd felt the temperature drop but paid little attention to it. The cloudy skies held the scent down; the falling temperature, now in the high forties, made for a glorious night of hunting about to be cut short.

A flash over the creek side stopped everyone in their tracks.

"Folks, I got to pick up. We don't want to be out here." Jack put his grandfather's huge cow horn to his lips, blowing in his hounds.

Joyce peered up at the sky. "Sure hope it's not like last night."

As the people turned to head back to their trucks the thunder moved closer and a light splattering of rain began.

Impulsively, Diego reached for Harry's hand, drawing her to him, and kissed her. She kissed him back, then they broke off, racing toward the trucks, laughing.

A glitter caught Harry's eye. "Hold up."

The rain fell steadier now but she moved to the left, off the path. Diego followed her. She knelt down, picking up the Mercedes star and a snapped chain. "The hubcap thief."

"Odd." Diego studied the object.

"He wore it around his neck." A bone-rattling clap of thunder convinced her to hasten back to the truck. Running, she pocketed the hood ornament. By the time she and Diego reached their safe haven they were drenched and shivering.

They'd parked at the end of a gravel road northeast of Crozet, the boundary between Booty Mawyer's farm and that of Marcus Durant. Durant, out of town this weekend, was an avid coon, fox, and rabbit hunter. He'd hunt just about anything. He'd built a twenty-foot-by-sixteen-foot shack. With a tin roof, a wood-burning stove, and two sets of bunk beds by the walls, he could roll in and sleep if his hounds kept running late into the night. A generous man, he shared his shack with his buddies, so long as everybody cleaned up.

Fair, using well-cured wood stacked outside under a protective overhang, started up a fire. Soon the little group was thawing out, passing the jug, and telling tales in the time-honored tradition of night hunters.

Thomas and BoomBoom sat next to one another on the edge of a bunk bed, as did Jack and Joyce. The others sat on upturned milk crates and wooden chairs in front of the stove.

Jim leaned back, putting his cold, wet feet in front of the stove. Everyone peeled off their shoes, boots, socks, hoping they'd dry before they had to put them back on.

"Ever tell you about the first time I coon hunted with Mim?" Jim cast his eyes around the room. "Guess not. Well, I'd come back from Korea in one piece and I hadn't been home three days when I spied Mim coming out of Crozet National Bank arguing with Aunt Tally. I stopped my truck, hopped out, took off my hat to the ladies, and asked Mim out then and there. Heard her family broke off the romance with another fellow because he wasn't high-class enough. Hell, he was more suitable than I but faint heart ne'er won fair lady and to hell with suitability. Aunt Tally looked me over like I was a horse to buy. Well, Mim said yes. So Tally says, 'Where you taking her?'

"'Coon hunting,' says I. 'See that's what you hunt, young man.'" He laughed, imitating Tally's voice. "A fine night. Crisp, you could smell the leaves turning. Marcus's father, Lucius, had a good pack of hounds, turned 'em loose, and what a hunt.

"Mim was a speedy little slip of a girl. She kept right up and the next thing we heard was screaming and cussing. Lord o'mighty. The hounds ran right up on Arnold Berryman, covering Ellie McIntire.

"She was screaming. He held up his coat over her. Scared

the hell out of the hounds. I thought that would be my last date with Mim.

"She enjoyed herself so much she asked when we could do it again." He slapped his thigh and laughed, the others laughing with him.

"Ellie McIntire." BoomBoom shook her head, remembering the spinster librarian who had struck terror in their hearts when they were children.

"Thank you," Thomas said as he received the jug from Fair. After a long draft he handed it to BoomBoom.

"Thomas, how do you like our country water?" Jack, who didn't drink, asked.

"Potent and smooth," the older man replied.

"Thomas, tell them how your grandfather brought the telephone to Montevideo." BoomBoom slipped her arm through his, leaning into him.

"Oh..."

"Tell," the others chimed in.

"My grandfather saw the telephone in London. He was our ambassador there before World War One. He formed a company and started the first telephone service in our country. Then my father, not to be outdone, founded the first television station. I remember when I was a boy being very disappointed to find out that Jojo, the clown on the children's show, emitted the distinct aroma of gin." They all laughed.

"Tell them what you did."

"My dear," he demurred.

"Thomas brought satellite technology to their communications company."

"BoomBoom, it was the logical progression. That didn't take the intelligence or courage of Grandfather or Father. Or the determination of my mother, who took over the television business. She's slowed down a bit by heart trouble but really, she's smarter than I am."

"The Steinmetzes are quick to see the future and profit," Diego said admiringly. "The Aybars are running cattle instead of satellites." He laughed.

"Nothing wrong with running cattle," Jim said. "You come on over and look at my Herefords."

"Hunting down your way?" Jack politely asked.

"Yes, and fishing. If you like deep-sea fishing, you must come down," Thomas said, a hint of pride in his voice.

"Sounds like machine-gun fire." Joyce looked up at the tin roof as the rain intensified.

The four hounds thought so, too, as they edged closer to their humans.

"You know, I'd like to come on down and go fishing." Jim smiled at Thomas. "Mim and I have never been to Uruguay. Is there something we could bring...like jeans? When you visit Russia you bring jeans. At least we used to in the seventies. People would pay a lot of money for jeans from the United States."

"Not a thing," Thomas replied. "We'll take care of everything."

"Some things cost three times as much and some things are extremely inexpensive," Diego added. "Now, we don't have foxhounds or coonhounds. Those would fetch a high price."

"They're my babies." Joyce laughed.

"Almost forgot." Harry pulled out the Mercedes star.

"Where's the car?" BoomBoom laughed.

"That's the only part I could afford." She laughed, too. "Actually, I found this on the path back a ways. When Tracy brought Wesley Partlow back to the house at Mim's party, he wore a star like this around his neck."

"Anyone report one missing?" Fair logically asked.

"Not that I know of," Jim answered, "but many of our guests were feeling no pain."

They all laughed.

"It can cost two hundred and ninety dollars to replace that star," Thomas said. "Hang on to it." He stopped a moment. "Had to replace one once."

Harry didn't get home until one in the morning. She headed straight for bed, missing the shredded needlepoint pillow in the living room, compliments of Mrs. Murphy.

18

A series of thunderstorms crackled across Crozet for twenty-four hours. A few minutes of calm would ensue, and occasionally the skies lightened, but within a half hour clouds darkened again, the rains came down, and the roar of deep thunder reverberated throughout the mountains and valleys.

Harry sorted mail amid peals of thunder. Tucker crouched under the small table in the back of the post office. Mrs. Murphy sat on the dividing counter between the public side of the room and the working side. The broad and smooth old wooden counter with a flip-up section so the postmistress could walk in and out had seen generations of Crozetians call for their mail.

The advent of the railroad, built by the engineering genius of the New World, Claudius Crozet, brought the mail and news faster to the hamlet named for him. Residents no longer waited for the stage. They could stand at the station to watch the mail sacks being tossed off the train. The mail from Crozet would be picked up as it hung from a yardarm, the sack hooked so it could be grabbed from the moving train. Trains had cars outfitted as post stations and often money would be in the post station car, the postal employee taking the precaution of wearing a pistol.

The town had built its latest post office at the turn of the nineteenth century, altering it only to make more room for parking, since cars take up more room than horses. The pleasant structure had been rewired three more times in one hundred years, the last rewiring occurring in 1998. Small though the station was, it was hooked into the national postal computer system. Miranda resisted using the computer. Harry, much younger, mastered it rapidly. Wisely, she never instructed Miranda in its use. She waited for Miranda to ask—which, finally, she did.

Technology, so beguiling in its promises, often only delivers a new set of problems. The postal computers coughed, sputtered, and took to bed quite often with virus infections. While they could weigh packages, give an instant answer on postage at home and abroad, anyone handy with a scale, an instrument thousands of years old, could give the information in about the same amount of time. And wonderful though the blinking screen may have been, letters still needed to be hand-canceled at times, postage-due markings in maroon ink required human hands, and the process of sorting the mail once it arrived at the local postal offices was done the way it had always been done—one letter at a time.

In short, the tasks of the postal worker had changed little over the last century. And the advent of the twenty-first century still hadn't altered those tasks.

Harry owned a computer from which she sent e-mail or occasionally logged on to the Internet to look up something. She spent an evening once reading about Hereford cattle on the Internet. Then she switched to the Angus site and compared notes. But mostly she thought the information revolution was more hype than reality.

And nothing could substitute for a love letter. The sensuality of the paper, the color, the ink, the contents, the privacy of it, were inviolate and perfect.

As she sorted that Monday's mail she thought about writing Diego a letter. Maybe she'd mention their kiss in the rain or how wonderful it was to dance with him on a cool spring night. Then again she could talk about grass crops. She hummed to herself as Miranda carefully pulled the striped dish towel off the orange-glazed cinnamon buns she brought to work. The fragrance of Miranda's best creation mingled with the pot of coffee brewing in the back.

"Heaven."

Miranda glanced at the old railroad wall clock. "Heaven at seven-thirty in the morning." A clap of thunder made her laugh. "I don't remember so many storms. One after the other. I'll get over there in a minute to help you. Oh, tea?"

"Yes, thanks. Don't rush. There's not that much mail, which is surprising. Enjoy the lull. The summer postcards will fire up soon enough. Before that we'll have the graduation notices. Never ends." She sorted postcards as though shuffling playing cards.

Miranda brought her tea. She herself poured a bracing cup of coffee. Miranda had let Mim talk her into joining a coffee club, so each month she received another type of pricey coffee from France, Germany, Spain, Switzerland. This delicious coffee was from a famous café in Vienna.

A light rap on the door, next to the animal door, brought forth a "come in" from both women.

"Hi." Susan quickly stepped in, for the rain had intensified. "Have you ever?"

"No," they said in unison again.

"What are you two, a duet?" Susan laughed, shaking the raindrops from her auburn hair, cut in a sleek pageboy.

"Hogendobber and Haristeen. Has a ring to it. How about H and H?" Harry laughed.

"That sounds like a candy." Susan breathed in the moist aroma.

"Vienna." Miranda poured her a cup.

"You'll be our expert. Next thing we know, Miranda, you'll open one of those upscale coffee shops where a cup costs three bucks."

"It is outrageous but a good cup of coffee is special, especially that first cup." A louder boom lifted all eyes to heaven. Miranda cast hers down first. "Oh, Tucker, poor baby, it's all right." She knelt down to pet the shivering corgi.

Pewter, deep in the mail cart, said in a high-pitched voice, *"I don't like it either."*

Harry walked over to give love to the rotund gray kitty.

"Chicken," Mrs. Murphy tersely criticized them.

"Hateful bitch," Pewter promptly replied.

"I'm glad I don't know what they're saying." Harry laughed. "Hey, we all went coon hunting last night with Jack and Joyce Ragland. Got soaked. Hunted until the storm really hit, but it was a great night anyway. The voices on those Ragland hounds are something special. Goose bumps. I didn't get home until one this morning."

"You didn't shoot any, did you?" Miranda hated the thought of shooting animals.

"No."

"Well, while you were coon hunting, I took my two cherubs to see their grandparents. Danny"—Susan mentioned her son—"wanted to see the new Audi sports car that Mamaw bought for herself. He told her she looked like a teenager in her TT. I think that's what it's called. Anyway, it's a fabulous design and drives nicely. There's my mother, seventy-one, driving a high-tech sports car. I love it! What'd you do, Miranda?" Susan asked.

"Sewed curtains for Tracy's apartment. He fixed my washing machine. Romantic. Actually, it was. We'd spent the weekend doing all the Dogwood Festival things. It was kind of nice to be home doing chores. You girls will have to see his apartment, right over the old pharmacy. He's got the entire floor for three fifty a month. It needs a lot of work but Eddie Griswald couldn't give it away. Everyone in Crozet wants their own house. Tracy's very happy for now."

"I can paint," Harry offered.

"He'd like that."

"Oh, I forgot to tell you. Look what I found last night." Harry walked over to her bag, an old Danish schoolbag, worn through in spots. She fished around in the bottom, retrieving the Mercedes star.

Susan took it from her. "Remember there was a fad in the eighties and early nineties? City kids would snap these off and wear them."

"Before my time," Harry joked.

"Oh, puh-lease." Susan's eyebrow shot upward as she dragged out the syllables.

"Where'd you find it?" Susan asked.

"Near Durant Creek, where we were hunting."

"That's what that boy had around his neck." Miranda reached for her first and only orange-glazed cinnamon bun, an act of discipline. Last year she would have had three eaten by this time but she'd cut back dramatically on sweets and had lost over thirty-five pounds in the past year. She could have worn her high-school clothes if she'd kept them.

"It might not be his," Susan volunteered. "Then again, how many disembodied Mercedes stars are there?"

"Here comes another one," Mrs. Murphy warned Tucker

and Pewter as a bright flash of lightning presaged a mighty rumble.

"So," Susan's voice rose merrily, "when do you see Diego again?"

"Uh—I don't know. If not next weekend maybe the weekend after. I like him."

"That's obvious." Susan smiled. "And he likes you."

"Seems to."

"What man wouldn't?" Miranda thought of Harry as her own daughter in ways.

"What a nice thing to say." Harry blushed.

"Was Fair at the coon hunt?" Susan's curiosity bubbled over.

"He was."

"And?"

"Pretty much as you'd expect," Harry said, tossing a package onto the A–B section of the package shelf.

Miranda and Susan looked at one another, then back to Harry.

"Jealous." Mrs. Murphy stated the obvious, something she usually didn't do but among humans it was often a necessity.

Little Mim drove up to the front of the post office. The rain poured. She sat in her $83,000 Mercedes waiting for the rain to lighten, but it didn't. It only rained harder.

Murphy, eyes sharp, noticed the star was missing from Little Mim's exquisite car. *"Aha."*

"What are you aha-ing about?" Pewter grumbled from the bottom of the mail cart.

"The star is missing from Little Mim's silver-mist Mercedes."

"Really?" Pewter clambered out of the mail cart, sending it rolling about a foot in the opposite direction of her progress. She jumped up next to Murphy. *"It is."*

The humans noticed the cats staring out at Little Mim so they looked, too.

"Oh, my gosh, the star is missing from her car!" Miranda noticed first.

"You're right." Susan giggled.

"Boy, Wesley Partlow will be sliced and diced." Harry sighed. "Guess I'd better give her this when she comes in."

"Well, what would you do with it?" Susan wondered.

"Mount it on a block of wood and put it on my bookcase. It's the closest I'll ever come to a Mercedes." Harry reached for an umbrella in the stand by the front door. "I'll go out and walk her in. You know, that kid must be dumber than snot."

"Harry, what a vulgar thing to say."

"Sorry, Miranda." She opened the door a crack. "I wouldn't want to be in his shoes."

Truer words were never spoken.

19

Cut him down," Rick Shaw ordered one of his men.

The photographs had been taken, the body dusted for fingerprints, the ground under the corpse inspected.

Two kids crossing in the rough patch of land behind Crozet Elder Care, a home for the aged, had found Wesley Partlow dangling from a fiddle oak. His tongue hung down on his chest, his face was purple-black, his eyes bugged out, and his feet and hands were swollen from the fluids collecting there. The storms hadn't improved his appearance but they probably saved his eyes from the birds.

Naturally, the gruesome sight scared the bejesus out of the kids, but they had the presence of mind to call the sheriff. Although Rick and Cynthia Cooper had witnessed plenty of unpleasant sights over the years, it didn't mean they liked seeing it.

The body was lowered carefully onto the gurney. If Wesley'd been cut down with a thud the corpse might have been even more damaged. The coroner couldn't save anyone, that's for sure, but he usually had the right answer about someone's health a day late.

As Diana Robb rolled away the mortal remains of a wasted life, Coop examined the bark of the tree. "If he shimmied up the tree, he didn't slough off bark."

"He would have made a long skid mark. The rains would have taken care of little marks, don't you think?" Rick looked skyward. "And here comes some more."

"I don't know, boss. He was light. He could have climbed up without much effort, without a lot of scraping and slipping. I looked for tire tracks."

"Yeah." Rick, too, had wondered if he'd been hoisted up on a truck bed. "Washed out."

Wesley Partlow didn't seem like the suicide type.

"I don't get it."

"Let's find Din Marks."

They drove out sloshing through ever-deepening mud holes. As they turned onto Route 240 the raindrops fell, fat ones making big splashes on the windshield.

By the time they reached Fashion Mall, some thirty minutes later, it was again pouring. They parked by the side door and made a run for the Sears store. Din Marks worked in the lawnmower section. He blanched when he saw them.

Rick spoke to the other man behind the counter. "Can you hold the fort? I need a minute or two with Mr. Marks."

"Sure." The middle-aged man nodded.

Rick motioned for Din to follow him. Together with Cynthia they walked into the center concourse of the mall. Few shoppers milled about, weekday mornings being sparsely populated.

"Would you like to sit?" Rick pointed to a bench.

"No."

"When you were locked up with Wesley Partlow, did he

say anything to you? He was mad at someone or someone was mad at him? Anything?"

Din shook his head. "No."

"Did he seem depressed?" Cynthia asked.

"Not him." Din ruefully smiled. "I was drunk but I remember his smart mouth."

"Did he mention cars, hubcaps?"

"No. Said he didn't do anything. He didn't belong there and he'd get out. I said I slugged a cop and he laughed. I didn't mean to hit Yancy. Didn't mean to—well, I was drunk."

"We know," Rick replied. "Did you notice anything unusual about Wesley himself?"

"No."

"Did Wesley mention doing business with anyone in town?"

"No."

"Did he mention a truck?"

"No."

Cooper spoke again. "Would you say he was calm, agitated, surly, afraid?"

"Uh. Watchful. We didn't say too much to one another. He told me if I puked he'd kill me. When I woke up he was gone."

"By the way," Rick said, "how'd you get to work this morning?"

"Walked."

"In the rain?" Coop inquired.

"I'll be walking in the rain for a long time. I'm gonna lose my license for three years."

"Maybe you should stop drinking." She handed him an AA number. "Can't hurt to try."

"Yeah," he mumbled.

"Call the number, Din," Coop urged him. "The next

time we pick you up it could be in a body bag or you'll have killed someone else."

"It'll be three years from now. I won't drive."

"Don't drink. You can't handle it," she flatly stated.

"Go on back to work," Rick told him.

Din turned to go, then stopped. "What happened to that kid?"

"Found him hanging from a tree."

Din blinked. "Shit."

"If you think of anything, call us."

"That asshole would have never hung himself," Din blurted out.

"That's our assessment of the situation, too," Rick said.

Back in the squad car, Rick and Coop wiped their faces, damp again from the rain.

Rick pulled out a cigarette and lit it. "Never received a report for a stolen truck."

"The eighty-seven GMC." She lit up as well. "Maybe it wasn't stolen."

"That has occurred to me."

"Who'd lend him a truck?"

"Someone stupid." Rick inhaled. "Or someone who's a fence."

"O'Bannons?"

"Thought of that. Tim O'Bannon would have killed his kids if they'd ever pulled a stunt like that. He was as honest as the day is long. He'd never take stolen goods."

"The old man's dead."

Rick paused. "Sean's not that stupid. Make a couple of thousand tax-free dollars but jeopardize your whole business by selling stolen goods? He wouldn't do it."

"Who knows?" Cooper opened the window a crack to let the smoke out but the rain snuck through the crack. Even though she quickly put the window up, her right thigh was wet. "Damn."

"No point driving until I can see where I'm going." He sighed. "Coop, apart from drugs, what could bring in big bucks? Moonshine can still make you rich if you're careful," he noted.

Neither one had to tell the other that they were treating the demise of Wesley Partlow as murder. It's true that people can harbor deep pain and secret losses and finally do themselves in. And sometimes a surly façade covers pain; but both officers of the law felt that wasn't the case. Someone threw a rope over that fiddle tree and strung up Wesley Partlow just like in the Wild West.

"I searched the computer for a criminal record. Wesley Partlow managed to keep his nose clean. He was smarter than I gave him credit for. I thought he was just a dumb punk."

"He goes in the ground after that autopsy." Rick squinted, the rain had let up a little. "How's your appetite?"

"Why?"

"Haven't lost it after this morning?"

"No. Have you lost yours?"

"Takes more than a hanged man to do that. Let's go to the Riverside Café."

"I'll call Big Mim on the way. The news will be spreading all over Crozet. You know those two kids will tell. They'll have nightmares for months."

"Yep." He turned right out of the parking lot, heading for the intersection of High Street and Free Bridge. "Wait a second before calling the Queen of Crozet. Did you check out the number of 1987 GMC half-ton trucks in Virginia?"

"Over twenty thousand, four-wheel drive and two-wheel, still on the road."

"How about in Albemarle County?"

"Yancy's on that since he has to sit around. Guess he'll be sitting around for a while."

"Okay."

"We don't know if the truck is registered here. Could be out of state."

"I know."

"Like a jigsaw puzzle," she said, "all the pieces have been dumped on the table in a heap."

He turned toward her. "Maybe all the pieces aren't on the table."

20

The word of the grisly find reached the post office by one-thirty. Big Mim stopped by after her errands.

"I feel terrible." Miranda meant it, too.

"You didn't know him," Harry hastened to comfort her. She knew how guilty Miranda could get.

"She's right, Miranda. You simply reported that your hubcaps were stolen and by chance or whatever he was parking cars at my party. And you can believe I have chastised that company. I'll never use their valet service again. Not that he did any harm but still, they ought to scrutinize their help more closely. Their excuse was he had a valid driver's license and they needed all the help they could get due to the dogwood parties." Big Mim shook out her umbrella. "I've made a mess. Sorry. I didn't think it would be so wet."

"Don't worry about it. I'll mop up the floor before I leave tonight. It's that kind of day." Harry scratched Pewter at the base of her tail.

"Do they know how long he was there?" Miranda asked.

"No. The coroner will figure it out," Big Mim replied. "Did you know our county is getting so populous we have two coroners now, full time?"

"I didn't know that," Miranda replied.

"I guess I'd better call Cynthia and tell her I found the Mercedes star and gave it back to Marilyn." Harry headed for the phone while Miranda filled in Big Mim. Big Mim hadn't seen Little Mim since breakfast so she knew nothing of the returned star.

"*I wish Mother hadn't found that star.*" Mrs. Murphy sighed. The low pressure was getting to her.

"*Who cares?*" Pewter purred. "*Wesley Partlow's nothing to her.*"

"*She's curious. She'll be especially curious now. You know how she gets,*" Tucker agreed with Mrs. Murphy.

"*If the kid killed himself, that's that,*" Pewter, the hard-boiled, replied. "*He didn't have much of a life to look forward to, did he?*"

"*I can't imagine a dog killing herself,*" Tucker mused. "*I think it's a peculiar thing to humans. Suicide.*"

"*If it's suicide we have nothing to worry about.*" Mrs. Murphy joined Pewter on the counter. "*But if it's not suicide then this will be a stormy spring.*"

"*Oh, come on,*" Pewter said, a touch sarcastically. "*Who would risk their own freedom to kill a loser like Wesley?*"

21

The sodden ground could suck the shoes right off a horse. It held onto human shoes, too, as Harry and Cynthia Cooper trudged along the deer path not far from Durant Creek. Tucker, up to her knees in the mud, accompanied them. Mrs. Murphy and Pewter, left back at the farm, planned even more retaliatory destruction.

Harry pointed. "Here we connect up to the old farm road. Jeez, it's loud."

Coop stopped at the crossroads of deer path and farm road. "The ground's soaked. If we get any more rain, the creeks and rivers will jump their banks."

"Spring."

"Yep."

"We were running back. I noticed a gleam. And that's about the size of it. We walked over, I discovered it was the hood ornament. I didn't notice footprints or tire tracks. It started to pour but it had been raining before, as you know.

If a car or truck had come back here there would have been deep ruts. There weren't." She moved over. "About here."

Tucker, senses much keener, sniffed around. No trace of human scent remained, although a hint of coyote lingered. She was glad her mother couldn't smell it because coyote spelled a great deal of trouble for everyone. The force of the storms beat down small branches, brush, stripped some buds off trees. She couldn't gather any more evidence than the humans.

"Where does the farm road lead?"

"To the creek."

"Any structures, sheds, anything like that along the way?"

"No. Marcus Durant's shack is the only building and that's back where we parked."

"Well, let's head back." Coop stuck her thumbs in her belt. "Whatever might have been on the ground is washed away by now, but"—she looked around again—"I've got to run down every lead I can. I just wonder what the hell he was doing out here, if he was here."

"Come on, Tucker."

"I'm coming," the dog replied, irritated that she couldn't locate more scent.

A sharp breeze picked up as the two women and dog walked back.

"Sure doesn't feel like spring today," Cooper commented.

"Cuts to the bone. Coop, what's going on? You wouldn't be out here with me if you weren't worried."

"I don't think Wesley Partlow committed suicide. Marshall Wells can't get to the autopsy until tonight. I'll withhold judgment until I get his results."

"Isn't it hard to perform an autopsy on an exposed corpse that's been hanging?" Harry grimaced.

"Those guys know what they're doing. They take tissue samples. I couldn't do it. I trust their opinion because they do such a thorough examination of the body, too. Rick and I have trained eyes but we're not doctors."

"I wouldn't think a kid like Wesley could be hanged without a fight. Surely there are easier ways to kill someone than to hang them."

"Not if all you have is rope. What if our killer, assuming there was one, didn't have a gun or a knife? Right now I don't know much of anything and I sure don't know why he was out here. I would figure from the time we released him to the time you found the Mercedes star would have been five to six hours."

"He wouldn't knowingly throw away the star." Harry was thinking out loud. "He could have lost it running or in a fight. From here to the elder-care home in Crozet is about three miles."

"Yeah." Coop opened the door to the squad car.

"Shut the door, Cynthia. Let me wipe off Tucker's paws first."

"I can wash them," Tucker grumbled.

Harry had had the presence of mind to throw an old towel in the squad car. She grabbed it, bending down to clean off the corgi's muddy paws "I'd never know you had white feet, Miss Pooch."

Coop leaned against the car door. "He wasn't on drugs. That's the first thing I think about. Wesley was clean as far as we know."

"I'd have thought he'd take anything he could get. Maybe he had more sense than I gave him credit for—what little I saw of him. Some people are life's losers. It sounds harsh but it's true. Miranda gets mad at me when I say that because she believes everyone can be redeemed through the Lord. I hope she's right."

"She hasn't been quoting as much scripture lately." Coop smiled. "Tracy?"

"Yeah, though she was never what I'd call a Bible thumper. Okay, there were times when she came close but she has toned down a little. I actually like it when she quotes the Bible. I'm learning something. I never did memorize much except for Hamlet's soliloquy, which I hate." Harry, meditatively rubbing Tucker's paws, got lost in thought.

"M-m-m, come on, she's clean enough."

"All right, Tucker. In you go."

"I told you I could wash myself." Tucker sat down on the backseat and began washing her paws.

As they drove down Whitehall Road, Coop asked, "Is there anything unique about the farms out here?"

"Unique? Well, some of them are very beautiful but I can't think of anything unique. Many of them were filled with wounded soldiers during the War Between the States. They'd ship them in by train and folks would pick up soldiers, ours and the Yankees, down at the train station and take them home. God, it must have been a mess. Just about every house in central Virginia had soldiers in it."

"Hard to imagine."

"You were in as much danger from the surgeon as you were from the enemy. But no, there's nothing special unless you count architecture."

"I sure wish I knew what he was doing down here."

"Did anyone pick him up from the station?"

Coop shook her head. "Walked right out and kept going."

"Creepy."

"Wesley?"

"The weekend. Kind of a weekend of death. Roger and then Wesley."

Cynthia said, "I heard Lottie Pearson hired a lawyer."

"You're kidding."

"Just in case we accuse her of poisoning Roger. Now,

there's a paranoid woman. No one is accusing her of anything. It was her dumb luck to hand him coffee and cake."

"Who told you?" Harry could think of a few people who would get the news first.

"Little Mim."

"Lottie's been shining her on."

"Oh, well, Little Mim knows it. She said she called BoomBoom to tell her she made the right decision in fixing you up with Diego and not Lottie."

"She did?" Harry was surprised.

"You're a lot more fun than tight-ass Lottie." Coop whistled. "And he is gorgeous."

"Pretty is as pretty does."

"Oh, Harry, that's what you always say about horses."

"Well, it applies to men, too."

Coop laughed as she turned right, out toward Harry's farm. "Who knows what men say about us?"

"That we're beautiful, sexy, and wonderful. Right?" Harry laughed, too.

"I'm sure."

"Do you have to go to the autopsy tonight?"

"No, I get the night off. Things are returning to normal, finally."

"Miranda, Susan, and I are going to Tracy's apartment over the pharmacy to paint. Miranda's bringing all the food. How are you with a paint brush?"

"Picasso."

When Harry walked inside her house she noticed how silent it was. Not a kitty in sight. It wasn't until she went into the living room that she beheld savaged lampshades, pillows tossed on the floor, and her bowl of potpourri strewn all over the carpet.

"Mrs. Murphy! Pewter!"

"You don't think they'll show their faces, do you?" the dog

intelligently asked. *"They're both in the barn in the hayloft, I guarantee it."*

Harry looked at the old clock on the mantelpiece. "Damn. Well, come on, Tucker, I was going to take them to Tracy's but not now."

She grabbed her old white painter's pants, a white T-shirt, then headed out the door with a bouncy Tucker at her side.

Once at Tracy's she blew off steam about the depredations of felines. It made her paint faster but she was careful with her brush and didn't make a mess. Miranda had chosen a rich, warm beige for the living room, the windows trimmed in linen white.

Once Cynthia arrived the pace really picked up. They had the living room and all the trim knocked out by eight. Miranda had set up two card tables in the kitchen. Susan went off her diet. She couldn't help it, the food was too good.

Tracy had fought in Korea right out of high school. He stayed in the army, got his college degree, and after years of outstanding service was wooed away from the army by the CIA. He wasn't a right-wing fellow; he'd seen enough government mismanagement to cure him of any blind patriotism. However, he revered the Constitution and loved his country, warts and all. He had a logical mind, a mind good at detail. When he retired to Hawaii he thought all would be well, but his wife had died three years earlier. His fiftieth high-school reunion brought him home and back to his high-school flame, Miranda, herself widowed. It was as though they had never parted. So he flew back to Hawaii, attended to business there, sold his house, and returned.

Both Tracy and Miranda were of a generation where you didn't live with a member of the opposite sex unless you married them. He could walk to Miranda's from his apartment and everything would be proper.

"When do you move the furniture in?" Susan asked. "Do you have furniture?"

"Some." He looked at Cynthia Cooper. "Did you notice the knot on the hanging rope? Not to change the subject."

"Just looked like a knot to me."

"You saved the rope for evidence, of course."

"Yes."

"Mind if I come down and look at it tomorrow? And who notified next of kin?"

"Augusta County Sheriff's Department." A cloud crossed Cooper's face. She didn't want to trespass on another law-enforcement agency's jurisdiction, but she thought she probably should have gone with someone from the Augusta department. She'd go over there tomorrow.

Already a few pounds thinner thanks to his wired-up jaw, Officer Everett Yancy hopped out of his seat when Deputy Cooper walked through the doors of the sheriff's headquarters.

"Coop!" He hustled her to his desk, sat her in his chair, leaned over, and punched in a code. "What do you make of this?"

On the computer screen appeared a message from their contact at Richmond's Department of Motor Vehicles, Carol Grossman. The DMV, efficient, processed information from satellite DMVs statewide as well as mailings from individual drivers.

The message read:

Hey, you asked for this driver's license Saturday night.
Here's our record.   •
Yrs, Carol

Yancy reached in front of Cooper to scroll up more text. Before her eyes was Wesley Partlow's license. But the photo on the license wasn't Wesley Partlow.

For the first time, Cooper felt the ground give way beneath her. She knew they were going out into deeper water.

She glanced up at Yancy. "These guys are good—real good."

No sooner had she studied Carol Grossman's message than the phone rang for her.

"Hello."

"Deputy Cooper, Officer Vitale. I'm sorry to be a little behind. I went over to the Partlows' like you requested. No one's dead."

"Thank you, Officer Vitale." She put the phone down. "Someone sure is dead, along with my brain!" She stormed out of the room.

22

You've got ants in your pants." Miranda re-inked the stamp pads, then closed the lids, sliding them under the counter.

"I want to know what's going on."

"We all want to know what's going on. That's why Tracy drove down to the sheriff's office this morning."

"Well, why hasn't he called?"

"Harry, he left a half hour ago. Will you calm yourself?"

"Yes. It's time for my morning nap. I need quiet." Pewter yawned.

The front door swung open. BoomBoom came in, wearing bib overalls, large hoop earrings, and a bright green T-shirt. "Good morning, ladies."

"I can see you're going to spend a day on the tractor." Harry thought she'd like to be on her old John Deere.

"No," came the brief reply as BoomBoom slid her key in the lock of her postbox, swinging open the brass door with the glass window.

"Bills," Tucker told her as the corgi helped sort the mail this morning.

"Why, hello, Tucker. I didn't notice you when I came in."

"Where are you off to in your overalls?"

"Harry, I'm not accustomed to you being so interested in my schedule." BoomBoom sorted through the envelopes as though they were cards in a deck. "What gives?"

"Nothing." Harry appeared nonchalant.

BoomBoom sashayed to the counter, leaned on it, and purred, "You want to know if Thomas has said anything about Diego."

"Not me."

"I hate it when humans try to purr." Mrs. Murphy stuck one leg straight up, contorted her head under it to lick the back side.

"If I made her do that people would say it's cruelty to animals." Harry pointed to the agile tiger kitty.

"You can't do that." Miranda smiled. "I know I can't. I bet the Dalai Lama couldn't do it either."

"What's the Dalai Lama got to do with it?" BoomBoom, mystified, wrinkled her nose, a habit when she was puzzled.

"Doesn't he twist himself into a pretzel, sleep on nails?" Miranda's eyes grew larger. "Walk through fire."

"No, that's a master yogi."

"Yogi Bear." Harry giggled.

BoomBoom said, "But honestly, they can do things like that. There are some who can have out-of-body experiences."

"I have out-of-body experiences when I get the flu."

"Harry, gross." BoomBoom stacked her mail on the counter, flipped it on the side, and tapped the envelopes evenly together. "Anyway, do you want to know what Diego said to Thomas?"

"Sure," she shrugged.

"Mother, don't try to be so cool." Mrs. Murphy still had her hind leg over her head.

Tucker walked back behind the counter when Harry tipped it up. *"Murphy, I wish you wouldn't do that. It hurts just to look at you."*

"If you didn't have such stumps, you could do it, too," the tiger cat said with malicious glee.

"Ha, ha," the dog dryly replied.

"Why isn't anyone paying attention to me?" Pewter pouted.

"You said you wanted to take a nap," Murphy fired back.

"Am I asleep?"

"Pewter, you are so perverse."

"All cats are perverse." The little dog headed for the back animal door.

"Where are you going? What are you doing?" Mrs. Murphy demanded.

"Hey, there's nothing in here but two bitchy cats."

"Is that so?" Pewter fluffed her fur.

"Guess you won't find out what Thomas told BoomBoom." Mrs. Murphy cleverly dangled the bait.

"Oh, yeah." Tucker stopped, returning to the counter.

"Well?" Miranda expectantly leaned over the counter.

"Thomas said that Diego hopes to see Harry again." BoomBoom hooked her thumb under her overall strap. "Has he called you?"

"No, Thomas hasn't called me," Harry said.

"You know what I mean. Don't be such a smart-ass, Harry."

"Yes, Diego has called me. Is everyone happy now?"

"You didn't tell me." Miranda was hurt.

"Because he called last night after our painting party. I forgot to tell you because there's so much else going on. Anyway, Diego has to fly back to Montevideo this week, but he hopes to be down for the Wrecker's Ball."

"Oh. What painting party?" BoomBoom asked.

Mrs. Murphy, bored with the humans, put her hind leg down finally, swept her whiskers forward, and stared right down at Tucker. *"What a pretty doggie."*

Tucker looked up but a fraction of a second too late because the cat swooped down on her, bowling her over. *"Oooph."* The dog had the wind knocked out of her and was rolled over by the force of Murphy's aerial bombardment.

Pewter, ears up, inched closer to the tangle. *"This looks good."*

"Banzai! Death to the emperor," Murphy sang out.

"You watch too many war movies," Tucker snapped as she scrambled to her feet. She bolted out the animal door, Mrs. Murphy in hot pursuit.

Pewter hesitated a moment. After all, puddles dotted the alleyway; but the screams from outside finally lured her out the animal door, where both cat and dog pounced on her, knowing she'd fall for it.

"Nonstop party." Harry laughed.

"What, painting?"

Both Harry and Miranda told her about the painting party at Tracy's apartment and Tracy asking Coop to see the rope.

Just then the phone rang. Miranda picked it up and Harry crowded next to her. BoomBoom hurried behind the counter to listen in.

"Oh, hello, Mim." Miranda tried to hide the disappointment in her voice.

"Has my package arrived from Cartier? I sent my tank watch up to New York to be fixed weeks ago." Big Mim emphasized "weeks."

"No package today. I'm so used to you being my first customer. Where are you?"

"I'm on my way to Richmond with Marilyn. I promised

I'd take her to Monkey's." She mentioned a dress shop much frequented by ladies such as herself. "I'm on the car phone. Clear as a bell, isn't it?"

"You two have a wonderful time. Bye now." Miranda hung up the phone.

Lottie Pearson walked through the door. "Hello." She opened her postbox, gathered her mail, and walked right out.

"Can you believe?" BoomBoom's eyebrows shot upward.

The phone rang again. They all reached for it but Miranda was first.

Miranda picked up the receiver. "Hello."

"Hi, sugar." Tracy's baritone sounded deep. "I'm heading back. Need anything?"

"What'd you think?" Harry, leaning over, spoke into the receiver.

"Did you grab the phone from my beautiful girlfriend?"

"No. She's right here. BoomBoom, too. We're hanging on your every word."

"Oh." He inhaled. "Heavy rope, climber's rope. You know when you see movies of hangings in the Old West, how the rope has a special kind of noose?"

"Yes," they said in unison.

"That's what I wanted to see. If Wesley took the time to make that noose, assuming he killed himself, or if his killer did, assuming he was murdered. The noose isn't as easy to tie as you would think."

"And?" Harry's tone raised up.

"No. A simple knot like you tie when you're tying up a package."

"Honeybunch, what does that mean?" Miranda breathlessly asked, having regained full access to the receiver.

"That either Wesley or his killer didn't know how to tie

the knot, didn't care, didn't have time. Or that the climber's rope would hold."

"I don't follow." BoomBoom honestly didn't.

"One of the reasons the noose knot was used to hang people is that it would hold the weight of the body and snap the neck. It's more humane than choking to death, which is what happens if you tie a common package knot. In time the common knot will give even on good quality rope."

"This gives me chills. You come on home." Miranda half laughed.

"I will. Say bye to the girls."

Miranda hung up the phone as the three animals pranced through the animal door, best friends again.

"I didn't know that about a noose." Harry's hand instinctively flew to her neck. "Choking and swinging at the same time. What an awful way to die."

"I think we missed something." Mrs. Murphy quietly sat down on a chair by the table in the back.

"We have only to wait. They're bound to tell another human. You know how they are." Pewter jumped on a chair at the table and began biting out the mud between her toes. She hated dirt.

"All this talk of death ..." Boom's voice faded away, then increased in strength. "Roger's funeral is tomorrow. Are you all going?"

"You know we will." Miranda frowned for a moment. "Now, why would you even ask?"

"I don't know." BoomBoom's shoulders hunched up, then she relaxed. "I'm a little distracted. Aren't you?"

"Well, it has been a strange couple of days but we may be making too much of it all." Miranda noticed the tiny mud pellets falling to the floor since Pewter was sitting in one of the chairs next to her. "Pewter, pick up after yourself."

"I'll clean it up." Harry opened the small broom closet in the back, fetching the dustpan and brush.

"Well, I'm off."

"You never said why you're wearing overalls." Harry knelt down, brushing up the mud bits.

"I'm going to work."

"What work?" Harry rather impolitely replied.

"Welding. I have an order to make a hen and chickens for Opal Michaels."

"Better make it a chicken with attitude," Harry said.

"If I were making it for Big Mim I'd put a crown on that bird." BoomBoom laughed as she opened the front door.

Miranda picked up Mrs. Murphy to pet her. "I'm glad to see you and BoomBoom are getting along better."

"She's always made more of an effort than I have."

"Well, I'm glad to see you recognize that. Remember your *Proverbs*. 'A friend loves at all times, and a brother is born for adversity.'" Miranda quoted Chapter Seventeen, Verse Seventeen.

"I wouldn't go that far." Harry winked at her.

Mrs. Murphy listened as the tiny mud bits hit the floor. *"Pewter, you have more mud between your toes than an elephant."*

"And you don't?"

"Not as much as you."

"Why aren't you grooming yourself?" the gray cat wondered.

"I'm waiting until she sweeps up your mess. Then I'll make another one."

"Murphy, you're awful," Tucker giggled.

23

St. Luke's Lutheran Church, pleasing eighteenth-century architecture with clean brick and white lintels, filled with those wishing to pay their last respects to Roger O'Bannon. The town residents crammed into the pews, the light streaming through the stained-glass windows.

All rose when Sean O'Bannon and his mother, Ida, entered by the door next to the lectern to take their seats in the front row. The once numerous O'Bannon clan had dwindled over the decades. As neither Roger nor Sean had ever married, the line might well end with Sean.

As the mother and son seated themselves, the congregation also sat down.

People were surprised at the change in Sean's appearance. He'd cut off his dork knob, gotten a good haircut, and was clean shaven. A well-cut dark gray suit gave him a substantial, solemn air. No one could remember Sean wearing a suit since high school; he'd always been low-key, counterculture. The Reverend Jones solemnly came out of a door recessed behind the pulpit. He bowed his head before the altar, then turned to face the congregation. Herb, no stranger to funerals, tried to invest this last event with meaning. He avoided platitudes, the easy phrase.

Fair sat with Harry. Susan and Ned Tucker, Miranda and Tracy were on the other side of Harry. After the service they drove to the cemetery south of town, a pleasant site with a beautiful view of rolling pastures. When the casket was lowered into the grave, tears rolled down Sean's cheeks. He'd held up until then. His mother put her arm around his waist.

When Harry drove away with Fair, Susan, and Ned in Ned's car, Sean was still standing at the gravesite.

"Depressing," Susan tersely said.

"Harry, do you want to go back to the post office or do you have time for lunch?" Ned turned left toward town.

"Work. Miranda's having lunch with Tracy."

"Want me to bring you a sandwich?" Susan volunteered.

"Yeah. How about chicken, lettuce, tomato, and mayo on whole wheat."

"Do you have cat and dog food at the P.O.?" Ned pulled up at the post office.

"Susan, you know I do. I'll go hungry before they do." Harry smiled as she hopped out of the car.

"I've got a call at Quail Ridge Farm." Fair rolled down the window. "Take you to the movies over the weekend?"

"Sure," Harry replied.

The post office was only fifteen minutes from the cemetery by foot but she had liked being in the car with her old friends. As Harry walked in the back door she caught a glimpse of the two cats, paws fishing in the backs of the postboxes. They jumped down as she closed the back door and walked across to unlock the sliding door—like a small garage door—that separated the public section of the post office from the workers' section.

"What are you two doing?"

"Nothing," both said unconvincingly.

She walked to the open backs of the postboxes, peering inside, shutting one eye for a better view. The torn ends of envelopes presented themselves. Irritated, Harry pulled them out. "Great, Big Mim and Fair. You would have to claw those two."

"We were just playing," Pewter replied. *"No real harm done."*

"For now." Tucker rolled over on her back.

"You're supposed to be on our side." Mrs. Murphy pushed the mail cart into the recumbent dog.

Before a first-class fight could erupt, Cynthia Cooper opened the front door.

"Hey, I thought I'd see you at the funeral," Harry said.

"I was picking up the coroner's report on Wesley Partlow."

"And?"

"Murdered."

Harry grimaced. "By hanging?"

"Ultimately. Apparently he was a hard bugger to kill. Given the rains and the condition of the body when we found him, we shipped him right off to the cooler. But on close examination, small hunks of hair were torn from his head, there were bruises on his torso. He put up a fight. He can't be exactly sure but Marshall Wells is ninety percent certain that Wesley wasn't dead when the rope was put around his neck. Unconscious, maybe, but not dead."

"That's gruesome."

"Yep. I was quite happy not to have to attend this coroner's exam."

"I don't think I could get through one with a body in good condition."

"You get used to it. Think of the body as a book. You open it up and read." The tall blonde pointed toward the divider.

Harry nodded, so Cooper flipped it up and walked toward the back.

"Coffee, tea, Coke. Susan's bringing me a sandwich. You're welcome to half."

"Actually, I just ate." She sat down in the chair. "No sign of the GMC truck either. I don't know if he stole it and returned it before the owner knew it, stole it and the owner didn't report it, or the owner lent it to him. I keep thinking the truck will get me on the rails.

"The other thing that bothers me is I can't find a police record. We sent out his dental information. That's often the easiest way to get something, that and the name. But Wesley Partlow isn't his real name."

"What?" Harry exclaimed as Cooper filled her in on the false photo on the driver's license.

"I'm going over the mountain to Waynesboro later today."

Harry sat down opposite Cooper as Murphy jumped in her lap and Pewter nestled in Cooper's. "It's almost as if he were a ghost, isn't it? A nameless, unknown person who"— she paused—"left no trace."

"Except for the Falcon hubcaps." Cynthia Cooper sucked in air between her teeth. "A kid like that collects bad marks, a real bad report card. I'll find it in time."

"Does that mean you have to keep the remains?"

"No. We've got photographs of the corpse. And we took mug shots and fingerprints when we booked him. There's not much point in keeping him in the cooler. A lot of times when a corpse is disfigured or decayed, people can't recognize it. Odd though, some corpses retain their features for a long time, the eyes can be gone, the lips, too, but they are still very identifiable.

"You know, I have this theory that fake boobs, plastic hips, the whole march of medicine will mean that corpses stay around longer. We don't just live longer, we die longer—sort of."

"You're punchy," Harry replied.

"A little."

"How's Rick?" Harry stroked under Mrs. Murphy's chin.

"You know how he gets when he has an unsolved crime. He's pieced together all the area topo maps and pinned them on the wall. Then he uses colored pins for the day. Day one, all the known movements of the victim are in blue. Day two, green and so on. It's a good system because Rick thinks better if he can visualize."

"He's a good sheriff."

"Yes, not that the county knows or cares." Coop sighed. "People take things for granted."

"In every endeavor." Harry started to reach across the table but it squeezed Murphy so she stopped. "The only reason to kill someone like Wesley is because he was caught red-handed stealing again or"—she stopped a second—"because he knew something."

"Revenge."

Harry thought a moment. "Maybe."

"Suppose he insulted someone on a deep level? You know, tried to seduce a man's wife or, worse, an underage daughter. Something like that can set a normal person right off. Murder is normal. That's why we don't want to look at it. The media is fascinated with serial killers, a fairly rare aberration, but most murders are run-of-the-mill affairs committed by run-of-the-mill people."

"That theory would place Wesley's killer in his own social

class. Wouldn't it? People like Wesley don't have a lot of contact with people higher up on the scale."

"My, what a pretty gray tummy and so much of it, too." Cooper laughed as Pewter rolled over in her lap. "Uh— I don't know. What if he did odd jobs on a big farm, made a pass at the lady of the manor?" She shrugged. "Who the hell knows?"

"He knew enough to sell hubcaps."

"And to park cars."

"My guess is he knew someone in Crozet. He wasn't just passing through. I mean, you don't just pass through Crozet. Charlottesville, yes, but not Crozet. We're a little off the beaten track." Harry's features brightened. She liked figuring things out.

"Route 64's not that far away, nor is Route 250."

"Yeah, but if you come to Crozet you usually have a purpose or a person in mind. We're a little bit nondescript, you know."

Cooper thought silently for a time. "I think you're right. What next?" She ran her fingers through Pewter's fur.

"I don't know but I can help."

"No," Tucker said from under the table.

"Oh, Tucker, don't be a poopface. This will liven up the spring," Mrs. Murphy chided her.

"You're the one who always counsels prudence," the dog reminded her.

"Maybe I'm bored." The tiger placed her paw on Harry's forearm. *"I'm ready for a little action."*

"Be careful what you ask for." Pewter turned her head so she could see Murphy from under the table.

"And what would you ask for?" the tiger replied.

"Steak tartare garnished with braised mouse tails."

24

Tucked on the west side of the Blue Ridge Mountains in the Shenandoah Valley sat the modest city of Waynesboro. While not wealthy like its eastern neighbor, Charlottesville, Waynesboro evidenced its own character, which was upfront, hardworking, and ready for a good time.

Cynthia Cooper liked the town, which was economically dominated by a DuPont chemical plant. Virginia Metalcrafters was also based in Waynesboro, and she enjoyed stopping by to watch the men create the beautiful brass door locks and other items for which the firm was justly famous.

She turned right past the Burger King and McDonald's, heading west. Then she turned onto Randolph Street, filled with neat, well-kept houses.

She parked in front of a brick rancher painted white with navy-blue shutters on the windows. The front door, red, had a large polished brass knocker, no doubt made at Virginia Metalcrafters.

She rapped on the knocker. Within seconds the door

opened, revealing a careworn woman perhaps in her mid-forties but appearing older at the moment. Glued to her side was a pretty golden retriever.

"Mrs. Partlow?"

The woman involuntarily took a step back. "You're the second policeman to come here. My son is not dead."

"Yes, ma'am, I know that and I'm sorry to bother you. I'm Deputy Cynthia Cooper from the Albemarle County Sheriff's Department. Is your son at home?"

"As a matter of fact, he is. He works the night shift at the DuPont plant. He's asleep."

"I see." Cooper smiled at the golden retriever. "Beautiful dog."

"That's Rolex. Wesley gave her to me on my birthday. He said he couldn't afford a Rolex but the puppy would make me happier than any watch. He was right, wasn't he, Rolex?" She patted the silky head as Rolex thumped her tail.

Reaching inside her chest pocket, Cooper pulled out a license, which she handed to Mrs. Partlow. "Is this your son?"

Her eyebrows darted upward. "No. Who is this?"

"We don't know."

Mrs. Partlow studied the rest of the license. "The rest of it is correct."

"We're hoping your son will know who the man is in the photograph. Do you mind waking him?"

"No, not at all. It's about time for him to get up anyway. Please come in, Deputy—"

"Cooper." She walked through the door.

The parquet floor in the entrance hall gleamed.

"Come on in the living room. I'll go wake Wesley." Mrs. Partlow disappeared down the hall, Rolex at her heels.

Cooper heard a few grunts and groans.

Mrs. Partlow returned. "He'll be out in a minute. May I get you something to drink?"

"No, thank you, ma'am."

Wesley soon appeared, wearing a blue T-shirt, jeans, and sneakers without socks. "Hi."

Cooper stood up to shake his hand. "I'm sorry to disturb you."

"That's okay." The slight, curly-haired young man smiled.

"Here's your driver's license."

He took the stiff card from her hand. "I have my license. I think. Let me check." He hurried back to his room.

Cooper could hear metal clothes hangers sliding on a metal closet pole. Rolex cocked her head. "Good ears, Rolex."

Wesley, perplexed, stepped back into the living room. "It's gone! I keep my license in the pocket of my bomber jacket except for when it's really hot, then I just stick it in the visor of my truck."

"Do you have any idea how long you've been missing your license?"

He thought a moment. "I remember getting gas. Had it then. Last week. I—" He paused. "You know, it's kind of hard to remember. I just never think about my license."

"Do you recognize the man in the photo?"

He peered intently at the likeness. "Kinda. I've seen him around but I don't know his name."

"Whoever he is, he can sure doctor a driver's license or he knows someone who can." Cooper smiled.

"Yeah. Looks valid to me."

"Me, too," Mrs. Partlow chimed in.

"Mr. Partlow, think. Any guidance you can give me will be a big help."

"He's dead, right? Mom said the Augusta cop came by to tell her I was dead."

"I think I surprised him more than he surprised me." Mrs. Partlow smiled tightly.

"Yes, he's dead. Could you have seen him at the gas station?"

"Uh, no." Wesley cupped his chin in his hand as he took a seat. "Might have seen him at Danny's, the bar behind the post office downtown." He furrowed his brow. "Yeah."

"And when you go to Danny's, what do you do with your coat?"

"Hang it up or put it over the back of the chair."

After a few more questions, Cooper left, driving over to Danny's. The bartender, Louis Seidlitz, was just setting up, preparing for the evening's traffic.

Louis recognized the face but couldn't recall a name to go with it.

As she drove back toward Charlottesville, climbing up over Afton Mountain, she thought how quick-eyed and light-fingered the false Wesley Partlow had been. Quick enough to pilfer a driver's license. How many pockets did he touch before finding pay dirt? Apparently he rifled them without drawing attention to himself. She was reminded of that expression, "Opportunity makes a poet as well as a thief."

25

Although the ground remained soggy, the next day the sky, a robin's-egg blue, presaged a spectacular spring day. The late-blooming dogwoods covered the mountainside. Earlier blooms had their petals knocked off by the storms but fire stars still dotted banks with their brilliant red.

Tucker inhaled the lovely fragrances of spring as she sat on the back step of the post office.

Harry often walked the four miles to work but given the rains of the past week she drove. On the way to work she'd swung by the small lumberyard outside of town. Luckily, there was enough sawdust to shovel into the truck bed. Usually by Wednesday or Thursday there was enough sawdust for the horsemen to drive down and load up. She'd filled up her truck, pulled a tarp over it, and arrived at work by seven-thirty A.M.

Tucker told the cats, once they arrived at work, that she was going on a jaunt alone.

"Suits me," Pewter declared.

Murphy, a little miffed, said, *"Why alone?"*

"Want to check in with my dog friends. Not all of them like cats."

"Get new friends." The tiger turned her back to her.

With anticipation and a heady sense of freedom, Tucker took another deep breath, then trotted merrily down the alleyway behind the post office. She turned north, which meant she would swing past private homes, past the new grade school, and then she'd be in the open countryside. Despite her short legs, the corgi moved at a fast clip. In fact, she could run very fast, and on occasion she enjoyed the delicious victory of outrunning a hound, a spaniel, or once even a Great Dane. It should be noted that the Great Dane had a splinter in its paw. Still, Tucker was a confident, cheerful dog. She edged along well-manicured lawns, dogs in the houses barking empty warnings. In no time she was in farmland.

Early corn, tiny shoots just breaking the furrows, gave the red clay fields a green cast. The hay in other fields already swayed over her head. She pushed through a field of rye and timothy mix. Tucker could identify any grass crop by its odor. She reached a rutted farm road and thought she'd go down to the old Mawyer place. Booty Mawyer, seventy-seven, farmed his three hundred acres pretty much as he always had. A shrewd fellow, he sank no money into large purchases like tractors, manure spreaders, hay balers, and the like. He kept four Belgian horses and worked them in teams of two. The cost of feeding and shoeing his horses proved far less than tractor payments. And he managed to get everything done. His grandson, Don Clatterbuck, helped him in the evenings, and during hay-cutting time, Don worked full-time with him.

Tucker could hear the old man and his horses in the distance. A faint whiff of onion grass floated across the light

southerly breeze. Tucker stopped and sniffed. Wind from
the south usually meant moisture and lots of it, yet the day
was achingly clear. Still, the dog trusted her senses. She figured she'd better get back to the post office by lunchtime.

She hurried down the road, eager to visit anyone at all,
first coming to the old tobacco-curing sheds. Booty
Mawyer, like many central Virginia farmers, once upon a
time made a good profit from his tobacco allotments. After
World War II the business slacked off, the cost of labor
zoomed upward, and many farmers allowed their allotments
to fall into disuse. But the accoutrements of a lively tobacco
trade still stood—curing sheds, storing sheds, and in town,
the old auction house.

Foxes especially like curing sheds. Just why, Tucker
couldn't understand, except that having a burrow under a
nice structure was always a plus. There were lots of sturdy
outbuildings, yet the tobacco-curing sheds held a fasci-
nation for *Vulpes vulpes*. Tucker didn't mind foxes. Mrs.
Murphy hated them and hissed with the mention of a fox's
name. From time to time the cat would declare a truce, but
the real reason Murphy loathed them was that they competed for the same game.

The milk butterflies flitted upward along with Tucker's
thoughts as she reached the shed. She walked around the
side of it and stopped. Sitting right in front of her was the
1987 GMC pickup, the faded Cowboys football team jacket
jammed up on the top of the seat.

26

Tucker blasted through the animal door at the post office with such velocity that her feet skidded sideways and she fell over, sliding. A bump into the mail cart stopped her unusual progress.

Scrambling to her feet she shouted, *"I found it! I found the truck."*

Mrs. Murphy, who watched the dog's slide with mirth, hopped off the table. *"Where?"*

"At Booty Mawyer's."

"What?" The cat couldn't believe her ears.

Pewter, roused from yet another slumber, shook herself, stuck her head up from the mail cart in which she was sleeping. *"Tucker, what are you talking about? And you woke me up."*

"I'm telling you that the GMC truck is parked at the old tobacco-curing shed at Booty Mawyer's place."

"How do you know it's the right truck?" Pewter, skeptical, asked.

"Has the Cowboys jacket on the seat. Like Sean said. Remember?" The dog's eyes shone with intelligence.

"He did say that, didn't he?" The gray cat pulled herself up and out of the mail cart using her front paws.

"What's the commotion here?" Harry smiled down at her friends.

"Oh, Mom, I wish you could understand me." The corgi's ears drooped a bit, then perked back up.

Harry handed the dog a Milk-Bone. For good measure she gave the cats a few bits of Haute Feline, then returned to her task of reorganizing the carton shelves.

"I think we'd better check this out. This just doesn't sound right." Mrs. Murphy brushed her whiskers with her paws. *"For one thing, Tucker, Rick Shaw and Coop could have traced the truck to Booty Mawyer easily enough. License plates alone would do that and even though Sean didn't get the number all they would have to do is tap into the Department of Motor Vehicle computers for 1987 GMC trucks in the county. So something's amiss."*

"That's just it, Murphy, there are no license plates. 'Farm Use' is painted where the plates should go. This truck is long off the records."

"Well, why didn't you say that in the first place?" The cat was already heading for the door.

"You didn't give me the chance. And you know, Murphy, 'Farm Use' trucks aren't supposed to go out on the roads. Who would remember this old truck?"

"Tucker, I'm sorry. Come on." She disappeared through the door, her tail swishing through last.

As Tucker hurried after the sleek tiger, Pewter wailed, *"I smell rain. I'll get wet."*　•

"Stay here, fatso." The corgi couldn't resist a parting shot.

"Don't leave me! I hate to miss anything." Under her breath the gray cat grumbled, *"I know I'm going to regret this."*

"What is going on?" Harry scratched her head as Pewter's gray bottom vanished through the door.

"Must be a good party somewhere." Miranda laughed. "Here, let me hold that package or you'll tip the shelf over."

The three animals streaked along the lawns. Tucker held other dogs at bay, declaring they were just crossing and would be off that particular dog's property soon enough. The corgi also advised other dogs they would probably be returning that way and she was sorry to disturb them but important business was at hand.

The other domesticated animals behaved reasonably, except for one Australian shepherd who mouthed off so abusively that Tucker told the cats to run on. She advanced on the medium-sized dog, who, seeing the determination of the corgi plus the bared fangs, decided that passage through his lawn might not be so offensive.

Tucker caught up with the cats as they entered the rye field.

"*Guess you shut him up.*" Murphy brushed the slender rye blades.

"*For now.*"

"*How much farther?*" Pewter sneezed as pollen tickled her nose.

"*I told you to stay at the post office,*" Tucker chided her.

"*I'm not complaining. I just want to know how far,*" she snapped back.

"*Ten minutes.*" Tucker pushed through the rye.

They journeyed in silence until emerging on the farm road. The ruts seemed even deeper to Tucker this time. In the near distance they could hear a tractor whine.

"*Doesn't sound right, does it?*" Pewter noted.

"*No.*" Tucker, spying the tobacco barn up ahead, put on speed. She rounded the structure, the long-distant whiff of decades of smoke still pungently perceptible. "*What!*"

The two cats almost collided into her.

"*Where's the truck?*" Pewter caustically asked.

"*It was here. I swear it!*"

"*That tractor sounds stuck. Let's find it. Maybe Booty's using the truck to pull it out,*" Mrs. Murphy suggested.

Finding Booty proved easy enough not only because of the whine of the tractor but because he was cussing a blue streak. The animals heard words they'd never heard before.

The tractor had sunk into a soft pothole that must have been deceptive from the driver's seat. The rear wheels were mired a quarter of the way up the large yellow hubcaps. Booty, overalls shiny with fresh mud, placed stones, anything he could find, in front of the wheels, then he'd swing back up into the seat to try again.

Abraham, a bluetick hound, mournfully watched his human have fits. Abraham, two years older than God, endured some loss of hearing, stiff hips, and fading sight, but his nose stayed keen.

"*Abraham,*" Tucker called loudly to him as they approached. "*How are you?*"

"*Tucker? Who's with you? Are those Chihuahuas?*" He squinted.

"*I resent that,*" Pewter flared up.

"*Pewter, he's nearly as old as Booty.*" Mrs. Murphy bumped the gray just to put her in her place.

"*Mrs. Murphy and Pewter are with me,*" Tucker answered.

"*Hello, girls,*" Abraham greeted them, his manner courtly. "*I apologize for my human but as you can surmise, he's struggling with the elements and if my nose is any good at all, we'll be wet within the half hour. He'll need another tractor to pull out this one. Oh, me.*" He let out a long, long sigh.

"*No need to ever apologize for a human.*" Tucker laughed.

"*He's right about the rain,*" Pewter whispered to Mrs. Murphy. "*I feel it coming. If I get wet it will take me hours to dry. I can't stand it when my hair gets matted down. Murphy, are you listening?"*

"Stop worrying." She edged up to Abraham, then rubbed against his chest.

"Mrs. Murphy, you smell like nutmeg." He chuckled. *"Pewter."*

"Here I am." Pewter rubbed against him also.

"We're hoping you can help us." Tucker sat down as Booty cursed to high heaven. *"There's a farm truck parked behind the curing shed. I chanced by not an hour and a half ago and now on my return, it's gone. Might you know of its whereabouts?"*

"No. I didn't hear the truck being driven off but then I don't hear so good anymore."

"Do you recall Booty driving the truck to town?" Mrs. Murphy spoke up.

"Farm truck. Don't know how it would make it to town and back, really," Abraham answered.

"I thought when I came by that Booty was out with his team of horses," Tucker wondered. *"And I thought he didn't own a tractor."*

"What a memory you have, Tee Tucker. He worked the little field, the garden patch field, I call it, with the horses but Dimples threw a shoe. So he unhitched the horses and he was going to hitch up the second pair, you know he has the young ones he's bringing on, fine matched pair, ah, but I digress here. Well, he checked the weather and thought he'd return Marcus Durant's tractor to him. He'd borrowed it to dig fence holes. Marcus has every attachment made in the U. S. of A. and Booty's getting on in years, he just didn't feature digging fence holes with the hand digger. Luckily he finished that job, earth's soft, has to set the fence posts, of course, so he wanted to return the tractor. Now he's got to hitch up the young horses to pull out

the tractor and he'd better wash off the tractor, too. Rain'll help." He exhaled and his flews fluttered out with his breath.

"*Abraham, would you do me a great favor?*" Tucker's pink tongue hung out slightly.

"*If I can, I would certainly not like to disappoint a lady.*"

"*Will you walk over to the curing shed with us and work the ground where the truck was parked? Your nose is better than mine.*" Tucker flattered the bluetick hound but in truth hound noses were the best of the best.

"*Why, I'd be delighted although I'm sure your nose is keen as can be.*" He stood up on all fours, stretched, and moved toward the shed, happy to be useful. Hounds need to be useful or they sink into a torpor.

Booty turned around and beheld the four animals leaving. "Abraham, Abraham, you are useless as tits on a boar hog." He sputtered, needing to take out his anger on someone.

"*Going deaf has its advantages,*" Abraham chuckled. Once at the shed, he put his nose to the ground, working in small circles around the spot where the truck had been parked. "*Grease. Gas. Now, that's odd. Pump's down by the shed. And—*" He lifted his head, sniffed in fresh air to clear his nasal passages, then put his nose to the ground again. "*Something, something, a chemical? Tucker, get over here.*"

Tucker also put her nose to the ground as the cats watched. A stiff breeze came up quickly, blowing their fur toward their heads.

"*It's not fertilizer yet it smells organic. The man-made chemicals are harsh. This is—h-m-m, familiar.*" Abraham inhaled another deep draft. "*Acidic. Natural. Ah, I have it. Yes, tannic acid. Yes. Use it sometimes on the backs of new Oriental rugs to make them look old. Use it on skins. That's it.*"

"*Any association with a human?*" Mrs. Murphy asked as she lowered her head, the wind picking up considerably.

"Don." Abraham nodded slowly. *"Guess he borrowed the truck. Funny, though, he didn't leave his car. I can't think of anyone else with that scent. The moisture's holding it down pretty good. I don't know if Don did take the truck but I'm sure this is tannic acid."*

"Forgive me, Abraham, I'm not an initiate into the mysteries of scent." The tiger smiled, her green eyes glittering. *"But isn't it possible that the odor could be from the leather on the bottom of shoes or from the leather upper? It's muddy enough here for a shoe to sink in."*

"Wouldn't be this pungent." Abraham's deep voice reverberated. He lifted his head south, to the wind. *"Going to be another blow. You'd better head back or stay here if you'd like. Booty will get over himself."*

"Thanks. We'll go back. Oh, one more question." Tucker also lifted her head. *"I don't recall Booty being a Dallas Cowboys fan. I thought he was Redskins all the way."*

"Is."

"There was a Cowboys windbreaker on the back of the truck seat," Tucker said.

"No one in our family roots for any team but the Redskins. I'm not a football fan myself but I can tell you that. Go on now. You haven't much time."

"Thanks again, Abraham," Tucker said.

"Yes, thank you," the cats replied.

"Glad to be of service." Abraham turned, ambling back to the house. He'd given up on Booty and the tractor.

As the three hurried back the first raindrop splattered down behind the grade school.

"I knew it. I just knew it," Pewter railed as Mrs. Murphy and Tucker forged ahead, and as the storm worsened her volume level rose. *"I should have never left the post office. I should have trusted my first impulse. When am I going to learn*

to do that? What do I care about an old truck? I mean I don't care about Wesley Partlow. I didn't know Wesley Partlow. I wouldn't care if half the human race vanished. All they do is make a mess. I should have never let Tucker talk me into this. I hate those two. I hate them. Really!"

27

Rick Shaw stopped off at Pantops Shopping Center to grab a snack. He'd slipped back into the car with the sandwiches as Cynthia Cooper returned with drinks and two cartons of cigarettes since the price was so good.

He turned on the engine. Just as he did he heard the dispatcher's voice. "Sheriff, Sheriff Zakarios of Culpeper needs to talk to you. I've been trying to get you."

"Say what he want, Sheila?"

"No. But he said it's important."

"See if you can get him for me. I'll be in the car."

"Righto."

"Wonder what Zak wants." Coop bit into a ham-and-cheese sandwich. She hadn't realized how hungry she was until she took her first bite.

"Rick," Zakarios's voice boomed over citizen's band radio.

"Yes, Zak. What's cooking in Culpeper?"

"Albemarle resident found on White Shop Road just

about a half hour ago. Shot through the temple, slumped over the steering wheel. Don Clatterbuck."

"I'll be right there, Zak."

"We sealed off the site. You know this guy?"

"Yes."

"Damnedest thing, he has a stuffed pileated woodpecker on the seat next to him. Thing's almost two feet tall."

"He's a taxidermist on the side. Sirens on, maybe I can get to you in a half hour. I don't know, rain's looking evil."

"How far down are you on White Shop Road? This is Deputy Cynthia Cooper."

"Hi, Coop. Not two miles. We're a little off the road to the right. You'll see the yellow tape and the squad cars. Ambulance will be here, too. Thought you'd want to see him before—" He was interrupted, then returned. "John says he thinks he's been dead less than an hour."

"Be there as fast as I can. Over and out."

A gushing rivulet of rainwater poured down in front of Rick Shaw's eyes each time he bent his head. The sheriff's hat, a modified cowboy hat that he and other officers wore, shunted water fore and aft, but the rains were so heavy the hat was soaked through in fifteen minutes.

Sheriff Zakarios mourned the loss of clean vehicle tracks next to the truck. Tracks could still be seen but the rain wiped out a tread imprint. "We've gone over his truck thoroughly." He wiped his cheeks, wet; his hands were wet, too. "Not a feather off this woodpecker."

Coop leaned against the 1987 GMC truck, now wearing real license plates, her back to it. "The woodpecker belongs to Mary Minor Haristeen. He must have just finished it."

"She into drugs or anything?" Chris Zakarios asked.

"No," Coop replied. "Straight as an arrow. Why, were you going to tear apart the woodpecker?"

"Not right off the bat but I'll impound it for a while."

"Neat. Small caliber." Rick opened the door a crack again, inspecting the wound. "Twenty-two, I'd reckon."

"Whoever it was walked right up to him," Chris theorized. "The driver's window wasn't down. The door was closed. So the door had to be opened, perhaps by Clatterbuck himself, *bam,* then the killer closes the door and drives off. Swift. No sign of struggle."

"Well, Don wasn't looking for it." Rick sighed. "Your people might as well take the body away. I appreciate you calling me. You'll keep the Cowboys windbreaker for evidence, too? You see, we've been looking for this particular truck and windbreaker."

"I don't suppose there was anything in the pockets that—" Coop hoped against hope.

"A matchbook. We dusted it. Here." He handed it to Coop, who bent over to shelter it from the downpour.

Beautifully colored with turquoise, airbrushed orange, and yellow with squibbles of purple, the matchbook was expensive to produce. Three inches by two inches, shiny coated paper, the proprietor intended to make an upscale statement. "Roy and Nadine's," with the Y of Roy as a martini glass, announced the restaurant in Lexington, Kentucky. The address, Palomar Center, Harrodsburg Pike and Man-O-War Drive, was printed on the back. The phone number was printed under the address.

Rick huddled next to Coop. "Don't jump to conclusions."

"I'm not but if this matchbook belongs to Partlow maybe he's from Kentucky."

"We sent the fingerprints out nationally," Rick replied.

"Doesn't mean he's got a record." She noted that at the

bottom of the matchbook, the black lip had printed in white ink, "Contemporary American Cuisine." The R in the restaurant's name was printed in yellow, the A in deep orange, and the N was hot pink. "Great design. I'll call the restaurant." She walked back to the squad car, scribbled down the information, then emerged into the deluge, handing the matchbook back to Sheriff Zakarios.

"Know much about the victim?" the Culpeper sheriff asked.

"Friendly. No record. A relaxed kind of guy."

Coop answered the good-looking, trim Culpeper sheriff. "It's hard to imagine anyone wanting to kill him."

"Half of what we do comes back to drugs." The sheriff squinted as the rain blew sideways. "Maybe he had a secret life."

"It's a damn national epidemic." Rick stepped away from the GMC as the ambulance crew pulled out the body. "Coop, get the license plate number."

"Yeah." She had written down the letters and numbers the minute she got out of the squad car. The license plate, white with blue raised numbers, appeared much older than the truck itself but it had the correct registration stickers on the upper left-hand and upper right-hand corners. She slipped inside the squad car, ran the information, and within minutes was back out. "Nothing. This license plate is from before computer records. Carol Grossman will check back in the files. But the stickers are certainly current. And there's no way you can peel them off another vehicle's plate without tearing the stickers."

"We've got a homicide. The victim was reported driving this truck."

"Kid hanging from a tree." Sheriff Zakarios stroked his long, square chin. "That's a hell of a note. So is this."

"Thanks for the call." Rick Shaw clapped Zak's back.

"I'll help in any way I can."

One of Zak's deputies called to him while wrapping the pileated woodpecker in plastic. "Good work."

"He did very good work." Cooper sighed. Don was a likeable man, clearly a man who had either been in the wrong place at the wrong time or had been involved in something she couldn't fathom right then. But she and Rick would figure it out. They usually did, and she always came to the same conclusion: it's easier to keep your nose to the grindstone and be honest. But she couldn't imagine what Don could have done that was dishonest. As far as she knew, criminals had no need of taxidermy skills.

As they climbed back into the squad car, Rick tossed his hat in the back, droplets flinging outward. Coop threw hers back there, too.

"I'll have to get my hat blocked. I forgot my plastic hat cover."

"Those things look awful." She shivered in her seat.

"Chill?"

"Yeah. Soaked to the bone."

"Me, too, but I've more protection." He pinched his spare tire, which was decreasing slowly. Rick struggled with dieting. The temptation was to roll into a fast-food joint.

"When we get back I'd better tell Harry her woodpecker has been impounded."

"This woodpecker is news to me. She shooting woodpeckers out there? Isn't that against the law?" He winked.

"Found it dead by the back porch. Actually, the cats found it."

"Those cats of hers." Rick laughed. "She'd better enlist them for Social Security numbers given all the work they do." He turned left down Route 29. After about five minutes he asked, "Any ideas?"

"The truck ties them together. Weird." She lapsed into

silence and then spoke again. "I'll track down Lottie Pearson, too."

"Why?"

"She dragged Don to Mim's charity dance."

"And wasn't it Lottie who brought O'Bannon the coffee? It was. Glad you were there. Lottie Pearson." He whistled low. "Want me to turn up the heat?"

"No. We'll suffocate. I've got a change of clothes in my locker. I'll talk to Lottie after calling Roy and Nadine's. She'll be a real treat." Coop folded her arms across her chest.

28

No." Lottie frowned as the rain slashed at the windowpane in her office.

"Lottie, no one thinks you killed Donny Clatterbuck. Don't get your nose out of joint." Cynthia Cooper, tired and frustrated, spoke bluntly. "But you were in his company recently. Anything you noticed might create a major breakthrough." Cooper thought to herself how onerous it was to butter up people like Lottie.

"Well." She tapped the desk with a pencil, rose from her ergonomically correct seat, crossed the tidy, attractive office, and closed the door behind Coop. "Of course I want to help. It's just that you put me off coming to my place of work in uniform. I have a position to uphold." She returned to her seat. "The university would take a dim view of anything incorrect." She lowered her voice on "incorrect."

Assistant Director of Major Gifts, Lottie was hypersensitive to social nuance. The job suited her and the day would come when old Vernon Miller retired and she would take over. Patiently she nurtured his social contacts as well as her own.

"I understand but *you* have to understand two men are dead, Wesley Partlow and Don Clatterbuck. There's a strong possibility that their murders are connected—"

"What?" Alarm registered on Lottie's face. "And who is Wesley Partlow? I read about him being found but the paper didn't say much."

"Because no one knows much. Partlow was a kid parking cars at Big Mim's fund-raiser."

"What's someone like that got to do with Donny?"

Coop leaned forward as the rain beat down. "Don Clatterbuck was shot in a truck Partlow had driven before he was killed. Sean O'Bannon described the truck when we— Well, it's a long story involving Mrs. Hogendobber's hubcaps but Sean correctly described the old pickup. We couldn't trace the truck. We had no license plate. We now have a license plate but it's ancient. The stickers are current. Carol Grossman down in Richmond, working on this since this morning, has tracked the old license plates to a Jaguar dealer down in Newport News. They used them as part of the decor."

"The dealer stole the plates." Lottie jumped to a conclusion.

"According to the dealer, he didn't. They turn the plates in. By law they must."

"Well, someone took them." She liked being right.

"Someone did. Someone also filched new date and month stickers. Dealers don't have those. You can't even peel them off someone's plates intact using a razor blade. As you can see, Lottie, this is becoming more and more interesting."

"I still don't believe Donny would know anyone like that hanged man." She stopped herself, regrouped, and continued, "There has to be a reasonable explanation. A coincidence. Maybe Partlow stole the truck and returned it. No one knew."

"That has occurred to us but what I need from you are details: Don's mood, did he say anything about plans for the future? That sort of thing."

"Would you like a beverage?" Lottie asked. "I apologize. I should have offered you one when you came through the door."

"A hot coffee would work wonders."

"Cream and sugar?"

"Heavy on the cream, light on the sugar."

Lottie pushed a button on her phone system. "Franny, two cups of coffee. The usual for me and heavy on the cream, light on the sugar for the other. Thanks." She returned her attention to Coop. Lottie thought Cooper, nice-looking, could look even better. With a bit of luck a tall, lean woman like Cooper could make a decent match in a county like Albemarle, but working as a deputy destroyed her chances of moving too far up in the world. Lottie wondered why women didn't think of those things. Life would always be easier if one was attached to a wealthy man.

They chitchatted until the coffee was placed before them. As Franny withdrew, Lottie took a deep sip, as did Cynthia.

"Thank you. This is just what I needed."

"For the record, Donald Clatterbuck and I weren't dating. He escorted me to Mim's party. I liked him, of course. Who didn't? You know why I, well, I won't go into that but it still bothers me that BoomBoom didn't allow me to show Diego Aybar the sights. I love doing that sort of thing and Harry already has a beau. It just upset me. That's how I wound up with Donald." She cast her eyes at Coop but Coop betrayed no feelings of her own so Lottie continued on. "He couldn't have been nicer. You see, I'd not been especially solicitous of him. Well, truthfully I ignored him. You know, he was just a working-class guy. But he actually had some ambition, which surprised me."

"In what way?"

"He said he was taking his leather-design business on the Internet. He'd been working on a website where he would display techniques. I don't know anything about leather design and repair but I remember he said something about showing the different quality of skins. He thought if he did that he'd get orders for special items like sofas, couch slipcovers, even boots."

"He was good." Cooper sighed.

"He also wanted to go on the Internet for his taxidermy business. He said he ought to preserve rich people and call the business Stuffed Shirts. He had a good sense of humor."

"So he seemed positive?"

"Yes. He mentioned saving to buy his grandfather's farm. Said it had been a good year so he was going to make Mr. Mawyer an offer. He mentioned that no one else in the family was interested. He's lucky there."

"No clouds on the horizon?"

"No. If there were he didn't mention it. You mean was he afraid of something or someone?"

"Considering he was shot, yes, I'd—"

Lottie interrupted. "What if the murder was a mistake? What if whoever killed him saw the truck and thought he was someone else?"

"Anything is possible." Coop drained her cup.

"Would you care for some more?"

"Thank you, no. I'm finally warming up. If I hadn't had a change of uniform in my locker I'd be sitting here dripping on your floor. It's not that cold but I took a chill."

"Don't you just hate that?" Lottie asked sympathetically.

"Did you think Don wanted to go out with you again?"

"We just didn't click on that level. What can I say? No chemistry." She dabbed her lips with the small napkin Franny had brought with the coffees. "Speaking of chemistry, Harry and Diego!"

Coop smiled. "Who knows?"

"Do you think she's done with Fair forever? I mean I thought that's why BoomBoom set her up. Boom wanted Fair away from Harry. She's like that."

"I don't know. That was a long time ago, BoomBoom and Fair. Five years . . . or close to it. I don't think she wants him back."

"She wants them all. She's not happy unless every man is circling around her like a honey pot."

"Then you would have thought she'd have kept Diego for herself." Coop shrewdly observed Lottie's reaction.

"Steinmetz is a bigger fish and probably a richer one, too. She doesn't miss a trick. I hate the way men fawn over her."

"She's beautiful."

"Artifice." Lottie sniffed.

"Don evidenced little interest."

"They grew up together. He saw right through her."

"But, Lottie, Fair grew up with her, too."

Not one to appreciate an errant detail in her argument being pointed out to her, Lottie's shoulders froze a bit, then relaxed. "Donald had more sense." She glanced out at the gloomy day, returning to meet Cooper's eyes. "I'm sorry he's dead. He was a nice person. I can't imagine why anyone would want to kill him."

29

Would you look at this!" Harry followed her observation
with a string of curses. One of the joints on the old disc used
to break up earth had cracked, small ball bearings scattered
underneath. The rain pelted the tin roof of the equipment
shed. She'd just gotten home after work and decided since
she couldn't work outside, she'd grease the manure spreader,
the disc, check the tines on the drag, the fluid levels in the
1958 John Deere tractor.

Mostly she couldn't bear the thought of being inside for
one more minute. By the end of the day at the post office
she wanted to be outside as long as possible.

The cats, less enthusiastic about her work ethic in the
rain, repaired to the house. Only Tucker accompanied her.
The shed, tidy and tight, kept the rain out, but the wind
added to the gloom.

"Boiling black out there." Tucker felt the electricity of the
storm building.

Harry reached down, rubbing one of Tucker's ears between her thumb and forefinger. "I can't complain, really. This disc is almost as old as the tractor. You know on the new ones the joints are sealed after being packed in grease. I guess that works, I don't know. Wonder how much it will cost to fix it? Oh, well." She leaned against the tractor. "What we need is a drill seeder. Fat chance." She laughed because the type she needed retailed for $22,000. That was practically a year's salary for Harry.

She lifted up the hood of the dually, checked the oil, the windshield fluids, and the pressure in the tires. She repeated the process on the 1978 Ford F150 which she'd pulled into the shed. Finally satisfying herself that everything was fine, she sprinted to the barn. She'd left the back stall doors open and the three horses had wisely chosen to come in from the storm.

"Phone's been ringing off the hook," Poptart told Tucker.

The corgi hopped up on the tack trunk to speak to the youngest horse eye to eye. She stood on her hind legs, sticking her head through the square opening with the big feed bucket underneath. *"Ever wish you could answer it?"*

"No." Poptart laughed. *"Makes more work. Every time one human calls another there's usually a chore attached or something that sends Harry flying out of here. Can't see why any reasonable human would wish to be interrupted like that."*

"And who would call you?" Gin Fizz, the oldest of the three, asked.

"Anne Kursinski." Poptart laughed, naming one of the most famous show-jumping riders in the world.

"Princess Anne would dial me." Tomahawk put in his two cents.

"Oh, I'm sure the next time the Princess visits America, she'll make a special request to come see workaday hunters right here in Crozet." Gin Fizz guffawed.

"And why not?" Tomahawk stoutly replied. *"Most horse sports come from foxhunting. Point-to-point races, steeplechasing, hunter shows, jumper shows."* He ended with authority.

"Three-day eventing," Tucker added.

"Thank you, Tucker. I forgot that one," Tomahawk called from his stall.

"I thought three-day eventing came from cavalry drills," Gin Fizz said.

"Cavalry were foxhunted. Eventing is still related to foxhunting," Tucker declared, although the connection was slender.

Harry walked in to close Tomahawk's back stall door. The wind blew with such ferocity she thought the doors would bend. "You all are so talkative."

"Evil out there, Mom." Tomahawk nuzzled her.

She kissed his nose, giving him a molasses cookie. She had two for each horse.

"Dressage doesn't come from foxhunting." Poptart was thinking out loud. *"Haute école. Guess it's centuries old. I can't do it. I can't canter in place, half halt at the letter B or whatever. Just can't do it. I want to run!"*

"Don't we all." Gin Fizz eagerly awaited Harry's visit to his stall. *"The trick is, Poppy, to stop."*

At this all four animals laughed loudly, even Poptart, since she had the tendency to run right through the bridle. Young, she'd become so excited when the other horses took off that she wanted to pass everyone. This wouldn't do. Harry schooled her but it was going to take time. There are no perfect horses just as there are no perfect people. Her one flaw was small compared to Poptart's gift: the ability to jump the moon. Nothing was too high or too wide and she was clever with her hooves.

Gin Fizz admired the youngster's ability but wished he

could give her some of his wisdom. Whenever she'd cut a shine the old fellow would sigh and murmur, *"Youth."*

Tomahawk, less impressed with Poppy's talents since he was fairly talented himself, usually responded, *"Mares."*

The two geldings felt that mares were emotional, erratic, and a royal pain in the ass. However, they loved Poppy despite her moodiness.

She thought highly of herself, too.

"You'd better not run away with Mom," Tucker warned her.

"I won't," Poppy said halfheartedly.

"I can bite your ankles before you can kick me. Fetlocks, I should say. Well, I can bite and bite hard."

"Squirt." Poptart pinned her ears but in good fun.

Harry closed the last outside door. "What's going on with you all? I've never heard such carryings-on."

"Just shooting the breeze." Gin Fizz laughed.

The phone rang again.

"You'd better pick it up, Mom. It's been ringing off the hook," Tomahawk advised the human.

With a great sigh, Harry trotted into the tack room to pick up the phone. "Hello."

"Hey, Donny Clatterbuck's been shot dead." Susan got straight to the point.

"What?"

"It must have just happened. Lottie called me and I tried calling you first, then called Miranda. Where have you been?"

"In the equipment shed." She drew in her breath, thought a moment. "Susan, where was he? I mean, what do you know?"

"He was found in Culpeper by the side of the road. Shot through the temple. Oh, he had your woodpecker."

"What!"

"Mim said he had your woodpecker and he was in the

truck Rick's been trying to find. The truck Wesley Partlow
drove. Am I making sense?"

"Kind of. Who's going to tell his parents? Oh, this is
really awful."

"Rick."

"Glad I don't have that job. I can't believe anyone would
shoot Donny Clatterbuck. And what was he doing in the
GMC?"

Tucker pricked up her ears since she could hear Susan's
voice, then tore out of the tack room, down the center aisle
barn, through the deluge, pushed open the screen door,
then barged through the animal door into the kitchen.

*"Mrs. Murphy, Pewter, Don Clatterbuck was found dead,
shot, in the farm truck."*

Mrs. Murphy, dozing on the bookshelf in the living
room, raised her head, her eyes now wide open. *"I knew this
would come back at us. Too close to home."*

"You knew no such thing." Pewter, also awake now, sat up
on the sofa.

"Whoever strung up Wesley Partlow was in Crozet. Right?"
the tiger argued.

"Yes, but that doesn't mean they live in Crozet," Pewter
countered.

*"No, but Donny sure did. I can't figure out what Wesley
Partlow and Donny would have in common."*

*"Maybe nothing. People die without there being a connec-
tion."*

*"Pewter, they didn't just die, they were murdered and within
a few days of one another. Think about it . . . and Partlow was
seen in the truck. Am I right, Tucker? It was Booty's farm
truck?"*

"That's what Susan told Mom." Tucker walked over to the
bookshelf as Murphy jumped down. *"I hope Booty's not in
danger. The truck's cursed."*

"*Oh, Tucker.*" Pewter sniffed. "*Inanimate objects aren't cursed.*"

"*The pyramids. The curse of the Pharaohs.*" Tucker thought objects did, indeed, carry curses.

In a way Tucker was right.

30

All that evening the phone lines hummed throughout Crozet and Albemarle County. Usually a crisis would propel people to one another but the weather, increasingly awful, kept them inside.

Harry tried calling Diego but gave up, defeated by international codes. Uruguay's code was 598 but she couldn't get the number of zeros and ones right to get a line out. She'd figured rightly that he was two time zones ahead of East Coast time. That was a victory. She had enough trouble keeping time in her own time zone. Finally she humbled herself and rang BoomBoom.

"I just heard!" BoomBoom's excitable voice sounded higher than usual.

They discussed the dolorous news, then Harry felt she'd minded her manners and could ask her question. "Have you heard from Thomas?"

"This morning." BoomBoom dangled the bait, forcing Harry to ask another question.

"The reason I'm asking you is because I can't reach Diego and well . . ."

"It seems their government is having some crisis over loans to the International Monetary Fund or something like that. Diego will call you as soon as he gets a minute."

"I thought that was a problem for Argentina, not Uruguay, but then what do I know?" She sighed.

"We tend to ignore South America, which, when you think about it, is really dumb. After all, we're all part of the New World."

"He's probably got a mistress in Montevideo." Harry wasn't focusing on American shortcomings. She was focusing on Diego.

"No, he doesn't. I wouldn't do that to you . . . not if I knew. But he doesn't. Feel better?"

"Sort of." She walked to the stove, turning the flame up under the kettle. "Boom, this welding that you do—could you cut locks?"

"Of course."

"Steel plates?"

"Yes, but it would take some time. What I work with is thin sheets. The cutouts are strong enough to stand on the base I make for them but a heavy steel plate like the kind put in the back of pickups to hitch trailers, that kind of plate, that would take a long time. Why?"

"Donny had one of those huge old stand-up safes. If Rick doesn't find the combination, he'll have to cut it."

"That will be a very difficult job."

"I know but if you volunteer we'd be there first. I could help."

"Harry." BoomBoom considered this. "What do you think is in the safe?"

"I don't know but I'd like to find out, wouldn't you?

Maybe it will tell us why Donny was shot. In fact, why don't you call Rick now, then call me back."

"Well—all right." BoomBoom hung up the phone. Within minutes she dialed back. "Harry, he's at Donny's shop now and said he'd be grateful for the help. I'll meet you there in fifteen minutes. I told him I need you to regulate the oxygen in the tanks."

"Did he believe it?"

"Uh—sort of."

"Okay, fifteen minutes."

31

As the blue flame slowly sliced into the heavy lock of the safe, Rick Shaw allowed as how the last person he thought would be wielding a torch would be BoomBoom Craycroft. He readily agreed to her offer, otherwise he'd have to wait a day while the safe company flew in an expert to open the lock. The county budget prompted him to make use of local talent even though it meant destroying the lock, which resembled the hatch locks of submarines.

"Harry, you drive me crazy sometimes, you and your amateur detective crap, but I hand it to you on this suggestion."

"Thanks, Sheriff." She stood by the oxygen tank feeding the welding torch.

"She'll live off that compliment for a month," Tucker remarked as she sat discreetly next to a finished stuffed elk's head on the floor.

Pewter, frightened by the noise of the welding torch, crouched behind Tucker. Mrs. Murphy perched on top of

Donny's worktable. She remained motionless, since she didn't want to rouse the sheriff's attention either.

"Think Harry will stuff us when we go?" She laughed as she surveyed Donny's handiwork.

"Vile!" Pewter leaned harder on Tucker, who licked her head.

Coop stood well behind Boom.

Arms across her chest, Harry murmured, "Tell Booty?"

"Yeah. Rick did."

"Did he know anything about the truck?"

"Said it was his but for farm use. Never took it off the farm. Didn't much use it anyway, he said. No license plate. You know, he took it like the soldier that he was. He asked if Marge knew and Rick said that I was with her. He got in his car and drove in her driveway just as I was leaving. Poor Marge. He was her only son."

"Yeah." Harry felt bad for Donny's mom, a much-liked woman.

Rick checked his watch. "Harry, tell me about the woodpecker."

"I brought it in just before the Dogwood Festival and Donny said he'd get right on it. Business was always slower in the spring, the taxidermy business, I mean. His leather business was doing well and he was making coffee tables, too, out of license plates. One's over there." She pointed it out. "He was bursting with ideas."

"Did he seem like himself?"

"Yeah." She shrugged.

"Did he look healthy?"

"Very." She waited a moment. "Sheriff, what's going to happen to my woodpecker?"

"It's my woodpecker," Pewter chirped up.

"Shut up. Don't attract Rick's attention," Murphy counseled.

"For now, nothing. I told them to run it through an X-ray machine." He turned to BoomBoom, who stopped for a moment, pushing up her protective face guard to check her work. "How you doing?"

"Another five minutes, I hope." She slapped the mask down and resumed cutting.

"Find anything besides my woodpecker?"

"A Dallas Cowboys windbreaker just as Sean described it." Cooper squinted when a shower of sparks flew off the safe. "And a matchbook from Roy and Nadine's restaurant in Lexington, Kentucky. Very colorful."

"Any ideas?" Harry asked.

"That's what I was going to ask you." Rick hitched up his belt. "You've known Clatterbuck all your life. Did you like him?"

"Yeah. Always seemed levelheaded. He didn't run with a bad crowd. Didn't have a lot of bad affairs with women. Stuff like that."

"Huh." Rick grunted.

"I guess you looked for the key to the safe?"

"Yes, we did. Why?"

"Oh." Harry turned her palms up for a moment as if in supplication. "Hate to see the safe ruined."

"It's not ruined. I can put it back together if Rick wants me to." BoomBoom turned off the torch. She waited a moment, then pushed the heavy lock with her gloved hand. "Sheriff, if you grab one handle and I grab the other I think we can pull it out. I'm afraid if I try to do this by myself I'll push it into the safe and that might damage whatever's in there."

"Good thinking." He grabbed a brass handle.

They both pulled on the count of three and the heavy lock and spinning handle fell out on the floor with a clunk.

Rick stepped aside as BoomBoom, gloves on, reached in and pulled open the door.

"Oh, my God!"

Each shelf contained bundles and bundles of crisp new bills, neatly stacked.

"That's a lot of stuffed deer heads," Mrs. Murphy laconically observed.

32

The shock of finding five hundred and twenty-five thousand dollars in Donny Clatterbuck's safe was nearly as great as finding Donny himself.

Harry and the animals drove to Miranda's, a place of sanity and common sense. To her surprise, BoomBoom wanted to go, too.

They found Miranda and Tracy playing gin rummy. Tracy was winning.

"Knock, knock." Harry let herself in, with Mrs. Murphy rushing first through the door. "I'm coming unannounced and BoomBoom's about two minutes behind me."

Tracy rose, as befit a Virginia gentleman. "You look a little peaked, Harry, my girl. Some fortification?"

She shook the rain off in the little back-door entrance-way. "How about a steaming cup of tea with a drop of Maker's Mark in it?" She mentioned the famous sipping whiskey distilled in Loretto, Kentucky.

"Why, Harry." Miranda stood up herself, heading to the teapot. "I don't remember you ever roping your tea."

"Well, I'm wet, I'm chilled, and I'm sorely vexed, as my grandmother used to say."

BoomBoom stepped in tight behind Harry. "Miranda, forgive me. I just had to see you."

"Are you two having another fight?" Miranda turned on the gas stove while Tracy opened the cabinet serving as a liquor chest. "BoomBoom, what can I get you?"

"A straight shot of gin will revive me considerably."

"What in the world is the matter with you two girls?" He put his hands on his hips.

Harry hung up her worn Barbour coat. BoomBoom did likewise, only her Barbour coat was new and longer. One couldn't reside in Albemarle without a proper Barbour coat, made in England and the best working raingear in the world. Tucker, anticipating treats, moved over to be near Miranda. Pewter, no fool, headed straight for the table.

"I don't know where to start." BoomBoom shook her long blond hair, droplets of water falling to the oak floor.

"I'll start." Harry pulled out a chair at the kitchen table. "Rick Shaw and Cynthia Cooper were called up to Culpeper this afternoon because Donny Clatterbuck had been shot through the head."

Miranda exclaimed, "Oh, no! We haven't heard—"

"He was in the truck Sean described Wesley Partlow as driving to his salvage yard to sell your hubcaps, and don't feel left out, the only people who know about this are Donny's family. Big Mim probably doesn't know yet unless Rick is calling her now."

Both Tracy and Miranda sat down at the table to listen to Harry as they waited for the water to boil.

"What in the world is going on?" Miranda rubbed her cheek with the palm of her hand.

"Nobody knows. It's scary." BoomBoom also sat down as Tracy rose to pull out a chair for her, then reseated himself.

"The truck had stolen plates, old ones with new stickers. Coop told me that. The plates are from a Newport News car dealership. The dealer has no idea how the plates were stolen. No cars were missing. Coop asked if he would send over his employee rolls so she could check for criminal backgrounds. Nothing. The truck, as it happens, is Booty Mawyer's old farm truck. He says it hasn't been off the farm. Been moldering in one of his sheds. That's what he told Rick when Rick gave him the bad news. But, of course, it *has*. He said sometimes Don would move hay from one shed to another—but, you know, Booty's getting on in years and it would be easy to fool him. Well, he wouldn't know anything unless he saw it with his own eyes.

"And before I get to why we're together—in the back of the truck, on the seat, was the Dallas Cowboys windbreaker exactly as Sean described it."

Tracy got up to pour the tea. He motioned for Miranda to stay seated. He put the pot on the table, set out four cups, smacked the Maker's Mark bottle directly in front of Harry, then opened the refrigerator and brought out cold cuts. He figured, correctly, that Harry and BoomBoom hadn't eaten. He also put a chilled green bottle of Tanqueray gin in front of BoomBoom.

"Honey, let me do that." Miranda got up to arrange the food, bringing out the homemade seven-grain bread, fresh butter, and local honey.

Within minutes an impromptu cold supper sat before the two hungry women.

"Thank you." BoomBoom gratefully buttered a piece of bread cut thick.

Harry chattered as she, too, made herself a sandwich, surreptitiously dropping food bits to her pets. "Coop said the only thing in the windbreaker was a matchbook from Roy and Nadine's, a hot restaurant in Lexington, Kentucky. She called the restaurant, gave them the fake Wesley's description, and the manager said he had no recollection of anyone like that, nor did it seem that would be the kind of customer Roy and Nadine's would attract. He did, however, promise to ask his employees if they remembered anyone looking like that. She's sending on the mug shot.

"But, well, Boom should tell you what happened next."

"Donny has that huge safe in his shop, the kind that's taller than I am. Harry suggested I call Rick and offer to open the lock using my welding torch. She was right because Rick couldn't get a service representative for twenty-four hours plus there was the expense of getting him here. So over I went, cut out the lock, and what do you know... there's a ton of money inside the safe! Five hundred and twenty-five thousand dollars. Five hundred and twenty-five thousand!" BoomBoom repeated.

"Stacked neatly. So new you could smell it. Rick says it isn't counterfeit either." Harry sipped her tea.

"Where in the world would Donny Clatterbuck get money like that?" Miranda brought both hands to her face in surprise.

"New? Directly from a bank or someone who had access to new bills, who dealt in large sums often." Tracy's mind whirred along. "Someone who either needed Donny to stash the money, giving him a cut, or someone who needed Donny."

"For what?" BoomBoom poured honey over a piece of buttered bread.

"He was good with his hands." Harry tried to feed Tucker another small piece of meat under the table. Pewter snatched it before the dog could get it so Harry tore another small piece for the corgi. The mild altercation revealed

Harry's feeding the "kids" from the table—not that anyone really cared that much.

"I'm here, too," Murphy reminded the humans.

Miranda gave her a tidbit. "This is so—so hard to believe. Donny never threw money around."

"No, he didn't," Harry confirmed.

"He could have put the money in the bank but he didn't. This points to his doing something illegal." Tracy, hand poised in midair with a butter knife, said, "And it seems obvious that he knew in some fashion the young man found hanged. The question is, how and why? That kid looked as though he didn't have a dime."

"Coop can't find a trace of him anywhere. Wesley's not his real name," Harry said.

"I wonder if Marge knows about the money." Miranda thought about Donny's mother, worrying for her welfare.

"Highly doubtful, my love," Tracy replied.

BoomBoom finished her sandwich, which made her feel more conversational. "Wait until Lottie Pearson hears this."

"What's Lottie Pearson got to do with this?" Miranda asked.

"She blew him off just like she spurned Roger. She wants money and prestige or what passes for it. When she hears that Donny Clatterbuck had a small fortune in his safe, she'll pass out."

"Five hundred and twenty-five thousand dollars." Miranda couldn't imagine that much money.

"We helped count it. Had to wear plastic gloves that Rick and Coop keep in the squad car. They have to avoid blood because of AIDS so they carry these hospital gloves around." Harry thought a moment, then excitedly said, "When I took my woodpecker to Don, I noticed the safe. I asked him if that's where he kept his millions and he said, 'Only half a million.' I thought he was kidding."

" 'He who loves money never has money enough, he who loves wealth never has enough profit; this, too, is vanity.' *Ecclesiastes*, Chapter Five, Verse Ten," Miranda quoted.

"What a memory," Tracy marveled.

"Miranda is a marvel." BoomBoom smiled.

"Mim really must not know what's happened." Harry's mind stayed on the murder. "Or she would have called you. Rick usually gets to her."

Miranda said, "She's in New York this weekend visiting Stafford and his wife."

Stafford was Mim's son, who rarely returned home as he loved his family more the farther away they were.

Mrs. Murphy washed her face with her paw. *"We've got work to do."*

"I'm not going out in the rain," Pewter stoutly stated.

"I didn't say we were."

Tucker nuzzled her pal. *"What do you have in mind?"*

"We need to get to Aunt Tally's and snoop around. I should have thought of it during the tea party but I got caught up in the commotion."

"Aunt Tally's is a long, long hike, Murphy. Talk Harry into driving us over there."

"Sure, Pewter. She listens about as well as any human."

Tucker thought about it. *"She's right, Murphy. The creeks are over their banks. We won't get across. We've got to convince Harry to drive us there somehow."*

The pretty tiger pondered this, then curled her tail around her. *"You're right."*

"Finally, someone's giving me credit around here," Pewter crowed, then for good measure reached up and hooked a piece of bread off the table before a human could stop her. Once the bread was on the floor she knew the humans wouldn't touch it even if they scolded her, which they didn't, as they were too busy deciding if Lottie Pearson really was a

gold digger. BoomBoom said yes. Harry said maybe. Miranda wanted to think the best of her and Tracy opted not to have an opinion.

"*Don't let it go to your head. Listen, we'd better get over there tomorrow. If this rain would only stop.*"

"*What's on your mind?*" Tucker respected the tiger's brain power, the quickness of her mind.

"*We need to examine the floor of the dining room, open the cupboards in the pantry, investigate the places where Tally keeps food. We might have to check the outbuildings. I don't know exactly but I can tell you this, if we find what I think we're going to find, either Sean O'Bannon is in on this or he's the next victim.*"

$$\boxed{33}$$

At twelve midnight on the dot the rain stopped. Mrs. Murphy had become accustomed to the incessant din on the rooftop. The silence awakened her. Curled up next to Harry, she lifted her head, then rose, stretching fore and aft.

Tucker, asleep on the rug by the bed, snored lightly, her parted lips revealing her considerable canines as well as the small square teeth between them.

Pewter, on the pillow next to Harry, was dead to the world. Her gray forehead rested next to Harry's pillow edge, her body formed a comma, her tail curled tight around her legs.

No point waking up the Princess of Sleep. Next to eating, Pewter loved sleep.

Murphy walked out of the bedroom, down the hall, careful to step on the old carpet runner. She liked feeling carpet beneath her paws. Then she bounced across the kitchen, out the animal door, and pushed open the screened porch door. The clouds, low and billowy, Prussian blue, flew across the sky, west to east. Puddles like black ice filled the small depressions in the driveway. Keeping that driveway in good working order gave Harry fits. She'd dutifully fill the holes only to have the stones eventually worm their way out to the side of the road. Every three years she would break down and hire Mr. Tapscott to bulldoze the long driveway, put down bluestone or crusher run, and then pack it as hard as possible. No wonder a large part of the state budget was siphoned off by road maintenance. If only Harry had the tiniest fraction of that budget, her road would be in tiptop shape.

Murphy often thought of human cares. Not that she thought road maintenance a foolish care. After all, she was a farm cat; she understood the importance of roads, tractors, and re-seeding pastures. But much of what humans fussed over seemed silly to her. They worried about their looks, about money, about their social standing.

Cats ignored social standing. To be a cat meant one was at the top of the animal chain. And since cats are not herd animals, each cat remained a complete individual. This didn't mean that Mrs. Murphy lacked kitty friends. It only meant that she didn't rely on them for a sense of herself. She simply *was*.

She hopscotched across puddles, entering the barn. The three horses, sound asleep, didn't hear her. She jumped on the tack trunk. Gin Fizz slept like Tucker, on his side and snoring. Tomahawk and Poptart slept standing up. Murphy couldn't imagine sleeping standing up.

She crept into the tack room. The mice were playing with a jacks ball, singing at the top of their lungs, "Take Me Out to the Ball Game."

She pounced, narrowly missing the fattest mouse.

"Eeek! Mad cat. Run for your life!" they screamed, scrambling for the hole in the wall. They all made it.

Murphy put a glittering eye to the hole shaped like an upside-down U. *"Have the decency to clean up after yourselves. My human doesn't think your games are funny. And you've left grain bits all over the floor. You'll get me in trouble and if you get me in trouble I'll nail one of you if it's the last thing I do!"*

"Bully," a high-pitched voice replied.

"We had a deal. You leave the tack room clean and I leave you alone."

"You surprised us. We would have cleaned up."

"Sure." Mrs. Murphy batted the jacks ball between her paws.

"Give us the ball back. We'll clean up. I promise."

"Maybe I will and maybe I won't." With that she catapulted straight up in the air, turned halfway round, dropping back on the ball. She flopped on her side, kicked the ball out with her hind legs, then chased it wildly under the saddle racks and bridle hooks. She whacked it hard with her right front paw. The little red jacks ball slammed against the wall, bouncing back almost into her jaws.

Murphy carried on like this for five minutes until she tired of solo handball. She tantalizingly deposited the jacks ball about a foot from the mouse entrance. Making a great show of leaving the tack room, she tiptoed back in, silently vaulting onto a saddle. Holding her breath, she waited until she saw tiny whiskers appear in the opening.

"She's gone," a voice said.

"Oh, no, she's not. I know Mrs. Murphy. She's clever," the original high-pitched voice replied.

"Mom, you worry too much. She's up in the hayloft with Simon."

"Bart, don't you go out there. You can play later."

But Bart, young and full of himself, thought he could dash out, grab the ball, and roll it back in. Even if the cat

happened to be in the tack room he thought he was quicker than she was. Wrong.

Bart no sooner scooted out than the full weight of Mrs. Murphy surrounded him. She'd jumped down, pinning him under her beige-striped tummy.

"Bart! Bart!" his mother screamed.

"Mom." His voice was muffled by all the fur.

Murphy, highly pleased with herself, twisted her body so Bart could stick his head out from under her but couldn't escape. *"Worm."*

"Oh, please, Mrs. Murphy, don't kill me."

"I'm going to play with you, I'll let you go, then smack my paw down on your tail. When I'm tired of your foolishness, I'll snap your neck and bite your head off. I'll leave your head right here so Harry can see what a mighty mouser I am. I'll eat the rest. Yum."

"Take me." Bart's mother boldly hurried outside amid screams from the other mice inside.

"I could have you both, you know, I'm that fast."

"You're a fabulous athlete, Mrs. Murphy." The mother walked right up to Mrs. Murphy's nose. *"But he's young. I'm not. Take me."*

Bart was sobbing. Mrs. Murphy considered the situation. She heard a soft flutter in the rafters. The owl returned from hunting.

"Go on. Get in there. She will eat you. I won't."

"Bless you, Mrs. Murphy." The mother hugged Mrs. Murphy as best she could as Bart scurried into his home.

"Just clean up around here. If you don't I won't be nice to you next time."

"We will!" the jubilant chorus agreed from behind the wall.

Satisfied that she'd struck terror into their hearts, the tiger emerged into the center aisle, then climbed the ladder up to the loft. Simon was asleep, his treasures surrounding him.

She looked straight up into the cupola as the owl, over two feet of her, peered down.

"Who?"

"You know who."

"Indeed I do. A saucy cat. A spoiled cat. Mrs. Murphy. What are you doing in here? Get caught in the rain?"

"No. I woke up when it stopped. Have you been hunting in it?"

"A foray when the worst was over."

Mrs. Murphy climbed to the topmost hay bale. "Come down here and talk to me so I don't get a crick in my neck. And I don't want to yell. Sooner or later Simon will wake up and whimper. You know how he is."

Although not close friends, the two predators had respect for one another even though the owl did not understand domestication one bit. She glided down, silent as the tomb. Gave Mrs. Murphy the chills because when the owl hunted you didn't know what hit you until it was too late. Even sharp cat ears could only discern her presence when she was already close.

The owl's bright yellow eyes blinked. "What's on your mind, pussycat?"

"I have to get over to Tally Urquhart's but I can't cross the creeks."

"Over the banks, debris hurtling in the water. The beavers don't even want to come out of their lodges and the lodges are getting holes punched in by tree limbs. You can hear the roar." The owl blinked.

"Yes, I heard it when I left the house. I suppose I could open the truck window when we pass Tally's drive and hop out of the car. Mother has to slow for the curve but I don't like her know-

ing I can manage the windows. It's not good for humans to know what we know."

She chuckled. *"That's very owl-like of you."* She fluffed her feathers, turned her head almost the whole way around, then settled herself. *"Want me to fly over?"*

"I need to get in the house."

"Ah, I can't help you there."

"You see, two humans have been murdered. One was hanged and the other was shot."

"I know."

"I guess you would. You're out and about. I didn't think you cared much about human affairs."

"I don't, but murder has a certain lurid curiosity. We owls don't murder one another. You cats might tussle, a bad fight, lose an eye, but you don't murder one another. It's one of those depressing curiosities about humans."

"So it appears." Murphy leaned toward the large bird. *"I think there's been a third murder. Roger O'Bannon. And either his brother did it or his brother is next in line."*

"Ah, so I am not my brother's keeper?" She rocked back and forth on her huge feet.

"Cain and Abel. Mrs. Hogendobber would know the exact quote from the Bible. I don't but I know the story."

"As do I. Cain slew Abel because he was jealous. The Hebrew God favored Abel. All religions have such a story. Being sacred to Athena, I'm partial to the Greek myths myself. But it would have to be a powerful motive for blood to kill blood. Either that or Sean O'Bannon is one cold-blooded creature."

"I don't think he is. I could be wrong. Crozet is so small. You think you know people but you don't. But I really don't think Sean is cold-blooded. What puzzles me the most is what the victims have gotten themselves into—over five hundred thousand dollars was found in Donny Clatterbuck's safe. So I would have to say that money is the motive and if that's just Clatterbuck's

cut then we are talking about a great, great deal of money. But I can't for the life of me think of what they could be doing to generate that kind of cash. It's not drugs, at least I don't think so, and we know the money's not counterfeit. I've thought and thought. I even thought what if they've been selling state secrets but there are no state secrets in Albemarle County. The government officials and military brass retired here are just that, retired."

"Slavery."

"Huh?"

"Mrs. Murphy, there's still slavery. Children are bought and sold. People from Asia and South America are sold as domestic slaves smuggled into the U.S. Oh, it's called something else but it's slavery. When you can't speak the language, you can't go out on your own. You work for nothing or next to nothing and another human, maybe the one who smuggled you in, controls your life. There's a lot of money in smuggling people across the border."

"I never thought of that. I don't know, but it's something and it's here. This I do know, if Sean O'Bannon isn't part of it he'll be dead before too long. If he lives, I have to assume the worst."

"Can't you set a trap for him? If he doesn't fall into it, he's innocent," the owl said with deliberation.

"That's just it, since I don't know what it is that they're doing, I can't bait a trap."

"You are in a pickle." The owl chuckled. *"But your human is safe. Why worry?"*

"No, she's not. She was there when the safe was cut open by BoomBoom Craycroft, of all people. So now her blood is up. She's as curious as a cat but without the nine lives."

"Harry does have an odd way of stumbling onto the truth." The owl scratched her head with her foot.

"You could do me a favor. When weather permits, fly over

O'Bannon Salvage. *See if anything looks peculiar from the air. Sometimes land betrays things. Oh, and there's a very offensive rat that lives there, he calls himself Pope Rat. I think he knows a lot."*

"If I catch him and carry him aloft he'll sing like a robin." She chuckled low and deep, the idea of swinging the rat in the air appealing to her.

"When we find out what it is we'll no doubt wonder how we missed it," the cat sighed.

"Or be completely amazed. Humans, for all their faults, can be damnably clever."

34

Although the rain had stopped, the runoff slopped over highways, and culverts, jammed with gunk, backed up and overflowed. Everywhere one looked there was running water. The shoulders off the sides of the roads shone with it.

Driving slowly, Harry gave thanks that her lands rested high above the floodplain. Structures built in lowlands had flooded basements at the least.

Mrs. Murphy, Pewter, and Tucker had been arguing since climbing into the truck. Murphy was determined to jump out when Harry slowed for the curve by Tally Urquhart's farm entrance.

Pewter vowed she would not launch herself from a moving vehicle. What did she care if Sean might be in danger? Besides, the long, long driveway meant she'd get her feet wet.

Tucker moaned because she might squeeze out the window but not being as agile as the cat, she feared the drop. No point in collecting broken bones.

"But I need your nose," Murphy pouted.

"Won't do you a bit of good if I can't haul myself up the driveway. It's not a good plan, Murphy. Be patient. Sooner or later, Mom will call on Tally."

"By that time it will be too late." The sleek cat put her paw on the window crank as the old truck didn't have electric windows.

"No, it won't." Pewter was nervous that if Murphy rolled down the window and shot out of the truck, Harry would swerve and they'd slide off the road into the muck. Not an appealing prospect to a fastidious cat.

Tally's farm lay up ahead, marked by a big rectangular sign with a white rose on a dark green background and the name "Rose Hill" swinging in the light breeze. Mrs. Murphy, using both paws, started cranking down the window when to her delight, Harry turned right onto the drive.

"Murphy, what are you doing?"

"Damn, now she knows I know how to roll down the window."

"I told you not to do it." Pewter smugly moved over to sit next to Harry.

"Brownnoser," Murphy spat.

"That does us no good at all. What if this is a short visit? We need a plan," Tucker, being practical, said.

"All right. When we get there, Tucker, go straight to the dining room. The flooring is old random-width. There are cracks between the boards. Sniff the cracks. Would be a bitter smell, I think. Pewter, go into the pantry. You do the same thing but get on the shelves. You'll have to stick your nose in sugar bowls, creamers, any small bowl, but be careful. You don't want to inhale anything into your system. Stuff would be lethal. Think how quickly it killed Roger O'Bannon."

"If it did," Pewter replied. *"We'll never know without an autopsy. He could have died of natural causes."*

"We'd best hope he did," Tucker grimly said.

"Sean should have ordered an autopsy." Pewter eagerly moved toward the passenger door as Harry parked at the back of Tally's beautiful house. *"It's weird."*

"Some humans feel strongly that the body shouldn't be disturbed. And no one thought of murder at the time. It's not so weird." Tucker allowed Harry to lift her down.

The blossoms, knocked off the trees and bushes, scattered on the grass like pink and white confetti. Harry rapped on the back door as she scraped the petals off her boots.

As no one came directly to the door she opened it a crack. "Aunt Tally, it's Harry."

The sound of footsteps reverberated through the back hall. Reverend Herb Jones appeared. "Harry, come in."

"Hi. I didn't see your car."

"In the garage. The storm was so bad I thought I'd better come out here and stay, especially since Mim and family are in New York." He closed the door behind Harry and the animals, who headed to their respective assignments. "When the help goes home she's out here all alone and those were nasty storms. One right after the other."

"Gee, I'm happy you're here. That's why I stopped by. I was worried about Tally being alone, too." She followed Herb into the huge kitchen.

Tally glanced up from yellowed hunt-territory maps, drawn in the 1930s. "I'm still alive, thank you."

"Never a doubt in my mind." Harry laughed. "Hey, those are something."

"Forgot I had them and then Herb and I were talking about the old Albemarle Hunt, which hunted the Greenwood territory. I was just a kid then but that hunt unraveled, odds and ends, and in 1929 Farmington took over the territory. Anyway, these old maps will show you."

Harry propped on her elbows to study the maps. She loved old prints, photographs, aquatints. "I think people had better lives back then."

"Well, I'm inclined to agree—until you had a toothache," Aunt Tally sensibly replied.

As the humans enjoyed one another's company, Tally recalling her girlhood, Herb remembering the big jumps from hunt days gone by, the animals worked quickly.

Pewter, nosy anyway, quietly pulled open the pantry cabinets. They had glass window fronts so she didn't waste any time. She pushed the lids off the two sugar bowls, one silver and formal, one informal. Plain white sugar rested inside. She sniffed. Plain white sugar, pure and simple.

For good measure she inspected every small bowl, tureen, creamer. Everything was in order. Disappointed, she hopped down, pulling open the bottom cabinets that didn't have glass window fronts. Nothing in there but big pots and pans and serving dishes.

Mrs. Murphy had intended to prowl around the kitchen but with the humans in there she decided to join Tucker.

The corgi, diligent and intelligent, carefully started with the joinings between two boards, following it from end to end. Murphy walked in just as she reached the place where the table had been set.

The cat sat on her haunches.

Tucker stopped, checked out a spot, lifted her nose up, then put it back down. *"Murph, try this."*

The cat joined her friend and although her nose wasn't as refined as the dog's, a scent so faint as to be ethereal wafted up from a crack. *"Bitter."*

"Smells like a bad poison, but we can't prove it." The dog cocked her head, then put her nose down again, wrinkled it, bringing her head up. *"Not rat poison. I've never smelled this."*

Pewter sauntered in. *"Big fat nothing."*

"Come here," Murphy said.

Pewter placed her nose where Tucker indicated she should. She sniffed, then blinked her eyes, jerking her head back. *"Nasty, what's left of it."* She turned to Murphy. *"You might be right."*

"You two slept under the table. What I remember"—the tiger jumped up on the fireplace mantel where she'd been sitting during the tea dance—*"is that Roger was already in the chair. Lottie came into the room. She'd been out dancing or in the garden. I don't know. The desserts had just been placed on the table. Everything was buffet style. People started to come in and crowd the table. They needed the coffee. Lots of drinking. Lottie picked up a piece of chocolate cake. She was in the line. Next she poured a cup of coffee from the silver samovar and then she put in three scoops of raw sugar. I remember it was raw sugar because she took a step back to put the sugar on the table, bumped into Thomas Steinmetz just as he reached for the sugar, and spilled it all over the floor. She apologized, he said it was his fault, and then she carried the cake and the coffee over to Roger, who was happy that she paid attention to him. I don't know what they said because I was, by then, watching the other humans."* She thought a moment. *"She'd made a mess of the sugar. Thomas cleaned it up before one of the kids hired to serve got there. He picked up the broken pieces of the bowl and swept up the sugar with his napkin. When one of the servers got there he handed it to him to put in the trash. He'd wrapped everything in his napkin. I didn't pay much attention to it at the time except to think that he was nice to do it because there was enough on the floor that someone could have slipped on it. Drunk as many were, I'd say that was a sound conclusion on his part. And, well, within ten minutes, Roger was dead. And quiet. No gurgling or choking. I was sitting right here. Quiet!"*

"Lottie Pearson gives Roger coffee and cake. She went with

Don Clatterbuck to the dance that night." Pewter frowned. "*Lottie Pearson.*"

"*And she's not very happy with Mom.*" Tucker flattened her ears.

"*Yes.*" Murphy remained silent for a long time. "*I was thinking that Sean—but now I don't know. But what would Lottie Pearson have to do with three dead men, Wesley Partlow, Donny Clatterbuck, and Roger O'Bannon? Is she a black widow or something?*"

"*She could have been killing men before now, but thinking on it, maybe her animosity toward Roger was a big act,*" Pewter, suspicious, said.

"*If she isn't acting, someone around here sure is.*" Tucker hit the nail on the head.

35

Harry, not knowing what her animals were thinking, was working from her own ideas. Satisfied that Aunt Tally flourished, she headed her truck toward the old folks' home, the highest building in Crozet, which wasn't saying much.

An expanse of asphalt surrounded the beige block building, still wet so the parking lot surface shone like mica. She pulled her truck to the back, cut the motor, and emerged followed by the "kids," Pewter shaking water off her paws at every step.

Harry walked around the building. Nothing unusual presented itself. She then stopped at the edge of the tarmac to study the railroad tracks that swooped right next to the building with a long curve. Wesley had been found near those tracks. The brush, already grown up at this time of year, could easily conceal activity. She pushed through the bushes and brambles, leaves spraying water on her. An old mud road pockmarked with huge holes filled with brown water followed the tracks. The hanging tree, a fiddle oak, sat just south of that road, maybe fifty yards. From the tree the distance to the tracks measured about two hundred yards.

Harry looked up at the strong, spreading limbs and shuddered. The sun peeked out from the clouds, then immediately disappeared again. Thunder shook the other side of the Blue Ridge Mountains. It was far enough away that it sounded like one of the gods, clearing his throat.

"Not more rain." Harry exhaled. "I tell you, it's either floods or drought these days."

"You're exactly right. Let's go back to the truck," Pewter strongly suggested.

"H-m-m." Harry walked around the tree, searched the ground, then checked the tree bark. Her curiosity was getting the better of her, a condition her pets feared.

After ten minutes she returned to the truck, Pewter racing ahead of everyone. The skies grew dark gray rapidly. Harry opened the driver's door a crack, reached behind the seat, pulling out a towel. She wiped off each animal's paws before allowing them in the truck. Then she climbed in herself, opened the window about two inches, and sat. A fine mist slowly enveloped the old folks' building.

The front door opened. Sean O'Bannon, his hand under his mother's elbow, guided her to her car. The mist thickened, heavy with moisture.

"I forgot about that," Harry said to herself as she observed Sean slide behind the wheel of his mother's car, turn on the motor, and drive out.

"What?" Mrs. Murphy nudged her.

"Sean's grandmother lives here now. She's too old to properly take care of herself."

"She understood you?" Pewter's jaw dropped.

"Coincidence." Murphy laughed.

Harry thought out loud. "Seems Wesley was murdered at night, during the storm—of course, it's been one storm after another. Even without the cover of rain it would be pretty easy to get back in there without anyone noticing. But why back there? There's nothing there and even if there had been fresh tire tracks they'd been washed away by the time the body was found. Maybe going behind the home wasn't in the plan." The first raindrop struck the windshield, a circle of tinier droplets spraying upward after the contact. "Maybe this was an easy place to meet or maybe it was an easy place to jump the train as it slows for the curve to go through town. Plus easy to find if one doesn't know Crozet. Big parking lot. In the rain you could sit here with your lights off and who would notice, driving by? The question is, how long was Wesley alive after he was released from jail? I found the Mercedes star three miles from here. What was he doing out in the woods? There's nothing there."

"Nothing that you know about," Murphy corrected her.

The rain arrived full force. Harry rolled up her window. The temperature dropped with the arrival of the rain, skidding into the low sixties so fast that the animals huddled together.

Harry reached behind her seat and pulled up an old sweatshirt, slipping it over her head.

"It's so raw."

"Let's go home where it's warm," Pewter pleaded.

Finally, Harry turned on the motor, reached over, flipping the heat on—low—as well as the windshield wipers. She cruised by Miranda's. Tracy's car sat in the driveway. Although he now lived within walking distance, he must have decided it was going to rain.

She turned out toward O'Bannon's. The rain fell harder. She could barely see the wrecker's ball. She drove east for a few miles, then turned back for home.

The second she opened the passenger door, the animals

flew from the truck to the house. She, too, dashed through the downpour.

No messages on her answering machine disappointed her.

Thanks to the constant rains she'd reorganized every closet, her library, the linens and towels, even the socks. The only indoor chore left to do would be to repaint the living room. She didn't feel up to that.

Restless, she rambled from room to room, then finally grabbed a county map from her map section in the library. She opened it on the coffee table, placing paperweights on each corner, shooing off Murphy and Pewter, who felt compelled to sit on paper, any paper.

She used a number four pencil, a light line, to trace the distance from the jail to the place at Marcus Durant's where she'd found Wesley's Mercedes star. Then she drew a line from there to the old folks' home. From the jail to Durant's would be a long distance to walk, close to twelve miles if you knew how to cut over meadows and pastures. Following Route 250 West to Route 240 West would increase the distance from the jail to Durant's by another two miles.

"Someone picked him up."

Murphy, back on the coffee table, but not on the map, peered down. *"Draw a line to Booty Mawyer's farm. Draw a line from the place where you found the star at Durant's to Mawyer's. Just for the heck of it."*

Pewter hopped up next to Murphy. *"Why not from the old folks' home to Booty's?"*

"Could but I don't think that's the way it played out."

Tucker, on her hind legs, studied the map also.

"I have an audience here." Harry smiled, then jumped when a loud clap of thunder exploded right over the house. "Big one." She sheepishly grinned. "Okay, what else? Murphy, get your paw off the map."

Murphy pointed from the river spot to Booty's. She did this three times before Harry caught on.

"Do you think their minds just aren't wired right?" Pewter wondered. *"They'd forget their head if it weren't attached to their neck."*

"No, the problem is their heads are filled with junk. Whatever they see on TV or hear on the radio or hear at the corner store. Empty stuff, eats up brain cells."

Tucker loved Harry so she felt she should defend her. *"But Mother's better than most."*

"H-m-m. Booty's backs up on Durant's. He could have hidden in the shack. It wouldn't be that far to park the truck and walk to the shack."

"Or to Donny Clatterbuck's!" Pewter raised her voice.

Harry, believing the cat was afraid of the storm, petted her. "Wesley wasn't seen driving the truck by the time Coop was looking for it. Unless he drove the old farm roads, but for what?" She bent low over the map. "Railroad's not far." She sat up. "Doesn't compute." Then she stood to get the county map of Culpeper off the shelf. She unfolded it as the animals watched. "White Shop Road."

"Right off Route 29. Easy to find," Pewter noted.

"Easier driving from the south to the north than vice versa unless you know the road. See, it's at a sharp angle," Murphy pointed out. *"But once you know where it is, it's easy."*

"Back way to Bull Run Kennels," Harry said.

"Hey, someone's coming down the drive. Intruder! Intruder!" Tucker raced to the back door, the fur on the back of her neck standing up.

A door slammed, feet could be heard running for the back door. The screened porch door opened with a creak and then a knock reverberated with the thunder at the back door.

"It's Lottie Pearson," Tucker barked.

36

Harry hopped up, surprised to see who stood at her back door. "Lottie, come in."

Lottie stepped through, removed her coat, hanging it on a peg. "I'm sorry to barge in."

"It's a pleasure to see you," Harry replied, just as her mother had taught her. "How about a hot cup of coffee or tea? I have cider and hot chocolate, too. It's easy to take a chill in this kind of weather."

"Actually, I'd love a hot chocolate." She moved toward the kitchen table, remembered her cigarettes, and returned to retrieve them and a matchbook from her coat pocket, which she slid under the cellophane of the cigarette pack. "This is the coldest, wettest spring."

"Sit down. I'll have this ready in no time." Harry pointed to the kitchen chair. "We could go in the living room."

"The kitchen is fine. Everything important happens in there anyway." She dropped in a chair, Tucker sitting next to her, on guard.

"*Let's plop by our food bowls. We won't look as nosy there,*" Mrs. Murphy whispered to Pewter.

"*Good idea.*" Pewter crouched, gathered steam, then soared up on the counter. Sitting by the food bowl was her natural position.

Lottie exhaled through her nostrils. "Do you get the Weather Channel?"

"Yes."

"Every blip is treated as though it's the beginning of some millennial trend. First there's a warming trend. Then it's El Niño followed by La Niña. Seventeen-year cycles more or less. How can anyone predict a trend? We haven't kept accurate records long enough."

"I wonder about that, too."

The milk warmed in the saucepan. Harry poured some cold milk for the kitties and gave Tucker a treat. When the temperature in the milk reached perfection, just before boiling, she poured the milk over the powdered cocoa, stirred it, grabbed a can of whipped cream out of the refrigerator, and spritzed a mound on top. Then she lifted an orange out of the fruit basket and skimmed a thin strip of orange peel. She placed that on top of the whipped cream, setting the concoction before Lottie.

"How pretty it looks."

"Give it a minute, still hot." Harry, with her extra-large mug of chocolate, sat down opposite her.

"I like the glaze on your mugs. They're almost big enough to be soup bowls."

"Bought them in the kitchen shop in Middleburg."

"Such a beautiful town. I wonder for how long." Lottie dipped her spoon into the whipped cream. "M-m-m." She grew serious again. "Washington encroaches. The big cities will swallow the entire East Coast in our lifetime."

"God, I hope not."

"West Coast, too." Lottie pressed on with her pessimistic conviction. "Everyone goes to the city then leaves the city and for whatever reason they all want to live in the beautiful countryside, which they immediately desecrate. If we were smart we'd restore passenger train service. Spur lines. Would cut the pollution by half if not more. Trains pollute eight times less than airplanes and four times less than cars. And you can read the paper while you commute. I can't read the paper while I drive. In fact, I can't do anything when I drive except drive. I'm so worried about someone slamming into me or jumping the meridian. You can't trust anyone these days."

"I suppose." Harry wondered how long it would take Lottie to reach the point of her impromptu visit.

Lottie fiddled with her cigarette pack, which she'd dropped into her lap. She couldn't light up until after the hot chocolate, much as she wanted to—wouldn't be proper to smoke and eat simultaneously.

"We've heard about the weather and urban sprawl." Pewter licked the milk off her lips. *"What's next?"*

As if in response to the gray cat, Lottie propped her right elbow on the table. It wasn't perfect etiquette but under the circumstances she thought Harry wouldn't mind. One can be too proper. "You know, Harry, that my position at the university requires a lot of socializing. I enjoy it. I enjoy meeting people and cultivating relationships. And," she quickly tacked on, "not all those relationships will result in major gifts to the university. Big Mim will never write us a check. Her money goes to her alma mater and I appreciate that. After all, when she was young the university was males only. Her son attended Cornell. So as I said not all of my socializing revolves around donations."

"That's nice to know." Harry drank half of her hot chocolate. She hadn't realized she was thirsty.

"I'm a people person." Lottie smiled.

"You'd have to be to be good at your job." Harry smiled back at her, wondering if she should heat more milk.

"I meet all kinds of people and I have to get along with all kinds of people. But mostly what I do is woo the wealthy. They are more alike than different." She drained her cup.

"I'm going to have some more."

"Oh, I couldn't."

"I bet you could and forgive me for not putting cookies on the table. I don't know where my mind is these days." She opened the cupboard, put some cookies on a plate, then heated more milk.

The rain drummed steadily outside; the night was blacker than black.

"Thank you. What I find is that most, now I said most, not all, people with money react to visual cues. They're quick to size other people up, if you know what I mean. What kind of earrings does she wear? What kind of watch does he have on and what does she or he drive? The cut of one's clothes. The cues are very, very important. The way in which one speaks. One's manners at the table. I swear that's why Southerners are so successful at fund-raising. We know how to act if nothing else."

"Good manners beaten into our skins." Harry laughed as she had heard a constant stream of corrections from her mother, aunts, adults as a child.

"That's one way to put it." Lottie turned in her seat toward the stove as the milk simmered. "You'd be amazed to know how much I spend on clothing alone. And I'm not really a clotheshorse but I have to look good."

"You're one of the best-groomed women I know. You, the two Mims, and BoomBoom, always."

"Boom's too flashy." Lottie waved her hand, dismissing even the thought of BoomBoom Craycroft. "It takes time, imagination, and money on my budget. After all, I wasn't born with a silver spoon in my mouth."

"I often wonder what life would be like if I had been," Harry mused as she finished making another delicious cup of hot chocolate. This time she shook a little powdered nutmeg on top, placing the orange rind on top of that. She'd forgotten the nutmeg the first time around.

"We'd both be in a better place." Lottie turned back toward the table as Harry sat down. "It's grinding. I love what I do but it's exhausting to pay bills, keep up appearances, pay taxes. There's so little left for me."

"Yes, I know the feeling but we have our health, we live in one of the most beautiful places in the world."

"That's true." Lottie breathed in, lifted her heavy cup, then put it down. Still too hot. She spooned up some whipped cream. "Apart from your company, I dropped by to pose two questions to you. The first is, did you put Cynthia Cooper up to questioning me?"

"No," Harry abruptly said. "I didn't know she had questioned you."

"You two are close. You're a, what shall I say, amateur sleuth. She came to my office and that really upset me. She could have picked another place."

"I suppose she could have but if she was really worried or suspicious she probably would have met you somewhere else or simply hauled you in. If she came to your office it means she needed your help. I'd think that your superiors would know that."

"Maybe. It made me quite nervous."

"Lottie, two men have been murdered. I should think that would take precedence over any of us feeling nervous or put out."

"Yeah, and Lottie may have poisoned one of them," Pewter catcalled.

"Hush, Pewter. Don't call attention to us. Besides, the humans think Roger died a natural death and our smelling what we think is poison in the cracks of Aunt Tally's floor doesn't constitute proof. For all we know it could have been ant poison."

"It wasn't," Tucker rumbled.

"Be that as it may, let's be quiet." Mrs. Murphy half closed her eyes, pretending to sleep.

Pewter followed suit so Tucker walked a bit away from Lottie's chair and flopped down with her head on her paws. She never took her eyes off Lottie, though.

"It is gruesome. I know." She sighed. "I never even saw that hanged man. He didn't park my car. And as for Donald, well, it's too bizarre, just too bizarre."

"Okay, I answered your first question."

"Thank you. I feel better. I was terribly upset when Coop came in uniform and everything."

"Lottie, I assume you explained her presence to the people around you. You're making too much out of it."

"You work in the post office. It's different for you. I'm judged by a different standard and I'm telling you, people are not fair, not for an instant. Furthermore, women are judged more harshly than men."

"Oh, Lottie, I don't believe that."

"I do. We're held to a higher moral standard."

Harry considered this. "Do the Ten Commandments come with gender specifications?"

"No." Lottie frowned.

"Then it's the same for everyone, male or female. If people want to use gender as an excuse for their behavior, have at it. The rules are the same for everyone."

"Harry, you've been around Miranda Hogendobber too long. The real world doesn't work like that. The real world is still controlled by rich white men and it is in their self-interest to have their cake and eat it, too. So when Bill

Clinton slept with every tart that came his way there was finger-wagging and fussing but finally people just figured that's what men do."

"Lottie, as I recall he nearly got impeached."

"I still maintain the standards are different. If I sleep around it's one thing. If Fair sleeps around, it's another."

"Lost him his wife," Harry coolly replied, then laughed.

"Uh—I'm sorry. Bad example." She blushed.

Harry leaned forward. "Lottie, what's the second question?"

"Oh, yes." She fiddled. "Do you mind if I smoke?"

"No."

She lifted her pack of king-sized filtered Salems from her lap, slid the matchbook out of the cellophane, tapped out a cigarette, and lit up, placing the pack and matches on the table.

Harry rose to fetch an ashtray, placing it to the right of her cup. "That's pretty." She picked up the matchbook. "Like a little work of art. Roy and Nadine's." She paused. "Roy and Nadine's." The matchbook Cooper had mentioned. "Lottie, where did you get this?"

"That? Oh, I don't know."

Harry turned it around. "Been to Lexington, Kentucky?"

"No. Let me think. I was at Aunt Tally's, needed a light. Uh—Roger. He wanted to light my cigarette; his hand was so shaky I had to hold his wrist. He gave me the matchbook." She paused. "Poor Roger. He was a pest but I didn't wish him dead."

"Lottie, this may be important. I'm going to call Coop."

"The matchbook?"

"Yes." Harry jumped up, lifted the receiver off the wall phone, and dialed Coop's home number. Luckily she was there. "Coop, hi."

"What's cooking? Or not cooking?"

"I'm sitting here in my kitchen with Lottie Pearson. She just lit up her cigarette with a Roy and Nadine's matchbook."

"Put her on."

Harry walked over to Lottie; the phone cord was long. "Here."

As Lottie repeated her story to Coop, Harry sipped her hot chocolate. Slender though the clue was, at least it was something. The other pack found in the Cowboys windbreaker could have belonged to either Wesley or Don, since the exact ownership of the windbreaker was undetermined. Identical matchbooks from Lexington, Kentucky, wouldn't just be floating around Crozet, Virginia. The connection could be something as simple and unsavory as Wesley selling Roger stolen hubcaps. She found the fact that Roger and Wesley must have known one another deeply disquieting. But what if the matchbook had been Don's? What else did they know? And what did Sean know?

Lottie's voice pierced her thoughts. "She wants you back."

Harry reached for the phone. "Well?"

"Interesting. Thanks for getting to me so fast. I'll drop by sometime when I get a minute."

"Okay." She stood to hang up the receiver, then closed the cupboard door that Pewter had opened when the humans were occupied. "Pewter, you're not getting that catnip until I say so." Harry closed the door.

"Meanie."

"She's going into a sulk."

"Cats are funny that way." Lottie sighed. "Everything is so strange right now. I'll drop this matchbook off at the sheriff's office on my way home. Odd." She pushed the matchbook around with her forefinger.

"Lottie, the second question."

"Oh, yes. I need a presentable date for the huge alumni dinner in two weeks. Someone very impressive, and I was wondering if you would mind terribly if I asked Diego. He'd be perfect at something like that."

"Yes, he would. I have no claim on him. If he wants to go that's his choice, not mine."

"Yes, but you like him. I don't want to step on toes."

"You're not stepping on my toes. It was good of you to ask me but it seems to me if a man and a woman aren't married they come and go as they please. Right?"

"It's not that simple. You see things in black and white."

"No, but I do think things are simpler than we make them."

"But you like him. You're attracted to him."

"I'll bet you just about every woman who sees that man is attracted to him." Harry smiled. "He's to die for, as they used to say."

Lottie puckered her lips, inhaled deeply, and exhaled. "There's been enough dying around here."

37

I asked around if anyone had a recent photograph of Don," Cooper said.

"Any luck?" Rick checked his watch. He was due at a county commissioners' meeting in a half hour.

"BoomBoom had one from the parade. Here." She handed him the Polaroid of Don, his face half turned to the camera, and Roger O'Bannon, standing by the float. No hoopskirted belles were in sight, fleeing the float the second the parade stopped.

"Better than nothing. Mug shots of Wesley?"

"Got those. I faxed them off about an hour ago to the dealer in Newport News and the manager of Roy and Nadine's. That car dealership is huge, by the way, two hundred and five employees. That's a lot of payroll."

"Sure is." Rick shrugged. "My idea of hell is a committee meeting." He checked his watch again. "I wonder if you have to take an IQ test before being elected a county commissioner. You know, you can't run for office unless it's below one hundred." He checked his watch one more time.

"What is it this time?"

"The bypass. Same old, same old. I deliver the accident statistics on the highways, the locations, the times of the accidents, and the volume of traffic. They have the Department of Transportation statistics on volume but they want to hear what I have to say, and what I really have to say but I won't is that sooner or later the damned bypass will go through. If we work together I think we can limit the damage." He ran his palm over the side of his head above his ear. "Truth is it will make an ungodly mess wherever the state puts it."

"And we need it."

"Hell, yes, we need it. Traffic grows, people's tempers shorten, and we'll be in gridlock before you know it. The commissioners don't want to face facts. The bypass is a necessity."

He opened the long middle drawer of his desk, then pushed it shut after retrieving a rubber band, which he slipped on his wrist.

Cooper, recognizing his jog to his memory, the rubber band on his wrist, asked, "You could write yourself a note."

"Yeah, stick it in my chest pocket and forget it. This way I don't forget." He snapped the band against his wrist.

"What do you need to remember?"

"Milk. The missus asked me to bring home a quart of two-percent milk. Well, I'd better push off. I'll see you in the morning."

"I've been thinking about the money in Don's safe. Would a merchant be able to get new money like that? A department store, a business like Wal-Mart, something with high volume?"

"I don't know. What would the purpose be? Money is

money. Customers at Wal-Mart don't care if they get change in brand-new bills. We know the banks get new money supplies, the old money gets burned. I don't think I could stand to see that." He stood up, clapped his hat on his head. "Daniel into the lions' den."

"Boss, I'll say my prayers."

"You do that." He clapped her on the back, snapped the rubber band on his wrist, and left.

Paperwork had been accumulating on Coop's desk at a geometric ratio. She straightened up the piles, sighed, then gave in, sat down, and started sorting into three piles. The first one hit the trash can, the envelopes and letters making a little pinging sound in the metal wastebasket. The second pile was more urgent and the third pile was less urgent. She hoped that time would solve some of the questions and problems presented by the third pile. Her rule of thumb was if she waited three weeks, often she didn't need to answer. It wasn't the most scientific system in the world but it worked.

She e-mailed replies to the most urgent pile. For those individuals and organizations lacking an e-mail address she wrote out letters on the computer, then printed them.

In the background she heard the metallic grunting of the fax machine.

"For you," Yancy said as best he could, since his jaw was still wired shut.

She rose and grabbed the fax from the dealer in Newport News. No one at the dealership recognized Wesley Partlow. "Rats." She slipped the fax into her file box under her desk.

"No luck," Yancy commiserated through clenched teeth. He'd gotten pretty good at talking despite his handicap.

"Hell, no. Say, Yance, when do you get the wires out?"

"Next week."

"Bet you'll be glad."

"Yep."

"Does it ruin your sex life?" she teased him.

"Nope."

She started to say something silly when Sheila at the front desk buzzed her. "Din Marks is here for you."

"Be right out. Yancy, your attacker is here. Maybe you'd better stay put."

"I'll get 'im in court."

"Right, buddy." She walked out front where a nervous Din Marks waited on a long wooden bench. An older man sat next to him.

"Mr. Marks."

Both men stood up so Cooper surmised the older man was Din's father.

"Officer Cooper, uh, Dad said I had to come down here."

"Pleased to meet you, Mr. Marks." She shook the older man's hand, rough with calluses. "Why don't we go in this room here? It's more private. Can I get you all a drink?"

"No, no, we're fine," the older Marks, rail thin, replied.

Once seated in the small room, Din squirmed in his seat. "I remember something."

"Let's hear it."

"Dad said I had to come on down."

"That's right, son." Mr. Marks was hoping his boy would make a good enough impression that perhaps the trial against him would not be so heavy to bear. Maybe Cooper would help Din.

"I remembered something that Wesley said. He said he was owed some money. Big money. He meant to collect it. Stealing hubcaps." Din shrugged. "Said it wasn't how he made real money. He said stealing was like, uh, pitching. You had to keep limbered up."

"Did he say who owed him?"

"No, ma'am."

"Did he say how much?"

"Fifty thousand dollars. Said he could make as much as he wanted. I didn't believe him but I was, well, you know."

"Did he say how he'd make more money?"

"No, ma'am, but I figured it wasn't in the stock market."

"Did he ever say what kind of work he did? Regular work? Like road work in the summer or roofing? Anything?"

"No."

"Well, you were right to come down here. Thank you, Din. Thank you, Mr. Marks."

As they stood up to leave, Mr. Marks, his eyes moist, said, "Will this help my boy?"

"Mr. Marks, the fact that he is cooperating with the sheriff's department can't hurt him. What can help him is if he goes to AA meetings. If he repents in front of the judge and produces evidence that he is mending his ways, going to AA, I think, will make a favorable impression on the judge. Hear?"

Mr. Marks nodded vigorously. "Yes, ma'am, I hear." With that he put his hand in the small of Din's back, directing him toward the door.

They were no sooner out the door than Yancy, bright-eyed, strode into the front room. "Coop, Coop, will you look at this?"

She grabbed the fax he handed her. "Jesus, Mary, and Joseph. This changes things."

The fax from the manager of Roy and Nadine's read:

Dear Deputy Cooper,

I do not recognize Donald Clatterbuck nor does anyone on my staff. However, we recognize the man with him. He comes in about once a month, usually in the company of a local businessman, Bill Boojum. Let me know if I can be of further service to you.

Yours truly,
Tara Fitzgibbon

38

Are you sure we should do this?" Harry asked Susan.

"Someone has to" was the terse reply.

"Why not BoomBoom? She uses the salvage yard. I mean she has to get sheet-metal scraps."

Susan considered this. "Maybe all three of us should go to Sean."

"I don't want to go." Harry stubbornly dug her heels in.

"Mother hates anything that might become emotional." Mrs. Murphy sighed. *"I don't know why. Humans have highly developed emotions to keep them alive."*

"When they lived in caves." Pewter shook herself, then sat down for serious grooming.

"What are you talking about?" Mrs. Murphy edged toward the door. If the humans were going to the O'Bannons', she was going with them.

"All that adrenaline worked when they lived in caves but I can't see how it does them a damn bit of good now. Just gets them in trouble."

"I'm not talking about violence, I'm talking about the whole range of emotion."

"Piffle," the cat sniffed.

"I don't think my emotions are any less developed than a human's," Tucker stoutly said.

"Did I say they were?" Murphy was irritated that her two cohorts missed her point and she thought they were being deliberately obtuse. *"What I'm saying is their emotions keep them alive. I am not saying those emotions are in the service of reality at this time in their evolution."*

"They haven't evolved. That's the problem," Pewter sharply said. *"They're walking around in clothing but they're still the same animals who lived in caves, feared the dark, and smashed one another over the head for beans. Trust me."*

"You have no faith." The dog thought humans were better than that, some of them, anyway.

"Faith, why should I have faith in human beings? You've got one man hung, one man shot, and we believe Roger was poisoned. That does not bespeak evolution." Pewter stated her case succinctly.

"I can believe Lottie Pearson would poison Roger. Poison is a woman's weapon. But I can't believe she'd hoist Wesley Partlow over a tree. She wouldn't have the strength. I doubt Lottie could heave a hay bale. Now, Mom could do it." Tucker quickly added, *"Never would, of course. Harry wouldn't kill anyone unless in self-defense."*

"Hey, cut the gab. I'm not missing this." Mrs. Murphy charged out the front door of the post office when Harry opened it.

"Girls, take your time." Miranda waved to Harry and Susan.

"You could go." Harry tried to wriggle out of this task one more time.

"I'm minding the store. And Susan asked you. After all,

you all are closer in age." Miranda wasn't afraid of emotional outbursts. She truly believed Harry was a more suitable emissary.

Defeated, Harry opened the door to Susan's Audi station wagon. The three animals hopped in the back where the seat was down, making it pleasant for them. Susan had called BoomBoom so by the time they pulled into the salvage yard, BoomBoom was also there.

Three small pieces of sheet metal rested in the bed of BoomBoom's brand-new Chevy Silverado truck. Boom, contrary to her appearance, was a motorhead. She loved machines almost as much as Harry did. Driving her BMW provided her with true delight. She felt the same way about her half-ton truck, too, although the road feel was different. She liked sitting high up, she liked the huge V-8 Vortec engine, she liked the stereo system.

"Does he know we're coming?" BoomBoom asked.

"I called ahead. He's working. I called Ida first"— Susan mentioned Sean's mother—"she said he'd be at the yard. Work helps him."

"So many memories of Roger." Harry thought it must be painful, for she knew how it felt after her parents died and she took over the farm. Before that she'd lived in a small apartment in town.

"Well?" Susan raised her eyebrows.

The three trudged together to the main building.

"I'm going to strangle Pope Rat." Tucker scampered off to the garage.

"She's a quart low." Pewter indicated the dog. *"Why tangle with a rat? I'm going inside with the humans."*

"I'm going to sit here and think." Mrs. Murphy padded over to the marble section.

When the three women opened the door, Sean glanced up. "Hi."

"Hi," they said.

"Can I help you?"

BoomBoom spoke first. "We don't want to intrude but we want you to know that if you want to move the Wrecker's Ball from here, we've found a place to have it. The salvage yard in Louisa County agreed to do it and we'll do the work, send out a mailing."

He smiled. "Thanks. That's good of you and good of Jonathan." He mentioned the owner of the salvage yard in Louisa County. "But I'll have it here. Roger loved that party. I thought I'd have it in his honor and accept donations to establish a scholarship in his name at Virginia Tech."

"That's a wonderful idea." Susan meant it, too.

"Do you need extra hands?" Harry asked.

"No, thanks. My crew can handle it. We've got ten days. We're okay."

As the three women left the building, Harry saw Tucker streaking from the garage to the caboose on the siding. The corgi raced around the caboose because the first step was so high she couldn't climb up.

"Pope Rat," Murphy told Harry.

"Vermin!" Tucker shouted.

"Nipshit!" the rat taunted from inside the caboose.

"Susan, I'm going to have to pick her up. She won't come voluntarily." Harry ran over to grab her dog before the barking offended Sean and the customers. "Tucker, come on."

The dog's soft brown eyes pleaded, *"I can get him."*

"Come on." Harry, curiosity aroused, stepped on the platform. The door was locked and the shades drawn. "Make a neat restaurant or even a place to live."

Pope Rat put his eye to the opening he'd chewed in the door. *"Another nipshit."*

Harry scooped up Tucker, returning to the station wagon, where Susan and BoomBoom were talking. "Wouldn't you love to have that caboose? They've got wood-burning stoves in them and I don't know, I'd sure like to have one. Wonder why he locks it up."

"Going to clean it up, paint it, and use it as a coffee-house, I think. At least that's what the plan was before Roger—anyway, I guess it's locked so people don't troop through and damage it." BoomBoom thought it would be a good place to gather. "And liability. I'm sure he needs to get everything perfect. What if someone fell off the steps before they're finished? Stuff like that."

"Yeah, I'm expecting someone to sue the post office if they get a paper cut opening their mail." Harry grimaced. "Hey, here comes Coop."

As she pulled the squad car next to the Audi, Tucker squirmed out of Harry's arms, tearing back to the caboose.

"Damn you, Tucker." Harry ran after her, grabbing her again as the dog challenged the rat.

"You're supposed to herd cows, not rats," Murphy dryly laughed.

"He called me a nipshit. Called Mom one, too." Tucker heaved, indignant.

"He's like the blue jay. Born trouble." Pewter harbored a plan to dispatch her tormentor. She wasn't telling anyone.

"So?" Everyone expectantly looked at the lean, long deputy.

"Can't tell you. Not until I speak to Sean." She picked her hat up off the passenger seat, then decided not to wear it.

Harry opened the driver's door for her. "I've been thinking."

"That's scary." Cooper laughed.

"Who knows that we opened Don's safe?"

"His mother and father. The sheriff. You. BoomBoom. I

know his mother and father won't speak of it. At least, not for a while. It's too overwhelming. Who did you tell?"

"No one," BoomBoom truthfully replied. "Harry told Miranda and Tracy but I was there. I guess in a way I told them, too."

"Susan. I told Susan," Harry stated.

"No one else?" Cynthia Cooper stretched her arms over her head. "Kinks."

"The older you get, the more getting out of bed in the morning becomes an athletic event." Susan shook her head in surprise at how rapidly the aches and pains mounted up and she was only in her late thirties, as were the others.

"What's your idea, Harry?" the officer inquired.

"Well, first let me ask you a couple of questions. Who had the combination to the lock? There wouldn't be a key to a lock like that, right?"

"Right. I thought when I first saw the safe that maybe there would be a key, you know, the big handles could be for show, but it really was a combination lock."

"A tough one," BoomBoom added.

"How do we know someone else didn't have the combination? The press doesn't know about the money. Rick withheld that information. Can it really be possible that all that money was Don's? And even if it was, whoever he was in business with had to know he wouldn't put a sum like that in the bank. That would be like waving a flag in front of a bull. So his partner or partners had to know Don's share would be in that safe. Which is exactly why Rick didn't tell the press even though they're hounding him for a development concerning the murder. He's hoping to flush them out," said Harry.

"Possible," Cooper drawled as BoomBoom and Susan stared at Harry.

"I think I know what comes next." BoomBoom, no slouch, put her hands together.

"Put the lock back. Fill the safe with fake money. Maybe we can flush them out faster." Harry beamed.

"His partner will come back to take Don's share," Susan thought out loud. "Yeah, but how are you going to know when he comes back or *if* he comes back?"

"Can't we put a small surveillance camera in the shop, the kind they use in the bank? It can't be too expensive. I know Rick is worried about the budget." Harry warmed to the task. "No one needs to be there. You'll see who it is and nab him later."

"In the best of all possible worlds, yes, but what if he comes in with a mask? Or she? I shouldn't assume it's a man." BoomBoom rubbed her hands together. The talk of aches and pains made her joints hurt.

"Yeah, but any picture is better than no picture and whoever this is knows no one is at Don's house. He won't even have to pretend to be a thief," Harry sensibly said.

Coop held up her hand. "Let me run this by the Boss. BoomBoom, can you weld the lock back?"

"If you all help me, I can. It's so heavy someone has to hold it in place. It's going to take a couple of hours to do it right. You don't want the seam to show, that's a big tip-off."

"How about Friday night? I have it off. Chinese." Coop meant bring Chinese food.

"I'll get the food." Susan thought this exciting. "We shouldn't park there."

"I've got to back up and drop off the oxygen. I need help with that, too. Harry, you're the strongest."

"Yeah, okay."

"We can park at the high school and walk over. There's so much activity there that our cars won't be noticeable," Susan said.

"Seven," Cooper said, then nodded toward the building. "I've got to get in there."

"Will you tell us later?" Harry couldn't stand not knowing something.

"Yes."

"Boy, it must be unsavory." BoomBoom, sensitive, felt Cooper's reluctance, as did the others.

"Uh, yes."

Later that day, Cooper dropped by the post office to pick up her mail. She told Harry and Miranda that she had dropped off papers requesting to exhume Roger's body. Sean hit the roof. He called his lawyer and threatened to drag this case out as long as possible.

Cooper then visited Ida O'Bannon, again patiently explaining the new concern that Roger did not die a natural death. She knew this would be upsetting and she knew that Sean would call a lawyer but she hoped Ida could talk sense into him. This wasn't about violating Roger's corpse, it was about bringing his killer, if he was killed, to justice. He could then rest in peace.

Ida, tearful and shocked, said she would reason with her older son. Legally, this was her decision and she agreed to it.

"Coop, what—?"

She leaned toward Harry, Miranda leaning in, too. "I sent photographs of Wesley and Donny to Roy and Nadine's."

Harry explained to Mrs. Hogendobber about the matchbook.

"And they recognized Don?" Miranda just couldn't believe this.

"No. The manager of the restaurant didn't recognize him but she did recognize Roger. She said he came in about once a month with a businessman named Bill Boojum."

"Who's Bill Boojum?" Harry asked the logical next question.

"He was easy to find. He's one of the biggest car dealers in Kentucky. He specializes in high-end car rentals and does a booming business with Thoroughbred trainers, jockeys, people who make money erratically. Sometimes it's a big paycheck, sometimes not. They find it easier to rent cars than to buy them."

"What did he say?"

"He seemed helpful enough. He said he knew Roger from college. They'd both gone to Virginia Tech. I checked that out with the alumni office. He told the truth. He said Roger was interested in getting into the racing game and he was putting him in touch with NASCAR people. He said Roger had already bought into a syndicate, a forty-thousand-dollar share."

"Forty thousand dollars—Roger?" Harry nearly fell over.

"I checked out the syndicate, too. Based in Lexington, Kentucky. Roger was, in fact, a member. They didn't know he had died. The share passes to his mother. The lady on the phone, Mrs. Higgins, pulled it up on the computer and read it right off to me. I asked Boojum why Roger came out so often and he said he just loved Lexington. I can believe that. Who wouldn't? And he said he was besotted with racing."

"Loved cars." Harry rubbed her chin.

"It truly was his passion." Miranda found this troubling, the forty thousand dollars especially.

"An expensive passion, I reckon." Harry spoke a little too loudly, which made the animals jump. "What did Sean know?"

"He says he didn't know a thing about it. I had the presence of mind to ask him about the syndicate before requesting exhumation. He said Roger did drive to Lexington about once a month and he'd stay two or three days. Roger's reason was he wasn't having any luck with Virginia girls so he thought he'd try Kentucky girls."

"Does Sean know Bill Boojum?" Harry asked.

"Yes, but not well. He said he met him once or twice when Roger was in college. Sean, being older, ran with a different set of friends, plus he went to the University of Virginia."

"A sore point between them." Miranda drummed her fingers on the countertop. "Roger in a car-racing syndicate."

"We'd better get that lock back on soon. All this talk of money takes me right back to Don Clatterbuck," Harry said, then told Miranda what they'd be doing that Friday night. "Oh, hell, I'm supposed to go to the movies with Fair. Coop, may I ask him to help us? He's stronger than the two of us put together and he'll never tell."

"Okay." Coop jiggled the handcuffs hanging from her belt.

"When do they dig up Roger?"

"Monday."

"Wish I could be there." Tucker wagged her nonexistent tail.

"Tucker, that is so disgusting." Pewter wrinkled her nose, gray like the rest of her.

39

Slowly the earth drank the rainwater. The ground remained muddy, the creeks little by little subsided. The scent of new blossoms began to overpower the odor of creek water.

Mrs. Murphy hastened to the barn at dawn as the owl returned from hunting.

"Did you get a chance to fly over O'Bannon's?"

"Yes. There are lights on in the garage but the curtains are drawn."

"Any cars or trucks parked outside?"

"No, which I thought was curious."

"I do, too."

"Of course, it could be someone left the light on during the day or it's been on throughout the storms," the owl thought out loud. *"Still, you'd think someone would go in there."*

"What about the caboose?"

"Your rat friend, an industrious sort, scurried from the garage to the caboose frequently. He had a bag of potato chips.

When he heard me—I swooped low for effect—he didn't drop the chips and run. A rough sort."

"If I could pour water in his hole, I bet I could get him to talk. I'd stop up the exits, of course." Mrs. Murphy envisioned this to her enjoyment. She heard Simon snoring in his nest. He looked ratlike yet was so different from Pope Rat; two creatures could hardly be more different in temperament.

"That rat has places and loot all over the salvage yard."

"No sounds from the garage?" Murphy hoped for more clues.

"Yes. I sat by the window and I heard human feet. I know someone was in there."

Later as Murphy walked back to the house she wondered if someone was working late because of the Wrecker's Ball. Then again, why not park out front? And why not work in the new building where the dance would be held? If it was on the up-and-up why hide your car? Maybe Sean was in the garage. Maybe he felt closer to Roger in the garage. So many thoughts jammed into her head she had difficulty sorting them out. One thing did help her focus. She certainly didn't want Harry snooping around the salvage yard.

40

Sean's assistant, Isabella Rojas, disdained Lottie but had to be nice to her. The customer is always right even though in this case Lottie wasn't a customer. Sean would fire her if she behaved rudely toward anyone. The truth was that Isabella, like many a woman before her, had fallen in love with her boss.

"He's out back, Miss Pearson." Isabella forced a smile. "Statuary."

"Thank you." Lottie, with a supercilious air, swished back outside and found Sean carefully positioning chains around a massive recumbent griffin. "Sean." She waved.

"Hi." He held up his hand to the operator in the small crane ready to pick up the heavy object to place it on a flatbed.

"Who has bought this beautiful piece?"

"H. Vane Tempest." He named a wealthy Englishman who owned a large estate west of town and whose symbol was a griffin.

"But of course." Her eyes swept from the griffin to the crane to the flatbed and the large diesel semi that pulled it. "You must have a small fortune tied up in equipment. I never really appreciated how much. I guess you get quite good at leveraging your debt."

"Hey, I'm a junkyard dealer. I have a nose for finding equipment at good prices. Take that crane there. New it would cost one hundred and thirty-nine thousand dollars. I picked it up for nineteen."

"Fabulous," she purred. "But how do you do it?"

"Contacts and"—he stared off into the distance for a moment—"Roger. He'd give the equipment the once-over, tell me how much it would cost to bring a piece up to speed, and then I could make an informed decision. And we always looked for reliable brands like Caterpillar. You pay more but you get more. You know, Roger really was a genius with anything that had a motor in it. He even kept that old wrecker's ball in perfect working order."

"I'm so sorry about Roger. I know I've said that before, but I don't know what else to say." She played with the ring on her pinkie finger, right hand. "When you worked as closely as you did with Roger it must be doubly disastrous."

"The Lord giveth and the Lord taketh away," Sean replied. "At first, I was so shocked I wanted to sell the business and walk away. Mom talked sense into me. Running away doesn't solve anything. Three generations of O'Bannons sweated into this ground. With any luck there will be a fourth and a fifth."

"I certainly hope so." She smiled. "You can imagine yourself an old man watching your grandson move statuary."

"By that time they'll beam it up. You know, rearrange the molecules and send it without a crane and a flatbed."

"Maybe." She shifted her weight to her left foot. "I heard

through the grapevine that you're going through with the Wrecker's Ball and I wanted to help."

"Thank you, Lottie."

"I thought perhaps I could perform some of Roger's chores."

"That's just it. I don't know the half of what he did. He'd burrow down there in the garage and I was up here. He took care of the catering. I did the decorations but there were so many things that just happened. I'm afraid I never closely examined Roger's contributions to the business, or my life. I feel so—so guilty."

"Sean"—she placed her hand on his forearm—"nobody does. It's not you. None of us knows what someone gives to our life until they're gone."

"Uh—thanks." He kicked the gravel path, then looked at her. "You'll be coming to the ball?"

"Of course. Well, I didn't mean to stay so long. I just wanted you to know I was available to help."

41

On a hunch, Cooper had sent out the mug shot of the false Wesley Partlow to all state agencies. At four-ten in the afternoon, she was sitting at her desk writing a presentation. Next Wednesday she was to give a speech at Western Albemarle High School about law enforcement as a career. Much as she loved her job, she was tired and drawing a blank.

Part of the exhaustion came from always dealing with people who were themselves under great stress. She'd received a blast from Sean about the exhumation next Monday. He was honoring his mother's wishes but he thought the request was ghoulish and would prove inconclusive.

Once he let off steam she asked him if he knew about Roger's purchase of a share of a stock-car syndicate for forty thousand dollars, a big chunk of change for a hobby, and Sean said it wasn't any of his business how his brother spent his money. He regularly visited the track at Waynesboro and it made sense that Roger would want to get involved at the higher end of the sport if he'd saved some money. Dale Earnhardt and Richard Petty were his heroes.

"You can't take it with you" is exactly what Sean O'Bannon had said.

Then Coop had to meet Don Clatterbuck's mother at the bank to open his safety-deposit box. The title to his truck, his birth certificate, a few stocks and bonds were in the narrow metal box along with the combination to the safe.

Mrs. Clatterbuck swore she didn't know the combination and thought the safe was another one of Don's finds. Sooner or later he might sell it. He liked to trade. She didn't know where he acquired that trait. Neither she nor her husband were traders.

No love letters were sheltered in the safety-deposit box.

Coop thanked Mrs. Clatterbuck, wrote down the combination, and finally returned to the office.

At four-twenty she wandered over to the coffeepot. A jolt of caffeine might trigger speech ideas. All she could think of was, "How would you like to pick up drunks, deadbeat dads, and squashed accident victims? For variety you could question a drug dealer with his jaw shot off." She knew if she continued in that vein she'd descend into the truly morbid. She no sooner had the coffee to her lips than Sheila buzzed her phone.

Returning to her desk, Coop picked up. "Deputy Cynthia Cooper."

"Louis Seidlitz, the bartender from Danny's."

"Yes, Mr. Seidlitz."

"I remembered that little puke's name: Dwayne Fuqua. It was driving me crazy."

"When I dropped by you said he didn't come in often."

"No, he didn't. Like I said, maybe once a month. Dwayne was on a mission."

"Sir?"

"Girls."

"Lucky?"

"No more than most." Louis laughed.

"Mr. Seidlitz, do you have a fax in the office there?"

"Yeah."

"Don't hang up. Give me the number and I'll fax you a photograph. Tell me if you recognize anyone."

He gave her the number. She faxed the photo of Donald and Roger.

She could hear the fax machine in his office grinding out the photo.

"Deputy?"

"Yes."

"The guy with his hands in his pockets. He'd hang out now and then. With Dwayne."

"Mr. Seidlitz, thank you so much. You've been a great help to me."

"Sure. Any time."

She hung up the phone, silently berating herself for being discouraged when she had first stopped by the bar. She'd felt she'd been sloppy. Well, Louis came through. He had just identified Donald Clatterbuck.

42

... Cool. A beautiful fall day." Diego described the day in Montevideo, for the seasons were reversed south of the equator.

"Raining here. When the animals walk two by two I'll worry." Harry laughed.

"Can you believe they're talking about the weather?" Pewter wrinkled her nose.

"And you don't?" Tucker felt a craving for bacon and wished Harry would make a bacon, lettuce, and tomato sandwich.

"So much has happened since you left." Harry didn't want to spend a lot of Diego's money on a long phone call. She had no idea how much money he really had but she certainly didn't want to waste any of it. "Don Clatterbuck was shot and killed. You might not remember him."

"Vaguely. Virginia sounds like the Wild West. Are you safe?"

"Sure. I'm of no importance to anybody."

"You are to me. I hope to see you again—soon."

"Thank you." She smiled, her voice lifted. "What do you have to do tomorrow?"

"Thomas and I fly over to Buenos Aires, which isn't far. If you look on a map you can see how the cities sit." A clock chimed behind him.

"Where are you now?"

"At my family's apartment in the city."

"I heard the chimes."

"A grandfather clock brought over from France in 1846. Oh, my father can tell you stories, but I didn't call to speak of my father. I called to tell you I will see you the weekend of the party, the ball." He paused. "I know you have a date for the ball. I will give him a run for his money."

"Please do."

"What can I bring you from Buenos Aires?"

"A picture of the polo grounds, where the Argentine Open is played. And you. I'd like to see you." This was about as flirtatious as Harry could bring herself to be.

"Sí!"

They said their good-byes, then hung up. Harry hummed to herself, then checked the kitchen clock.

"I'd better get moving."

"Take us."

43

What a crackbrained idea," Pewter complained.

"Unfortunately, humans don't consult us before they go off on a toot." Mrs. Murphy agreed with her friend's assessment of the situation. *"Silly of them, I know."*

"In theory it's a good idea." Tucker stayed on the other side of the room, away from the welding torch. The odor, the sparks, the flame bothered her more this time.

"If whoever is doing this stuff is dumb, it's a good idea." Pewter sniffed. *"But I doubt they're that stupid. They'll see the camera. It's like a bank camera."*

"We know it's up there in the corner but the thief doesn't know it's there and it might work. There's an outside chance." Tucker remained dimly hopeful.

"We'll see. Also, I'd amend thief to killer," Mrs. Murphy said.

The animals watched as BoomBoom patiently restored the huge lock to its place. Fair held it up but even his strong arms wearied. Harry took a turn to spell him.

As Boom worked, Cooper told the group about Dwayne Fuqua. "...on the fringes."

"What about a high-school counselor? He must have made an impression on someone," Susan said.

Cooper shook her head. "Not much. Didn't get his diploma. The father abandoned him. The mother turned to drink and drugs. No one knows where she is or even if she's alive. He lived in a room in a small house past the old Ford dealership, I mean before they moved. Checked with his landlady. She said he was quiet. She didn't know much about him except he'd be gone for days at a time. Paid his rent on time."

"Did he have a criminal record?" Harry called out as she was holding the lock.

"No. That surprised me."

"Odd." Fair stepped in as BoomBoom turned down the flame. "My turn."

"Thanks." Harry was relieved. "And he knew Don. That's really—I don't know. It confuses me. Waynesboro's just over the mountain. There's plenty of ways people can meet one another. I guess criminal intent doesn't have to be party to it." She shrugged. "But with both of them dead—well, what could they have known?"

"Or done?" Coop rested her elbow on the carton of phony money.

"I still say it's drugs. People don't have cash like that unless they deal drugs," Fair said.

Boom, mask up for a quick breather, added, "Diamonds. Gems. There's a lot of cash in that business."

Susan lovingly looked at the fake money, wishing it was real and wishing it was hers. "Well, what about rubies or sapphires?"

"Susan, what are you talking about?" Fair raised his voice over the sound of the torch.

"Okay, you intend to get engaged. You aren't sure what stone your fiancée would like. The jeweler shows you loose stones. You pick one and the others go back. Retail jewelers don't keep a lot of loose gems. Not here, anyway. We're too small a market. So Don could have illegal rubies. I mean it wouldn't have to be diamonds, given what Harry said about the dirty diamonds. I'd forgotten about that, the press calls them dirty diamonds."

"Gold, silver, platinum. Maybe it was metal." Harry was curious.

"Yeah, but the next question is, Where would Don Clatterbuck or Dwayne get the gold, who would buy it from them, and why?" Cooper sighed, her head spinning.

Harry smiled at Cooper. "What you're telling us is you don't think this money is about stones or precious metals."

"Right."

"Drugs," Fair persisted.

"The kingpin used Wesley, I mean Dwayne, and Don as mules." Coop rose to take her turn holding the lock in place. "That's more likely."

"Don could hide drugs in the animals he stuffed," Susan said brightly.

"What an awful idea." Pewter made a face.

"What? You don't want to be stuffed when you die?" Murphy laughed uproariously.

"I'll outlive you!" Pewter flared, flashing her fangs.

"Who knows? Anyway, it doesn't do you one bit of good to think about death. There's nothing you can do about when you die but there's sure a lot you can do about living."

"Murphy, Pewter, let's not talk about dying." Tucker hated the thought of dying.

The torch cut off, BoomBoom flipped back her face guard. "Done!" She inspected the seam as she tried not to inhale, because the metallic fumes made her eyes water. "Not bad if I do say so myself."

The others crowded round as the fumes dissipated.

"Let me clean up the floor." Harry had brought a dustpan and hand mop with her, anticipating this. "It wouldn't do for someone to open the safe only to hear tiny metal bits crunch underfoot."

Once the floor was cleaned Coop stacked the fake money in the safe. "Okay, let's shut it, lock it, and then unlock it to make sure his combination works."

"No." Boom put her hand on the door to keep it open. "Test the combination before you shut the door."

"Right." Coop let BoomBoom twirl the handles, then stop them. Then she carefully rotated the center dial according to the directions found in Don's safety-deposit box at the bank.

The clicking of the tumblers filled the room as everyone remained quiet.

"Works." Boom smiled. "Want me to shut the door now?"

"Sure." Coop nodded.

The door shut with a satisfying, heavy sound.

"What do you think about my idea of Don hiding drugs in deer heads?" Susan reminded them of her idea.

"God, I hope there's nothing in my woodpecker." Harry wanted to get that woodpecker back from the Culpeper sheriff's department.

"My woodpecker," Pewter corrected her.

"Nothing has turned up in your woodpecker." Coop allayed her fears. "But hiding drugs in stuffed animals would be a good way to transport them. Maybe you're on to something, Susan."

"Wonder how Don got into it?" Harry asked.

"Greed. That's how everyone gets into it," Fair said.

"Where would they get that quantity of illegal substances to begin with?" BoomBoom checked her tools.

"If they were selling marijuana that's not hard. It's grown here in the state and no amount of surveillance by helicopters at harvest time locates all of it. And people can grow it in greenhouses, too. If they sold cocaine, heroin, those drugs, they'd need a source in a big city. If that's what they were doing." Coop picked up the empty carton.

"What about legal drugs? Why couldn't they sell Darvon and Valium and Quaaludes?" Harry thought they were as bad as the illegal drugs.

"Sure, but they'd have to have a contact. Either a corrupt physician or a company salesman. You can't just go out and get your hands on a jar of muscle relaxers." Fair, being a vet, had a keen appreciation of legal drugs, since he was pestered by salespeople at regular intervals.

"What about steroids?" Susan wondered.

"Same difference." Fair picked up the heavy oxygen tank. "Even someone good at chemistry can't cook that up in the kitchen. Like I said, you'd have to have a corrupt source or steal them from a patient."

"Are there drugs you can make at home?" Harry innocently asked.

"Amyl nitrite," Coop answered. "But it's a liquid, wouldn't be that easy to transport. It's the kind of drug that someone with skill could cook up in the kitchen but your customer would come to the kitchen to buy. Liquids are too much of a pain to transport great distances and the profit isn't that huge. The profit margin on illegal drugs or designer drugs from the big drug companies is huge. Don isn't going to have five hundred and twenty-five thousand dollars in his safe from amyl nitrite."

"What if they stole frozen semen from high-priced stallions in Kentucky? What if the business was that? Some of those stallions stand for over a hundred thousand dollars. I know how the semen is cooled and shipped. If Roger kept going to Lexington he could be bringing back stolen semen. With DNA testing he'd have to have the real stuff. But he could do it. Maybe the car racing was a cover."

"He could. I never thought of that but I don't associate Roger with horses." Fair put the oxygen tank down. "I guess he could have done it. Are we ready?"

The others nodded; they checked and rechecked the place, then turned out the light and left. Fair gallantly carried the oxygen tank up to the truck just as he had carried it down.

"Strong bugger," Pewter said admiringly.

"You didn't live with us when Mom was married to him. He really was worth his weight." Mrs. Murphy remained neutral about whether or not Harry should get back together with Fair but she certainly appreciated his hard work on the farm.

Fair pulled Harry aside after he loaded the tank on BoomBoom's fancy truck. "Have you heard from Diego?"

"He called late this afternoon from Montevideo. He'll be in town next weekend. He's escorting Lottie to an alumni fund-raiser."

"Oh." Fair smiled.

"She asked him."

"Oh." His face fell.

"And?"

"She's making it hard for him." Tucker loved Fair.

"He's gotten better at expressing himself." Mrs. Murphy was proud of Fair's progress and although she wasn't a big believer in therapy she thought it had helped him. He liked structure even for his emotions, and therapy gave him the illusion of that. She knew one could never structure one's emotions but Fair's sessions helped him gain insight into himself.

"I thought we were going to the Wrecker's Ball."

"We are. I haven't changed my mind. You asked me at New Year's. As I recall you said, 'Plan ahead.'"

"I did, didn't I?" He was tremendously relieved, then he tensed again. "Is Diego coming to the ball?"

"He is and I'll dance with him. I dance with all the fellows. I even dance fast ones with Susan if you all are pooped out."

44

At eight o'clock Monday morning Roger O'Bannon was exhumed from his grave. As he hadn't been in the ground that long, he retained all his features and his digits but the body was filled with gas.

Rick detested exhumations. They were unpleasant affairs but he felt he had to be at this one in case Sean showed up. Although Sean had promised his mother he would comply with her wishes, people could snap, change their minds. Emotions were like quicksilver even in the best of times. This, hardly the best of times, called for extra vigilance.

Rick accompanied the body to Marshall Wells. As he worked, the new coroner said he couldn't promise when Richmond would return the results but he didn't think it would be longer than a week at most. Fortunately, this was a slow time.

As he drove away from the coroner's office, Rick called Coop, alone in her squad car that day.

"Coop, meet me at O'Bannon's Salvage."

"Trouble with Sean?"

"No. But I want to go over those grounds again."

"Might it be a good idea to wait for another day? I would expect Sean's a little raw today."

"In a perfect world, you're correct and sensitive. But if he is in on this or if he did kill his brother, he might drop a card, you know?"

"Okay. I'll be there in ten minutes. I'm at Route 250 and 240, want a sandwich?" A good deli was at that intersection.

"Not hungry."

"Sorry. I forgot." She was glad she wasn't at the exhumation.

Sean was curt but not openly rude. He told them to go wherever they liked.

First they walked the perimeter of the four acres. Rick liked to make sure he knew the terrain. Nothing unusual presented itself except for the fact that the business had room to grow physically, always a plus.

The few small outbuildings contained gardening tools or small pieces needing cleaning. Some salvage yards left the cleaning to the customer. Sean discovered if he cleaned, put in a little time, he could command bigger prices. It was worth the effort.

Then they pushed open the door to the garage. The large sliding door, big enough for vehicles, was locked but the small door, to the left of that, was open.

"Neat as a pin," Coop said.

"Yeah." Rick walked over to the hydraulic lift. "This is something."

"Nothing much here. I guess he wasn't working on anything. The books showed the last old car he sold was a week before his death. A 1932 Ford coupe. He got twenty-seven thousand for it. Deuce coupes. I'd love one."

"Yeah." Rick wasn't a motorhead but he appreciated old

cars. They were more individual or so it seemed to him. "Nothing out of line. He picked up most of his old cars in South Carolina and Georgia. The sources checked out. Guess he was waiting to find the next one or two. He seems to have contributed to this business. He wasn't the front guy but he worked. For one thing, Sean wouldn't have put up with it."

"Here's a bag of popcorn." Coop bent over to pick up the empty foil bag. "That's the only debris." She tossed it in the trash.

They left, walking through each of the large outdoor piles of offerings. They tried the door to the caboose. Locked. Coop dashed back. Sean gave her the key. She dodged the puddles back to Rick.

She opened the back door, then ran up the shades on the windows. The light streamed in. "Cool."

A potbellied stove sat in the middle. The floor, hard oak, was clean and no dust was on the two chairs and the heavy desk in the corner.

"Sean's a neat freak, too," Rick noticed.

"This would make a neat restaurant. I hope he goes through with it," Coop said.

They opened the drawers of the desk. Nothing but an old cracked celluloid fountain pen.

"Well, that's it," Rick said. "I wish I knew what we were looking for."

"I'd have been happy with one marijuana plant in the window." Cooper sighed. As she walked toward the door, she said, "I feel bad, we're tracking some mud in here. I'll tell Isabella we did. I'll even clean it up."

"Coop, it's not as though we've brought in slops. If Sean is that anal retentive, he can sweep it out." As Rick headed for the door he looked down at the wet footprints. A beam of light shone on dried footprints, light mud. "Hey." He knelt down. "This can't be more than a few days old."

Coop knelt down with him. "Yeah." She followed the tracks: one person, big feet. Two strides and then back out, footsteps overlapping the entrance footsteps. "In and out."

"H-m-m."

"Boss, you worried?"

"Yes."

"Me, too."

Pope Rat, observing them from his cozy quarters, growled, *"Nipshits."*

45

Coop sent photographs of Dwayne Fuqua and Donald Clatterbuck to Bill Boojum in Lexington, Kentucky. Bill couldn't or wouldn't identify either man. He'd never seen them with Roger.

Refusing to give up, Coop sent photos back to the dealer in Newport News. She asked him to show all his employees photographs of Dwayne, Roger, and Donald. Although none of those men ever worked at the dealership, it would have been possible that one or more of them could have dropped off a vehicle or picked one up to be delivered to Boojum's in Lexington, since a leasing agent would purchase cars from big dealers all over the U.S.

Within two hours of faxing the photographs she received a phone call from Fisher McGuire, the general manager. One of his office workers remembered giving Dwayne the registration papers for him to drive a Jaguar to Boojum's. He even remembered that the car was a three-year rental.

Large rental dealers like Boojum's would get a request for

a specific vehicle, in this case a new Jaguar sedan, British racing green, tan interior. The salespeople at Boojum's would call their contacts at various Jaguar dealers until they found one matching their client. They would then pay for the car, have it driven to the dealership, and rent it to the customer. If the residual value of the car is accurately figured, a dealer can't lose on car rentals because the customer eats the depreciation, not the dealer. The customer is responsible for maintenance and is allowed a certain number of miles per year, usually twelve to fifteen thousand. Any mileage over that is charged at ten to fifteen cents a mile. If the wear and tear on the vehicle is excessive, the customer is responsible for costs when the lease term expires. Once the car is turned back in at the term of the lease, usually three years, the dealer sells it at retail value. The customer has the right to purchase the car at retail value.

The program works nicely for those people not wishing to tie up a lot of money in a car. However, since they don't own the vehicle it is never counted as an asset but only as a liability. The tax write-offs and depreciated value present another labyrinth of issues that only an accountant can decipher. A renter needs a lawyer before signing a contract. The renter might be able to write off the monthly rental fee if the vehicle is used for business. However, as is often the case, what you save with one hand the IRS steals from the other.

Cooper nabbed Rick as soon as he walked through the door. He listened intently to her findings.

"Boojum can't identify Dwayne?"

"No, but it's possible he never saw who dropped off the car. Dwayne may not have been a regular."

"True." Rick dropped heavily into his chair. "Who paid for the delivery?"

"It was prepaid by Boojum's. They didn't specify a driver. Fisher McGuire, the general manager down there in

Newport News, faxed all the paperwork, including the release form, to Dwayne Fuqua. McGuire was under the impression that Dwayne was a driver for Boojum's. Bill Boojum says no one at his dealership has ever seen Dwayne Fuqua or Wesley Partlow, pick your name."

"I can guarantee you someone had seen him!" Rick slammed his hand on his desk out of frustration. His coffee mug rattled.

"Yeah, someone is lying through their dentures." She held her hand on his coffee cup in case he lost his temper again. "So what's the deal? Are they running drugs in these rented cars? Each time over the mountain a different car is used. Maybe even a different driver. Lexington and Louisville are good drug markets."

"Hell, they're so rich in Lexington they can fly the shit in," he growled.

"Well, not everybody is that rich, Boss."

"It makes sense and yet it doesn't make sense. If Boojum is in on this he—" Rick stopped in mid-sentence, grabbed his address book. "Just one minute." He found the number he was looking for and dialed. "Sheriff Paul Carter, please." He waited a moment. "Paul, Rick Shaw from Albemarle County, Virginia. Buddy, I need a favor."

"What?" the sheriff, an old friend from Washington County, asked.

"I'm going to fax you three photos. Will you take them to Boojum's in Lexington, avoid Bill Boojum, and see if anyone can identify any of these men?"

"The big dealership there? Very high-end."

"High seems to be the operative word," Rick said. "That's it. I'm conducting a criminal investigation here and I have strong reason to believe that Bill Boojum may be involved."

"How criminal?" Paul laughed.

"Two murders and when the lab reports come back from an exhumation, I may have three."

"Jesus." Paul whistled. "I'll do it myself—out of uniform."

"I really appreciate it and, believe me, I'll return the favor if the opportunity presents itself."

"Don't mention it."

After hanging up the phone with Paul, Rick bounded up from his chair, striding over to his maps pinned on the corkboard on the wall. Coop followed.

"Boss, want a map of Kentucky?"

"Yeah."

Coop buzzed Sheila. "Hey, check the metal file cabinet out there for a recent map of Kentucky."

There was one and Sheila brought it in. Rick pulled extra pins out of the corkboard, opened and straightened out the map. He put it up as Coop, anticipating his next request, brought him a state map of Virginia. Once up they both stared at it.

"Here's what I don't get." Cynthia stuck her finger on Newport News. "Over a million people. A huge naval base. Wouldn't there be a big drug market there? Has to be. Why fool around with Lexington?"

"Organized crime owns Newport News. A small-fry could survive for a time but they'd be squeezed out eventually. Maybe mid-South cities are more open." He touched each of the pinheads representing the murder sites. "I'm not convinced this is about drugs, even legal ones as you've suggested."

"Whatever they're doing, it has to be easy to transport."

"No. Whatever they're doing simply must not call attention to itself. It doesn't have to be easy. They could be transporting stolen cars."

"Yeah, but we'd know if the cars were stolen around here.

Besides, would Don have five hundred and twenty-five thousand dollars in his safe from stolen cars? These guys would have to be running one of the biggest rackets in America for that kind of money—and just for one guy. He probably wasn't even the head of it."

"I know. I know. That doesn't quite fit either. When we went to Roger's garage I was looking for a chop shop. Not a sign. Hauling in a car, stripping and selling off the parts, hell, there'd have been junk everywhere. That place of Roger's was immaculate."

Coop said, "His garage was cleaner than some people's houses."

"Scratch chop shop. I've even thought about counterfeit money. Unless there's a buried bunker or another place hidden, that's not going to work either. I know that drugs are the one logical piece in what is illogical right now but, Coop, I don't think it's drugs. I don't know if Don Clatterbuck and Roger could deal without dipping and that always shows."

"Roger liked to drink but remember Diana Robb says he did coke, too. I remember going over there to check on Mrs. Hogendobber's hubcaps and there was a line of beer cans to his shop. Never found a trace of drugs though." Cooper crossed her arms over her chest.

Rick paced in front of the maps. "It's difficult, hey, almost impossible to imagine Don or Roger organizing some kind of criminal business. Neither one struck me as that smart. Someone has to be on top, someone much more intelligent."

"Most murders occur within families or between people well known to one another. And most of those murders involve alcohol, drugs, or are crimes of passion. These murders are dispassionate, cool. The murder of Dwayne was opportunistic but not a crime of passion. The body wasn't mutilated, he'd been hit over the head; for whatever reason the killer couldn't finish him off with a blunt instrument so he strung him up."

"Maybe the weapon wasn't heavy enough or the killer wasn't strong enough. That points to a woman."

"Hoisting Dwayne over a tree couldn't have been light work."

"Push him on the back of a truck, throw the rope over the tree, and drive off. It rained so hard nothing was left. There could have been a truck in there or even a car, slide him over the trunk. It's messy but not all that hard."

"And Dwayne wanted more money. After Din Marks's talk with you that would appear motivation enough. If he wanted more now, he'd want more later. Or maybe he wanted promotion inside the company." Rick shook his head. "Greed leaches out every other emotion, doesn't it?"

"Yes, it certainly seems to do that. People become bloodless."

"I'm going to wait for the lab reports on Roger. If he was murdered then I must consider my first suspect Sean O'Bannon. He had the most to gain by his brother's murder, separate from whatever scam Roger was into. Sean inherits all of a lucrative business. Maybe he even inherits a lucrative illegal business."

"Maybe the safe full of money will lure the killer to put his foot right into the trap."

"A poster about selling off Don's goods might help. I spoke to his parents. They agreed and we won't put their phone number on there. Just an auction date, location, and time. Ought to light a fire under his ass." Rick's one eyebrow arched upward. He could be clever.

46

The daily sun and wind reduced the size of the puddles, the depth of the mud. Still not trusting the ground, Harry didn't drive her tractor to the creek. Large tree limbs were wedged along the banks; a few weak trees had crashed into the creek, their uprooted trunks looking like paralyzed squid tentacles. She needed to chainsaw the trunks into smaller portions, wrap heavy chains around them to drag them out. Once the wood dried she'd cut it for firewood, stacking it neatly on the porch. She'd also built a weather-tight woodshed next to the shavings shed. As spring and summer progressed she'd slowly fill the woodshed until full. That would hold throughout the next winter.

The mercury climbed to sixty-four degrees at noon, just warm enough to shed a coat but still cool enough for a mid-weight shirt. Harry took the opportunity before the weather shifted to hot and hotter to crimp a standing tin seam on her barn roof. The seams separate sometimes. You fold the longer piece over the shorter and squeeze them together.

Her father had taught her how to do it. She wore sneakers, the rubber soles helping to give her traction on the roof pitch. Only one seam needed work, which made her happy.

Pewter and Murphy reposed under the large white lilac bush. Tucker slept under the lavender lilac bush. Both cats were awake but stretched on their sides to their full length.

"Do you like bacon?" Pewter reached out to bat at an ant, who easily avoided her.

"You know I like bacon."

"If you had to choose between bacon and beef bits what would you choose?"

"Beef."

Pewter rolled on her back. *"What about between beef and tuna?"*

"Tuna."

"Tuna and salmon?"

"H-m-m, tuna." Mrs. Murphy had to think about that one. *"Why are you asking me? Are you hungry again? You ate a huge breakfast."*

"When I'm not eating I like to think about food. Food preferences are clues to personality." This was said with great conviction.

"Pewter, you need sunglasses."

"Huh?"

"You're getting West Coast."

"Close-minded," she sniffed. *"Figures. Tuna, a most conventional cat."*

Mrs. Murphy lifted her head. *"She's stopped."*

Pewter lifted her head off her outstretched paw also. *"What improvement will she tackle next? She's exhausting. She needs to learn to take naps."*

Out of nowhere the blue jay screeched by them, shaking the lilacs. *"Mouse breath!"*

Pewter leapt up, shaking herself. *"Death!"*

"Don't go out. Move back. Let's see if we can draw him into the bush. Then we've got him."

The blue jay turned, flew around the walnut tree, diving for the lilac bushes, too smart to be lured in. He screamed, *"Tapeworm host."*

"That does it!" Pewter shot out of the bush but he'd already begun his climb.

To show off he flew in the center aisle of the barn and out the back side.

"If we find his nest we can climb up and kill him." Mrs. Murphy logically suggested. *"If we can't get him or his mate we can push their eggs to the ground."*

"I'd love to hear them splat, little tiny splats since they're little tiny eggs. Death to the next generation." Pewter's pupils enlarged in excitement.

The only other excitement of the day was Diego calling Harry in the evening. He was back in Washington and looked forward to seeing her the next weekend. Since Fair was taking her to the Wrecker's Ball, he asked her to check her calendar so he could take her to the next dance, picnic, anything. Then he said they'd make their own picnic. She agreed. They'd enjoy a repast Saturday noon and if it rained, they'd eat in the barn just to be halfway outside.

She hung up the phone and began whistling.

"What an awful sound," Pewter meowed.

"It is," Mrs. Murphy agreed, running to Harry, begging her to stop.

"Sorry, girls, I forgot how sensitive your ears are." Harry laughed and stopped whistling.

"Doesn't bother me," Tucker said. *"If you whistle I come running."*

"Don't brownnose, Tucker, it's such an unattractive trait," Pewter grumbled.

"You know, Pewter, you're so fat I bet there are shock absorbers on your cat box."

That made Murphy laugh so hard she rolled off the sofa, hitting the floor with a thud.

"Murphy, you're supposed to land on your feet." Harry picked her up, kissing her forehead while Pewter, enraged, thumped down the hall into the bedroom.

The phone rang again. Harry walked into the kitchen to pick it up. On hearing BoomBoom's voice she squeezed her eyes shut for an instant.

"What worthy cause are you roping me into now?"

"Well—the Special Olympics need volunteers. They're going to be held at Wintergreen"—she named a local resort—"and we need people who know sports. I thought maybe you could be the starter for the races."

"Oh. Sure."

"That was easy."

"I like the Special Olympics." Harry smiled, then changed the subject. "Think our little trap will catch a mouse?"

"I hope so."

"I keep forgetting to ask you, how did you meet Thomas?"

"Big party at Vin Mattacia's." Mattacia had been Ambassador to Spain in the late 1970s. An urbane, outgoing man, he was at the hub of those people retired from the diplomatic corps who lived in the area.

"Oh."

"Great party. A Valentine's party. I enjoy him but I don't think the relationship will go anywhere. It's just—fun."

"Oh."

"I don't know if I ever want to marry again. Some days I think I do and some days I don't."

"It's a quandary."

After a bit more chitchat Harry hung up the phone, realized it was getting late, and took a shower.

Pewter, on the bed, ignored both Murphy and Tucker, who sat on the hooked rug by the bed.

"Can you imagine standing in a shower? It's like standing in the rain," Mrs. Murphy asked the dog, settling down for a good night's sleep.

"It's a human thing." Tucker half closed her eyes. *"It's right up there with using a knife and fork."*

47

Coop breezed in the back door of the post office at seven-thirty in the morning. She tacked up the bogus auction poster on the bulletin board in the front part of the building.

Miranda and Tracy both knew what was afoot. Every single person who came into the post office commented on it that day.

Lottie wondered if the Clatterbucks were that hard up. She then sarcastically said she thought Harry would be in the first row of the attendees since Harry couldn't resist sticking her nose in other people's business.

Mim, just returned from New York, thought it much too soon. One needed time before sorting and selling.

Little Mim questioned who would want to buy bears' paws and the like.

Jim Sanburne merely shrugged. He accepted a broader range of behavior than did the women in his life.

The Reverend Herb Jones thought the whole thing was too sad.

Sean O'Bannon read the notice without comment.

At the end of the day, Rick Shaw listened to Marshall Wells on the phone. The lab report had come back with all due speed. Roger O'Bannon had been poisoned with quinidine, a drug which, taken in excess of one gram, kills within fifteen to twenty minutes. It can be administered in pill or powder form. Unlike most other poisons, this one kills without producing horrible convulsions. It is sometimes given to heart patients to suppress acute arrhythmias.

Coop, standing next to him when he hung up the phone, simply said, "Do we arrest Lottie Pearson?"

"She handed him the coffee. Can you prove she poisoned him? *Intentionally?*" He emphasized the word.

"Not just yet. She's not going anywhere."

At three o'clock that night, a car, lights off, glided down Don Clatterbuck's short driveway. The driver emerged, noiselessly closed the door, and walked to Don's shop. What no one had noticed when they left Don's shop after reinstalling the lock was that the tiny red light on the video camera was reflected in the windowpane. The thief noticed and left.

48

The week roared by in a welter of chores, seemingly so important at the time yet quickly forgotten. Fortunately, mail volume was light, so Harry skipped out Friday morning to do her grocery shopping. Miranda, whose refrigerator remained full, gladly gave her the time. Tracy kept Miranda company at work.

"Have you decided what color dress you're wearing?"

"The magenta, the color of my peonies."

"You'll be the prettiest girl there." He smiled, deciding that either a white or pink corsage would complement her dress. "I don't remember Tim O'Bannon being so interested in charitable pursuits."

"Tim was tight as the bark on a tree. He used to embarrass Ida. When the boys took over the business they became involved in community affairs. I think they did it out of the goodness of their hearts but I don't expect it hurt business either. 'Each one must do as he has made up his mind, not reluctantly or under compulsion, for God loves a cheerful giver.' *Second Corinthians*, Chapter Nine, Verse Seven."

"What a memory."

"We're back!" Tucker announced gaily.

"Mom drove home, put stuff in the fridge, gave us a treat, and now I'm ready for the mail cart." Pewter hopped in, causing the cart to roll a bit.

"I bought pork chops." Harry sounded triumphant, up to the challenge. "I'm going to make stuffed pork chops according to your recipe. The only thing is, does Diego like pork? Some people don't."

"Feed him a loaf of bread, a jug of wine, et cetera...." Tracy slapped her on the back.

"You men. All alike." She teased him for quoting the *Rubaiyat* because the next line was "and thou." Tracy assumed all Diego needed was Harry.

"Gender wars!" Pewter called out from the bottom of the mail cart. *"I pick women to win."*

"Of course you'll pick women, you twit. You're female." Mrs. Murphy jumped in the cart, too.

A loud discussion followed, after which Mrs. Murphy jumped right out, hit the floor front paws apart, and pretended to chase a mouse into an opened mail sack.

Tucker stuck her nose in the sack. Murphy batted at the dog, who snapped her jaws, appearing quite ferocious.

"Oh, to be a cat or dog." Harry admired their untrammeled joy.

"Your cat or dog." Tracy waved as Coop passed by in the squad car.

Within minutes she came through the back door. "Hi. Didn't want to park out front. I'll only be here a minute."

"More news, I hope?" Miranda offered her a cookie, which she took.

They knew about Roger. Rick had allowed Cynthia

Cooper to tell them. After all, they were in on this mess. They'd helped with the safe and they'd not gotten in his way. He couldn't decide if he was mellowing or if he was too tired to bitch and moan.

"The sheriff from Washington County, Paul Carter, called. Two people at Boojum's recognized Dwayne Fuqua. Said he dropped off cars regularly. They also recognized Roger, of course, but what was interesting is that Roger would pick up Dwayne from Boojum's. Bill Boojum had to know."

"Hi." Susan popped through the front door followed by her youngest, Brooks.

"And why aren't you in school, young lady?" Miranda pointed her finger playfully at the high-school girl.

"Teachers' conference day." Brooks smiled.

"They didn't have those when I was in school." Miranda frowned. "I remember George Washington was good at math." She broke into a tinkling giggle.

"Oh, Miranda." Harry rolled her eyes.

"Brooks, I'm glad you're here. I was going to come over tonight and ask you some more questions. I wish they'd occur to me all at once but they don't." Coop leaned over the dividing counter as Brooks came up to lean on the other side.

"Will you stop running around," Harry commanded Mrs. Murphy, who had abandoned the mail sack to play tag with Tucker.

"Spoilsport." Murphy did sit down, though, as Tucker crashed into her, rolling them both over.

"Sorry, my brakes don't work." The dog licked Murphy's cheek to make up for the block.

"Ha, a likely story," Pewter called out from the mail cart.

"When you brought sugar to the table, who handed you the sugar bowl?" Coop pulled out her small notepad.

"Chef Ted."

"Did anyone stop you on the way to the table?"

"No."

"And it was a bowl of raw sugar?"

"Uh-huh." Brooks folded her hands, leaning harder on the divider. "I put it next to the silver creamer at the end of the table."

"The broken sugar bowl was china." Mrs. Murphy jumped up with a start. *"China. Oh, now why didn't I notice that at the time?"*

"And you weren't called in to clean up the sugar on the floor?"

"No. Someone cleaned it up. One of the guests, I guess."

"Thomas Steinmetz. Lottie backed into him." Coop had several eyewitnesses who corroborated that fact. "When you put the sugar bowl on the table, did you see who reached for it first?"

"Uh—Daddy. He was fixing a cup of coffee for Aunt Tally."

"Then why isn't Aunt Tally dead?" Susan held up her hands in frustration.

"You know, people have been asking that question for years," Harry devilishly replied.

"But that wasn't the bowl!" Murphy yowled.

"Save your energy," Tucker advised.

"I can't believe I was so stupid." Murphy was distraught.

"Don't be so hard on yourself, pussycat. Roger O'Bannon was sprawled on the floor with Little Mim yanking on his arm. That would get any cat's attention," Tucker soothingly said.

"Right under my nose." Murphy bent her head, putting her forehead on Tucker's chest.

"Hey, it's right under their noses, too. They haven't figured it out and they think their intelligence is superior to every other

creature on the face of the earth." Tucker levelly offered that criticism.

"Ha," Pewter called out.

"Do you remember party guests walking into the kitchen?" Coop asked.

Brooks thought a moment. "Mrs. Sanburne, Little Mim, Aunt Tally, Sean—"

"Sean?"

"He came in to ask when the coffee would be ready. There might have been a lot of other people because I was carrying dishes out. Action central."

"I believe that," Miranda said.

"Anyone going into the kitchen passes through the large pantry for china and silver. The food pantry is on the other side of the kitchen." Coop was thinking out loud. "Brooks, do you remember if all the silver bowls were used?"

"No, ma'am."

Coop smiled. "Well, there's no reason for you to have noticed. How were any of us to know what would happen? Sometimes I think solving a crime is like putting together a mosaic, it's thousands and thousands of tiny bits of information until finally a picture emerges."

"What an interesting thought." Miranda passed the cookie dish over the counter.

Brooks happily ate one. Susan resisted, willpower to the max.

"You've questioned the chef, of course?" Tracy asked.

"Yes. I was impressed with his memory for detail, especially about food." She smiled.

"Mind if I call Aunt Tally?" Harry asked.

"No," Coop said.

Harry dialed.

Tally picked up, greeting the caller. "Queen Bee and it better be good."

"Hi, Aunt Tally, it's Harry."

"Do I have a package?"

"No, I'm here in the post office with Deputy Cooper, Miranda, and Tracy, Susan, and Brooks."

"A little party."

"It would be much livelier if you were here."

"You're right about that." She laughed. "Now, what's on your mind, Mary Minor Haristeen?"

"When you hosted the tea dance, you used your own silver, china, and crystal, right?"

"Of course."

"How many silver sugar bowls do you have?"

"Two. One for white cube sugar and one for raw sugar. I use cubes because what people don't use that day I'll give to the horses."

"And both were in use at the tea dance?"

"My, yes, I think I had just about everything out there on that table."

"Ask her about her china!" Murphy hopped up on the table in the back and kept hopping, up and down.

"Calm down," Harry admonished the cat.

"I am perfectly calm," Tally answered.

"I'm sorry, Aunt Tally, I didn't mean you. Mrs. Murphy is pitching a fit and falling in it. Would you mind terribly going into your pantry and counting your sugar bowls, including china bowls if you have any?"

"No, but it will take me a minute."

"That's fine."

As Harry waited the others chatted. Mrs. Murphy anxiously ran over to Harry. She sat so she could hear Aunt Tally's response. As her hearing was acute she could hear if she was close to the receiver. She didn't have to have her ear smack on it.

"I'm back," came the authoritative voice. "I have two silver sugar bowls. Same as when I started. It's a good thing, too, because they cost far too much to replace. I also have only one china sugar bowl, my breakfast set of china. Does that help?"

"Aunt Tally, you've been a *major* help. I'll see you tomorrow night at the ball."

"Won't be the same without Roger. He'd get so loaded he'd start up equipment, make a mess, pass out on the railroad tracks. Everyone else will behave reasonably, I'm afraid."

"You never know."

Aunt Tally laughed. "Harry, in Crozet that's the truth, absolutely! Bye-bye."

Harry hung up. "Her two silver sugar bowls are there. Her china bowl is there yet the china sugar bowl broke. How could we have missed that? It means the broken china bowl wasn't Aunt Tally's." She smashed the palm of her hand to her forehead.

"We all did," Murphy commiserated.

"That doesn't solve our problem but it gets us closer to understanding just how Roger was poisoned." Miranda sighed.

"Roger was poisoned!" Brooks's voice squeaked.

"Yes, dear, now keep it to yourself." Susan's tone ensured obedience.

"Are you going out to Lexington? Sounds like Bill Boojum needs a face-to-face interrogation." Tracy thought any transaction stood a better chance of success if conducted in person.

"Next week. We know the three murders are tied together. We know Boojum knows something he's not willing to share but we still don't know why. If we just knew why."

"Always comes down to that." Tracy nodded his head.

"Drugs. The setup was perfect but Rick's not buying that. At least, not yet." Coop drummed the countertop. "We need one little slipup, one tiny mistake. Just one."

She was about to get it.

49

A light southerly breeze carried the fragrance of honeysuckle over meadows and mountains. The bumblebees showed up in full force, as did the carpenter bees. Tiny praying mantis babies crawled over trumpet vines, greening up nicely but no deep-orange blooms as yet.

A curving hill at the back of Harry's land provided the perfect spot for a picnic. Still not trusting the footing, she didn't drive the truck back there but loaded up the hamper and cooler with drinks on the John Deere tractor. She made it in one trip, spread out the checkered tablecloth blanket, and put a spray of thyme tied with ribbon in the middle of the blanket. A votive candle in a clear glass holder was next to the spray.

When Diego arrived he sat in the tractor seat while she stood in front of him, driving.

Tucker ambled along since she didn't pop out of second gear. Mrs. Murphy and Pewter stayed back, laying a trap for the blue jay. They carried sweet feed in their mouths to the lawn near the lilacs. They opened their mouths, dropping it. Three trips and they'd created an enticing pile. They repaired under the lilacs to wait.

Up on the hill, Harry and Diego chattered away, never experiencing that awkward lull that sometimes occurs when people are getting to know one another.

". . . swollen from handshaking." He recalled how Lottie introduced him to anyone and everyone at the alumni dinner.

"She was in her glory."

"She was and she's good at it. She'll pry money out of those old men and maybe even some of the middle-aged ones. Oh, why does it take so long to make money?" He laughed. "We need it most when we're young."

"You think?"

"Oh, yes, while we're still open for adventure, before we become too accustomed to creature comforts, before the children arrive." He surveyed the pastoral scene. "Perfect."

"That it is." She leaned against the maple tree. "What adventures would you like to have before settling down?"

His eyes sparkled. "Rafting the rivers on the western side of the South Island of New Zealand. Riding through Patagonia at springtime. Hiking Wyoming's Grand Tetons and the Bighorn Mountains. Sailing throughout the Greek isles, although one could do that with children, I think. Ah, I'd love to play tennis in Cape Town, croquet in England, polo in Argentina. I want to see the aurora borealis and I want to have more picnics in Crozet, Virginia. What about you?"

"The Dublin Horse Show. I'd like to see that. I'd like to see the south of France and Tuscany and the opera house in Vienna. I'd like to see the Ostsee and then go over to Stockholm and tour the Swedish countryside. And I'd like to see the British Museum, but if I don't get to see any of those things I can read about them. Mostly, I'm happy with what

I have. It isn't much by the standards of the wealthy and the powerful but it pleases me, and, Diego, how much does one need to be happy?"

"For some people, enough is not enough. They have cracks in their soul. No?"

She nodded. "Here I am, the postmistress in Crozet, Virginia. Most of humanity has never heard of Crozet and certainly not of me. But I think about the world. I wish people good lives and I know there's not much I can do to help them except take care of myself and not be a burden to others. I don't know if the human race can be helped."

"A very Protestant concern." He smiled, his teeth white against his tanned skin.

"I suppose it is, isn't it? This dreadful concern to improve one's self and the world. You'd think after all these centuries we would have learned to thank God for what we have and leave well enough alone." She smiled sadly.

"Do you believe in fate?"

A honeybee darted down on the mayonnaise while Harry considered this, then darted off again. "Yes."

"So long?" He laughed.

"I had to think about it. It drives my friends crazy. I'm not very spontaneous. I think things through and I don't know if I make fewer mistakes that way but it's just the way I am."

"I can see that. I'm the opposite, naturally. Opposites attract."

"I wonder." She laughed; his bubbling spirits delighted her. "Another sandwich?"

"Yes." He knew the ham sandwiches would make him too thirsty.

She handed him a sandwich, then pulled a small piece from her sandwich for Tucker, who devoured it instantly.

"Forgot to light the candle." She reached into her jeans pocket. "Oops, forgot to bring matches, too."

Diego fished in his pocket, pulling out a brightly colored matchbook. "Here."

Harry stared at the Roy and Nadine's matchbook in his hand. "Diego, where did you get those matches?"

"These?" He read the address. "Lottie's car."

Harry fervently hoped he was telling the truth. She knew the minute the picnic was over she'd call Coop.

"Have you ever been to Lexington, Kentucky?"

"No. I'll add that to my list of adventures."

Back at the house another small adventure was unfolding. The blue jay, perched on the weather vane on the roof, had observed the two felines laying the trap. He waited until the humans returned, Diego left, and the cats, disappointed, walked back into the house. Then he swooped down, gobbled up the grain, shouting in triumph. By the time the cats raced back out of the house half the sweet feed was gone.

"I hate you!" Pewter yowled at the top of her lungs.

"Ha ha," the blue jay called from atop the weather vane.

Before dressing for the ball, Harry dialed Cooper to report Diego's possession of the Roy and Nadine's matchbook.

"I'd call and ask her myself," Harry offered, "to save you the call but she'd think I was calling about Diego. It's as plain as the nose on your face she means to have him."

"You'd call because you're as curious as your cats," Coop responded. "However, I'll make the call. What time do you think you'll get to the ball?"

"Oh, seven. Starts at six-thirty, uh, wait, the invitation is on the fridge. Let me double-check. Okay, open bar at six-thirty, dinner at seven, dancing at eight. So I suppose we'll get there at six-thirty. Fair enjoys a drink. I'll pass."

"Did you ever really drink?"

"Not really, a beer here and there. Champagne at a wedding. What about you?"

"College."

"What time are you arriving?"

"Six-thirty." She laughed.

"Are you on duty tonight?"

"Yeah, but I'll be dressed to the nines. Rick, too."

"The minute you see me, tell me what Lottie said about the matchbook. I hope he picked it up off the floor of her car. If he didn't—"

"Yeah, I know."

50

The floodlights illuminating the old wrecker's ball shone cool blue. The lights on the sign for O'Bannon Salvage remained white but all around the edges of the yard that faced the road into the yard, lights cheerfully beamed in red, yellow, green, more blue, some pink, some white.

As celebrants drove in they cruised through an allée of light.

The new main building, the site of the dance, drew gasps of admiration from guests. Sean had built all his shelving on rollers so the shelves were rolled to the sides of the large building. In front of these, painters' spattered drop cloths were suspended from the ceiling to the floor. Beautiful salvaged objects, old fireplace mantels, marvelous huge coaching lights were arranged around the room or hung from the rafters. The centerpiece of the room, an Art Nouveau fountain complete with living nymph and satyrs, overflowed with flowers instead of water. Sean had filled the fountain with wisteria, hiring the gymnastics team from the university to display themselves in costume. The sculpted form of a stag stood atop the fountain, an unusual but dramatic symbol.

Each table's centerpiece boasted wisteria wrapped around salvage—a hand-carved finial, a porcelain wash pitcher, a mound of crystal doorknobs. People, drinks in hand, walked from table to table admiring the centerpieces, all of which were for sale for the benefit of the charity.

Other beautiful items, like old gold picture frames, had been bought by committee members and then donated for the charity ball. No one expected Sean to foot the bill for everything. As it was he'd gone to quite a bit of expense buying and painting the drop cloths à la Jackson Pollock. He and his staff cleaned the building, moved back the shelves, hung the cloths, and brought in the heavy statuary on a forklift. Fortunately, the floor was concrete. Plus he donated the fountain to be sold. He built the dance floor with a raised platform for the band. He told everyone he needed the work to keep his mind off Roger.

Miranda posed for a photo in front of the fountain with a satyr. The photographer was also paid by Sean. People bought the pictures, the proceeds going to Building for Life.

Aunt Tally was a sensation wearing a white tuxedo, a red rosebud in her lapel. Big Mim brought down a gentleman in his eighties to escort her aunt but Tally proved too much for him, ditching him for a forty-year-old lawyer dazzled by her wit.

Mim, herself swathed in St. Laurent from head to foot in colors as bright as a macaw, darted here, there, everywhere.

Harry and Fair looked as handsome together as they did when married. She wore her mother's beautiful classic Christian Dior dress and he wore a tuxedo that he'd bought from Bergdorf Goodman's over Christmas.

Susan chose lavender and Brooks chose white, for her first grown-up ball.

Lottie, sticking close to Sean, wore a simple but elegant off-the-shoulder black gown.

Diego escorted Little Mim, which set tongues wagging. Declaring independence from her mother, Little Mim was sponsoring a struggling designer in New York known as Mikel. He probably wouldn't struggle after the Wrecker's Ball because he made Little Mim look ravishing, not always the easiest task. Her emerald-green dress, exquisitely beaded, made a soft, unusual sound when she walked. It wasn't that Little Mim was bad-looking—far from it—but she was usually overshadowed by her mother. This dress ensured she wouldn't be tonight.

Coop, blond head towering above the other ladies, chose red for the simple reason that blondes usually don't. She felt like breaking rules tonight.

By seven, everyone was there, even a few uninvited guests. Mrs. Murphy, Pewter, and Tucker knew how to soften up Fair.

Fair had bought a new black Volvo station wagon. He grew tired of showing up everywhere in his vet truck so he finally sprang for the Volvo. Harry told him to leave the pets home before she remembered the knocked-over lamps, shredded lamp shades, books on the floor. The depredations escalated with feline anger. A put-out puss might stop at knocking over a glass but to be left out of a big occasion called forth torrents of destructive abuse. She agreed to allow them to attend the ball. After all, they knew their way around the salvage yard and it was far enough off the paved state road to pose no danger to them. Fair opened the back hatch so they could come and go as they pleased. Harry put down a beach towel so they wouldn't get the beige car mat dirty.

"Let's find Pope Rat," Tucker panted, eager to chase the rascal.

"No." Murphy reposed in the back of the Volvo. *"Let's sit here for a while and eavesdrop on conversations as people park or come back to their cars. I want to know if anyone comes back for a toot of cocaine."*

"You're going with Coop's theory?" Pewter happily snuggled onto the beach towel.

"It certainly makes the most sense and yet—let's keep our eyes and ears open. No one expects us to be here. If they see us they'll make kitchy-coo sounds. They'll never know what we're up to—humans are dependable that way." The tiger laughed.

"But, Murphy, even if people do come back here or find a place outside for a snort that doesn't mean they're in on the murders," Tucker sensibly reminded her.

"I know that. I'm hoping we'll glean something."

"Pope Rat knows." Pewter scratched behind her ear. *"What a rat."* Realizing he *was* a rat, she burst out laughing.

Rick Shaw pulled up in the next lane of parked cars. He looked good in a tuxedo and his wife wore a white floor-length dress that was very becoming.

The animals could hear their discussion.

"Honey, if my beeper goes off I've got to go. The Reverend Jones said he'd take you home."

"I know, dear." She smiled, accustomed to his odd hours and sudden departures. "I'm just thrilled to be here."

They headed toward the strains of the string quartet. The dance band would rock out after dinner.

The chimes sounded, signaling that dinner would be served. Guests checked their table numbers, moving to their assigned seats.

Sean, as host, sat with the director of Building for Life. Lottie sat on his right. BoomBoom, who'd been head of publicity on this one, sat with Thomas, who was a darker shade of tan than he had been at the Dogwood Festival.

As Diego guided Little Mim to their table, number two, he winked at Harry, who winked back. Fair chose not to notice.

Liberally lubricated by the open bar, the conversation flowed, the volume rising with the courses of wine attending dinner. The nymph and satyrs in the fountain, having sampled drinks offered them by admirers, became friskier than intended, the satyrs most particularly. It wouldn't be long before they took their mythology literally.

After dinner, liqueurs were served along with a staggering array of desserts, fruits, cheeses, and sherbets.

Sated, the guests sat, eyes glazed with happiness.

As the tables were cleared, Sean stood up. "Excuse me, folks, I'm going outside for a smoke."

"I didn't know you smoked." Lottie stood up, too.

"I didn't until now. They can say what they want about nicotine, it really does soothe the nerves." He smiled wanly.

"I guess a little puff can't hurt you too much." Lottie smiled indulgently.

Other people filtered out. Thomas, chest pocket filled with divine Cuban cigars, trailed men behind him. They resembled penguins following the Big Penguin.

Lottie ducked off into the ladies' room before joining the smokers. Harry was in there brushing her teeth.

"Harry, I can't believe anyone is that obsessed with their teeth." Lottie turned up her nose in disgust.

Harry rinsed out her mouth. "Those nuts on the chocolate cake got stuck in my teeth. It drives me crazy."

"H-mmph." Lottie marched off.

As Harry emerged she bumped into Aunt Tally. "Isn't he divine?"

"Who, Aunt Tally?"

"The Marine." She indicated with her eyes a fit man in early middle age wearing his Marine uniform for just this occasion, a carryover from the nineteenth century and one that delighted ladies. His short waist-length tunic fit him tightly, his medal ribbons, four rows deep, bedecked his left chest. His blue-black closely fitted trousers carried a thin red stripe on the outside. His patent leather dancing shoes gleamed.

"What happened to your date?"

"Harry, too old. I can't stand old men." Tally flicked up her cane.

"Well, what about that other guy?" Harry hadn't met the lawyer.

"Uh." She shrugged. "Dull. But now this one, he's a man all right." She covered her mouth with her gloved hand and looked exactly as she must have looked at seventeen at her coming-out debutante ball—minus the wrinkles, of course.

Harry lowered her voice conspiratorially. "I know you can't be good but go slow."

"At my age, sugar, there is no slow. Get it while you can! And I will, I will!" Tally giggled, then hurried into the ladies' room.

Rick, dying for a smoke, had been waylaid by Jim Sanburne. As they were talking Rick's beeper went off.

"Excuse me. I'd better take this." A little printout read DON. Rick's face registered no emotion. "Jim, I've got to go." He briskly walked to Coop, herself walking outside for a smoke. "Come with me."

Hoping not to call attention to themselves they walked fast but not frantically to Rick's car.

"Something's up," Mrs. Murphy noted.

51

Pulling into Don Clatterbuck's, they grabbed their guns and opened the car doors, crouching behind them. Coop dearly wished she weren't in a ball gown.

Rick moved away from the door, running low. He stood outside the shop door, reached over, and opened it. He flattened himself against the building. Nothing.

Coop, keeping as low as her dress would allow, joined him on the other side of the door.

Rick reached in, flicking on the light switch.

No sound. No movement. He ran inside, diving for the workbench. Nothing.

"Coop, come on." He scrambled to his feet, brushing off his tuxedo.

The door to the safe hung wide open. It was empty.

"Our birdie can't be too far away." Coop grabbed a chair, placing it under the camera. She turned off the camera, removing the tape inside.

Yancy had set it up, locking the tiny TV playback box in

Don's broom closet. Coop hiked her long skirt up, stepped down as Rick opened the closet. They quickly plugged in the small monitor.

"Dammit!" Rick exploded.

A masked figure. A black cloth covering the face, slits for eyes and mouth, wrapped in what could be a black bedsheet or long cloak, it stopped in front of the camera after emptying out the safe to give them the finger.

"I'd like to see his face when he discovers the money's no good."

"Won't discover that until he gets it in a bright light." Rick slipped his gun back in his chest holster. "Whoever did this knew we'd be at the ball tonight."

"Boss, that's no surprise. Everyone's at the ball tonight."

"Maybe, but we know this—he knows that we're here. I think we've just been suckered." He sprinted for the car, Coop right behind him. She turned out the lights as she ran out.

"Boss, Boss, I can't run as fast as you."

He waited the extra twenty seconds it took for her to fold herself into the car. "Coop, I wouldn't give you a nickel right now for Sean's life or Lottie's."

"We'll nab them."

"That's not what I mean. One of them is going to be dead." He peeled out, spewing stones everywhere.

52

Mrs. Murphy stretched herself. Out of the corner of her eye she saw Pope Rat, scurrying from the direction of the caboose, carrying a bag of popcorn toward the garage. *"Hey, Tucker, there's the rat."*

Tucker vaulted off the Volvo, racing toward the large, glossy rat.

"She can move," Pewter admiringly said.

"Yeah, maybe we'd better provide backup." The tiger paused. *"Here come Rick and Coop."*

"You cover Lottie. I'll cover Sean," Rick ordered as they raced back to the ball.

"H-m-m, Mom's in there." Murphy gazed after the dog, who ran after the rat, unwilling to part with the popcorn. Instead, Pope Rat turned and scooted back into the caboose. He had cleverly gnawed an entrance right over the coupling and just to the right of the human-sized door.

Tucker had hit this impasse before, so she ran around and with great effort pulled herself up on the first step and was at the caboose door in the rear, the last thing one sees as the train rides by. But this time it wasn't locked. She pushed it in, surprising the foulmouthed creature who was sitting in front of the wood-burning stove.

Pope Rat bared his fangs. He picked up the popcorn bag, slowly backing away toward his hole.

Tucker stopped for a moment. A gunnysack of money sat in the middle of the floor. Much as she wanted to break Pope Rat's neck she turned and bounced down the steps, running flat-out for the Volvo. *"Murphy, Pewter, the play money is in the caboose!"*

"We'd better get Mom." Murphy moved toward the main building, great purpose in her stride. They had noticed cars coming and a few going while lounging in the back of the Volvo but nothing had captured their attention as out of the ordinary. Now all three animals wished they had climbed on the roof of the car to see exactly who was driving in and driving out.

The band played old tunes, new tunes. The dance floor was crowded. Rick and Cooper entered the building a few moments apart. Mrs. Murphy, Pewter, and Tucker followed Cooper in.

Harry, sitting this one out to drink a cup of tea, saw her three pets. "Oh, no." She got up but noticed Cooper's face. "Are you all right?"

"Yes."

"Hey, you never told me about the matchbook."

"Diego told you the truth." She scanned the room for Lottie, out on the dance floor with the Marine, much to Aunt Tally's disgust.

"I'm so glad." Harry exhaled in relief. "All right, you varmints, we're going back to the car."

She walked out, the three following her much too

obediently. As she reached the car all three took off toward the caboose.

"Dammit." Harry felt the cool night air, wishing she had a wrap. She trudged in her high-heeled shoes, those instruments of torture, to the caboose.

Tucker and the cats pushed open the door, driving Pope Rat back into his hole one more time.

"Nipshits," he taunted.

"Who cares about you?" Tucker's voice carried great self-importance.

Harry slowly climbed the steps, walked into the caboose. Her eyes took a moment to focus, adjusting to the dim light. She then saw the opened sack. Kneeling down, her knees cracked. She winced, reached in, retrieving a neatly bound stack of one-hundred-dollar bills.

Holding them close to her eyes, she whistled. "The fakes? Jesus."

Slipping one fake bill into her cleavage, she hurried back to the ball. She had sense enough not to burst in. A few people called to her, she smiled and called back. Her entourage followed behind her, Murphy in the lead.

Fair came up. "I've been looking for you."

"Fair, Cooper is on the dance floor. You can push through that throng better than I can. Will you bring her to me? It's important." She lifted the hundred-dollar bill from her cleavage.

"I guess it is." His long strides carried him to the dance floor in a second, although he had to dodge an amorous nymph.

Cynthia Cooper, dancing with the Reverend Herb Jones, kept Lottie in her field of vision. Rick, dancing with his wife, did the same with Sean.

Fair whispered in Coop's ear, she hesitated, he whispered

again, she thanked Herb for the dance, disengaged as subtly as possible, then joined Harry, who showed her the money.

Coop tried to catch Rick's eye but he was glued to Sean. "Fair, ask Lottie to dance. Keep her tied up," Cooper ordered the vet. "Tell Rick I'm going to the caboose."

"I'll go with you," Harry happily volunteered.

"You keep Lottie tied up." Fair didn't want Harry in danger. "Coop, I'd better go with you."

"I'm not asking her to dance," Harry stubbornly said as she pushed a none-too-compliant Fair toward the dance floor.

The two women hurried out, the animals again going with them, but before Fair could reach Lottie she had quietly disengaged from the Marine, walked behind the band, and walked out the back door. She saw the animals and humans going to the caboose. Looking over her shoulder, Lottie walked to her car.

"Over here." Tucker excitedly circled around the gunnysack in the caboose.

"What is this, Grand Central?" the rat complained from his quarters. As he had finished the popcorn his mood was improving considerably. The only reason he was taking the popcorn to the caboose in the first place was that he was tired of the music, of hearing the humans. He had resigned himself to staying in the caboose until the obnoxious pet threesome left him in peace.

Harry, a step behind Coop, knelt down beside her. Neither one had a flashlight but Coop fished a lighter from a small hidden pocket on the side of her dress. She clicked it on and the cheap plastic light shot out a long flame.

"It's our little bag of tricks all right."

"You think he knows it's fake?" Harry asked.

"I don't know but whoever threw it in here didn't lock

the door, either because they knew this money was worthless or because they didn't have the key."

Moving at a slow trot, Fair came out of the main building. He scoured the parking lot, finding Lottie as she opened the door to her car.

"Lottie."

"Fair, you getting your exercise?" She smiled.

"I was hoping you'd dance the next dance with me."

"Of course." She put a fresh pack of cigarettes in her evening purse, closed the door, and walked back with him.

Back at the ball they started to dance when the band stopped. Jim Sanburne strode up to the raised dais, taking the offered microphone from the lead singer.

Thomas groaned in BoomBoom's ear, "Spare us a long-winded speech. I hear enough of them."

"As mayor, I will say a few words. I'm never too talky. Now if Little Mim, as vice-mayor, gets the mike we might be here for a while." He winked at Little Mim as everyone laughed.

"I'm going to slip out for a smoke." Thomas kissed her on the cheek, stood up, then adroitly moved along the edges of the crowd until he walked out front. He inhaled the cooling night air and reached in his pocket, pulling out an aromatic Portages cigar.

He could hear Jim laud the charity's director, then continue. "I am grateful for so many of you coming to support Building for Life. Those of you who have attended the Wrecker's Ball in the past know that anything is possible . . ."

"Footsteps," Mrs. Murphy warned.

"Come on." Tucker nipped Harry's ankle.

Harry opened her mouth to chastise the corgi when she, too, heard the crunch of footsteps on the pea gravel. Putting her finger to her lips she motioned for Cooper to follow her.

They quickly opened the door on the coupling side of the caboose, grabbed the long iron handrails, cold now as the temperature continued in its plunge, and swung themselves out, Harry flat against the caboose on the right side, Coop on the left.

The footsteps passed them, the metallic steps vibrating as the individual stepped up onto the back platform, then opened the door to enter the caboose.

Mrs. Murphy and Pewter jumped down with ease. Tucker hit the ground with an *oomph,* rolled over, scratched to her feet, and followed the cats under the caboose as Harry and Coop dropped to the ground. The two women quietly crept along the side of the caboose opposite from the main building. It was even darker on that side.

They heard someone else walk toward the caboose, coming from the direction of the party.

Both women looked at each other. They hoped their feet wouldn't show.

Mrs. Murphy peeped out from under the caboose. *"Sean."*

"I knew it," Pewter crowed.

Not a moment later, Lottie's voice called out, "Sean, where are you going?"

Whoever was in the caboose froze.

"For a smoke. Thought I'd walk around the yard."

Fair walked out trying to shadow Lottie, but it's difficult for a six-foot five-inch man to be unobtrusive.

Lottie turned toward him, "Fair, what's going on?"

"We never had our dance."

"Oh." She faced Sean. "For some inexplicable reason I've become attractive to Fair." This was said with irony.

"May I have this dance then?" Fair persisted.

"Let me smoke a cigarette with Sean and I'll be right back in."

Fair beat a retreat toward the ball, all the while racking his brain for a place to hide so he could spy on Lottie. Rick, meanwhile, leaned against his car for a smoke, his eyes darting back to Sean from time to time. Diego came out, asked Fair where Harry was. Fair shrugged. He had no intention of helping Diego. Diego returned inside.

"Would you like to walk with me?" Sean evenly asked Lottie. "My first stop is the caboose. I don't believe I've ever showed it to you."

"That would be lovely." She raised her voice in that falsely feminine way.

Cooper and Harry heard whoever was in the caboose tiptoe to the coupling door in the back, the same one they used. The door opened and closed but no footfall followed. Whoever it was was hanging on the handrail. The two women looked at one another. Cooper silently cursed herself for leaving her evening purse in Rick's car. A small pistol was in it.

Just as Sean and Lottie reached the caboose steps, Lottie said, "Sean, I'm just freezing. Let me run back to the car for my wrap."

"I can go faster than you can. High heels." He smiled, pointing to her feet, then headed toward Lottie's car about one hundred yards away.

No need for her to describe her car. In Crozet everyone knew everyone else's wheels.

With lightning speed, Lottie climbed up the steps, pushed open the door, grabbed the sack, and walked back out again, the sack over her shoulder. She shoved it under the caboose and as she did, she saw Harry's and Cooper's shoes. She started running for her car.

Whoever was hanging on the caboose dropped.

"*Thomas!*" Pewter exclaimed.

"No, you don't." He tackled Lottie just as Sean opened Lottie's car door, unaware of the drama at the caboose.

"The money's under the caboose." She hissed a whisper, hoping that Cooper would nail him. He let her go. She hurried for her car, Tucker right behind.

Thomas bent down and grabbed the sack just as Coop stepped out from behind the caboose.

"Hands up, you're under arrest."

He saw Cooper was unarmed, hit her in the midriff with the sack, and tore after Lottie, who pushed Sean out of the way as she was plucking the keys out of her bag.

"*Stop.*" Tucker bit her on the ankle.

Lottie howled but managed to shake the dog off, hitting Tucker in the head with her purse. She slipped in the car, slamming the door shut while Tucker barked for all she was worth.

"You okay?" Harry bent over Cooper.

"Stop them," the tall woman gasped.

They could hear more running footsteps and hoped some of them belonged to Rick and Fair.

Harry, unarmed, heard a gun fire, felt wind by her temple, and hit the ground.

The cats were right with her. A sensible person would have rolled under cars for cover. Not Harry. She ran for all she was worth to the front of the main building.

"*What's she doing?*" Pewter kept up with the human. As humans aren't that fast, the cat didn't have to overexert herself, but she was out of shape.

"*There's only one way out. She's going to block it.*" Mrs. Murphy knew how her human thought.

"*They'll blow through that chain-link gate.*" The gray cat was really worried now. She had visions of Harry being run over and then realized that same fate could apply to her as well.

At the gate Harry rolled it shut, then climbed up on the crane. She sat high in the cab. She could see Sean crawl out of the way, Tucker helping by tugging at Sean's collar, as Lottie started her engine. She was ready to run them both over.

Thomas had sprinted to his car, a Mercedes sports car. He shook his fist as Lottie roared by him.

They would have to drive around the full car lot, around the side of the building, and then out the front drive to the gate.

Rick figured that out. He ran through the cars toward the front gate.

"Push over flowerpots, Pewter, anything to slow them," Mrs. Murphy hollered.

Tucker, rounding the corner at warp speed, heard the tiger, and started slamming into the wooden trellis, whiskey kegs, empty, old wooden milk cartons. *"I bit her on the ankle!"* the mighty little dog barked.

Fair Haristeen also figured out where the crisis would be. He, too, was running through the parked cars as fast as his legs would carry him.

"Got it." Harry fired up the crane, the heavy diesel motor rumbling.

People, hearing the commotion, began to pour out of the building. A few were unsteady on their feet. Those might have thought it was the ghost of Roger O'Bannon, loaded again, creating another memorable drunken scene.

Harry, nervous, forgot exactly which calipers controlled what. She swung the ball over the festooned building, causing those outside to scream and hit the dirt.

"Dammit!" Harry cursed, took a deep breath, gently squeezed the correct calipers, and swung the ball back.

Big Mim, back on her feet, realized what Harry was doing.

The roar of car engines and squeal of wheels were heard from behind the building. People scattered again.

Harry ran the ball up to the nose of the crane, positioning it directly above the gate. She blessed Sean for putting out the colored floodlights.

She didn't know the exact time it would take from when she squeezed the calipers to when the ball would hit, dropping straight down vertically. She prayed she'd get it right as she kept her hand on those calipers.

Lottie took the corner around the main building on two wheels. She crushed the trellis. Tucker dodged out of the way. The cats fled to the safety of hiding under the crane.

"Hurry, Tucker, Thomas will be right behind," Mrs. Murphy called to her dear friend.

Tucker ran for all she was worth.

Rick, gun in hand, reached the corner of the building, too. He fired at Lottie's tires but she saw him and swerved. Thomas, not ten feet behind her now, also saw Rick and he turned his vehicle straight at the sheriff, who tucked and rolled as Thomas swerved to miss the side of the building, narrowly missing Fair, who leapt on top of a car hood, then onto another one.

The guests, mesmerized, watched.

Diego, realizing Thomas was part of the drama, stepped away from the crowd as he edged toward the parked cars closest to the gate.

Tucker made it to the crane in the nick of time.

Cooper, shoes off, ran over the pea gravel in her stocking feet. She'd grabbed her gun. She hurried around the other side of the building.

"My God, she's going to ram the gate!" Big Mim screamed.

Just as the nose of Lottie's car hit the gate, Harry squeezed the release calipers and down dropped the wrecker's ball.

Smash! The ball hit the hood, driving the engine out the bottom. Lottie, no seat belt on, flew through the windshield with such force that she catapulted into the caved-in gate, killed on impact.

Harry picked up the ball and swung it toward Thomas. She lowered the ball. He had little room to maneuver with Lottie plastered in front of him. The ball crashed into the passenger side of the Mercedes with a metallic splintering sound.

Diego Aybar ran to the car, pulling out a dazed and bloody Thomas.

53

Monday morning, Rob Collier tossed the mailbag through the front door of the post office. "Harry, way to go, girl." He held his thumbs up.

"Thanks." She sheepishly smiled.

By then most of Crozet had filtered into the post office for their mail and to talk over events.

"I figured it out. I don't know why people are complimenting her," Pewter groused.

"Yeah, yeah." Tucker, tired from greeting everyone, sat by the table.

Miranda must have hugged and kissed Harry ten times. Every time she thought of the younger woman's quick thinking and cool head—after all, Lottie or Thomas could have shot her right out of the crane if they had kept their wits about them—Miranda had to hug and kiss her again.

A tired Coop finally rolled in at eleven. "Hey, partner." She smiled. "I think we've dotted the *i*'s and crossed the *t*'s."

"Will Thomas live?" Miranda asked, always concerned even when people were worthless.

"His face is a mess. He's full of broken bones but amazingly that's all."

"It was Lottie who opened Don's safe, wasn't it?" Harry figured that out.

Coop curled her upper lip. "Thomas blanched when I gave him a wad of bills to inspect. He's blaming everything on Lottie and she's not here to give her version of events."

"Was it drugs?" Miranda offered Coop a cup of steaming tea which she gratefully accepted.

"No. No, it wasn't. It was a lot more sophisticated than we realized. They were selling stolen cars in Uruguay. A four-year-old Mercedes sedan can bring as much as two hundred and twenty thousand dollars, a new car brings three hundred thousand. Thomas, thanks to his job, could ship stuff down there very easily."

"Cars, entire cars. Wouldn't the airlines or the shipping companies check the registration numbers?"

"That's where Roger and Dwayne came in. Roger would grind out the number on the inside of the front door and make a new plate. Who's going to check the engine number? He'd repaint the car. Rick and I thought he might be running a chop shop but this was less work and more profit thanks to Thomas. People in Uruguay and Paraguay will snap up expensive cars like candy. Thomas, of course, knew everybody, as did Lottie. It was Lottie who brought Thomas to Roger."

"I'll be, poor Roger."

"He said one time too many that he was a rich man, trying to win Lottie. The more he drank, the more he boasted. Roger was becoming a liability. She put on a big show, too big a show of disdaining him. Both she and Thomas figured Roger'd blow it somewhere soon. In time they'd find someone else to punch out new plates. Roger was dispensable. Thomas put the poison in a china sugar bowl along with a handful of raw sugar. Thomas's mother, sick, was on quinidine. We think he simply pilfered her prescription. They had a china bowl. It wasn't Aunt Tally's. He said Lottie was in charge of putting the bowl in the pantry. He picked it up. It was hidden behind plates. I don't know how she did it. He says he doesn't know but their plan was to kill Roger in front of everyone. The more people around the safer they'd be. Lottie made the coffee for Roger and she backed into Thomas as he was reaching for the bowl. It hit the floor and broke as planned. They wanted his death to appear natural. Sean's views on honoring the dead were well known."

"Bold though. They were certainly bold," Miranda acclaimed.

"What about Dwayne?"

Coop answered Harry. "He stole stickers, license-plate registrations, titles. Bill Boojum, on the Kentucky end, had someone doing the same thing at their Department of Motor Vehicles."

"He funneled stolen cars through the business?"

"Boojum, like all the big dealerships, had a body shop. What they stole from Louisville or Lexington or across the river in Indiana, they'd quickly paint over. Dwayne would drive it back and hide it in Roger's shop. Roger took care of any details left unfinished from Boojum. His drop-offs to Boojum from the Virginia end were legitimate."

"What Dwayne occasionally stole from Newport News, Richmond, and Staunton, Roger would paint, grind out registration numbers, and so forth. It was a lucrative setup and Thomas paid everyone in cold cash."

"Did Sean know?" Miranda wondered how wide their net cast.

"He swears he didn't know."

"Why didn't Sean recognize Dwayne?"

"He was out of it but I think Dwayne might have threatened him. I don't know and I'm not one hundred percent convinced that Sean didn't know more than he's letting on. If it turns out he was an accessory, well, he'll be needing a good lawyer." Coop shrugged. "It might come down to 'Am I my brother's keeper.' Maybe Sean did know and was trying to get Roger out of the business."

"Why did they kill Dwayne?" Harry asked.

"He wanted more money. He said he was taking the most risk in driving the cars and stealing them. He wanted more, a lot more. Thomas said he'd give him fifty thousand cash and arranged to meet him at the elder-care home. He had to act fast because Dwayne knew he killed Roger. That didn't take a rocket scientist to figure out. He was pushing Thomas and Lottie hard. Fifty thousand dollars was no longer enough." She mused, "I guess Dwayne wanted to move up, so to speak, in his profession. Boy just couldn't stop stealing, little things, big things. He was a born thief."

"I don't know if I would have ever figured it out," Harry thoughtfully said. "What did Don have to do with it?"

"He could repair damage to upholstery. He could change the whole color of an interior if need be but he also stole cars. The money was good—Thomas swears he didn't kill Don. He said it was Lottie. I think Don was delivering something to Lottie or Thomas—cash, fake titles, something. And before Dwayne was killed he may have been back by Durant Creek with Don. He probably stayed in the cabin back there. How he lost his Mercedes star—could have been a fight with Don. He was probably putting the screws to all of them. My hunch is once Don realized Roger was murdered he was scared shitless—a liability in crime. Dwayne wasn't scared. Thomas said he never acted scared, just greedy."

"Cooper, was all that five hundred and twenty-five thousand dollars Don's?"

"Yes. It's what he acquired over the last three years. Thomas, by the way, believes he has diplomatic immunity. He thinks he won't have to stand trial. We are pretty sure the business raked in close to four million a year."

"Does Thomas have immunity?" Miranda asked.

"Yes." Coop put her cup down. "But his government promises to prosecute him in his own country. For all I know he'll walk free."

"What a scam!" Harry shook her head.

"Lottie fell into it. She met Thomas at a party held in Washington. She'd make the rounds but that's part of her job. He sensed she was bright, cold-blooded, on the make. And she was."

"Coop, what an awful story." Miranda sighed. "'And He said to them, "Take heed, and beware of all covetousness; for a man's life does not consist in the abundance of his possessions."' *Luke*, Chapter Twelve, Verse Fifteen."

"I'm glad Diego wasn't in on it—was he?" Harry's voice dropped.

"We don't think he was but his career will be tarnished by it. That's the way the world works." Coop accepted a refill. "His government has already called him back to Uruguay. He'll have to testify at the trial."

"Their families are old friends. I wonder what pressures will be brought to bear on Diego?" Harry sadly said.

"You know," Coop mused, "Rick and I found the registration blanks and the title blanks. They were in Roger's files in his shop. We went over those files, so they had to have been moved there after we combed the shop. Funny thing, a monster rat, absolutely unafraid, watched us."

"Bet we know what he called them," Tucker laughed.

"Oh, Harry, I've got something for you." Coop walked

out the back door, returning with the pileated woodpecker, which she placed on the table. "Released from jail."

"Isn't he beautiful." Harry admired Don's work.

"And so big." Miranda had never seen a woodpecker up this close. "I'd stay on the good side of him."

"I can't wait until she takes him home. I am going to shred him. It's my woodpecker. Feathers everywhere," Pewter promised.

"You wouldn't." Mrs. Murphy tilted up her head.

"Just wait and see." The gray cat puffed out her chest, laughing.

Dear Reader,

My big news is I've found three fox dens, two reds and one gray. I watch from a distance. Foxes and cats are natural enemies since we compete for the same game. However, there are enough field mice this year to keep us all busy.

Oh, I've seen more hawks, falcons, and raptors than I can ever remember. And green herons as well as the big blues. Birds make me cackle, I can't help it.

Thank you again for the photographs you send me. Even horses send their photos.

It's been a good time on the farm. The hay crop was really good. Next year comes the timber harvest, all things being equal. Mom still can't afford to build a new bridge but she did patch up the old one. John Morris and Robert Steppe used the big tractor and did a pretty darn good job with Dana Flaherty directing all. Really fixing the bridge is about a $15,000 task but we all did our patch job for $1,700 worth of stone.

Part of the roof blew off in high winds. That hurt. Poor Mom. She was able to fix up the roof but she still doesn't have the money to repair the inside of the house and it does look pretty awful.

But we all have each other. We're all healthy. The fences are strong. The cattle are fat and the horses are so happy, they're silly.

Farming is a hard life if your goal is to be wealthy but I agree with Mom and Harry, it's the only life for us. When the sun rises and the Blue Ridge Mountains turn scarlet, the roosters wake up, the horses, too, and I can smell the earth, oh, I tell you, this is as close to paradise as a kitty can get. Sometimes, I climb into the big wisteria twining on the front entranceway to the house. The leaves flutter over my head, the praying mantises are everywhere, birds dart in, and sometimes they don't even know I'm there! It's the best of the best and I hope you are having half as much fun in this life as I am.

Yours in catitude,

Sneaky Pie
www.ritamaebrown.com

About the Authors

Rita Mae Brown is the bestselling author of several books. An Emmy-nominated screenwriter and a poet, she lives in Afton, Virginia.

Sneaky Pie Brown, a tiger cat born somewhere in Albemarle County, Virginia, was discovered by Rita Mae Brown at her local SPCA. They have collaborated on nine previous Mrs. Murphy mysteries: *Wish You Were Here; Rest in Pieces; Murder at Monticello; Pay Dirt; Murder, She Meowed; Murder on the Prowl; Cat on the Scent; Pawing Through the Past;* and *Claws and Effect,* plus *Sneaky Pie's Cookbook for Mystery Lovers.*

Don't miss the new
Sneaky Pie mystery

The Tail

of the

Tip-Off

Coming from Bantam Books
in March 2003

PLEASE TURN THE PAGE FOR A PREVIEW

A gray sleety drizzle rattled against the handblown windowpanes in the rectory at St. Luke's Lutheran Church. As if in counterpoint, a fire crackled in the large but simple fireplace, the mantel adorned by a strip of dentil carving. The hands of that carver had turned to dust in 1797.

The members of the Parish Guild were seated in a semicircle around the fireplace, at a graceful coffee table in the middle. As anyone knows, serving on a board or a committee is a dubious honor. Most people recognize their duty in time to avoid it. However, the work must be done and some good folks bow their heads to the yoke.

Mary Minor Haristeen had succumbed to the thrill of being elected, of being considered responsible, by the congregation. This thrill thinned as the tangle of tasks presented themselves in meeting after meeting. She liked the physical problems better than the people problems. Fixing a fallen drainspout was within her compass of expertise. Fixing a broken heart, offering succor to the ill, well, she was learning.

The good pastor of St. Luke's, the Reverend Herbert C.

Jones, excelled at both the people problems and teaching. He gladly gave of himself to any board member, any parishioner. As he'd baptized Mrs. Haristeen, nicknamed Harry, he felt a special affection for the good-looking woman in her late thirties. It was an affection bounteously returned, for Harry loved the Rev, as she called him, with all her heart.

Although the guild was bickering at this exact moment, it'd be fair to say that every member loved the Reverend Jones. It would be also fair to say that most of them liked—if not loved—Harry. The one exception being BoomBoom Craycroft who sort of liked her and sort of didn't. The feeling was mutual.

Like large white confetti, papers rested on the coffee table along with mugs. The aroma of coffee and hot chocolate somewhat dissipated the tension.

"We just can't go off half-cocked here and authorize an expenditure of twelve thousand dollars." Tazio Chappars crossed her arms over her chest. She was an architect and a young, attractive woman of color, with an Italian mother and an African-American father.

"Well, we have to do something," Herb said in his resonant, hypnotic voice.

"Why?" Tazio, combative, shifted in her seat.

"Because the place looks like hell," Harry blurted out. "Sorry, Rev."

"Quite all right. It does." Herb laughed.

Hayden McIntyre, the town's general practitioner, was a fleshy man with an air of command if not a touch of arrogance. He slipped his pencil out from behind his ear and began scribbling on the budget papers which had been handed out at the beginning of the meeting. "Let's try this. I am not arguing replacing the carpet in the rectory. We've put this off for four years now. I remember hearing arguments pro and con when I first came on board. This is one of the loveliest, most graceful churches in the Piedmont and it should reflect that." An appreciative murmur accompanied this statement. "I've broken this down into three areas of immediate need. First the sacristy: must be done." He held up his hand as Tazio opened her mouth. "It must. I know what you're going to say."

"No you don't." Her hazel eyes brightened. "Well, okay, maybe you do. Pick up the carpet and sand the floors."

"Tazio, we've been over that. We can't do that because the floorboards are so thin they can't take it." Matthew Crickenberger, head of Charlottesville's largest construction firm, clapped his hands together softly for emphasis. "Those floorboards are chestnut. They've been doing their job since 1797 and frankly they're tired and we can't really replace them. If you think the bill for new carpeting is high, wait until you see the bill for chestnut flooring even if we could find it. Mountain Lumber up there off Route 29 might be able to scare some up and give us a preacher's price, but we're still talking about thousands and thousands of dollars. Chestnut is as rare as hen's teeth and we'd need a great deal of it." He glanced down at his notes. "Six thousand square feet if we were to replace everything now under carpet and this doesn't factor in the other areas currently in use but not quite ready for recarpeting."

Tazio exhaled, flopping back in her chair. She wanted everything just so but she didn't have to foot the bill. Still, it rankled to have a vision amputated because of a small pocketbook. Such was an architect's fate.

"Hayden, you had a plan?" Herb pushed the meeting along. No one wanted to be late to the basketball game and this discussion was eating up time.

"Yes," he smiled, "what people see first is the sacristy. If we can't come to an arrangement among us, can we at least agree to go ahead with that? The cost would be about four thousand."

"If we are going to have the place ripped up, then let's just get it over with. We know we have to do this." BoomBoom, gorgeous as always, shimmered in her teal suede dress.

"I agree. We'll find the money someplace."

"We'd better find the money first or we'll have to answer to the congregation in the church, in the supermarket, and"—Matthew winked at Harry—"in the post office."

Harry, the postmistress, sheepishly smiled. "And you know my partner in crime, Miranda, is a member of the Church of the Holy Light, so she won't bail me out."

The little gathering laughed. Miranda Hogendobber, who was a good thirty years older than Harry, quoted Scriptures with more ease than the Reverend Jones and while she tolerated other faiths she felt the charismatic church to which she belonged truly had the best path to Jesus.

As the humans batted around the cost, the need, and the choice of color for the carpeting, Harry's three dear friends lurked in the hallway outside the large room.

Mrs. Murphy, a most intelligent tiger cat, listened to the intensifying sleet. Her sidekick, a large round gray cat named Pewter, was getting fidgety waiting for the meeting to end. Tucker, the corgi, patient and steady as only a good dog can be, was happy to be inside and not outside.

The Christ cats—as Herb's two cats were called by the other animals—had escorted Murphy, Pewter, and Tucker around. They'd gossiped about every animal in the small Virginia town of Crozet, but as the meeting was entering its second hour, they'd finally exhausted that topic.

Cazenovia, the elder of the two cats, nestled down, her fluffy tail around her nose. A large calico, she had aged gracefully. The young foundling which Herb had taken in a few years ago, Elocution, had grown into a sleek pretty cat. A touch of Siamese in her, she never stopped talking.

"—*tuna breath!*" Elocution uttered this insult. "*How can you stand it?*"

"*She doesn't.*" Mrs. Murphy giggled.

They'd been discussing the blue jay who tormented Pewter. He also tormented Mrs. Murphy but with less enthusiasm, probably because he couldn't get a rise out of the tiger.

"*Oh, I will snap his neck like a toothpick someday. You take my word for it,*" Pewter promised.

"*How thrilling,*" Cazenovia purred.

"*And un-Christian,*" Tucker chuckled.

"*Well, we are cats,*" Pewter sniffed.

"*That's right. Our job is to rid the world of vermin,*" Elocution agreed. "*Blue jays are beyond vermin. They're avian criminals. Picking up stones and dropping them on neighbors' eggs. Dropping you-know-what on freshly waxed cars. Do it on purpose. They'll sit in a tree and wait until the job is finished and then swoosh.*" Elocution glanced up at the rat-a-tat on the window. "*Not today.*"

"*Why don't blue jays go south in the winter?*" Pewter mused. "*Robins do.*"

"*Life in our barn is too good, that's why. Harry puts out birdhouses and gourds and then she plants South American maize for the ground birds, cowpeas, and bipolar lespedeza. The winter might be cold but she serves up all kinds of seeds for those dumb birds.*"

"*Birds are descended from flying reptiles,*" Elocution announced with vigor. "*That alone should warn us off.*"

"*What in the world is going on in there?*" Tucker listened as Matthew Crickenberger raised his voice about labor costs.

"*Say, have I shown you how I can open the closet where*

Herb stores the communion wafers?" Elocution puffed out her chest.

"Elo, don't do that," Cazenovia warned.

"I'm just going to prove that I can do it."

"They'll believe you. They don't need a demonstration."

"I wouldn't mind," Pewter laconically replied.

"Thanks, Pewter." Cazenovia cast her a cold golden eye.

"Come on." Elocution, tail held high, bounded down the hall.

The others followed, Cazenovia bringing up the rear. *"I know I'll get in trouble for this,"* the old girl grumbled.

Elocution skidded at the turn in the hall where it intersected with another hall traversing the width of the rectory, itself an old building constructed in 1834.

Pewter whispered to Mrs. Murphy, *"I'm hungry."*

"You're always hungry."

"I know, but you'd think the Rev would put a bowl of crunchies out somewhere. And I don't smell anything edible."

"Me neither," the mighty but small dog whispered, *"and I have the best nose."*

"Here." Elocution stopped in front of a closet under the stairwell that ascended to the second story. *"You all stay here."*

"Elocution, this really isn't necessary," Cazenovia sighed.

Ignoring her, the shiny cat hopped up the stairs then slipped halfway through the banisters. Lying on her side she could reach the old-fashioned long key which protruded from the keyhole. She batted at it, then grabbed it with both paws, expertly turning the key until the lock popped.

"Oh, that is impressive." Pewter's eyes widened.

"The best part is, Herbie will flay Charlotte for leaving it unlocked." Elocution laughed.

Charlotte was Herb's secretary, second in command.

As the lock opened, Elocution gave a tug and Pewter,

quick to assist, pulled at the bottom of the door with her paw. The door swung open revealing bottles of red wine and a shelf full of communion wafers in cracker boxes with cellophane wrappers. Elocution knocked one on the floor then squeezed her slender body all the way through the banisters, dropping to the floor. Within a second she'd sliced the cellophane off the box, and using one extended claw, she opened the tucked-in end.

The odor of wafers, not unlike water crackers, enticed Pewter.

"Elocution, I knew you were going to do this," Cazenovia fretted.

"Well, the box is open. We can't let it go to waste." The bad kitty grabbed a wafer and gobbled it down.

Temptation. Temptation. Pewter gave in.

Cazenovia suffered a moment. *"They're ruined now. The humans can't eat them."* She, too, flicked out wafers.

Tucker, being a canine after all, rarely worried about the propriety of eating anything. Her nose was already in the wafer box.

Mrs. Murphy allowed herself the luxury of a nibble. *"Kind of tasteless."*

"If you eat enough of them you get a bready taste, but they are bland." Cazenovia's statement revealed she'd been in the communion wafers more than once.

"Does this mean we're communicants?" Pewter paused.

"Yes," Mrs. Murphy answered. *"We're communicats."*

"What if I'm not a Lutheran? What if I'm a Muslim cat?"

"If you were a Muslim cat you wouldn't be living in Crozet." Tucker laughed.

"You don't know. This is America. We have everything," Pewter rejoined.

"Not in Crozet." Cazenovia wiped her mouth with her paw. *"You've got Episcopalians, Lutherans, and Catholics.*

More or less the same thing and I know Herb would have a fit, a total fit, if he knew I'd said that, but fortunately he doesn't know what I or any other cat in this universe has to say." She took a deep breath. *"Then you've got the Baptists busily fighting among themselves these days and then the charismatic churches and that's it."*

"Let's open a Buddhist shrine. Shake 'em up a little." Elocution hiccuped. She'd eaten too many wafers too quickly.

"No. We build a huge statue of a cat with earrings like in ancient Egypt. Oh, I can hear the squeals now about paganism." Mrs. Murphy laughed as the others laughed with her.

Tucker swiveled her ears. *"Hey, gang, meeting's breaking up. Let's get out of here."*

"Help me push this back in the closet and close the door," Elocution said with urgency.

Cazenovia knocked the box in as though it were a hockey puck. Tucker, larger than the cats, pushed against the door. It closed in an instant. They scrambled out of there. Luckily for them, the doors to the meeting room weren't yet open. They made it back in the nick of time.

"—tomorrow afternoon," Matthew told Tazio.

"I'll be in the office."

"I know you're disappointed about the chestnut flooring but, well." Matthew shrugged.

"I guess I'm a perfectionist. That's what they say back at the office and on the sites, only they say it a lot more directly there." She smiled.

"You've got a lot on your plate, young lady." Hayden McIntyre joined them. "Your design for the new sports complex is just the most ingenious thing. Is that the right word?"

"As long as it's a good word." Tazio picked up her coat hanging in the hall.

"I know H.H. has none for me." Matthew shrugged.

"He'll get his shot." Hayden shrugged right back.

Tazio pointedly did not comment on the animosity between Matthew and H. H. Donaldson, head of a rival construction firm. The bad blood had been made worse when Matthew won the bid to construct Tazio's new stadium. She had hoped H.H. would win the bid because she especially liked him, but she could work just fine with Matthew.

Herb walked out with Harry and BoomBoom. "I sure appreciate you girls coming on over here. You're a welcome addition to the guild."

Both women had just begun their first terms, which lasted three years.

"I'm learning a lot," Harry said.

"Me, too."

"Look at these little angels." Harry knelt down to pet all the cats and Tucker.

"If she only knew." Elocution giggled.

"Don't be so smug," Cazenovia chided her. *"Humans don't know what we're talking about but they know smug."*

"I don't know what I'd do without those two." Herb smiled benevolently. "They help write the sermons, they keep an eye on the parishioners, they leave little pawprints on the furniture."

"I'm sure they've left them on the carpets, too." BoomBoom liked cats.

"Well, that they have but I can hardly blame them for wearing those carpets out. Fortunately we are a well-attended church, but it does put wear and tear on the building." Herb checked his watch. "Game's in an hour. You all going?"

"Yes," the two women said in unison.

"Well, I'll see you there. I'd better go through the building and shut some of the doors. On these cold nights it saves on the heat bill. Gotta save it where I can."

As he headed down the hall, Mrs. Murphy urged Harry, *"Come on, Mom, let's get out of here!"*

Cazenovia and Elocution hurried into the meeting room, flopping themselves on the sofa with a great show of nonchalance. Too great a show.

"See you, Rev," Harry called out as she tossed on her coat, opening the door for her pets and BoomBoom.

"Whew," Pewter breathed as she stepped outside into the nasty weather.

Welcome to the charming world of
Sneaky Pie Brown.
Don't miss these earlier mysteries . . .

CLAWS AND EFFECT

Winter puts tiny Crozet, Virginia, in a deep freeze and everyone seems to be suffering from the winter blahs, including postmistress Mary Minor "Harry" Haristeen. So all are ripe for the juicy gossip coming out of Crozet Hospital—until the main source of that gossip turns up dead. It's not like Harry to resist a mystery, and she soon finds the hospital a hotbed of ego, jealousy, and illicit love. But it's tiger cat Mrs. Murphy, roaming the netherworld of Crozet Hospital, who sniffs out a secret that dates back to the Underground Railroad. Then Harry is attacked and a doctor is executed in cold blood. Soon only a quick-witted cat and her animal pals feline Pewter and corgi Tee Tucker stand between Harry and a coldly calculating killer with a prescription for murder.

"Reading a Mrs. Murphy mystery is like eating a potato chip. You always go back for more . . . Whimsical and enchanting . . . the latest expert tale from a deserving bestselling series." —*The Midwest Book Review*

PAWING THROUGH THE PAST

"You'll never get old." Each member of the class of 1980 has received the letter. Mary Minor "Harry" Haristeen, who is on the organizing committee for Crozet High's twentieth reunion, decides to take it as a compliment. Others think it's a joke. But Mrs. Murphy senses trouble. And the sly tiger cat is soon proven right . . . when the class womanizer turns up dead with a bullet between his eyes. Then another note followed by another murder makes it clear that someone has waited twenty years to take revenge. While Harry tries to piece together the puzzle, it's up to Mrs. Murphy and her animal pals to sniff out the truth. And there isn't much time. Mrs. Murphy is the first to realize that Harry has been chosen Most Likely to Die, and if she doesn't hurry, Crozet High's twentieth reunion could be Harry's last.

"This is a cat-lover's dream of a mystery. . . . 'Harry' is simply irresistible. . . . [Rita Mae] Brown once again proves herself 'Queen of Cat Crimes.' . . . Don't miss out on this lively series, for it's one of the best around." —*Old Book Barn Gazette*

CAT ON THE SCENT

Things have been pretty exciting lately in Crozet, Virginia— a little *too* exciting if you ask resident feline investigator Mrs. Murphy. Just as the town starts to buzz over its Civil War reenactment, a popular local man disappears. No one's seen Tommy Van Allen's single-engine plane, either—except for Mrs. Murphy, who spotted it during a foggy evening's mousing. Even Mrs. Murphy's favorite human, postmistress Mary Minor "Harry" Haristeen, can sense that something is amiss. But things really take an ugly turn when the town reenacts the battle of Oak Ridge—and a participant ends up with three very real bullets in his back. While the clever tiger cat and her friends sift through clues that just don't fit together, more than a few locals fear that the scandal will force well-hidden town secrets into the harsh light of day. And when Mrs. Murphy's relentless tracking places loved ones in danger, it takes more than a canny kitty and her team of animal sleuths to set things right again. . . .

"Told with spunk and plenty of whimsy, this is another delightful entry in a very popular series. " —*Publishers Weekly*

MURDER ON THE PROWL

When a phony obituary appears in the local paper, the good people of Crozet, Virginia, are understandably upset. Who would stoop to such a tasteless act? Is it a sick joke—or a sinister warning? Only Mrs. Murphy, the canny tiger cat, senses true malice at work. And her instincts prove correct when a second fake obit appears, followed by a fiendish murder ... and then another. People are dropping like flies in Crozet, and no one knows why. Yet even if Mrs. Murphy untangles the knot of passion and deceit that has sent someone into a killing frenzy, it won't be enough. Somehow the shrewd puss must guide her favorite human, postmistress "Harry" Haristeen, down a perilous trail to a deadly killer ... and a killer of a climax. Or the next obit may be Harry's own.

"Leave it to a cat to grasp the essence of the cozy mystery: murder among friends." —*The New York Times Book Review*

MURDER, SHE MEOWED

The annual steeplechase races are the high point in the social calendar of the horse-mad Virginians of cozy Crozet. But when one of the jockeys is found murdered in the main barn, Mary Minor "Harry" Haristeen finds herself in a desperate race of her own—to trap the killer. Luckily for her, she has an experienced ally: her sage tiger cat, Mrs. Murphy. Utilizing her feline genius to plumb the depths of human depravity, Mrs. Murphy finds herself on a trail that leads to the shocking truth behind the murder. But will her human companion catch on in time to beat the killer to the gruesome finish line?

"The intriguing characters in this much-loved series continue to entertain." —*The Nashville Banner*

PAY DIRT

The residents of tiny Crozet, Virginia, thrive on gossip, especially in the post office, where Mary Minor "Harry" Haristeen presides with her tiger cat, Mrs. Murphy. So when a belligerent Hell's Angel crashes Crozet, demanding to see his girlfriend, the leather-clad interloper quickly becomes the chief topic of conversation. Then the biker is found murdered, and everyone is baffled. Well, almost everyone... Mrs. Murphy and her friends, Welsh corgi Tee Tucker and overweight feline Pewter, haven't been slinking through alleys for nothing. But can they dig up the truth in time to save their humans from a ruthless killer?

"If you must work with a collaborator, you want it to be someone with intelligence, wit, and an infinite capacity for subtlety—someone, in fact, very much like a cat.... It's always a pleasure to visit this cozy world.... There's no resisting Harry's droll sense of humor... or Mrs. Murphy's tart commentary." —*The New York Times Book Review*

MURDER AT MONTICELLO

The most popular citizen of Virginia has been dead for nearly 170 years. That hasn't stopped the good people of tiny Crozet, Virginia, from taking pride in every aspect of Thomas Jefferson's life. But when an archaeological dig of the slave quarters at Jefferson's home, Monticello, uncovers a shocking secret, emotions in Crozet run high—dangerously high. The stunning discovery at Monticello hints at hidden passions and age-old scandals. As postmistress Mary Minor "Harry" Haristeen and some of Crozet's Very Best People try to learn the identity of a centuries-old skeleton—and the reason behind the murder—Harry's tiger cat, Mrs. Murphy, and her canine and feline friends attempt to sniff out a modern-day killer. Mrs. Murphy and corgi Tee Tucker will stick their paws into the darker mysteries of human nature to solve murders old and new—before curiosity can kill the cat ... and Harry Haristeen.

"You don't have to be a cat lover to love *Murder at Monticello*." —*The Indianapolis Star*

REST IN PIECES

Small towns don't take kindly to strangers—unless the stranger happens to be a drop-dead gorgeous and seemingly unattached male. When Blair Bainbridge comes to Crozet, Virginia, the local matchmakers lose no time in declaring him perfect for their newly divorced postmistress, Mary Minor "Harry" Haristeen. Even Harry's tiger cat, Mrs. Murphy, and her Welsh corgi, Tee Tucker, believe he smells A-okay. Could his one little imperfection be that he's a killer? Blair becomes the most likely suspect when the pieces of a dismembered corpse begin turning up around Crozet. No one knows who the dead man is, but when a grisly clue makes a spectacular appearance in the middle of the fall festivities, more than an early winter snow begins chilling the blood of Crozet's Very Best People. That's when Mrs. Murphy, her friend Tucker, and her human companion Harry begin to sort through the clues . . . only to find themselves a whisker away from becoming the killer's next victims.

"Skillfully plotted, properly gruesome . . . and wise as well as wickedly funny." —*Booklist*

AND DON'T MISS THE VERY FIRST SNEAKY PIE BROWN MYSTERY . . .

WISH YOU WERE HERE

Small towns are like families. Everyone lives very close together . . . and everyone keeps secrets. Crozet, Virginia, is a typical small town—until its secrets explode into murder. Crozet's thirty-something postmistress, Mary Minor "Harry" Haristeen, has a tiger cat (Mrs. Murphy) and a Welsh corgi (Tee Tucker), a pending divorce, and a bad habit of reading postcards not addressed to her. When Crozet's citizens start turning up murdered, Harry remembers that each received a card with a tombstone on the front and the message "wish you were here" on the back. Intent on protecting their human friends, Mrs. Murphy and Tucker begin to scent out clues. Meanwhile, Harry is conducting her own investigation, unaware that her pets are one step ahead of her. If only Mrs. Murphy could alert her somehow, Harry could uncover the culprit before another murder occurs—and before Harry finds herself on the killer's mailing list.

"Charming. . . . Ms. Brown writes with wise, disarming wit." —*The New York Times Book Review*